DETERMINATION

C. P. ODOM

Meryton Press

OYSTERVILLE, WA

DETERMINATION

ISBN: 978-1-68131-045-9

This is a work of fiction. Names, characters, places, and incidents are products of the author's imagination or are used fictitiously. Any resemblance to actual events or persons, living or dead, is entirely coincidental.

Cover design by Janet B. Taylor
Book design by Ellen Pickels

Published in the United States of America.

DEDICATION

To my long-time friend and neighbor, Del Merrill.

Our kids went to the same schools all the way through college, and we coached sports teams and did Boy Scouts together. Besides that, he's a fellow Marine from the Vienam years and a retired educator who is totally committed to his students. Amazingly, he has read all my books and was instrumental in getting me off my duff to write this one. Diabetes affects his vision, and we work together to get my books downloaded to his tablet so he can enlarge the font. We fellow Jarheads have to stick together!

— *C. P. Odom*
December, 2020

CHAPTER 1

If your determination is fixed, I do not counsel you to despair.
Few things are impossible to diligence and skill. Great works are
performed not by strength, but perseverance.

— Samuel Johnson

Thursday, April 14, 1812
Rosings, Kent

Colonel Richard Fitzwilliam, second son of the Earl of Matlock and commander of His Majesty's Sixth (Guards) Regiment of Dragoons, felt a familiar flash of exasperation as he espied his cousin Darcy making a furtive exit from the room. The two men were having tea with their aunt Lady Catherine along with her guests from the Parsonage, and her ladyship was at present engaged in instructing the clergyman's wife on the proper way to clean dining room furniture. Being, as always, fascinated by her own words, she did not see her nephew depart, but Fitzwilliam knew she would discover Darcy's absence sooner or later—probably sooner. And it was pre-ordained that her displeasure at that time would be directed towards the nephew who remained rather than the one who was absent.

Consequently, Fitzwilliam lost no time in beginning an equally surreptitious disappearance in Darcy's wake, thinking sardonically, *After all, if I am to be the recipient of one of Lady Catherine's celebrated tantrums, I would rather share the experience with Darcy than endure it alone.*

But, whilst avoiding conflict with his aunt was sufficient reason for a strategic retreat, Fitzwilliam had another reason for following Darcy: to try to find an explanation for the unusual behaviour exhibited by his cousin since their arrival at Rosings.

More unusual than normal for Darcy, that is, Fitzwilliam corrected himself. *The cousin I greeted after returning from Spain was not the cousin I remembered. He changed substantially while I was gone, and little of that change was for the better. That was true even before it was time to visit Lady Catherine, and he has changed again during this visit, adding unpredictability and foolishness to the harsh stiffness and icy reserve I had already noted. He bears little resemblance to the friend and near-brother I knew five years ago when I left for Egypt. Undoubtedly, part of it is due to the disaster that nearly befell Georgiana at Ramsgate, but that is not the whole of it. Other influences have been at work, and I cannot sort them out. Perhaps if I can entice him into discussing something other than trivialities—with a few glasses of brandy thrown into the mix—I might learn something about what is affecting him. After all, as is said: in vino, veritas.*

Fitzwilliam had returned to England with his regiment only six months before, having seen action in Egypt, Italy, and then Corsica in support of Britain's many campaigns against the tyrant Bonaparte. Those duties not only had kept him actively employed, they also had provided rare opportunities for an officer of His Majesty's ground forces to attain recognition and distinction. Fitzwilliam was well aware that the great bulk of the war against the Corsican oppressor had been borne by His Majesty's naval forces, so he was grateful to have received promotions to lieutenant colonel and then to colonel. When his last promotion had been accompanied by his posting to the command of a quite prestigious cavalry regiment, all at the age of twenty-nine, his satisfaction was profound.

Yet, however fortunate the period might have been in professional terms, Fitzwilliam was aware that it had come at no little cost, for he had been separated from England and his Darcy cousins for most of those five years. His absence had kept him from exercising his responsibilities as one of the dual guardians for Darcy's young sister, Georgiana. It also caused a painful separation from Darcy, who had been more of a brother than his own siblings had been.

And now he had returned, only to find both cousins markedly changed in manner and behaviour. Georgiana's reticence and lack of confidence had a reason, and he hoped the fullness of time would lead her to recover her former cheerfulness and optimism. But Darcy's natural reserve and silence seemed to have become a coat of armour during his absence. Fitzwilliam had observed the changes unhappily as Darcy appeared to view the entire world with a rigid detachment that sometimes passed into prideful arrogance. It was most unlike the cousin who had freely given him warmth and comradeship during his own rather unhappy childhood, and Fitzwilliam had not been able to puzzle out what had happened nor why.

Fitzwilliam grinned to himself as he quietly closed the door, having successfully managed his exit, cutting off the words of his aunt. The wry thought ran through his mind that, if Darcy was different from what he had been five years earlier, Lady Catherine was most decidedly unchanged.

Briskly, he set out to see whether Darcy had returned to his room.

However, while passing a hallway window, he saw his cousin bounding down the front steps of Rosings and setting off along the drive towards the park. Fitzwilliam quickly reversed his steps, but by the time he made his own exit from the house, Darcy was completely out of sight.

Confident that his cousin must be heading for the Parsonage,

Fitzwilliam set off in pursuit. They had been making the same trek almost daily since first arriving at Rosings, and there simply was no other destination in that direction. Fitzwilliam frowned in concentration as he walked, wondering why his cousin might risk the anger of his aunt by visiting the Parsonage when its residents were visiting with her ladyship. It was a difficult question to answer.

Can Darcy intend to visit Miss Bennet? I suppose it is possible since she did not accompany her cousins to tea. But the question is—why? Several times, I have wondered whether he might be interested in her, but his behaviour is so changed since I returned to England that I cannot confidently decipher his thoughts. Certainly, he never acted as most men would if they had an interest in a young lady. And Miss Bennet seems to regard him with more than a little antagonism.

Shaking his head in consternation at the puzzle, Fitzwilliam continued towards the Hunsford Parsonage. Surprisingly, though Fitzwilliam walked swiftly, Darcy must have progressed more rapidly since the colonel never caught a glimpse of him. He even took the time to climb a small hillock and look around, suddenly doubting his assumption of his cousin's destination.

Only when he drew near the entrance to the Parsonage did he gain any evidence that his conjecture had been correct. As he was about to ring the bell, he heard his cousin's voice through an open window. However, as he perceived the content and passion of Darcy's voice, he stopped suddenly.

"And this is all the reply which I am to have the honour of expecting?" he heard his cousin exclaim in obvious anger. "I might, perhaps, wish to be informed why, with so little *endeavour* at civility, I am thus rejected. But it is of small importance."

Fitzwilliam was so astonished that he was unable to consider fully the import of Darcy's words. However, he was staggered by an even more furious response delivered in the soprano tones of Miss Elizabeth Bennet.

"I might as well inquire, why, with so evident a design of offending and insulting me, you chose to tell me that you liked me against your will, against your reason, and even against your character? Was not this some excuse for incivility, if I *was* uncivil? But I have other provocations. You know I have. Had not my own feelings decided against you—had they been indifferent, or had they even been favourable—do you think that *any* consideration would tempt me to accept the man who has been the means of ruining, perhaps forever, the happiness of a most beloved sister?"

Fitzwilliam paled as he realized Miss Bennet must be referring to the conversation he had with her earlier in the day. He also appreciated that his inadvertent mention of Darcy saving his friend Bingley from a "most imprudent marriage" must have concerned one of Miss Bennet's sisters.

Truly alarmed now, Fitzwilliam quickly reached the front door in a few steps. He purposefully did not knock but rather eased open the door and entered quietly but rapidly. Losing no time, he moved down the hall towards the voices he was still able to hear, though he could no longer decipher the words. But, as he gently opened the door, he heard Miss Bennet exclaiming, "But it is not merely this affair on which my dislike is founded. Long before it had taken place, my opinion of you was decided. Your character was unfolded in the recital, which I received many months ago from Mr. Wickham. On this subject, what can you have to say? In what imaginary act of friendship can you here defend yourself? Or under what misrepresentation can you here impose upon others?"

Fitzwilliam had been debating whether he ought to simply close the door and return to Rosings since the conversation—rather, the quarrel—was obviously intensely private and emotional. But this last comment was so shocking that he stopped his retirement before it had fully begun. He knew Miss Bennet had good reason to be angry with his cousin if he had prevented Bingley from marrying her sister, but what reason could possibly have inspired her to take up the cause of George Wickham?

"You take an eager interest in that gentleman's concerns," Darcy said, and Fitzwilliam winced as he clearly discerned the cold fury that was barely contained. He doubted Miss Bennet could know just how angry his cousin was at this instant.

"Who that knows what his misfortunes have been can help feeling an interest in him?" Miss Bennet responded coldly.

HIS misfortunes? Fitzwilliam thought in amazement mixed with not a little anger. *George Wickham's misfortunes? This cannot be allowed to stand.*

So focused was each participant on the other that they were unaware of the partial opening of the door.

"His misfortunes!" replied Darcy, cold contempt dripping from every word. "Yes, his misfortunes have been great indeed."

"And of your infliction!" cried Miss Bennet. "You have reduced him to—"

"Miss Bennet!" blurted Fitzwilliam, throwing open the door as he was unable to restrain himself any longer. The two antagonists whirled towards him in astonishment as he stepped fully into the room.

"Miss Bennet," Fitzwilliam said again, his tone calmer as the other two stared at him with wide eyes. "I apologize for inserting myself so rudely into your private conversation, but you were both so loud that I could not help but overhear what you said about George Wickham. And I could not allow an otherwise sensible young lady to entertain such falsehoods about that man without refuting them. It is not my cousin who has acted infamously with regard to Wickham, I assure you. The situation is, in fact, the diametric opposite."

Elizabeth looked at Fitzwilliam in shock and embarrassment. The embarrassment was due to having her quarrel with Darcy overheard by another, but the shock was due to his firm and even angry repudiation of her charges against Mr. Wickham. She opened her mouth to respond vigorously to what he had said, but whatever she had intended to say was instantly lost since three heads swivelled quickly towards the open window due to the sound of a carriage pulling up in front of the house.

"It is clear there is no time to continue this conversation," Fitzwilliam said crisply. "Lady Catherine appears to have sent her guests home early. She was already upset by the way you absented yourself, Darcy. When I also disappeared, I am sure what little patience she possesses was expended."

Darcy had been standing at the fireplace, almost leaning on it for support, but now he stood up straight and mumbled an indecipherable apology as he made a perfunctory bow. He then rushed blindly from the room, causing Fitzwilliam to step aside quickly since he saw that Darcy's eyes were glazed and unfocused. Indeed, after the door closed sharply, he heard Darcy blunder into the wall on his way to the front door.

Fitzwilliam turned back to Elizabeth, who also made for the door.

"Miss Bennet, I must have a moment before you go. There is no time to continue, but I cannot leave this misunderstanding in place."

"There is no misunderstanding, sir," Elizabeth began coldly, but Fitzwilliam interrupted her in a manner completely at odds with his usual polite and civil composure.

"I am greatly afraid you are completely and utterly mistaken," he said, both politely and firmly. "I cannot let this stand."

His words were brisk and forceful as he fell unconsciously into the mannerisms of a military officer. "You return to London Saturday week, I understand. And you will stay there how long…?"

"A week or more," Elizabeth answered without thinking, automatically responding to the voice of quiet command.

"And you will reside there with your uncle. Did you mention his name?"

"Gardiner. Mr. Edward Gardiner."

"And where does the gentleman live?"

"In Gracechurch Street. In Cheapside." Elizabeth had regained enough of her usual composure to make this final comment in a sarcastic tone, her anger overcoming the previous automatic responses to Fitzwilliam's questions. She refused to feel any embarrassment for an uncle who made a living by trade.

"Excellent—then I shall wait on you the Monday after your return. I can then provide more details regarding the misunderstandings between you and my hapless cousin. I wish you good evening and a safe journey to town." He bowed quickly before smoothly exiting the room.

"Wait!" Elizabeth cried. "There is no need—"

But Fitzwilliam was gone, and Elizabeth stamped her foot in anger and frustration. She heard the sound of voices in the hall as he paid his respects to the Collinses and Maria Lucas, and then she heard the front door close behind him.

"There is no need for what, Eliza?" asked Charlotte Collins as she came into the room, obviously having overheard Elizabeth's last words.

"It is nothing, Charlotte, just a misunderstanding. Just a stupid, stupid, stupid misunderstanding. But I must beg you to excuse me. My headache has returned."

With that, Elizabeth fled for the stairs and the comfort and safety of her room.

CHAPTER 2

Blessed is the servant who loves his brother as much when he is sick and useless as when he is well and can be of service to him. And blessed is he who loves his brother as well when he is afar off as when he is by his side, and who would say nothing behind his back he might not, in love, say before his face.

— St. Francis of Assisi

Thursday, April 16, 1812
Rosings, Kent

Fitzwilliam had many things on his mind as he walked back to Rosings, mostly based on two central and amazing items: first, that Darcy had proposed marriage to the charming and amiable Elizabeth Bennet and, second, that she had soundly refused him. It was clear that the two of them had experienced more contact in Hertfordshire than he would have anticipated from what Darcy had told him. It was equally obvious that, whatever his cousin's feelings about *her*, the lady had formed a most profound dislike of *him*.

Darcy must have been shocked beyond all measure at her refusal, Fitzwilliam thought, and despite his compassion for his cousin's thwarted hopes, he could not help being somewhat amused by the irony that Darcy, having made up *his* mind, was found wanting by the object of his affections.

After the way he has been pursued through all the corridors and byways of London society by a multitude of available young women—and their mothers—he never could have entertained the possibility of being rejected at all, much less being rejected so utterly.

From the little I heard tonight, Miss Bennet has two reasons to reject any intentions on Darcy's part. She may have more, given the anger in her words. While she cannot know how utterly worthless Wickham is, her second reason—the one involving Darcy's separation of Bingley from her own sister—is almost certain to be well justified. Darcy told me himself that he saved a friend from an unwise marriage, and I assumed it was Bingley he meant. Now, not only do I know my assumption was correct, I also know it was Miss Bennet's sister. In fact, it must be her most beloved sister, the elder, given Miss Elizabeth's age of barely twenty, according to Lady Catherine. So I have been incorrect in calling her Miss Bennet, since that title belongs to her sister until she marries.

In any case, I have to wonder just how justified Darcy was. Given Miss Elizabeth's qualities, I have difficulty believing that a sister she values so highly would truly be such an imprudent choice. This seems to be a part of Darcy's increasing lack of consideration for those who are not part of his family or circle of friends. What a mess he has made for himself!

Well, one can do only what one can do. I have already tried to speak with him about these changes, but he simply ignores my questions. The open and friendly young man of my youth has been replaced by a version of…well, yes, of my father.

Fitzwilliam shook his head in sorrow as he walked, remembering the unhappy years of his youth after he had refused to comply with his father's edict that he begin studying for a life in the church. His father, as was common for the times, had determined his younger sons would find employment in the church, in the navy, and in the army—and in that order. His father had been beyond furious when Fitzwilliam defied him, and the two of them had been mostly estranged since that time. The Earl of Matlock was not a forgiving man, especially towards a son who refused a direct parental command.

Most of the subsequent years had been spent with the Darcy family since his father would not allow a disobedient son to live under the same roof as the rest of the family, and Fitzwilliam had not been inclined to sleep in the stables. During those years, he could have had no better friend than Darcy, and old Mr. Darcy had been more of a parent to him than his own father had.

Now, I find a cousin grown increasingly haughty and disdainful towards those he does not know well, and while Darcy does not challenge the justice of my charges, he gives no indication that he is inclined to mend his ways. Perhaps, tonight's events might be momentous enough to make him realize just how much he has been the architect of his own misfortune.

Certainly, there have been events in his life that would incline him to step back and away from a world that seems determined to either trap him or exploit him. There was that Marshall fellow from Cambridge who presumed on their friendship at school to try to get Darcy to invest in his ill-fated shipping venture shortly after old Mr. Darcy passed on. And there was that mother and daughter—what were their names?—who tried to trap Darcy into marriage by an artfully arranged clothing mishap—with witnesses, of course! Their plan very nearly succeeded if not for Darcy's wariness. But he has obviously gone too far in this matter, and I shall have to convince him of that. His own actions and habits of defence have caused him to give great offence to a young lady he hoped to make his bride. If I can make him see and understand his errors, he might yet mend his manners towards others and redeem himself in her eyes.

As for Miss Elizabeth, I shall do what I said and visit her in town to acquaint her with Wickham's true character, especially his skill at deceit, though it is unlikely she would be suitable prey for the scoundrel. She is not rich enough to tempt him. But I cannot see any way to repair the injury Darcy has done her sister.

A sudden thought struck him, and he wondered in what manner Miss Elizabeth had come to know Wickham.

He must have taken up residence in Hertfordshire and then spun her some kind of fairy tale about being badly treated by Darcy. But if Darcy knew before today that the rascal had defamed him, why did he not make known the history between them?

He realized the answer to that question even as the thought occurred to him.

Of course, Darcy would not want to reveal any aspect of Georgiana's near elopement with Wickham to those he does not know. Regardless, his overly fastidious concern about concealing such private family matters has become a partial reason for Miss Elizabeth's disdain and helps explain tonight's disastrous events.

Fitzwilliam heaved a sigh as he approached Rosings.

This is a fine farce to entangle a colonel of dragoons. What would my fellow officers think if they knew I had taken on the role of matchmaker for my cousin? Darcy is not likely to thank me for my interference were he to know its extent. Of course, he will never learn of my efforts unless Miss Elizabeth's attitude towards him changes. I certainly shall not inform him.

As for my chances of changing her mind, I cannot hold out much hope. That is unfortunate for Darcy because she might be just the tonic to restore him to some semblance of humanity. In addition to what I heard, I suspect she simply does not like him. Even after she learns of her mistake with Wickham, she is likely to remain so opposed to him that nothing further can be done. In which case, that will be an end to it. I shall have done my duty and corrected her errors, and I can then go about my business, leaving Darcy to deal with his own mistakes.

And, now that I think on it, when I talk of Wickham to Miss Elizabeth, I probably should not mention what the blackguard attempted with Georgiana, at least not directly.

Fitzwilliam clattered up the front steps, his hand automatically controlling his sword so it did not drift between his legs as sometimes happened to younger officers. As soon as he stepped inside Rosings, he was unsurprised to find Lady Catherine and Darcy engaged in an argument at the foot of the stairs. Rather, his aunt was engaged; Darcy was simply standing, listening silently to his aunt with ill grace.

"I demand to know why you absented yourself in such a manner, Darcy!" she scolded. "I was mortified to find both you and Fitzwilliam had disappeared—simply disappeared!—without even a word of explanation!"

Her ladyship must have seen something in Darcy's eyes, for she rounded on Fitzwilliam. "There you are! The other culprit responsible for making this a most embarrassing evening. Where did you and Darcy get to, Fitzwilliam? I want to know what is going on, and I want to know it right now!"

It had been a tactical blunder for Lady Catherine to turn her back on Darcy, and Fitzwilliam could not completely repress a smile as his cousin simply turned and began to mount the stairway. Lady Catherine turned away from Fitzwilliam with her questions unanswered and followed Darcy, continuing to chide him as he stalked mutely down the hall. Her remonstrations only came to a halt when Darcy entered his room, Fitzwilliam so close on his heels that he could not close the door.

"Please excuse us, Aunt," Fitzwilliam said smoothly, as he effortlessly pulled the door out of Darcy's grasp and stepped into the room. "We shall see you at breakfast, but now I shall wish you a good night." He closed the door securely behind him and locked it, cutting off his aunt's remonstrations.

Darcy looked at him with ill-concealed disfavour. "I do not feel particularly convivial tonight for obvious reasons. I would much prefer solitude, so it would be most pleasing if you would hie yourself to your own room."

"Nay, nay," responded Fitzwilliam cheerily. "You brood far too much these days. And you share your thoughts even less. For example, if you had shared with me your intention of offering marriage to Miss Elizabeth Bennet, I could have told you that your venture was ill-advised."

Darcy gave Fitzwilliam a black glare then looked away. "Who says I offered marriage? We were having a dispute regarding that scoundrel Wickham."

"It will not do, Darcy. It does not even come close. I heard too much. The windows to the front room were open to the evening air, and I could not fail to hear your words and hers. I clearly heard Miss Bennet state categorically that she could never accept the man who had ruined the chance of happiness of a most beloved sister. Were those not her exact words?"

Darcy said nothing and merely flung himself into a stuffed chair, so Fitzwilliam continued.

"I thought I had heard correctly. So, you offered marriage and she refused you, stating as one of the reasons that you had done injury to her sister. It does not take a high intellect to connect what she said tonight with what you told me about saving a friend from an ill-conceived marriage. The friend must have been Bingley, and the lady in question must have been Miss Elizabeth's sister. Am I correct?"

Darcy looked at Fitzwilliam hard for a moment and finally nodded grudgingly. "I have nothing for which to apologize in that matter."

"Yet, you were willing to make a match with the sister whose relations were *not* a suitable match for your friend. Does this not seem a trifle inconsistent?"

"It is not the same." But Darcy showed his discomfort by springing to his feet and beginning to pace the room.

Fitzwilliam shook his head in bemusement. "Darcy, you can be so blind sometimes. Did you never consider what the response of Miss Elizabeth might be when she learned of your interference between her sister and Bingley?"

Darcy looked quite uncomfortable at this and would not meet Fitzwilliam's eyes. "To be honest, I simply did not think of it. When you say it like that, I suppose I should have suspected she would learn of it at some time or other, which she obviously did. But I simply overlooked the matter. It appears to be yet another mistake on my part."

"I fully agree. But, because I was completely ignorant of your intentions, I have to admit that I am the one who accidentally brought the issue to her attention. Just this very day, I was walking with Miss Elizabeth in the park, and the conversation came around to you and Bingley. She challenged your friendship with him, implying you only associated with him because he witlessly followed your lead. In your defence, I asserted that you took care of him in those areas where he needed it and had lately saved him from a most imprudent marriage."

"What?" Darcy exclaimed in consternation, stopping to stare at his cousin.

"Sorry, old fellow, but I was completely unaware of your attachment to Miss Elizabeth at the time. She questioned me sharply as to the cause of your interference, and I told her what little I knew—that there were objections to the lady's family. I saw my comments did not please her, but she quickly changed the topic. I forgot about it until now."

Darcy threw himself back into his chair and closed his eyes in dismay. Fitzwilliam eyed him sympathetically for a few seconds before continuing. "Now that I know this much, perhaps you had better tell me the rest. What was the reason for your interference? I cannot believe any sister of Miss Elizabeth could be so completely unworthy of Bingley."

Darcy was unable to answer for some moments as his usually impassive face showed a succession of conflicting and intense emotions. His despair was obvious, and Fitzwilliam realized his attraction to the young lady must be great indeed if it was beyond Darcy's ability to conceal it. Darcy also showed flashes of anger, bewilderment, and grief, and it was some time before he was able to get himself in hand and respond to Fitzwilliam's question.

"The sister in question is her elder sister, Miss Jane Bennet, and she is in actuality a well-mannered, polite, and charming young lady. In fact, she is probably more so than even her younger sister, and you have evidence of how I feel about *her*. If it were only a question of Miss Bennet's propriety, I would not have stepped in. There were two matters that concerned me. The first was those members of her family who did not have the same manners. The two youngest sisters, for example, are exceedingly wild, unrestrained, and utterly foolish. I cannot see how they have been permitted to be out in society. And their mother is actually worse. At the ball held at Bingley's estate shortly before I left Hertfordshire, she was positively gloating at how her eldest daughter was as good as installed as mistress of Netherfield. She went further to say she was depending on that connexion to throw her remaining daughters into the path of other rich men. This is not rumour or hearsay. I actually overheard her say just that. Further, she knew I could not help overhearing her, yet she made no attempt to restrain herself—none at all. It was more than I could stand to see Bingley connected to such a family, so that was one reason I acted as I did. In fact, Mrs. Bennet reminded me of another mother seeking to get her daughter well married. You may remember Mrs. Northridge, the one who...who..."

"Contrived to have you discovered in private with the upper part of her daughter's dress fallen to her waist? Was that the one?"

Darcy nodded soundlessly, his eyes closed but with revulsion evident in his expression at the memory.

"I remember the affair," Fitzwilliam commented, "but I had forgotten the name. That would be a mark against the young lady, but—"

"I said that there were two matters, and I agree that the first is concerning but not absolutely conclusive in and of itself. The more pertinent reason was that I believed Miss Bennet's attachment to

Bingley was not nearly as deep as his. After her mother's comments and from other conversations I overheard in which their marriage was considered as good as fixed, I took it upon myself to observe them both closely. This was not difficult since they did not leave each other's side for the rest of the evening.

"I could see that Bingley's partiality for Miss Bennet was beyond what I had seen before, but about Miss Bennet I was more doubtful. Her look and manners were as open, cheerful, and engaging as ever, but I could not discern any evidence of particular regard. She received his attentions with pleasure but did not show any attraction similar to Bingley's. In honesty, I admit I was desirous of believing her indifferent since I knew she would accept if Bingley made an offer of marriage. Her mother would see to that. Even so, I took pains not to allow those facts to influence my observations, and my conclusion as to her indifference was based on impartial conviction—not because I wished it so. Until today, I have had no reason to doubt my analysis."

"Yet it appears, based on what I overheard, that you came to a wrong conclusion. Which makes Miss Elizabeth's resentment all too justified."

Darcy nodded in unhappy agreement, so Fitzwilliam continued.

"But you still have not answered my original question. If you feel that strongly against at least part of the Bennet family, how is it you were willing to offer marriage to Miss Elizabeth Bennet when you acted to prevent Bingley from doing the same with her sister?"

Darcy tried to laugh, but his effort sounded more like a hollow cackle, and it took a drink of brandy before he could answer.

"I have been trying to resist just such an attachment for some months. I know my parents would tell me she is not at all suitable since she has neither fortune nor social position. She could do nothing to enhance the Darcy name."

"Are you certain the Darcy name really needs enhancement?"

"Exactly the question I have been asking myself, and I have struggled to act as I thought my mother and father would wish me to act. You were witness to just how unsuccessful I have been in hewing to their guidelines. Everything came to a crux last night with our departure imminent."

"You could delay it again, you know."

"Yes, but I have already done so once. To delay again would just sidestep the issue, and last night I finally reached a conclusion that seemed inescapable. I realized that I simply could not face the rest of my life without her at my side. I...I need her, Richard. Without her, I am...incomplete. I know it, but I do not know how to correct my...defect."

Fitzwilliam looked at Darcy thoughtfully before speaking. "And you believe Miss Elizabeth can fix what you call your 'defect'? Since returning to England, you know I have frequently asked what caused you to change while I was gone, yet you always managed to avoid giving me clear answers. I cannot see how Miss Elizabeth can fix anything."

"Not by herself, no," Darcy said miserably. "You are correct about there being a problem, but I have no idea what happened, and I simply do not know what to do. The problem is mine, and I have to fix it, but I do not know how. That is why I evaded your questions."

He looked up at Fitzwilliam with haunted eyes. "I do not believe I possess the courage to even try without her. She haunts my thoughts. Without her, it would be easier...safer...to just go on as I did while you were on the continent and devote my energies to making sure Georgiana finds a suitable husband so her children can carry on the family line."

He shook his head, and Fitzwilliam could easily read his cousin's confusion.

"I do not understand how I could have been so wrong," Darcy said. "I was certain she discerned my interest and knew of my intentions. I was convinced she was only waiting for me to declare myself."

Fitzwilliam was shocked at this statement. "You thought she recognised your interest and returned it?"

"Of course. How could she have failed to discern my attraction? I showed no interest in any of the other young ladies in Hertfordshire and twice went so far as to ask her to dance. And my attentiveness while she has been visiting her friend Mrs. Collins has been too marked to be overlooked. There seemed no reason to doubt my inferences."

"Darcy," Fitzwilliam said wearily, "there is a saying that there is no fool like a fool in love, and you are living proof. If your attitude towards Miss Elizabeth Bennet was supposed to indicate an *interest* in her, *I* never recognised it. And as for her attitude towards you, I am afraid I have to tell you: it more resembled concealed hostility than anything else."

Darcy seemed to sink further down into his chair as he received these words. Silently, he drained the little brandy in his glass and looked about for the bottle. Fitzwilliam leaned over to fill his glass. He knew Darcy was looking to dull his pain, and while there were problems in turning to spirits as a refuge from despair, there was little else he could suggest in the short term.

A more comfortable, companionable silence held for some minutes, more intimate than any Fitzwilliam had shared with his cousin since returning. Fitzwilliam had little advice to give, and it was Darcy who finally broke the silence.

"The part about her sister surprised me. It shocked me, to tell the truth. I could see why Mrs. Bennet would be furious at seeing her plans thwarted, but I did not think either of her daughters would be greatly distressed."

"In line with your assessment that Miss Bennet's feelings towards Bingley were not that involved."

"Correct."

"So you were surprised to learn from Miss Elizabeth that there was a great depth of feeling towards your friend."

"Exactly. Oh, she received his attentions readily enough, but I could not see anything particularly fervent. When I made that point to

Bingley, it was not difficult to convince him to give her up. Certainly, if the positions were reversed, no person or argument could have convinced me to give up Elizabeth Bennet."

Darcy was silent after that, and Fitzwilliam could see the effect on him of these unprecedented confessions of doubt and uncertainty. Seeing such an intense emotional reaction in his normally imperturbable cousin shocked him to his marrow, and if he had not previously been convinced by Darcy's words, his cousin's unmistakable angst put an end to the matter.

Without a word, he filled Darcy's glass again and set the brandy within easy reach. He considered telling him of his intention to visit Miss Elizabeth in town to disabuse her of her mistaken attitudes regarding George Wickham, but he decided not to engender hope where there might be none. And Darcy might even forbid him to do anything like that on his behalf.

Not that it would affect my intention, Fitzwilliam thought as he closed the door softly behind him, *but it might increase the tension in a situation with too many heightened emotions.*

But the discussion just ended had convinced him that he needed to do more than just acquaint Miss Elizabeth with Wickham's character as he had originally planned.

Given what has already passed between them, I doubt I can truly change Miss Elizabeth's opinion of Darcy, but I can at least inform her of the pressures that have shaped him these last years. Also, if she is at all interested in my opinion, I can venture that I do not believe him beyond redemption, at least for the right woman. Darcy is right in one thing. Despite the shambles he has made of their acquaintance, I believe her to be a woman who would complement him in those areas where he is wanting. Perhaps she might keep that thought in mind for the future, though she is likely not willing to consider it right now. In addition, though I dare not make the point explicitly, she really ought to consider how he might complement certain facets of her own character.

By the time he reached his own chambers, Fitzwilliam's attitude had shed the gloom that had surrounded him in Darcy's room, and he was already considering how he should phrase what he had to say to Miss Elizabeth Bennet on his cousin's behalf.

CHAPTER 3

Conscientious people are apt to see their duty in that which is the most painful course.

— George Eliot

Monday, April 27, 1812
Gracechurch Street, London

At just after two o'clock on Monday, Colonel Fitzwilliam turned down Gracechurch Street. None of the respectable-looking but rather plain houses were numbered, but a street vendor directed him to a house further down the street. This information was quickly confirmed since the house had a bronze plate over the door with the legend, *E. Gardiner.* He appraised the house as he dismounted, noting that it appeared well built and maintained and was of a simple architectural style common about fifty years previously.

I know little about architecture, he thought wryly. *But while this house is more fashionable and larger than my own town house, they look to be built in a similar fashion.*

The door was answered promptly by a young woman wearing the simple dress and apron of a servant.

"Colonel Fitzwilliam to see Miss Elizabeth Bennet if she is available," he said, presenting his card. From the quick examination the maid gave his card, he wagered the young woman could read, which was vanishingly rare amongst most household staff.

"Certainly, sir," she said with a curtsey. "Will you be staying long enough to need your horse cared for?"

"If possible, yes," he responded, and the maid smiled at his obvious surprise.

"Mr. Gardiner shares a stable with the house next door. My brother is the assistant groom. I shall inform him after I conduct you upstairs. If you would come this way, Colonel?"

As he followed the maid, Fitzwilliam was somewhat surprised he had not been left waiting in the hall while the maid took his card to her mistress. Either Miss Elizabeth had given warning of his possible visit, or else the family allowed their servants considerable latitude in admitting visitors.

"Colonel Fitzwilliam," the maid announced after opening the door.

As soon as he entered and saw the four women who had risen to their feet, Fitzwilliam knew his arrival had not been expected. The look of polite inquiry on the face of an older woman, whom he assumed to be Mrs. Gardiner, would have been enough to tell him as much, even if he had not seen the look of shocked surprise on Miss Elizabeth's face. Maria Lucas was also present, as he had expected, as was another young lady who could be none other than Miss Jane Bennet.

So much for Miss Elizabeth having given warning, for it appears she did not believe I would really come, he told himself in amusement as he cordially greeted the two ladies he already knew. *She appears rather irritated as well as surprised, and I wonder whether she has told her aunt and sister any part of what occurred in Kent? Perhaps she does not want to discuss such sensitive matters where Miss Lucas might overhear. But what did she think I intended to do? I told her I would call on her, and here I am.*

Whether Elizabeth was surprised or irritated, he saw it did not appear to affect her manners as she quickly turned towards the older woman at her side.

"Colonel Fitzwilliam, may I present my aunt, Mrs. Gardiner? Aunt Gardiner, this is Colonel Fitzwilliam, whom I met in Kent. He is Mr. Darcy's cousin and a son of the Earl of Matlock."

"Your servant, madam," Fitzwilliam responded with a bow over Mrs. Gardiner's hand, and he raised it towards but not quite all the way to his lips.

"I am delighted to meet you, Colonel," Mrs. Gardiner said easily. "And if I may, allow me to introduce another niece, Miss Jane Bennet, Lizzy's eldest sister, who is also visiting us.

"Yes, Miss Elizabeth has mentioned her often. I am pleased to make your acquaintance, Miss Bennet," he said as he turned and bowed to her politely.

"And I, yours," Jane said in a soft voice as she curtseyed, and it was only when he rose from his bow that Fitzwilliam got his first good look at the young lady who had been the subject of so much intense discussion between Darcy and him.

She's certainly lovely, especially with those violet eyes. It is the eyes that are the most overwhelming, he thought, as he moved to seat himself in the free chair next to Mrs. Gardiner and her younger niece. *But then, Miss Elizabeth is quite striking also. Darcy mentioned that both sisters were considered among the most handsome young ladies in the neighbourhood of Bingley's estate, and Miss Elizabeth has definitely had an impact on Darcy unlike any of the more fashionable ladies here in town.*

Fitzwilliam sighed internally as he thought of Darcy's poor method of dealing with this whole affair, but he was determined to correct Miss Elizabeth's wildly mistaken notions about George Wickham. He also wanted to repair Darcy's character in her eyes as much as possible, but he knew that would be the more challenging part of his visit today. Still, he would do his best for his cousin, partly because of their long friendship but also because of his immense gratitude to the entire Darcy family.

After being essentially cut off by his father, the Darcys—especially Lady Anne—had helped him immensely. As well as providing a home to replace the one he had fled, she had arranged for the purchase of his lieutenancy in the cavalry as well as outfitting him with horse, saddle, uniforms, and arms. That generosity had made it possible for him at least to support himself in life. After such unexpected beneficence, he had resolved that the only chances he would take in the future would be those that might occur on the battlefield. After all, he told himself at the time, those chances had to be taken, or else he would never distinguish himself. And taking risks in battle was necessary; he knew a number of forty-year-old lieutenants who had served honourably but had never achieved promotion because they had never done anything particularly distinguishing. However, in his private life, he had steered a path that avoided entangling connexions of many types, whether associated with a risky financial enterprise or perhaps involving a fashionable young lady who needed money as badly as he did and simply could not believe the son of an earl could be a near pauper.

Well, he was no longer a pauper, thanks to careful management of his finances and the bequest he had received after Mr. Darcy's death. The latter, he was certain, had been the work of Darcy's mother, for she had been managing the affairs of her increasingly distracted husband for years before her own untimely death. But at least he could support himself now and for the rest of his life, even if he was placed on half-pay.

These thoughts went through his mind as the initial pleasantries were proceeding and he explained his acquaintance with Elizabeth. He was about to proceed with the substance of his mission; however, he was a little reticent about talking openly about Darcy in front of so many. He looked closely at Elizabeth, wondering whether he might solicit a private interview with her, when she suddenly leaned over and began whispering urgently into her aunt's ear. Mrs. Gardiner looked rather startled at what her niece told her, and she glanced over at Fitzwilliam in sudden concern.

But her civility went too deep to continue to whisper in front of a guest, and she suddenly put her fingers up to stop her niece. Gracefully, she came to her feet, and Elizabeth rose with her, discreetly guided by her aunt's hand on her elbow. Fitzwilliam was caught off-guard, but he quickly scrambled to his feet in turn.

"Colonel Fitzwilliam, my niece has just imparted some information that was previously unknown to me. From what she tells me, you likely have a good idea of the matter she wishes to discuss with me. Please accept my apologies for such a breach of civility, but might I ask Jane and Maria to entertain you while Lizzy and I have a private chat?"

Fitzwilliam gave her a quick bow of acquiescence. "Certainly, madam. I can indeed imagine how…surprising…Miss Elizabeth's news is to you. Take all the time you need. I shall be quite happy in the meantime."

"You are too kind," Mrs. Gardiner returned. "Now, come, Lizzy. We can use your uncle's study. Ah, here is tea just arriving. Jane dear, would you serve the colonel while I have a private talk with your sister? Thank you, my dear."

WHEN MRS. GARDINER CLOSED THE DOOR BEHIND ELIZABETH and took a seat in her husband's study, she had to control her anger since she was rather upset with her niece. However, knowing Elizabeth as she did, she had to believe that only some undue distress could have caused her to behave with such incivility. Nevertheless, explainable or not, it was her duty to ensure such behaviour was not repeated.

Accordingly, her voice was cool and firm as she fixed her niece with an unyielding eye. "You should well know, Elizabeth, that it is not the custom in the Gardiner household to allow people into our home and then ask them to leave," she said sternly, and Elizabeth had the grace to blush in embarrassment.

"I am sorry, Aunt," she said, eyes downcast. "I do know better. I just…was not prepared to talk of what Colonel Fitzwilliam wishes to discuss."

"That may be, but what you suggested to me in the front room was not at all proper. You do understand, do you not?"

"Yes, I do. It will not happen again."

"I am sure of it, Lizzy. But remember that manners were invented in order to be our guide when our tempers are high and our blood runs hot. Manners are what keep us from each other's throats."

"I agree. I was mistaken in my attempt to deal with the matter."

Mrs. Gardiner nodded agreement before continuing. "Now, before we consider the visit of this colonel—who, by the bye, seems to be quite a pleasant young man—I must insist you explain the nature of his visit. From what you whispered to me, Mr. Darcy evidently made you an offer of marriage while you were visiting Mrs. Collins. Is that correct?"

Elizabeth nodded without saying anything.

Mrs. Gardiner raised an eyebrow at Elizabeth's response. "That was rather surprising, was it not?"

Again, Elizabeth made no response, and Mrs. Gardiner continued. "Considering what you told me at Christmas, I would have thought he disliked you as much as you disliked him. That evidently was not true, was it?"

Elizabeth gave a forced laugh at this comment. "Evidently not, Aunt. I was completely surprised."

"I daresay. And, having heard his proposal, you refused it, rather forcefully from what you said. Is that correct?" Again, Elizabeth only nodded.

"How forcefully, Lizzy?"

"Not as forcefully as I had intended," she admitted rather sheepishly. "Colonel Fitzwilliam barged into the room and interrupted us before I could even get to the strongest parts of my rejoinder."

"Hmmm…" Her aunt eyed Lizzy and wondered whether her niece had ever considered why she let Mr. Darcy affect her so strongly. The Lizzy she knew would have simply laughed at the man rather than taken such offence. However, she could discuss this later with her husband, who would be greatly surprised at the day's events.

"And that brings us to the most surprising part of what you told me: that you are afraid his cousin has now come to make excuses for Mr. Darcy, and therefore you wished me to ask him to leave immediately. That, Lizzy, will not do. I must know much more before I would ever agree to such a rude and impolite request."

Elizabeth was reluctant to discuss the matter, but she realized she had no choice. She tried to temporise by giving her aunt the highlights of the proposal and its interruption by Fitzwilliam, but Mrs. Gardiner was far too shrewd to let her evade disclosing all the details. She shrewdly probed and questioned, despite Elizabeth's discomfort, until her niece finally confessed that it was her assertion of the many wrongs Mr. Darcy had committed against Mr. Wickham that had been the reason for Fitzwilliam's visit that day.

"So the good colonel does not share your admiration for Mr. Wickham, does he? Well, I have now met them both, though I have only met Colonel Fitzwilliam for a few minutes. Certainly, there does not appear to be anything on the surface of either man that would make any judgment easy, but it is clear there cannot be two right views in this matter. Mr. Wickham asserts that Mr. Darcy is a blackguard, and the colonel insists the opposite—that Mr. Wickham is the villain of the piece. Now, what else transpired while you were visiting Charlotte?"

She continued to draw reluctant information from Elizabeth until she was finally satisfied that she had the entire story regarding not only every word spoken at Hunsford that disastrous night but also what had transpired previously. Elizabeth was loath to disclose everything: Mr. Darcy's many visits, their frequent meetings in the park, and even Elizabeth's original mortification when Darcy pronounced her only "tolerable" at the Meryton assembly.

"It would appear your young man is so captivated by you that he cannot make his tongue work in your presence," Mrs. Gardiner said in amusement.

"Mr. Darcy is most certainly *not* my 'young man'!" Elizabeth retorted.

"Perhaps not, but you told me of your respect for and friendship with his cousin. Should we not listen to what he has to say, at least in the matter of Mr. Wickham? It certainly sounds as if there is another side to *that* matter than the one related by Mr. Wickham. After all, Mr. Wickham has had his innings. It should now be only fair to allow Mr. Darcy's cousin a turn as batsman."

Elizabeth could not disagree with her aunt's logic, but she decidedly did not wish to do what her aunt—and her own better nature—insisted was the right thing to do. However, her love and respect for her aunt left her no recourse but to return to the front room…and confront Colonel Fitzwilliam.

CHAPTER 4

To him who is determined, it remains only to act.

— Italian Proverb

Monday, April 27, 1812
Gracechurch Street, London

After Elizabeth and her aunt departed, Fitzwilliam's attention turned to the elder sister and Maria Lucas. As Miss Bennet poured and passed out tea, he refrained from engaging in the usual inanities and trivialities so often considered to be perfect examples of amiable discourse among upper-class British society. He had done so on many occasions when he was simply filling the void and conversing with those uninteresting people who seemed to attend every gathering. But he knew and liked Miss Elizabeth Bennet too well to follow such a common and sterile exchange with this young lady.

Instead, knowing from conversations with Elizabeth that her sister had spent several months visiting their aunt and uncle, he enquired about social diversions she had been able to sample during her time in town.

"I have had a very pleasant visit, though I knew before I came that

34

my aunt and uncle do not go out often," Jane said. "We went to view the shops several times, of course—"

"Of course," Fitzwilliam said agreeably.

"—and visited with their various friends. But I was especially pleased at the opportunity to visit Astley's Amphitheatre. The acrobatic riders as well as the clowns and comic sketches were very entertaining. And we also visited the Vauxhall gardens to see an orchestra and singers. I especially enjoyed the boat trip across the Thames to the candle-lit gardens. It was very beautiful. But what about you, Colonel? You must have spent far more time in London than I have."

"Not as much as you would think, though I do look forward to a visit to the theatre or to the philharmonic when I am able to visit Darcy in town. But my duties keep me quite busy and often well removed from London. And I have been gone from England for the last five years."

"Five years! That is a very long time. You must live a very hard life."

"The exigencies of the service—as we so often jest with each other in that black humour common among soldiers," Fitzwilliam said with an uncomfortable shrug. "It happens during wartime, I am afraid. But no more on that topic. Even if you have had a pleasant visit, I have to believe you are very anxious to return home."

"Yes, indeed. We shall be returning in a week, though my aunt says she has planned a number of engagements before we leave…"

Fitzwilliam found it quite easy to maintain a conversation with this lovely Bennet sister. Her observations were sage and thoughtful, and he could already discern an inner sweetness of temperament coupled with the same excellent manners as her sister, save that Miss Bennet did not appear to have the wry detachment of Miss Elizabeth.

With the skill of long practice, he gradually shifted the conversation to other subjects, including herself, her sister Elizabeth, her aunt and uncle, her enjoyment of the company of her young Gardiner cousins, and even her life back at her home. He attempted to draw Miss Lucas into the conversation, but she was even less talkative in this environment than she had been at Rosings.

It was not long before Fitzwilliam began to wonder why Bingley had allowed himself to be separated from this charming young lady. That she was beautiful had struck him on first introduction. But physical beauty could not compensate for the haughty airs so often displayed by the aristocratic young ladies who decorated the more popular salons, especially during the London Season. Though the blood of the nobility flowed in his own veins, Fitzwilliam had, over the years, grown increasingly unimpressed with its importance or even its tolerability. He repressed a shudder at the memory of several interesting but rather embarrassing incidents from his few ventures into that maelstrom of the marriage mart when he was younger and more foolish.

He had always had an appreciative eye for the ladies, though his financial situation and his own nature had prevented him from cutting a particularly wide swath through the feminine population. In his opinion, Miss Bennet possessed a rare beauty that does not fade with the passing of youth. He thought this young lady would become more lovely as she aged—one of those ladies whose hair simply turned grey while the rest of her retained a remarkable similarity to that of her youth.

Because of the accident of his noble birth, Fitzwilliam had gained extensive experience in talking with ladies, both those of society and from the more ordinary occupations. It was a manner he had with both men and women of looking directly at the person, concentrating on what was said, and asking the short questions that, little by little, convinced the other person of his true interest in what he or she had to say. It was a talent that came somewhat naturally, but it was also one he had developed and extended. Such capabilities could have been a manipulative tool in the hands of a scoundrel, but Colonel Richard Fitzwilliam had not an ounce of scoundrel in him. Further, if he was not a scoundrel with men, he was equally not a rake with the ladies.

Fitzwilliam knew he was not particularly handsome. In fact, a fellow officer had bestowed the most flattering description of him when he termed him "rugged" and "pleasantly ugly." Added to that was the fact of his profession as a cavalry officer, which had necessarily led to a degree of muscular development more common for a dockside labourer than the son of an earl. It was perhaps in partial compensation for his deficiencies in physical appeal—about which he could do nothing—that he began to cultivate his skill in discourse.

He had planned his future carefully, and he intended to avoid marriage until his years of active service were over or almost over. He had ways of making his intentions clear to the ladies with whom he enjoyed flirting. Certainly, there had been occasions when a lady desired a more intimate relationship, but he prided himself on the fact that she always knew the true situation. He also prided himself that those few intimate encounters had ended without acrimony, for he had a sixth, seventh, and even an eighth sense that warned him away from those nervous or erratic females who might profess to understand his intentions but would then turn vindictive when he had orders to depart once more in the service of his king.

Those special senses now told him this young lady was hiding a subtle sadness, probably related to having lost the affections of Darcy's friend Bingley. She was concealing her discontent with skill, but he set about trying to dispel that sadness since this young lady did not deserve such melancholy. He believed he was making a bit of progress towards that end when Mrs. Gardiner and a rather downcast Elizabeth returned to the room.

"Please accept my apologies, Colonel," Mrs. Gardiner told him, as she and her niece returned to their seats. "After talking with Lizzy, I believe I now understand the reason for your visit. I have no objections to the conversation Lizzy believes you desire, but I do have a condition, which is that I remain present. I can assure you of my complete secrecy on such a delicate topic, but Lizzy's feelings are running so high I believe a more useful communication will be facilitated by my remaining."

"I certainly have no objections, Mrs. Gardiner," Fitzwilliam said quickly. He had seen evidence of Elizabeth's temper at the Parsonage, and he believed Mrs. Gardiner would be able to moderate what promised to be a quite intense conversation.

"But I believe no useful purpose will be served by my remaining, Aunt," Jane said, rising gracefully to her feet. "It will afford you more privacy if Maria and I take the children to the park in the meantime."

Fitzwilliam noted that Jane's plan, while admirable for its civility, was not one that Miss Lucas desired; it was clear from her expression that she would much rather stay and listen.

"Very well, Jane," Mrs. Gardiner said. "Please ask Mary Alice to go with you, though. James still has the sniffles, and she might need to bring him back early."

Jane returned an elegant curtsey to Fitzwilliam's bow before leaving the parlour and closing the door behind her.

As Fitzwilliam returned to his seat, Mrs. Gardiner looked at him expectantly while Elizabeth looked down at the floor.

Fitzwilliam cleared his throat, mentally going over the points he wished to make.

But first, I need to find out how much background I need to provide, he thought.

"Mrs. Gardiner, from the length of time you were gone with Miss Elizabeth, would I be correct in assuming that she has acquainted you with the particulars of what occurred between her and Mr. Darcy in Kent?"

"I believe she has now done so—not willingly, you understand, for our Lizzy is a very self-reliant young lady and does not usually seek the counsel of others. But I believe she has told me everything of importance."

"Very well, then. The primary purpose of my presence here is to right a certain misconception of your niece regarding my cousin. As you should know from her narrative, I interrupted the quarrel between them when I heard her accuse my cousin of, among other things, having thwarted the hopes of, and inflicted misfortunes upon, one George Wickham. I had arrived at the Parsonage shortly before that point and, upon realising the sensitive and private nature of the conversation I heard through an open window, had been about to withdraw when I heard the charge regarding Wickham. Neither Darcy nor Miss Elizabeth appeared to be aware of my presence, and I am certain I could have left quietly with no one the wiser.

"But I reversed my course at that point. Whatever else my cousin is or is not, has done or has not done, I simply could not stand aside and see him accused of any malfeasance whatsoever towards one of the most ungrateful scoundrels it has been my misfortune to encounter."

Elizabeth looked at him with open disbelief, but Mrs. Gardiner wore a look of intent interest as he continued.

"Those are strong words, ladies, and I do not make them lightly. But George Wickham has been given opportunity after opportunity by the Darcy family and has repaid generosity with disloyalty, avarice, and deceit. You do know George's father was old Mr. Darcy's steward, do you not? Very well, then. Know also that the elder Mr. Wickham was a loyal and capable man, faithful to the Darcy family and to his position. And, in return, Darcy's father stood godfather to the son and provided the same schooling and education for young Wickham as his own son received."

"Exactly as Mr. Wickham related," Elizabeth snapped. "He never tried to hide his background."

Fitzwilliam responded calmly. "Ah, the best lies are always built on some foundation of truth rather than being complete fabrications from beginning to end. For example, did Wickham disclose that he amassed considerable debt at Cambridge? Or that Darcy discharged those debts out of his own allowance?"

Elizabeth paled at this charge, and Fitzwilliam thought he could see her confidence waver.

"And perhaps he forgot to mention that Darcy did the same in Derbyshire when Wickham had finally worn out his welcome there? Strange that Wickham should have forgotten such unusual generosity on the part of his arch-enemy, is it not? Well, actually it is not strange at all, for these two items are but mere snippets among the other black marks that may be set against his name. For example, did he mention that Darcy's father intended to provide for his future after he was gone?"

"Yes, he did," Elizabeth said slowly, feeling her certainty begin to weaken. "He was supposed to be provided a living by the Darcy family patronage."

"Of course he was. Old Mr. Darcy, may God bless his soul, only saw the best in George. He did not know him as Darcy and I knew him, and both of us knew Wickham should never be a clergyman. But our concerns became somewhat moot when his father passed on about five years ago. Wickham received a bequest of a thousand pounds from the elder Mr. Darcy's will—"

"A thousand pounds?" Mrs. Gardiner exclaimed. "A princely sum for a young man."

"Yes, it was, and Wickham evidently thought the same, for he left Pemberley shortly afterwards, leaving behind the debts I mentioned. Darcy heard nothing from him for about half a year, at which time Wickham wrote to Darcy to say that he had decided against the church and wished to read law. The problem, he wrote, was that the interest on a thousand pounds would not be enough to support those studies, and he wished to negotiate a more immediate monetary payment rather than to wait for the family living the elder Mr. Darcy wished him to have when it became vacant. For my part, I am certain that Wickham ran through his entire legacy in about six months and came up with the story of studying law to replenish his empty purse."

"That is a most unjustified assumption," Elizabeth said hotly.

"I admit I do not have absolute proof," Fitzwilliam said with a nod, indicating he accepted her point in part. "However, since I lived at

Pemberley from the age of twelve and visited often after I received my commission, I had many occasions to form my opinion of Wickham—occasions based on personal knowledge and not the result of a convincing story spun by an amiable man skilled in deceit. I witnessed Wickham use his smooth tongue more than once to either seduce or attempt to seduce the daughters of servants at Pemberley or shopkeepers in Lambton. I *know* George Wickham, Miss Elizabeth."

But Mrs. Gardiner had noted a point in Fitzwilliam's comment and wished it cleared up. "You say you lived at Pemberley since you were twelve? Was that all the time, or did you spend part of that time at your father's estate?"

"It was all the time, Mrs. Gardiner, but that is another story, which I can explain more fully later. But to return to Wickham's letter, he and Darcy struck a bargain: Wickham would receive an outright sum of three thousand pounds, and in return, he signed a paper agreeing never to seek the living Darcy's father had intended for him. I had already left for Egypt some time before, so I was not personally present at Pemberley for that interview, but I would have advised against such a bargain. But Darcy is—or at least he was then—a less cynical man than I, and he thought there was a chance Wickham meant to do as he said. In any case, he agreed to Wickham's bargain and gave him the three thousand. As witnesses to the truth of what I am saying, Darcy will back me up, as will a number of the servants either at Pemberley or at Darcy's house here in London."

"Lizzy, are you feeling well?" Mrs. Gardiner asked in concern, for Elizabeth had gone pale as a ghost at this last recitation. If Elizabeth had doubted Fitzwilliam previously, she could not do so now. She had never considered that he would lie outright to absolve his cousin of his offences, but she had been certain he must have been unaware of what occurred between Darcy and Wickham.

Instead, he appeared not only to be completely informed on all particulars but also to be cognizant of a number of additional facts of which she had been unaware—all based on personal observation. A number of these fit what Wickham had related, and she understood and agreed with Fitzwilliam's statement that a good lie must have a core of truth. Given his offer to provide witnesses, even beyond the testimony of his cousin, she could not evade the certainty that everything else he was saying about Mr. Wickham must also be true. Either that or he was lying himself, but that was now hard to believe since he had offered to provide witnesses. And, if she had been wrong about Mr. Darcy being the cause of Mr. Wickham's misfortunes, what else had she been wrong about?

"I am…feeling a little faint, Aunt," she said miserably.

"I know, child. I can already see we have been completely deceived by an absolute miscreant."

"Too true, madam, but I cannot let it stand here," Fitzwilliam said, his face stern. "You need to know the entire story about this…as you said…miscreant. That was not the last Darcy heard from Wickham though the previous exchange had essentially ruptured all ties between them. The man returned to my cousin's notice about three years later. This part I know only from letters, for I was in Italy by that time, trying to escape with my regiment before either the French overcame us or our Italian allies betrayed us. But I can still remember the anger in Darcy's letters telling me Wickham had written him when the parson at Kympton died. That was the family living to which the elder Mr. Darcy had made reference. Wickham had evidently spent all the money Darcy had given him—"

"In only three years?" Mrs. Gardiner exclaimed incredulously. "That is…is…"

"Profligate, to say the least. In addition to his legacy, that makes four thousand pounds in about three and a half years. Wickham now requested the appointment at Kympton. He almost demanded it in fact, making reference to the elder Mr. Darcy's intentions. He seems to have believed Darcy would accede to his demand and forget about everything else out of respect for his father. But, unknown to Wickham, Darcy was no longer willing to be deceived by Wickham or to entertain emotional pleas to the memory of his father. He rejected Wickham's appeal and its several repetitions, and he appointed a good and deserving man to the post."

"As was his responsibility. Well, Lizzy, are you convinced now? It seems obvious to me that Mr. Darcy is completely blameless with regard to Mr. Wickham, that he had just cause to refuse to greet and associate with him as would be expected between gentlemen."

"I can provide several witnesses to verify parts of my story within a couple of hours," Fitzwilliam said eagerly. "After having listened to one man spin a convincing tale, I would not take it amiss if you would like additional verification."

"That will not be necessary, sir," Elizabeth said, her voice barely audible and her eyes focused on her lap. "I agree with my aunt, and I feel like an utter fool to have allowed myself to believe what Mr. Wickham said about Mr. Darcy. I remember that Charlotte never thought highly of Mr. Wickham, thinking it very improper for him to be impugning the character of Mr. Darcy in the way he did, especially upon being first introduced to me. It pains me that I was so proud of my judgment that I never considered there might be another side to this dispute."

Mrs. Gardiner looked at Fitzwilliam closely. "There seemed to be something in your eyes just now, Colonel. Was there more? You appear to be somewhat conflicted."

Fitzwilliam squirmed a bit in his seat before meeting her eyes. "There is another item on the scale in this matter, Mrs. Gardiner, but I would much prefer to leave that topic unmentioned unless absolutely necessary because of its privacy. I am prepared to discuss it though I have not secured Darcy's permission, but I would need a pledge of absolute secrecy before I did. Suffice it to say that this single item, weighed upon the scales of anguish to the Darcy family, would outweigh everything

I have already told you. But, because it is of such a sensitive nature and touches so closely upon private, family matters, I would prefer to avoid it if possible. But I *will* discuss it if required."

"I scarcely think that will be necessary. There is one item, however, that does surprise me, and that was your statement that you had not secured Mr. Darcy's permission. Does your cousin not know you are here?" Mrs. Gardiner's surprise was evident. She had supposed Fitzwilliam was acting with the knowledge and approval of his cousin.

"He does not, madam," Fitzwilliam said firmly. "I am acting completely on my own today with the primary object of setting the record straight with respect to George Wickham's deceit of your niece. Darcy is at home, I suppose, though I do not know for certain since I have been with my regiment since returning from Kent. But I would not have mentioned it to him in any case since I thought it possible he would try to forbid me from coming. Your niece, you see, is not the only person involved who is quite self-reliant and unwilling to take the counsel of others. My cousin is such a person as well—too much, perhaps, for his own good."

Fitzwilliam and Mrs. Gardiner exchanged knowing smiles at this comment though Elizabeth completely missed the interplay. Her eyes were focused on her hands in her lap, and she showed no willingness to meet the eyes of either Fitzwilliam or her aunt.

However, Fitzwilliam did need to confirm that he had fully convinced Elizabeth with what he had related, so his next words were addressed to her.

"Miss Elizabeth, I must know for absolute certain that you also believe what I have told you of the history between Wickham and Darcy. Your aunt appears to be convinced, but I came to convince you personally. From what you said, you appear to be persuaded, but I must be certain. I can, as I said, provide evidence if you need additional proofs. Some proofs could be provided rather quickly, such as corroborative testimony by several of Darcy's staff here. Several of those who were at Pemberley during the events I have related are now at Darcy's house here in town. Other evidence might take somewhat longer. I daresay Darcy still has his receipts for his discharge of Wickham's debts, and I am equally sure he has the letter Wickham signed renouncing the living at Kympton when he received his three thousand pounds. And I could, if necessary, relate the other matter I mentioned."

Elizabeth shook her head quickly. "No, that will not be necessary. I am well convinced by what you have told me, and as I said, I should have known better than to allow myself to be deceived in such a manner. I had heard from my sister through Mr. Bingley that Mr. Darcy was known to be an honourable man, and I had not heard any wrong of him other than his actions towards Mr. Wickham. It should have been obvious to me that an otherwise honourable man would not confine his dishonourable deeds to only a single individual. No, I have been blind—wilfully blind. It is most…mortifying."

"Then may I ask whether my information has altered your opinion of my cousin and especially of your reaction towards the addresses he made to you?"

Elizabeth managed a rueful laugh. "You are indeed a faithful agent for your cousin, sir. I am sure he does not deserve you."

Then she grew more pensive and finally shook her head. "No, I am sorry, sir, but even knowing of how badly I estimated his character regarding Mr. Wickham, I have other offences to lay at his feet, especially what he did to separate Jane and Mr. Bingley. And, while I am willing to admit you have rehabilitated part of his character, there remains the simple fact that I simply do not like him and have no desire to change the answer I gave him that evening. I wish I had been more temperate in my response, and I wish I could give you a different answer, for you have shown yourself to be a true and loyal friend. But I simply cannot do so."

"Do not apologize, Miss Elizabeth. I asked the question because I had to, but I expected the answer you gave me. In fact, I agree with you in part. Darcy is not a very sociable person in many ways, especially with respect to those who are not part of his own inner circle. But—and this may surprise you—he was not always that way."

Elizabeth was startled enough by this remark to look sharply at Fitzwilliam, and he nodded in response to her look.

"I assure you: the Fitzwilliam Darcy I found when I returned to England six months ago was not the warm, open man I knew when I departed for Egypt five years ago."

"And why is that?" asked Mrs. Gardiner quickly since she saw Elizabeth was prepared to dispute this statement. "Was there some cataclysm in his life? I know he has come into his fortune at an early age. Five years ago, you said? The death of a parent is always a difficult time for a young man."

"Actually, both his parents are dead, Mrs. Gardiner. And it is not a single event but a succession of events, and I am not sure that even I could ever figure out the root cause. But this I know: for much of my life, I was closer to Darcy than I was to my own brothers. I would like to have that Darcy back, for I am convinced he has fallen into bad habits rather than become a bad person. And I think he is not yet beyond redemption—with the right impetus."

"Or, more exactly, the right woman," Mrs. Gardiner said with a rather sly smile.

"Yes, ma'am, I believe so, hence my presence here today. I shall be perfectly honest with both of you: I am acting as I have done with the hope I might help restore my cousin to what I believe to be his true nature before he becomes too practiced at ignoring the entire world and past saving. I wish I could say my cousin might perform a similar task on your behalf, Miss Elizabeth, but I cannot, for you are whole and not in need of healing."

"Well, we can certainly testify that you have been forthright in your loyalty to your cousin, Colonel," agreed Mrs. Gardiner.

"And just as I expected," said Elizabeth angrily. "It is as I feared, Aunt Gardiner. He will not be content until he has changed my mind. Why cannot my answer be left to stand by its own right?"

Fitzwilliam looked at her calmly, and she glared back at him, her small fists clenched and two bright patches of red on her cheeks that showed her blood was up. Rather than confront her charge directly, he decided on an indirect approach.

"Do you know anything about the Matlock family, Miss Elizabeth? Mrs. Gardiner?"

"Outside of the fact that your father is an earl, I know almost nothing, sir," Mrs. Gardiner said.

"Then I should relate at least a little of my own story since it bears on Darcy's character and my knowledge of its dramatic change. First, my elder brother, George, will inherit the title and all the associated properties and fortune. He will thus become the next Lord Matlock. Since he has already married and sired two sons, neither I nor my other brothers will inherit. One of his sons will do so. Thus, I had to find a profession to support myself, and I chose the army."

He smiled ruefully at Elizabeth, who still glared at him. "As you know, I sometimes commented on being a younger son. It is really a half-joking act of mine, one that has proven effective over the years as an explanation for my lack of funds. You even commented to me: 'What could an earl's son know of true want?' You were partly right, you see, but not completely."

Elizabeth looked a bit uncomfortable at that, and Fitzwilliam could see her certainty waver as he continued. "When I was twelve years old, my father decided my profession would be the church. My younger brothers would go, in turn, to the navy and to the army. But as the next eldest, he declared I would go to the church and would thus receive a religious education.

But I was of a different mind, even at so young an age. I had no interest whatever in being a clergyman. So I refused my father's order.

Again he ordered, and again I refused. I knew I was not right for the church and the church was not right for me. Also, I shall not disguise that I inherited a full measure of the stubbornness my father possesses. The upshot was that he essentially cut me off."

"Cut you off?" Mrs. Gardiner exclaimed. "At the age of twelve?"

"He did indeed, Mrs. Gardiner. He ordered me to live in the stables with the staff and also directed that I should not be allowed to eat my single meal a day until I had done a full day's work. Well, I was not afraid of work, but I had my pride—all the pride of a twelve-year-old boy added to my consciousness of my noble heritage and possibly made worse by that heritage. I left Matlock with the clothes on my back, less than a pound in coin from my mother, and a letter to her sister-in-law, Lady Anne Darcy. It took a fair amount of time to make the journey, most of which I walked since the pittance my mother could give me paid for little post fare at two to three pence per mile. Nor did it buy much food—I spent a considerable time working for my board. But I eventually reached Pemberley and gave my mother's letter to Lady Anne."

Fitzwilliam's eyes were unfocused. "I can still see the calm, queenly features of my aunt as she put down the letter. 'Well,' she said to me, 'my sister asks if we could find room for you at Pemberley, and we have rooms in abundance here. You shall have the one next to Fitzwilliam.'"

The colonel's gaze came back from across the years. "She ordered a bath drawn for me, and the staff managed to find me some clothes, for mine were rags by that time. And she saw to my education. Later, when I confessed my desire to be a soldier, she saw to the purchase of my commission as a seventeen-year-old lieutenant of cavalry, complete with horse, saddle, uniforms, and arms. When she died suddenly a year or so later, I thought my heart would break."

He shook himself, and his voice lost the soft wistfulness it had possessed. "So I grew to adulthood with Darcy, and he has been closer to me than my brothers. My mother and my sister wrote regularly, but my brothers wrote seldom, and my father not at all. I have not, in fact, been face to face with my father in the last seventeen years. The Darcy family—brother, sister, mother, father—were all closer to me than anyone other than my mother and sister.

"So," he continued briskly, "what happened to change Fitzwilliam Darcy? Life did, I suppose—life and stress and the betrayal of trust he found in so many places outside the circle of his family and his closest friends. How long," he asked suddenly, turning to Elizabeth, "has Darcy been managing his own estate, Miss Elizabeth?"

"Why, I…I am sure I do not know," she stammered. "You said the elder Mr. Darcy died some years ago."

"Five years ago, Miss Elizabeth, and so you would say he has had the responsibility for Pemberley and all who depend upon that great estate for the last five years, would you not?"

Elizabeth nodded warily, not at all certain of just where Fitzwilliam was taking this conversation.

"And you would be dead wrong, Miss Elizabeth. He has actually been managing everything since his mother died when he was but eighteen. He is now eight and twenty, so that was ten years ago. How old were you ten years ago? Nine years old? Ten?"

"Ten," mumbled Elizabeth in confusion. "Barely."

"His father," interjected Mrs. Gardiner. "He must not have been capable of it, and Lady Anne had been performing his tasks."

"Exactly," Fitzwilliam said with a nod, impressed by her quickness of mind. Even Elizabeth, well known for being quick-witted, had not yet gotten that far. She was still looking at her aunt in complete confusion.

"Did the younger Mr. Darcy know?" Mrs. Gardiner asked softly.

"No, not really, nor did I because his father outwardly seemed the same as always. But Darcy found out when he was called home from Cambridge after his mother died suddenly. When he arrived at Pemberley, in the midst of his shock and dismay, the elder Mr. Wickham had to tell Darcy that his father had grown increasingly incapable of managing the estate and his mother had gradually assumed the part her husband had previously played. The change did not affect my uncle's nature—he remained as cheerful and amiable as ever. But his cogitative skills had simply vanished, and Mr. Wickham entreated Darcy for help. The affairs of the estate had been at a standstill for more than a fortnight, and decisions were needed immediately. So, in the midst of his grief, Darcy had to learn how to manage an estate the size of Pemberley and to assume the responsibility of everyone who depended on it—the staff, the tenant farmers, the villagers—everyone, including his sister. And, by the bye, including a young cavalry officer who was just learning his trade as a very junior and inexperienced officer."

Fitzwilliam took a sip of tea, which Mrs. Gardiner had just replenished. "I did not learn all the particulars for some months. I did not find out about Lady Anne's death until she was already buried, and it was months after that before I was able to return to Pemberley. Darcy was home from Cambridge, and I shall never forget that interview in his father's study. I was a year older than Darcy at the time and fancied myself as maturing quickly, but already I could recognise that he appeared to have caught me up and surpassed me."

"Cambridge?" asked Mrs. Gardiner in confusion. "Why did he go back to Cambridge?"

"Because his mother had made him promise he would finish his studies there, no matter what else happened. She wrote down a considerable set of instructions in her last weeks—she must have felt her demise coming on. She had also written a letter to Darcy just the night before she died in which she charged him to remember his oath to her, even if he had to close down much of Pemberley in order to make it possible to be away. But Darcy was as stubborn in his own way as I am. He knew that many of the tenant farmers and much of the staff would be out of work and unable to feed their families if he did that, and he arranged for a personal express service to shuttle documents and instructions from Pemberley to Cambridge and back.

So, while the rest of the students were sleeping, wenching, or drinking, Darcy was devoting his late nights and weekends to maintaining a continuing correspondence with the elder Mr. Wickham and with his housekeeper in London. And even then he managed to place near the top of his class every year."

Mrs. Gardiner was shocked to hear this tale. "So young, so young. All those years were taken away from him. And this, I suppose, is the reason for the change you mentioned?"

"If it was, I saw no signs of it at the time though I am sure the strain played its part. He came to visit me when he finished at Cambridge, and he was as warm and cheerful as ever. In fact, he was looking forward to returning to Pemberley and spending more time with his sister, who was then approaching ten years old. And things did go rather well for Darcy, though I know from his letters that he was irritated by the way his father seemed to want to spend so many hours with George Wickham. His father was sleeping sixteen hours a day by that time, and his sleep was getting longer. And Darcy had so many things to do during his father's waking hours that he was not able to spend the time with him he desired.

"And then," Fitzwilliam said, pausing for effect, "his father died. And Wickham's father died only months later."

"I can see how that might have changed him," Mrs. Gardiner said, "but I suspect you are going to contradict that."

Fitzwilliam nodded. "As you suspect, it did not appear to make much difference. In fact, Darcy appeared much the same to me until I was ordered to Egypt. It was only when I returned that I found a different Darcy. Oh, he was much the same with me in private, as well as with some other close friends, and he never changed his relations with the staff of his estate, but he had become stiff, formal, and distant with everyone else. Much as you have described him to me, Miss Elizabeth."

Elizabeth looked up at him wordlessly, and from her expression, Fitzwilliam knew then he had failed in his mission. He could see she was affected by his recital, but if it made her see Darcy in a more sympathetic light, it did not change her basic reaction to him.

But her aunt was not yet ready to let this mystery lapse. "So it would appear that a continuing series of emotional bereavements as well as extremely intense pressures may have been working on your cousin before you left but it appeared to do little to change his basic personality. So, it might be that events took place while you were away that caused him to change."

"Or it may have been that he simply grew arrogant and prideful because he had learned that other people were not worthy to associate with such an august personage as himself," Elizabeth said bitterly.

"Elizabeth, that is not at all polite," her aunt retorted sharply.

"But look what he has done to Jane!" Elizabeth cried. "He has destroyed her most cherished hopes, perhaps forever, and for what reason? Because she was not wealthy enough for his friend? Because her family did not have the standing or the connexions to be worthy of a friend of Mr. Darcy? How do you explain that, Colonel Fitzwilliam? Just how?"

"Because Darcy made a mistake," responded Fitzwilliam, struggling to hold on to his temper.

"Mistake? I think not, sir. He accomplished just exactly what he intended to do: separate Jane from the man she loved."

"No, he did not," Fitzwilliam said, his voice calm but unyielding.

"What? How can you dispute what happened? He even admits his interference. He said he had nothing of which to be ashamed and rejoiced in his success."

"His intent was not to separate your sister from a man she loved. His mistake was that he did not detect that your sister actually loved Mr. Bingley. I also asked him about that subject, and he could not understand why you were so upset. He truly believed that, while your sister enjoyed Mr. Bingley's attentions, her affection was not commensurate with his friend's for her."

Elizabeth was struck speechless by this comment, and Fitzwilliam hurried on. "His mistake was just that—a mistake. His intent, however, was not as you phrased it. His intent was to save his friend from marrying a woman whom he loved but who did not love him and whose mother would force her to accept a proposal of marriage for the benefit of his friend's fortune."

"What?" Elizabeth exploded.

"Moreover, Darcy knew this not only from his own close observations," Fitzwilliam continued relentlessly, "he also knew it because your mother openly boasted that your sister would soon be mistress of Netherfield and their marriage would throw her daughters into the path of other rich men. That is what he heard, Miss Elizabeth. Does my cousin lie? Did your mother really say these things, knowing he would overhear them?"

Elizabeth had turned pale at this recitation, and a stricken look was on her face as she collapsed back into her chair.

"Lizzy, what is it? Did your mother really say that in front of Mr. Darcy?"

Elizabeth hated the thought of having to answer, and tears were running from the corners of her eyes as she finally nodded and then buried her face in her hands.

"I am sorry, Mrs. Gardiner," Fitzwilliam said remorsefully, rising to his feet. "I should not have stated my case so forcefully, but my anger carried me away. I believe I should leave. No useful purpose can be served by continuing this. I can see your niece is not at all inclined to give my cousin a chance to redeem his character."

"No," Mrs. Gardiner said forcefully, "sit back down. We started this, and we shall complete it. I knew it would be difficult, and so it has proved, but we *will* finish it."

Fitzwilliam collapsed back into his chair, and soon Mrs. Gardiner had comforted her niece. Once Elizabeth had stopped crying, Mrs. Gardiner spoke again. "You said your cousin made a mistake,

Colonel. I suppose his mistake was in not recognising Jane's feelings for Mr. Bingley. In the family, we know how reserved Jane is in public—well-mannered and polite but not at all inclined to show her emotions—not like our Lizzy at all."

"You are correct, and after Miss Elizabeth responded so forcefully in charging him with destroying her sister's hopes, Darcy has been forced to admit his error. But, and I hate to state it like this, he was not aided by the response of your niece's suitor, who allowed himself to be persuaded that Miss Bennet did not return his affection. Bingley must shoulder a share of the blame."

Fitzwilliam paused for several moments to gather his composure and marshal his thoughts before he was ready to continue.

"What little I do know of the years I was gone is that Darcy was one of the most pursued bachelors in our society. He also was dogged by any number of sharp-tongued operators who sought to entice some part of the Darcy fortune into their own pockets. With regards to both the romantic and the financial pursuers, he wrote me about several incidents that occurred shortly after I left England. Evidently, he was both skilled and fortunate that the traps did not ensnare him, and he wrote that one case involved a friend he would have previously considered completely trustworthy. I had no real information after that because his letters became more cautious. I wonder whether such a change was not happening to his character in a similar fashion. If he could not trust even those who were part of his inner circle, how much less was he prepared to trust those who were not even part of it?"

Mrs. Gardiner nodded thoughtfully. "Perhaps we have found a key element, Colonel. It is too bad life has to force lessons like that upon us."

"I have stayed long enough, and my mission is accomplished, even if the result is not what I had hoped. I want to thank you for your support, Mrs. Gardiner. And I want to thank you for listening to me, Miss Elizabeth. I hope you will be able to forgive me for having inflicted myself and these emotional conversations on you."

"I do not blame you. You have acted as a good and loyal friend ought to do. I do not even blame Mr. Darcy," Elizabeth said wanly. "I hope we, you and I, shall meet again in the future and in happier circumstances."

"I, too, Miss Elizabeth. And it was a pleasure to make your acquaintance, Mrs. Gardiner. Your nieces are fortunate to have such a sensible and insightful aunt."

"Thank you for the compliment. I hope you will not mind seeing yourself out, and when you get your horse from the stable, will you tell John to send one of his sons to the park? It is time for Jane and the children to return."

"Perhaps *I* could convey the message? I saw the park as I rode down the street, and I shall pass it on the way back to my regiment."

"I would appreciate your help." Mrs. Gardiner smiled and then turned back to Elizabeth, who still appeared shaken by the bruised feelings occasioned by the interview. They were talking in low tones as Fitzwilliam left the room.

CHAPTER 5

Who ever loved that loved not at first sight?

— Christopher Marlowe

Monday, April 27, 1812
Gracechurch Street, London

Despite her calm demeanour, Jane was actually as consumed with curiosity as Maria Lucas regarding the event transpiring at her aunt's house, but she was too well mannered to engage in idle speculation. However, she was not averse to learning a few hard facts, so when she noted Colonel Fitzwilliam riding down the street towards the park where her aunt's children were playing, she was eager to collect them and return.

However, she was surprised to see the red-coated officer stop and dismount before tying his horse at one of the hitching rails that bordered the park. She was further surprised when he began to walk unmistakably towards where she and Maria stood as they watched the children dancing and running about among the grazing sheep. The calm animals must have been accustomed to a profusion of people since not even the occasional collision with a child disturbed the serious business of cropping grass.

"Oh, I wonder whether the colonel might tell us what is happening," Maria said suddenly, and Jane, while she might prefer that Maria reined in her curiosity, could not deny that her own interest was every bit as great.

"Good afternoon, Miss Bennet, Miss Lucas," he greeted them, a cheerful smile on his rugged, sun-browned face. "Mrs. Gardiner sends word that dinner is being prepared and the children should return, which appears to be occurring even now."

Indeed, Mary Alice was at that moment calling the children together in preparation for trooping back to the house. Jane made to follow her but paused as Colonel Fitzwilliam seemed to be looking at her oddly. His distraction took no more than a few seconds, however, and he visibly seemed to shake himself as he stirred into motion and easily fell into step beside her. She noted his glance towards Maria Lucas as the younger girl cast a surreptitious look his way, and she knew he could easily discern that Maria was almost hopping up and down in her eagerness to know what had occurred while they were away. But Jane was more adept than the other girl, and she was confident that the colonel could not detect her own curiosity as he asked whether the children had been a burden.

"No, of course not, sir. They are very active, of course—even James, who is supposed to be sick. But they have such dear, sweet hearts that it is impossible to be cross with them."

"When I remember the trouble my brothers and I got into when we were young, I can only wish Mrs. Abbot, our governess, had possessed some of your disposition. Luckily, she was only able to catch us at a portion of the trouble we caused, so I was able to escape many a thrashing that I well deserved."

"You make me laugh," Jane teased. "I cannot believe such a soft-spoken man could have been the scamp you describe."

"I was a thorough scamp, and I heartily deserved every switching

Mrs. Abbot administered. But we all loved her fiercely, though she scolded us sternly every time she caught us. I often thought she could read my mind as I was growing up, and all my brothers thought the same. She now lives with my older brother, George, and I have no doubt she will be as effective with his brood as she was with us, though she is not as young as she once was."

"Then you have no sisters? I have no brothers, only four sisters."

"Only one, and I have seldom seen her. She was born after I left home; fortunately, her faithful correspondence has allowed us to grow to know each other as well as we do. She is eighteen now and experiencing her first Season."

Jane looked over at Fitzwilliam in surprise. *He cannot be much older than thirty,* she thought in surprise. *How long has he been away from home?*

"We have nothing in Hertfordshire comparable to the London Season, and my two youngest sisters constantly complain that Father will not take us to town. He does not like London, you see."

Jane was careful not to mention that her sisters only complained about that when they were not discussing various officers in the militia regiment in winter quarters near Meryton.

They would not believe I am talking to a colonel, much less one who is also the son of an earl, she thought. *It is just as well he will not have occasion to meet them. They have already caused me embarrassment enough.*

She winced as she remembered them the night of the ball at Netherfield. *What should have been the happiest night of my life was marred by their wild and improper behaviour, as well as the conduct of my mother,* she thought sadly. *I wonder whether that was a premonition of the unhappiness to come.*

"And do you know whether your sister is enjoying the parties and balls of the Season?" Jane asked in an attempt to turn her mind from gloomy thoughts rather than satisfy her curiosity.

"Not exactly. She wrote that she feels like a piece of prime livestock being inspected by all the young men since she is presumed to have a substantial dowry, being the only daughter of the Earl of Matlock."

Jane heard this simple statement, but she was certain that more was contained in the words than the mere meaning imparted. *But it is none of my business,* she thought, *so I shall not worry about it. I wonder whether I shall see this man again. And I particularly wonder what happened to Elizabeth while she was visiting Charlotte. The sudden appearance of a relative of Mr. Darcy who desired to talk privately with Lizzy and Aunt Gardiner—what does it mean? And what did Aunt Gardiner mean when she said she understood but that she needed to stay while the colonel talked to Lizzy? Oh, mystery, mystery. Can I ask him? No, not with Maria walking beside me. Oh, for just a few minutes of privacy!*

As Fitzwilliam had approached the park, he had wondered at his impulsive offer to deliver Mrs. Gardiner's message instead of leaving it to one of the groom's sons. He had been feeling all the bruised emotions that would be expected after such an intense and confrontational conversation, and he was ready to return to his house and a healthy glass of brandy. Instead, he had volunteered for this errand, and he now saw the three young ladies and their charges as he dismounted and tied his horse to a hitching rail. He lost no time in hurrying towards them to deliver his message and be on his way.

There was only one problem: when he glanced towards Miss Jane Bennet, a sudden shock rippled through his being as if he were seeing her for the first time.

Only a lifetime of stern instruction and practice in the civilities expected of a gentleman prevented his making an utter fool of himself at that moment, for the jolt to his inner self stunned him like nothing he had ever experienced. He struggled to speak, to defeat the paralysis that gripped him and threatened to embarrass him in front of this angel, and stirring himself into motion was one of the most difficult things he had ever done. He desperately wanted simply to stand and study this young lady until he could recall every facet of her features from memory.

It is the eyes that are the most overwhelming, he thought as he somehow managed, despite his inner stupefaction, to walk beside her. *I cannot understand why it struck me so unexpectedly, but her eyes seem to pull me into them—eyes of the purest violet, sparkling with life, and with the longest, darkest lashes I have ever seen. And her smile! So soft and gentle yet bearing that touch of sadness I noticed—unless I am deceiving myself because I know of the disappointment she has suffered.*

Desperately, Fitzwilliam tried to recover his composure and bring his racing thoughts and emotions under control. He was so distracted that he could scarcely believe Miss Bennet and her friend had not discerned the state he was in, yet they seemed to notice nothing untoward. But when he glanced towards Miss Bennet again, meaning to ask her whether the children had been difficult to control, he found he could say nothing; his composure was still shattered.

There are some who say that violet eyes do not exist, he thought, mesmerized by their clear gaze that briefly rested on him. *But I can now testify that such people are ignorant though I have never seen eyes of that colour until today. And the eyes are only the final complement to the exquisite beauty of her face, to the perfection of her figure. She is quite the most angelic female I have ever met.*

Sternly, he demanded of himself to shift his attention away from Miss Bennet and control his raging thoughts.

What is happening to me? he thought desperately. *I came to help DARCY with his quixotic problem, not to be smitten myself!*

He clamped down on his distraction, but it was extremely difficult, especially for someone who had disciplined himself to be guarded and thoughtful about making the important choices in life. He had grown so used to calm consideration and deliberate thought that he had never imagined he might be caught defenceless by an event that avoided the rational part of his nature.

What a fool Bingley was to walk away from this woman! He struggled to listen to Miss Bennet and respond in a civil, thoughtful manner as they approached the hitching rail where his horse was tethered. *Did Darcy ever take a close look at her before he advised Bingley to cast her off? I have to wonder whether my cousin, even then, was not so smitten by her sister that he never even looked at the lady he was convincing Bingley to discard. No, Bingley is not just a fool—he is a veritable idiot.*

But then he demanded of himself, *What am I going to do? I cannot just mount my horse and ride on my way. But think, man, think. What can I do? I have to do something, but what?*

Jane was surprised when Fitzwilliam collected his horse as they walked past the hitching rail but did not mount. Instead, he continued to walk with them as they returned to her aunt's house, and his conversation was friendly, open, and cheerful, though she continued to struggle to restrain her curiosity. It was only when they reached the house that his face grew solemn.

"Might I have a few words with you before you go inside, Miss Bennet?" he asked politely. Jane heard a bit of stiffness in his voice, but since they were standing before the front door, she had no hesitation in agreeing. However, when Maria Lucas lingered at her side, she realized from his expression that he wished to speak to her in relative privacy.

"Please go ahead without me, Maria," she said to the younger girl, "and tell Aunt Gardiner I shall be inside directly."

Again, Maria Lucas wanted to stay and listen, but she could not gainsay such a clear and polite request. After she entered the house, Jane turned expectantly to the colonel, only to find that he seemed to be having trouble finding the words he wanted to say. The hesitation, however, was no more than a few seconds, and she saw him visibly gather his composure.

"Miss Bennet, you will no doubt soon learn that the reason for my presence here today involves certain issues between your sister and my cousin from their acquaintance at my aunt Lady Catherine's estate. I do not know how much your sister or your aunt will share with you, so I shall only say that my mission today was only partly successful. That is, I corrected a problem that needed to be corrected, but I was unsuccessful in my ultimate goal. Accordingly, I shall have no further cause to return to your aunt's house on that matter."

Jane stiffened as Fitzwilliam's eyes caught hers and held them. They were dark, rather ordinary eyes, but they blazed now with an intensity completely at odds with his pleasant manner.

"However, it happens that I *do* desire to return to your aunt's house, though my mission this time will be on an affair of my own rather than my cousin's. Miss Bennet, I would like your permission to call on you tomorrow."

Jane was taken aback by this unexpected request. She had only met this man today, and such a request was normally made as part of a ritual involving a couple with considerably more knowledge of each other than was true in this case.

Thoughts flashed through her mind as she considered how to respond. She noted the sturdy planes of his face and the well-tanned skin, indicating a life spent mostly outdoors. She also noted the laugh lines at the corners of his mouth, indicating this was a man who laughed frequently. And, while he was not particularly handsome, he was certainly not ugly.

What should I say? she thought quickly. *Do I want this man to call on me? He is not like any man I have known, certainly not at all like Mr. Bingley. Do I dare take a chance? And what of Mr. Bingley? Can I take a chance on being hurt so badly again? No! I cannot go through it again. Better to decline. Far better.*

But his eyes still held hers, and she had to give him an answer.

Oh, I wish I could talk to Lizzy. She would know how to advise me.

In later years, Jane could never determine just when or how she made her decision. Perhaps it was a conviction that, whatever else might happen, this man would never simply disappear as Mr. Bingley had done. But whatever the reason, she always remembered hearing her voice, as if it belonged to someone else, saying calmly and without conscious volition, "Yes, Colonel Fitzwilliam, you have my permission to call."

Those dark eyes of his now almost disappeared as a broad smile came over his rugged face.

Why, he is really quite nice looking when he smiles, Jane realised. And then she thought in confusion, *When did I think he was not handsome? I do not remember thinking it, but I must have. Oh, I am so very confused!*

"Excellent," Fitzwilliam said enthusiastically. "Then, with your permission, I shall call at two o'clock. Perhaps, if the weather is obliging, I might assist you in escorting your cousins to the park again."

He gave her a quick bow, but then he rather surprised her as he grasped the front of his saddle and seemed almost to levitate onto the back of his horse with just a heave of his arms. Once in the saddle, his feet found the stirrups with an ease borne of long years of practice in inclement weather and the dead of night.

"Until tomorrow, then," he said, tipping his hat to her.

"Yes. Until tomorrow."

As he clattered away down the road, she could hear him whistling a cheerful tune, and she was struck by the breadth of his back and shoulders above the narrow waist of an experienced horseman.

My word, the man is huge, she thought in surprise. *Why did I never notice that before? What have I got myself into now?*

Her thoughts were both troubled and elated as she closed the front door, and somehow the resolution of Lizzy's mysteries seemed to have lost all its intensity.

WHEN JANE WENT INSIDE, SHE FOUND HER UNCLE HAD ARRIVED in her absence, and he and her aunt were closeted in his study with the door closed. Undoubtedly, they were discussing the day's mystifying events, but that provided no means of assuaging *her* curiosity. When she found Maria sitting alone in the front room, attempting to read a book, Jane smiled inwardly. Lizzy had told her she had suggested to Maria that she should read more so as to enlarge her horizons, but the younger girl found the process harder than she preferred. Maria informed her that she had not seen Lizzy on her return and assumed she was in the bedroom upstairs. A quick look in the dining room told Jane that preparations for supper were only beginning, so she went upstairs to the room she shared with her sister.

Upon entering, Jane saw Elizabeth in the window seat, her knees pulled up to her chest while she rested her chin on her knees and stared out the window. Her mood was difficult to decipher since she did not look around when Jane entered the room. Even when Jane removed her gloves and deposited them in a drawer along with her shawl and bonnet, Elizabeth did not look around.

But Jane was in no mood to be deterred, so she pulled a chair over to the window, placed it directly in front of the window seat, and sat herself down firmly. Even then, Elizabeth did not look around and remained gazing out the window.

Finally, Jane could stand no more. "Well?"

"Well, what?" came Elizabeth's barely audible reply.

"Well, what shall I have to do to have the complete story from you? From what you said before Colonel Fitzwilliam's arrival, I would have assumed you had nothing but a rather dull and uneventful visit with Charlotte and her husband as well as occasional visits to the home of Lady Catherine de Bourgh. You made no mention whatever that Mr. Darcy was visiting, and you never mentioned his cousin at all. Yet today, that same cousin visits, and I would be willing to wager he has done so in the service of Mr. Darcy, and you try to avoid speaking of it. This will not do. *Something* happened in Kent, and you shall have to tell me at some time, so it might as well be right now."

Elizabeth had been overjoyed to be reunited with her beloved sister when she had arrived on Saturday, but her attempt to study Jane's spirits had not been especially fruitful. She thought Jane looked well, but then Jane always looked well. Thus, she had decided to wait until they returned to Longbourn before attempting to delve any deeper. Besides, there would be little opportunity during the remainder of their visit since their aunt had a variety of engagements planned that would keep them quite busy.

She had also been tempted to tell Jane of Mr. Darcy's surprising proposal, but upon reflection, she had decided that subject ought also to wait until they returned to Longbourn. For one thing, she had not yet decided how much to tell Jane of Mr. Darcy's interference between her and Mr. Bingley. She had been of a mind that revealing that fact would only grieve Jane further.

Now, after Colonel Fitzwilliam's astonishing visit, she would have preferred to be left in solitude. While she had learned much from what he related, she was even more confused about Mr. Darcy and his formerly unknown attraction to her.

Then, there was the information Colonel Fitzwilliam had related about Wickham. She had attempted to forget what he had told her at the Parsonage, reasoning it was predictable that one cousin would try to protect the other. But the evidence the colonel had given, in addition to that at which he had merely hinted, had destroyed her previously held beliefs completely. More galling was the uncomfortable realisation that vanity and pride in her assessment of others' characters had been most responsible for such a grievous error. Since she had only begun to accept that unpleasant fact, she would have preferred to ignore the whole subject completely for days or even weeks, at least until her own thoughts were more settled.

However, that option was obviously not possible—not with Jane's curiosity now aroused. So Elizabeth sighed and turned away from the window, leaning back against the wall and curling her feet beneath her.

Jane smiled at Elizabeth's obvious acquiescence and leaned over to pat her on the knee. "Much better, Lizzy. Now, tell Sister Jane everything. Do not omit a single detail."

"Oh, very well," Elizabeth said, managing a rueful smile. "And, since so many people already know all the sordid details of my private life, it is not right that *you* should be the last to learn of it."

Jane laughed at Elizabeth's glum expression. "Please, no melodrama. Now, tell me."

"Since I appear to have no choice, I had better begin. As you have undoubtedly deduced, I did indeed see more of Mr. Darcy than I mentioned last night. But I thought nothing of it at the time, considering it merely an inconvenience that he frequently stopped by the Parsonage and happened to be walking in the park at Rosings at the same time as I. His cousin, whose unexpected appearance here has caused all this uproar, accompanied him on his visit to his aunt. I actually grew to know the colonel well, and I quite like him since he is as well mannered and civil as Mr. Darcy is cold and rude. I am sure he visited us at the Parsonage because he was friendly and glad of the conversation, but I completely deceived myself as to the reason for Mr. Darcy's visits. Despite the fact that Charlotte several times mentioned the possibility that he might be in love with me, I disregarded it. As a result, I was completely unprepared for Mr. Darcy's visit to the Parsonage on a night when the others were taking tea with her ladyship. He came alone that evening, which was only a day or so before he was scheduled to leave Rosings…"

Jane listened spellbound as Elizabeth related the scene in which Mr. Darcy made his proposal and the resulting acrimonious exchange that followed her rejection of it. Jane could not conceal a wince when Elizabeth told of learning from the colonel that Mr. Darcy had played a large part in separating her and Mr. Bingley. Once she had begun her story, Elizabeth had decided she should not hold back anything. In light of Colonel Fitzwilliam's visit that day, she believed that concealing Mr. Darcy's interference was no longer possible. Already, the colonel,

Aunt Gardiner, and probably Uncle Gardiner were fully acquainted with all the particulars, and Jane would surely learn of the facts sooner or later.

She also related that the growing quarrel between herself and Mr. Darcy had been suddenly interrupted by the colonel, who had shocked her to her core by claiming she was completely wrong in her support of Mr. Wickham.

"I was about to dispute those unbelievable statements regarding Mr. Wickham when we heard the carriage with the Collinses and Maria arriving at the front door, so both of the gentlemen departed. However, Colonel Fitzwilliam lingered behind a little and said he would visit me here in town in order to provide more information regarding his claims about Mr. Wickham. I confess I rather deceived myself into thinking he would not keep his promise, and you saw the results of my error today. He arrived, and I was completely unprepared to hear what he had to say."

The information Elizabeth had told her about Darcy's proposal amazed Jane more than anything she could remember, but even learning of the part he had played in separating her and Bingley could not long lessen the strong sisterly partiality she felt for Elizabeth.

"I am as astonished by these events as you must have been, but now I wonder why it should be so surprising that Mr. Darcy would find you attractive enough to marry. In fact, he appears to have been so completely overcome by the strength of his love for you that he could not manage to deliver his sentiments in a manner that might have recommended them. He must have been afflicted with emotions that were so strong they overcame his normal mode of address."

"That is no excuse for being rude and arrogant. Why, he insulted me and our family in every possible manner."

"It does appear so, but is that really surprising for such a reserved and private person as Mr. Darcy? I am certain he had never felt anything similar and had nothing in his experience that could possibly provide him guidance."

Elizabeth shook her head at Jane's comments. "Can you possibly be serious?" she said in disbelief.

Jane just looked at her in confusion, and Elizabeth quickly amended her comment. "Of course you are being serious. Of what am I thinking? You are always serious. And you always seem to see good in people, even when it is totally lacking."

"Despite how badly he made his addresses to you and despite his being so sure of the success of his suit, think of his disappointment." Jane was thinking of her own distress after Bingley left Netherfield, and she felt a surge of empathy at the thought that Darcy must be experiencing misery as extreme as her own.

But Elizabeth appeared not at all inclined to sympathy. "Perhaps I should feel heartily sorry for him, but I am sure he has other feelings that will probably soon drive away his regard for me. I am concerned, however, that you might blame me for refusing him. If I had accepted, it would have guaranteed security for Mama and our sisters."

"Blame you? Oh no, how could I blame you for refusing a man you found so objectionable? Security, I would hope, should not be purchased at such a price."

"You would be correct, however, in blaming me for having been so deceived by Mr. Wickham."

"I cannot tell. All you mentioned is that Colonel Fitzwilliam disputed your opinion, but I cannot determine which of you is right."

"Listen, then, and I shall inform you of how greatly my highly valued perception of others has been in error. When the colonel visited today, he told me he had known Wickham since he was twelve years old, and…"

Jane could not believe what she heard, but she had Elizabeth's merciless dissection of her own errors to prove that the general perception of George Wickham had been mistaken. She would willingly have gone through her whole life without believing a man of such pleasing manners and carriage could have been so base as to repay the generosity of the Darcy family with ingratitude and infamy. Not even learning of Mr. Darcy's innocence was enough to console her for such a discovery. Such was her discomfiture that she even went so far as to wonder aloud whether there might have been some mistake, some error that might lessen Mr. Wickham's offences without transferring blame to Mr. Darcy.

"This will not do, Jane," Elizabeth said with a bitter laugh. "Not even you could make both of them good. You can choose one or the other, or you might say they are both half-good and half-bad. But after listening to what our visitor related, I really have no choice but to lay the good, what there is of it, to Mr. Darcy's account. But I would not be surprised if you cannot be as callous as I am."

However, such was Jane's despondency that not even this witticism was enough to extort a smile from her.

"I do not know when I have been more shocked," she said dolefully. "Mr. Wickham so very bad. It is almost past belief."

"And that does not even include the other matter the colonel would not mention because it was sensitive and involved a private family matter."

Elizabeth's comment made both sisters look at each other in consternation since they had both leapt to the same conclusion.

"Mr. Darcy's sister," Jane said miserably.

"Yes, it must be. Colonel Fitzwilliam has been gone from England these five years, and there is no one else. It must be his sister. And, no matter how much I might detest Mr. Darcy, I witnessed that he held his sister in high esteem. He has no other brothers or sisters."

"But what could even Mr. Wickham have done against such a girl? How old was she?"

Elizabeth wrinkled her forehead. "I am not certain I ever heard it mentioned. But she is not yet out in society. Perhaps Wickham tried to force his attentions on her?"

"No!" exclaimed Jane. "Could even Mr. Wickham have done that?

Would not Mr. Darcy have set the authorities on him?"

"I suppose it depends on how he tried to do it. Perhaps he only tried to pay attention to her when Mr. Darcy did not desire it."

"But she is not yet out. Oh, miserable day, to think of Mr. Wickham doing such a thing! Poor Mr. Darcy. And then to think of the disappointment he has suffered—not only your refusal but also your ill opinion of him."

"He is fortunate that his cousin came along when he did, then," Elizabeth said grimly, "for I had only begun to express myself when we were interrupted."

"But it is so distressing to consider how miserable he must have felt. Surely you must also have felt it."

"Oh no, my regret and compassion are all done away by seeing you so full of both. In fact, with your determination to be sympathetic for his feelings, I find I am growing every moment more unconcerned and indifferent to them. Actually, if you continue to lament over him much longer, my heart will become as light as a feather."

"Poor Wickham—there is such an expression of goodness in his countenance. Such openness and gentleness in his manners and address."

"True, true, but as I mentioned before, they cannot both be good, and Mr. Wickham seems to have only the appearance of goodness, not the reality of it. As for Mr. Darcy…"

"I never thought Mr. Darcy so deficient in his manner as you did, Lizzy. He seemed mainly to be very quiet and reserved."

"Perhaps," Elizabeth said sceptically, "and yet I thought myself uncommonly clever to form such a dislike for him. I considered it a spur to my genius and an opening for my wit. It allowed me to be quite abusive without requiring me to justify what I said. And now I find it just one among several mortifications I need to rectify, if only I knew how."

"Lizzy, I am sure you could not be so casual and dismissive about the matter when you were talking with Colonel Fitzwilliam."

"Indeed I could not. I was quite uncomfortable, even unhappy, with many parts of what he said. But now I feel better, for I have you to comfort me, and since you have demanded that I tell you everything, I have no further secrets to withhold from you. I feel as if a great weight has come off my shoulders."

DESPITE HER OWN RELIEF, ELIZABETH NOTED THAT JANE DID NOT share it; in fact, she had a pensive look on her face that indicated she was still troubled.

"What is the matter, dearest?" she asked in concern. "Has my mention of Mr. Bingley brought back troubling memories? Oh, I am so sorry, Jane. I thought it best to conceal nothing, and now I have caused you pain."

"It is not that. I am glad you related what you knew. It is something else entirely. Before he left today, Colonel Fitzwilliam asked whether he could call on me tomorrow."

"He what?" Elizabeth said in astonishment.

"He delivered my aunt's message that it was time to return home, and he escorted us back to the house. Then, before I went in, he asked my permission to call on me."

"But...but..." Elizabeth stammered, and then she stopped. For a moment, she simply did not know what to say. Then a thought occurred to her. "What reply did you give him?"

"I decided to give him permission." Jane stopped in sudden shock and asked in horror, "Why do you look at me that way, Lizzy? What is it? Do *you* have an interest in him?"

Jane's expression turned to confusion as Elizabeth recovered herself and gave a strained laugh.

"Oh no, no, nothing like that. I had just...well, I do not have any feelings for him though I did find him quite amiable at Rosings. My surprise is due to the fact that I would not have expected him to show *any* interest in one of the Bennet sisters."

"I am sorry. I do not understand what you mean."

"Simply this: Colonel Fitzwilliam several times mentioned the misfortune of being a younger son. I teased him that I could not imagine the son of an earl ever wanting for anything, and I also mentioned that such men often seemed to marry women of good fortune. He admitted the truth of my comment and replied that their habits of expense usually made it necessary to pay some attention to money when marrying. It is one of the reasons I knew he had no intentions towards me. Despite how well we got on, I had no fortune—nor do any of us."

Jane merely nodded at this, but Elizabeth was struck by a sudden thought. *Why did Colonel Fitzwilliam agree with my comments about never wanting for anything as an earl's son? From what he told me, he actually did want for almost everything. He was fortunate in having an aunt with the generosity and the means to purchase a commission for him. How could he now show any interest in Jane when he ought to be in even more financial distress than the usual younger sons of nobility?*

Jane could know nothing of what passed through Elizabeth's mind since she had not related that portion of the colonel's conversation in any detail. The questions in her mind made Elizabeth distinctly uneasy, and she resolved to have a word with her uncle after the evening meal. She could not believe the colonel had any dishonourable intentions towards Jane, but her uncle ought to be aware of her misgivings. While she and Jane were visiting, he had the responsibility for their protection, and he took those duties seriously. He might well wish to have a word with the man when he called.

WHEN he calls, Elizabeth thought in renewed amazement that it would really happen. *It is too unbelievable. And what about Mr. Bingley? From the way Mr. Darcy reacted when I castigated him for his interference, I actually wondered whether he might feel compelled to inform his friend that he had been mistaken about the nature of Jane's feelings. What might happen then?*

What if Mr. Bingley tries to renew the acquaintance and finds the colonel in attendance on Jane? Would that not confirm Mr. Darcy's opinion that Jane's feelings were not a match for those of Mr. Bingley? That would certainly drive Mr. Bingley away forever, and he is a far superior future husband for Jane than an impoverished officer, no matter how heightened his affection for her might be. I would sooner match him with Lydia, who would be ecstatic at the very idea.

In the meantime, Elizabeth did not want to burden Jane with her disturbing musings, so she did her best to disguise her actual thoughts. "However, no matter what Colonel Fitzwilliam may have said at Rosings about his financial situation, it appears he must have found *something* to change his mind."

"Lizzy, I just met him today. And all he asked was permission to call on me. Nothing more serious than that."

"Of course, of course. But he did not ask permission to call on *me*, and I knew him first. So I cannot be blamed for making of it what I would."

Jane could only manage a sheepish smile in response to her sister's teasing, but further conversation had to wait as supper was announced. Elizabeth was pleased to see the sparkle in her sister's eyes as they descended the stairs, but she felt compelled to suggest that their uncle ought to be informed of the colonel's request. Jane coloured at this comment and flashed her sister a remorseful look, but Elizabeth's only response was a smile.

It is not what I expected to make her stop thinking about Mr. Bingley, though it has certainly had that effect, she thought. *I shall speak with my uncle, and he will almost certainly want to talk with Colonel Fitzwilliam. But, no matter what Uncle Gardiner might say to him, I shall also have a talk with the good colonel. Even though I like the man, I will not see Jane hurt.*

CHAPTER 6

Love at first sight is only realizing an imagination that has always haunted us; or meeting with a face, a figure, or cast of expression in perfection that we have seen and admired in a less degree or in less favorable circumstances a hundred times before.

— William Hazlitt

Tuesday, April 28, 1812
Gracechurch Street, London

I t is often the small things that are unexpected, Richard thought sourly as he guided his horse towards Gracechurch Street. His problem this afternoon was the unanticipated apprehension roiling his stomach. It was as bad as anything he had experienced before battle, and the affliction had proven quite beyond his ability to quell.

Stop it, he told himself firmly for the twentieth time. *I am NOT some adolescent suffering a case of first love. This is beyond ridiculous. I am almost thirty, for God's sake. I am born of the nobility, a veteran of numerous conflicts with the tyrant's minions, able to mix and mingle in any milieu, no matter how fashionable, and not completely inexperienced with the opposite sex. It is embarrassing to be unable to control my innards when making a simple social call. It is not as if I were making a visit to court after all. Miss Bennet may be a veritable angel in appearance, but common sense says she is actually a rather undistinguished young lady, at least from the point of view of her family and connexions.*

But it was all useless. No matter how harshly he castigated himself, he was completely unable to effect any change, and he had to resist the temptation to kick his horse into a gallop in order to have the journey finished sooner rather than later.

The reason for his sedate pace was to avoid kicking up dust. He had dressed with special care, donning well-tailored and fashionable riding clothes that had been a gift from his mother upon his return to England. While his father had no use for him after his defiance so many years ago, the earl at least had put no impediments to Richard's associations with the rest of the family. But he had expressly forbidden his wife to provide his wayward son with funds of any sort, so Lady Matlock had acquiesced to her husband's orders, and she got around them by providing gifts of clothing and furniture to her son that Richard's own frugality would have otherwise avoided.

So today Richard was dressed in the most fashionable manner, which was possibly also a factor in his agitation. He had briefly considered wearing his uniform when choosing his dress, but he had worn his uniform the previous day, and he wanted to make a good impression today.

For the most part, he paid little attention to fashionable dress; a uniform was almost always acceptable for a serving officer in time of war. And for those few events in which fashion mandated a more elegant mode of dress, Richard was not above trading shamelessly on his status as the son of an earl in order to avoid the dictates that forced other men into less comfortable attire than his own well-tailored uniforms.

There are some aspects of being the son of nobility that not even the earl's disfavour can take away, he often thought with a touch of sardonic humour.

But he had decided he wanted to look the part of a gentleman on this occasion and, for that reason, had solicited the assistance of Darcy's valet to tie his cravat. His orderly, Sergeant Bascomb, was more than capable of assisting him with the rest of his attire, but such intricacies as tying a cravat were beyond his experience. Once that task was completed, he had left Darcy's town house and travelled at a moderate speed and on less travelled avenues. Thus, he rigidly controlled his pace, and he was therefore condemned to the flutterings of trepidation until he arrived.

When he was ushered into the parlour, Richard was surprised to find Mrs. Gardiner awaiting him with a man beside her. The obvious deduction was that this was her husband, and so it proved as Mrs. Gardiner performed the introduction. Before further conversation, however, Mr. Gardiner asked Richard whether they might have a few words in the privacy of his study, and he politely, if a little confusedly, agreed.

As he followed the older man, Richard's usual sensibility finally put a halt to his internal qualms as he comprehended that Jane's uncle intended to interview the complete stranger who had suddenly appeared in his niece's life. Richard had more or less anticipated something of the sort if this first call was followed by others, but the fact that the occasion came on his first visit was somewhat surprising. He now realized the suddenness was likely due to Elizabeth enlisting her uncle's aid in her desire to protect her sister.

"Please, have a seat, sir," Mr. Gardiner said as he closed the door to his office. "May I offer you some tea, or perhaps you would care for something a bit stronger? A glass of port, perhaps, or even brandy?"

Richard raised an eyebrow at the tone in Mr. Gardiner's voice, and he quickly concluded that some type of test was being offered. Given the popular attitude towards soldiers, it took little imagination to determine what it was, and it was with a touch of malicious humour that he replied.

"Well, sir, thank you for the offer, but even considering the popular image of those of us who wear His Majesty's coat, it is a bit early for brandy, and I usually prefer port after a meal. So, perhaps I might trouble you for a cup of tea or, better still, coffee?"

Richard's tone was bland, but Mr. Gardiner immediately coloured as he realized his rather clumsy attempt to determine whether Richard was overly fond of the bottle had been deciphered.

"Touché, Colonel," he said with a rueful smile as he pulled on a cord to ring for a servant. After he had ordered coffee for both of them, he continued.

"I apologize for my ruse, but I am out of my normal fishing pond here. What my wife related of your visit yesterday was both surprising and unforeseen. When I was also informed that you had asked my niece's permission to call on her, I simply had no idea what to expect. But I should have been more discreet."

"I understand your position of responsibility, and I assure you I do not possess a volatile temperament. Regardless of discretion, then, might I suggest you ask whatever questions you need to ask?"

"Very well, then, I shall do exactly that. As of yesterday morning, you were completely unknown to everyone in my family except for Lizzy, and she had not so much as mentioned your name or even your cousin's astonishing offer of marriage. Given the pain my elder niece has suffered due to the disappearance of your cousin's friend from his estate, I do not want to see her hurt further. So, therefore, I would like to ascertain your intentions towards Jane."

Richard nodded at this statement. It was clear, direct, and even blunt. In fact, its clarity crystallized the amorphous emotions that had been churning beyond the conscious part of his mind. And now that he had the courage to look deeper, he found that his inner self had already made decisions he had not yet comprehended. Therefore, to answer Mr. Gardiner's questions was quite easy, but the answers needed to be phrased with a certain delicacy in order to make them both understandable and believable, even to him, for they were quite new. Accordingly, a somewhat circuitous approach was indicated, and his gaze was intent as he began.

"Mr. Gardiner, you appear to be a man of some experience in the world. And I am not exactly an innocent young lad. So would you not agree that both of us regard the concept of *love at first sight* as something more appropriate to a writer of fiction than to a man of good sense and experience?"

Mr. Gardiner's eyebrows furrowed at this unexpected answer to his question, and his answer, therefore, was rather tentative. "While what you say is sensible, I do not know what relevance it has to my question."

"Just this: you stated that your objective was to make sure your niece would not be hurt further, with the obvious implication that I might be the occasion of such pain to her feelings. I assure you, I share your objective to spare Miss Bennet any further misery, and I shall do all in my power to avoid it. Do you follow me so far?"

Mr. Gardiner was still puzzled, but he nodded in agreement.

"In fact, the true situation is that Miss Bennet should not suffer further infliction of pain in any way. If the sensibilities of anyone are at hazard, they will be my own."

"You mean…"

"I do, sir. Yesterday I would have laughed with you at the notion of *love at first sight* and confined such a ludicrous concept to that literature written exclusively for the diversion of the fairer sex. But today, I no longer find the idea laughable. In fact, I tell you frankly: not only are my intentions towards your niece honourable, but it is my firm intention to win her affections and eventually make her my wife."

Even as the words fell off his tongue, Richard's mind was still reacting to what his heart had already decided, and Mr. Gardiner was caught so completely off guard that his mouth was still open in surprise when the coffee was delivered.

Dismissing the servant and pouring coffee for both of them gave

Mr. Gardiner time to come to grips with his amazement. Finally, he ventured, "I cannot help but comment that what you have told me seems somewhat precipitate. You have, after all, only just met Jane."

"You are saying nothing to me that I have not said to myself in the past twenty-four hours and with considerably more vehemence. And *your* words are having no more effect on my intentions than my own did."

Mr. Gardiner considered this comment in silence as he sipped his coffee, then he began to see the more amusing side of what he had just been told.

"Ah, the impetuousness of youth," he murmured with a small smile.

"I have never been impetuous in my life, Mr. Gardiner; else, I should not have evaded the snares of at least a brace of society daughters who were certain the younger son of an earl could not be a pauper."

"Ah, so you are a pauper, then?" Mr. Gardiner asked intently.

"No, sir, I *was* a pauper. But Darcy's father left me a generous bequest, part of which I used to purchase a house here in town. It is smaller than your own but still sufficient in size for a wife and family. It even has a small stable that I share with my neighbour. The remainder of my bequest was invested in the Funds, along with what I have been able to save over the years from my army pay and from rents of my house when I was gone from England."

"I see. I also share a stable with a neighbour."

"So I was told when the girl who admitted me arranged to have my horse cared for."

"And an excellent mount, as I saw from the window of the parlour."

"Maximillian has rescued me from more than one tough situation, sir. A cavalryman lives and dies by his horse, and he was a gift from my mother before I left for Egypt more than five years ago. Magnificent beast. In any case, along with the interest from my legacy and my army pay, even if it goes to half-pay when these disagreements with the Mad Corporal are put to rest, I can state confidently that I have sufficient solvency to support a wife and family—in comfort if not in luxury."

"But you seem to be saying you were not looking for a wife when you met Jane."

"Entirely correct, though I was not explicitly avoiding the subject either. I had a plan in my mind that marriage would be more appropriate when I pass on command of my regiment to another officer rather than at the present time. There is a certain saying in the army that goes like this: a subaltern may not marry, captains might marry, majors should marry, and lieutenant colonels must marry. That usually meant that officers would not marry until their mid-thirties. The fact that I am a full colonel is balanced by my age of thirty, so I am able to choose at my discretion."

"Pardon my ignorance of military matters, but my experience is that you are rather young to already hold such a high rank," offered Mr. Gardiner.

Richard shrugged. "A matter of fortune, though whether it is good or ill depends greatly on your point of view. Being the son of an earl helps somewhat, though your wife likely told you of my...let us say, *strained* relations with my father. He certainly has never actively exerted any patronage on my behalf. But there is another facet to my rank: promotion comes easier on the battlefield, especially when higher-ranking officers keep getting shot out of the saddle. I was fortunate that the campaign was concluded before my turn arose to be shot out of the saddle, and equally fortunate that my rank was confirmed when the regiment returned from Italy. On the subject of my Italian service, I would only say that I have sworn a vow never to willingly set foot in Italy again unless it is as part of an army bent on conquest and subjugation—with the addition of a copious amount of looting and burning. I might even turn my eyes away from a judicious amount of rape. I can point out a few residences and government edifices that would make excellent bonfires and a few treacherous noblewomen who deserve the fate worse than death."

"I take your point, Colonel. So it was Italy where you received your promotion?"

"It was. A disastrous campaign, sir, simply disastrous: intrigues, betrayal, cowardice, retreat, disorder. It was nightmare piled upon nightmare."

"It definitely sounds like one. Now you make me rather nervous that you might leave my niece a widow."

Richard shrugged again. "While soldiering is not a safe profession, death will come for all of us sooner or later. And if it should befall me, my wife would at least have the security of an adequate income, a home, and a pension from the King, which is more than most men can promise."

"True, but why my elder niece? Why not Lizzy? You knew her before you knew Jane, and her manner and deportment is similar to Jane's."

"I am not sure I can answer your first question for the reasons I've stated. I cannot even explain how it happened to me—at least not yet. Your second question, however, is much more straightforward. Even before I knew of my cousin's interest in Miss Elizabeth, I knew she and I might be friends—even good friends—but nothing more serious. We are quite dissimilar, you see. She and my cousin Darcy would actually be much more suited to each other if it were not for the dislike your niece has developed for him. They are both quick-witted—much more so than I am. They are very private, subtle, well-read, and they both delight in verbal rhetoric and debate. I am a much more ordinary sort of person—slower, good-natured, and happiest when in cheerful company."

"And that is more Jane's nature than Lizzy's. Yes, you do have a point. But still, it is so unexpected. Jane could have all sorts of deficiencies you know nothing about. She might be a spendthrift, for example."

"Then I shall have to make sure to keep her on a tight allowance, sir."

"And she does have three rather silly sisters and a rather silly mother, though she is my own sister."

"I shall not be marrying either sisters or mother. And if they come to visit, I always have my duties to keep me busy."

"Or she could have…"

"It is no use, sir. I beg you to desist. The situation is hopeless, quite hopeless."

Mr. Gardiner nodded slowly, a broad smile coming over his face. "I begin to agree with you, Colonel. And, despite the upheaval of the last day, I can find no reason not to allow you to seek your destiny—commensurate, of course, with the usual dictums of propriety."

"I understand and agree, sir."

"Does Jane have any idea of your…impetuosity?"

Even Richard had to smile at this jibe, and he shook his head. "I think not, sir, though she has to understand I have some interest, or I would not have asked to call in such a hasty manner. But it is too soon for her. I can see she has suffered hurt, and I shall give her sufficient time to heal before I press my suit."

"Excellent, Colonel, excellent. I can only applaud your thoughtfulness—unlike, I might add, the young man who caused her pain in the first place."

That idiot Bingley, Richard thought, though he was careful not to voice such thoughts aloud. He only shrugged and tried to be calm as he replied, "How Mr. Bingley could ever let such a treasure slip out of his grasp is beyond me, sir, but I shall not say I am sorry, except for the pain your niece has suffered."

His attempt to maintain his composure was not very successful, however, as he instantly saw from Mr. Gardiner's expression.

I must have let some of my venom show, he thought. *However, he is a sensible man, and he must realize I am already aligning my nature to protect a loved one, even though, strictly speaking, that responsibility still remains with him as long as Jane stays in his house. And it is likely he agrees with the sentiments I unconsciously revealed since they likely parallel his own.*

"Very well, sir. I do want to apologize for the question about your financial situation. I had been informed it might not be of the best, but it seems my information was in error."

"It was, but that is probably not the fault of your...informant. She was correct that I have had no financial help from my father since I was twelve, but she took my comments about younger sons a bit too broadly. I remember the conversation when she mentioned that younger sons often sought wealthy wives. I commented that their habits of expense made such a consideration necessary. But I was speaking in generalities. I never said it pertained to me."

"That is entirely more than I need to know, and I shall not detain you longer. I wish you luck in your endeavour, and I shall maintain our conversation as completely secret."

"Thank you, sir. I hope I shall not ever disappoint you."

"I rather think you will not, young man. Now, I hope you will do us the honour of dining with us tonight?"

"Thank you, it will be my pleasure."

"Excellent. Now, my wife should be in the front room with my nieces. I am sure you can find your own way back since I have to return to my warehouse after I have written a note to Jane's father relating our conversation. Have a good afternoon, Colonel."

"Good afternoon, sir."

JANE LOOKED UP AS COLONEL FITZWILLIAM ENTERED THE ROOM, and her heart was warmed by the instant smile that came over his face. She was not aware that her eyes no longer saw his blunt features as might a stranger; his rough-hewn face complemented his sturdy frame so sensibly that she could no longer remember her initial impression of the man.

She had been rather put out with Lizzy earlier when she learned her uncle was determined to have an "interview" with Colonel Fitzwilliam before granting permission for him to call. She thought that her permission alone should be sufficient since she was of age, but she had not been prepared to contest the matter—at least, not yet. But it appeared her worries had been for naught and the requisite permission secured; otherwise, Jane was sure her uncle would have escorted him back to his horse.

The colonel lost no time in making his introductions and finding a seat in the closest proximity to Jane. He had to take the chair across a small table from her, for Elizabeth was firmly planted in the chair next to her sister, her sewing in her lap and her sewing basket on the chair beside her. He gave Elizabeth a stern look but received only a beatific smile in return, which elicited a reluctant chuckle at her impudence.

Jane raised an interrogatory eyebrow at this interchange, which led Richard to respond to her sister's impudence with impudence of his own.

"I am amused at the solicitude of your sister, Miss Bennet. You will note that she has carefully acquired the chair closest to you, which I surely would have claimed. Moreover, she has asserted that her possession of the chair will not be of a transitory nature since she has brought her sewing basket and will thus have no need to leave her seat to find either thread or another needle. Have I covered all the high points of your strategy, Miss Elizabeth?"

Elizabeth blushed bright red at having her scheme revealed in such accurate detail, which drew a laugh from both Jane and her aunt. Maria Lucas, however, who was sitting next to Mrs. Gardiner, looked on with confusion, having failed to follow the colonel's meaning.

"Then you have completed your conversation with my uncle, Colonel Fitzwilliam?" Elizabeth asked, trying to divert attention from his well-placed barb.

"I have, Miss Elizabeth, and he appeared to be extremely well informed on many aspects of my life. He was particularly concerned with my finances since he seemed to be under the impression that I was all but destitute. I cannot fathom where he may have obtained such an idea. But, once I was able to assure him that a cell at debtor's prison was not being reserved in my name, he said he had to get to his warehouse and invited me to dine tonight."

By now, Elizabeth's face was the brightest red Jane had ever seen it, and her aunt was having a difficult time restraining her mirth. Suddenly, Jane realized her sister must have told her uncle information about the gentleman that was not to his credit, and obviously, the colonel had been able to assure him that he had been misinformed.

"Elizabeth," she hissed in mingled mortification and irritation, which only made Elizabeth lower her head further as if she were buffeted by raging winds.

"Perhaps we should take pity on your sister, Miss Bennet. I believe she only had your welfare at heart. After all, she had been deceived by one bounder in uniform, and she may have been overly concerned I might be another."

"Well, you are not in uniform today, sir," Jane replied. "In fact, I do not believe your cousin could be better dressed."

"I do thank you, Miss Bennet, but all the credit belongs to my mother. She is completely au courant when it comes to fashion, has impeccable taste, and presented this to me after I returned. This is the first occasion I have had to wear it."

He leaned closer and said in a conspiratorial tone, "I admit I usually wear a uniform because it saves me from having to make those sartorial choices for which I am completely unprepared. A sudden outbreak of peace would be disastrous to whatever claim I have to possessing a gentleman's wardrobe."

"So you admit you are not a slave to fashion, then?" Jane asked slyly.

"Nay, I do not *admit* it. I *proclaim* it. At least, I do to those I trust."

"So you feel you are in trustworthy company, sir?"

"Partially, Miss Bennet, partially. I must, however, be honest and report there appears to be at least *one* in our party who has been known to tell tales out of school." His easy smile took the sting out of his words, and Elizabeth's first impulse to glare at him only caused him to smile more broadly. She was quickly driven to cover her discomfiture by sipping at her tea, but she could not be truly angry with him since it was clear that he was not offended and completely understood her concern for her sister.

Mrs. Gardiner now failed to restrain her mirth and excused herself hastily from the room. She loved her niece dearly though she had often warned her that a satiric manner might cause embarrassment in the future, and the chance to see the tables turned on her was priceless. Jane was more successful in containing her amusement and confined her own laughter to muffled giggles. Meanwhile, Elizabeth tried to concentrate on sipping her tea though she flashed occasional furious looks at both the colonel and her sister and muttered dire threats of retribution under her breath, none of which seemed to trouble either of them.

Maria Lucas, as usual, had not an inkling of what was being referred to, and she could only look on in confusion as the conversation turned to more amiable topics.

"I DO WANT TO THANK YOU FOR A MOST PLEASANT AFTERNOON and evening," Jane told Fitzwilliam as she and Elizabeth escorted him to the courtyard behind the house where his horse waited. "I have not enjoyed myself so much in months."

Richard had to swallow as the tenderness of her smile touched his very heart. "I am pleased beyond measure that I was able to provide a little entertainment today."

He tried to cover up the emotional huskiness of his voice as he spoke, and he seemed to have been successful with Jane. At least she did not show an awareness of the effect her comment had on him. Her sister, on the other hand, looked at him with steadfast intent.

"Oh yes," Jane said. "Everyone agrees that your stories of what you saw in other countries were enthralling. It makes our lives here seem so commonplace."

"Miss Bennet," Richard said intently, "commonplace is not all bad. My experiences may sound exciting, but I am greatly relieved to be returned to England. It is my serious desire to experience more of the commonplace pleasures of life."

"Oh yes, I do understand," Jane said more solemnly, remembering his brief mention that few of his men and fellow officers had survived to return with him to England. "I imagine we always think the other person has the better life, while that same person often wishes to change places with us."

"Quite true. But now, here is my horse, and I must bid you and your sister good night."

"Good night, Colonel, and I do hope we shall see you again," Jane said. She had thought on what Charlotte had told Lizzy—that a young woman ought to show more than she felt if she wanted to make an impression on a young man. And she had decided to take Charlotte's words to heart, for she *did* desire that this particular young man might return. He made her sadness disappear. *I have not thought of Mr. Bingley since the colonel arrived,* she thought, *not until this very moment.*

"Would the day after tomorrow be soon enough? I am engaged tomorrow. The regiment goes to the field."

"The day after tomorrow would be most agreeable," Jane said with a smile.

"I shall see you then, Miss Bennet. And Miss Elizabeth," he said, shifting his attention to her sister. "I note your gaze, and I would advise you to speak with your uncle to assuage your curiosity. Tell him I recommended it and asked that he be completely forthright with you."

With a final tip of his hat, Richard clattered out of the lamplight in the courtyard and disappeared into the darkness of Gracechurch Street.

"I wonder what he meant by that last comment?" Jane asked curiously.

"I doubt he meant anything. Now, let us hasten inside, for the night air is growing chill."

And I need to see Jane to our room so I can step back downstairs to speak to Uncle Gardiner, Elizabeth thought dourly. *Oh, the impertinence of this man! My every sense tells me he has already made his decisions and is proceeding to implement his plans. But all my powers of deduction have abandoned me. I cannot determine whether his devices might mean good or ill for Jane.*

On the other hand, Elizabeth had to admit that the colonel's visit had certainly brought cheer to Jane's demeanour. Her cheeks were slightly flushed, and her eyes sparkled. He was definitely an amiable man, and she was leaning towards the conclusion that his steady regard towards Jane indicated a concern for her sister that might approach her own.

But I need more information. Obviously, he is not as destitute as I indicated to Uncle Gardiner. But how can he look at her that way when he did not even KNOW her yesterday morning?

And the associated unwelcome musings concerning his cousin continued to plague her. *How can a man as well behaved and affable as Colonel Fitzwilliam say he was closer to Mr. Darcy than to his own brothers? How can he say Mr. Darcy has changed and he wants that old Darcy back? Is he correct, or is he just trying to act on behalf of his cousin? Certainly he owes much to the Darcy family. Is it just loyalty that impels these remarks from him? Oh, I need more information about everything!*

CHAPTER 7

Nothing in this world can take the place of persistence. Talent will not; nothing is more common than unsuccessful people with talent. Genius will not; unrewarded genius is almost a proverb. Education will not; the world is full of educated derelicts. Persistence and determination alone are omnipotent. The slogan 'press on' has solved and always will solve the problems of the human race.
— Calvin Coolidge, thirtieth president
of the United States

Tuesday, April 28, 1812
Gracechurch Street, London

"He said what?" Elizabeth asked in disbelief.

"He told me it was his intention—his *firm* intention, as he phrased it—to win Jane's affections and to eventually make her his wife," her uncle replied patiently.

Elizabeth sat back in her chair, stunned by her uncle's statement, and it was some moments before she could say anything.

"I am beyond astonished," she said slowly. "I am absolutely taken aback. Possibly I should not be, given that he came to call after being introduced to Jane only yesterday. It is far more precipitous than anything I would have expected. It is difficult to believe—incredible, in fact."

"He seems to be quite a determined young man in my opinion." Mr. Gardiner had not intended to discuss Jane's situation when Lizzy first asked to speak with him. He had promised secrecy to the colonel, but he had relented when Lizzy told him of Fitzwilliam's recommendation to her.

"It is not his resolve that disturbs me. It might even be admirable in other situations. But it is so hasty—too much so."

"He mentioned being quite surprised himself and explained that he was not an impulsive person. But he went on to say that he has been completely smitten and simply cannot help himself."

"I cannot bear to see Jane hurt further."

"None of us want Jane to endure any further sorrow."

"I know, I know. But the very suddenness of Colonel Fitzwilliam's interest worries me. It worries me greatly."

"I really believe you are concerned over nothing, especially after what your aunt told me of his seeming to cheer Jane. And, as he said to me, if anyone will be hurt over this sudden interest of his, it will be him and not Jane. He is the one putting his feelings at risk."

"But Jane is not cautious enough. How can we be sure she will make a decision based on her best interests? I worry that she might agree to his addresses because she is unwilling to hurt his feelings and not because of a similar desire on her part."

"Do you not believe that we must leave those decisions in Jane's hands? We cannot live her life for her after all. I believe you are doing your sister a disservice, and I am not disposed to interfere in the case of an honourable young man who seems to have caught her interest and has certainly brought a smile to her face. I think you would be advised to act in a similar manner."

"But look what happened to her with Mr. Bingley."

"You know, I have come to the conclusion that I no longer approve of Mr. Bingley. To be perfectly honest, he all but abandoned her just when she was most justified in believing some kind of declaration would be forthcoming. Jane deserved something more than a brief note from Bingley's sister telling her the whole party was leaving for town and would not return. But there was nothing from Bingley himself. No matter what arguments Mr. Darcy made—the ones that so incensed you—Bingley himself had a responsibility to explain his actions in not returning."

Elizabeth said nothing to this and did not lift her eyes, so her uncle continued. "And it is a simple fact that Mr. Bingley is *not* here and Colonel Fitzwilliam *is*. Further, he has clearly and openly stated his intentions, which Bingley never did, and he also makes it clear that nothing except a rejection by Jane will deter his quest."

"I am just so confused. I can find no basis for such a sudden fixation on Colonel Fitzwilliam's part," she said plaintively, returning to her original contention.

"So you disapprove of him?"

"Disapprove? On the contrary—I quite like him. He is amiable, well-mannered, and well-informed. But I had formed the distinct impression that he was not in search of a wife, especially one who could not bring any financial advantage to the marriage."

"From what he told me, he would agree with you, at least in part. He had not anticipated looking seriously for a marriage partner until his active service was near an end, but once he met Jane, he was completely overwhelmed. And as for the financial side, it seems he must have been more circumspect with you than you were able to detect. He appears quite capable of supporting a wife and family. 'In comfort,' as he put it, 'if not in luxury.'"

"That part is quite surprising, but I suppose your information is superior to mine."

"He admitted you might have been justified in your supposition, but he pointed out that, when the two of you discussed the subject, he was agreeing with you about younger sons of the nobility in general, not about himself in particular. And, as he said, he may not be a pauper now, but he once was."

"I suppose you are right," Elizabeth conceded unwillingly.

"Both your aunt and I were quite favourably impressed by his visit here today, Lizzy. From my opening interview, which must have been rather stressful for him, to the manner in which he conducted himself all evening, he was a perfect gentleman. His interest in Jane was clear, but he was neither obsessive nor improper in his attentions. He simply made it eminently clear that he was interested. And you saw the way his visit has raised her spirits."

"I do, but I still think Jane is more suited to Mr. Bingley. They are so similar, and I cannot forget that their separation is due to Mr. Darcy. And it was only by accident that Jane and the colonel met when he called yesterday. Jane had mentioned taking the children to the park an hour earlier, and it was only by chance that she was in the front room when he arrived. And then she left before he began his discourse on Mr. Wickham."

"Ah, Mr. Wickham."

"I have to confess I made a disastrous error there," she admitted with a blush.

"And also in laying the blame on Mr. Darcy without adequate justification."

"Well, yes, I suppose I was in error there also," she mumbled unwillingly.

"Your aunt wonders whether you have not been precipitous in summarily refusing to reconsider what occurred between you and Mr. Darcy in Kent."

"You cannot mean that you blame me for refusing Mr. Darcy," Elizabeth said angrily.

Her uncle shook his head. "I would not blame you for refusing any young man so long as your decision was made after due consideration.

You are the one who will have to live with that decision, and it is not my part to say yea or nay. What I am concerned with is the possibility that your conclusion was made in haste, spurred on by anger rather than real reflection, especially since you now know you erred in your assessment of Mr. Darcy's treatment of Mr. Wickham. Remember, it was quite a compliment that Mr. Darcy admired you enough to offer marriage, despite facing the same drawbacks that pertained to Mr. Bingley and Jane."

"Well, yes, I must admit I did enjoy a certain amount of gratification from that thought. But he was so proud and haughty to everyone. I simply could not accept such a man even if I *was* wrong about his harm to Mr. Wickham."

"Lizzy, Lizzy, you are not *listening* to me. I am not questioning your decision. I am only saying that I am uneasy about the *haste* with which you reached it—and, of course, with the possibility that your emotions rather than your judgement are responsible for your decision. If you are uneasy about the speed with which Colonel Fitzwilliam became enamoured of your sister, then can you not see how I am uneasy with the similarly rapid fashion in which you rejected any possibility of a connexion with Mr. Darcy? It is a connexion, after all, that might have many advantages, not only to your family but also to you. I am also perplexed that a man highly valued by both Colonel Fitzwilliam and Mr. Bingley could possibly be bad enough to warrant such a hasty decision."

This argument finally penetrated the wall Elizabeth had erected, and she was quiet for a time as she considered what he had said. Finally, she said reluctantly, "I am forced to confess you may be right. On the matter of Mr. Darcy, I seem quite unable to think clearly. Certainly, I should have considered what Colonel Fitzwilliam had to say for a little longer than I did."

"That is all I am concerned about. Naturally, your aunt and I support whatever decisions you and Jane might make. I simply want you both to take the time to think them through. If you do that, then you will justify the faith we have in both of you."

"Very well, Uncle. Your point is well taken, at least on my part."

"And I shall have the same discussion with Jane if the occasion arises before you both return to Longbourn. But you should consider what you said when you described the colonel as being amiable and well mannered since Jane also shares those attributes. I certainly found him quite pleasant, clear-thinking, and cheerful when we talked. So, while you say Jane and Mr. Bingley are better suited to each other, this may only be in some respects. In other ways, the colonel may be a better match than Mr. Bingley is. For certain, he is more firm and stalwart than her wealthier suitor."

Elizabeth nodded thoughtfully. "Perhaps you are right, yet he is so *different* from Mr. Bingley. However, I realize I shall have to restrain myself on that topic from now on."

"And," suggested Mr. Gardiner with a wicked grin, "he might also be right when he noted the similarities between you and Mr. Darcy. The way you are both quick-witted, private, and—I like this one very much though I have never met Mr. Darcy—both of you are adept at verbal repartee and debate."

To this comment Elizabeth made no response. She simply blushed and bade her uncle good night.

IT TOOK SO LONG FOR THE BUTLER TO RESPOND TO HIS KNOCK that Richard at first thought Darcy might already be in his bedroom, despite the fact that candlelight was visible behind the curtains of his study. But the butler finally answered the door, apologising that he had been assisting the housekeeper with her bookkeeping. When Richard entered the study, he could see that Darcy was busily engaged in working through the backlog of paperwork that had built up while he was at Rosings. Papers, notes, and bills were stacked in piles all over his massive desk.

"You are up rather late, Richard," Darcy said, looking up. He waved his cousin towards a comfortable chair on the other side of his desk and offered a glass of port and a cigar, both of which were gratefully accepted.

"I wanted to thank you again for the loan of Jennings," Richard said as he puffed his cigar alight. "Tying this neck cloth was quite beyond the capability of Sergeant Bascomb. He is perfectly capable of fitting me out in full dress uniform to appear before the major general on a moment's notice, but he simply threw up his hands at the thought of essaying one of the more fashionable knots."

Darcy steepled his hands as he looked his cousin up and down. "You are certainly welcome, but you were in such a hurry that I never did get an answer to where you were going and why you were dressed in such unprecedented style."

"I was visiting a young lady. I think I did mention that."

"You did, but I have seen you call on young ladies before. You always seemed to find your uniform perfectly acceptable on those occasions. But today you could rival Brummell for sartorial elegance. So why is *this* young lady so special? And do not trot out the old adage that 'this is the one.' That line has been used to death in far too many cheap novels."

"Then I can say nothing," Richard said with a smile, "especially since this young lady *is* the one, and I *am* going to marry her."

"Oh, saints preserve us," Darcy muttered, rolling his eyes. "First me and now you. Dare I even ask the identity of this vision of female perfection who has finally caught your eye and secured your heart?"

"Actually, she is someone you already know," Richard said seriously. "Miss Jane Bennet."

Darcy froze in the process of lifting his cigar to his mouth and simply stared at his cousin in stunned amazement.

Finally, he shook himself and carefully replaced his cigar in the ashtray. "How can this be? You do not even *know* Miss Bennet."

"Ah, but I do. I met her yesterday when I called on her sister at their uncle's house in Cheapside."

"Sister? Which sister are you talking about?"

"You know which sister. The sister we both know so well. Miss *Elizabeth* Bennet."

"What is going on here, Richard? Just why are you calling on either of the Bennet sisters? I do not care for the fact that you would go behind my back on this."

Richard was unaffected by his cousin's visible anger and blew out a cloud of fragrant smoke. "I was not going behind your back. From what you told me last week, all discourse between you and Miss Elizabeth was presumed to be at an end. However, there remained an unfinished question between Miss Elizabeth and me, a question concerning George Wickham. I burst into your abortive proposal, if you remember, at the moment she was taking his part, and I did not have time to explain to her just how badly she had misjudged both him and you. I resolved instantly that I would revisit the question when she returned to town, which I have now done. I simply could not leave her in any doubt as to the true worthlessness of that man."

"And just how much did you discuss with her?" Darcy said, his eyes icy with anger.

"I did not mention Georgiana if that is what you are worried about. But I did tell her everything else. All of which, I might point out, she should have learned months ago and from you. From what you have said, you knew Wickham was spreading lies about you when you were both in Hertfordshire, and you did nothing."

"I was determined that my actions would speak for my character without having to lower myself to Wickham's level to debate his falsehoods."

"No, Cousin, you would not lower yourself to confront his lies because the country gentry you met were not part of your circle and thus deserved no explanation from a Darcy."

Darcy said nothing, just looked angrily at his cousin, but Richard returned his challenge glare for glare until Darcy finally looked away. His anger was ebbing, and he knew it was unjustified in any case. It was patently obvious that *someone* had needed to disabuse Elizabeth and probably the rest of the neighbourhood of their delusions about Wickham. And he was forced to agree with Richard that it should have been done by him, and much earlier.

Perhaps if I had openly discussed Wickham at that time, told her clearly what lay between us, and even offered evidence of my truthfulness, then many things might have been different. But I was determined not to admit I was attracted to her, so I resolved to keep my distance. Accordingly, I suppressed my own emotions and never bothered to assess hers, so I had not the slightest idea of the disdain in which she held me. Until that horrible evening…

Finally, he drew a deep breath. "And did Miss Elizabeth believe you?"

"She did. Her aunt sat with us because the manner in which I arrived at their door was rather unusual, but she will, I am sure, be discreet about what I told her. Not that there is a real need for secrecy, you understand, but I know how obsessive you have become about not revealing any aspect of your private affairs."

Darcy coloured but nodded again. Then, clearing his throat, he asked, "And was Miss Bennet present for these discussions? Was that how you met her?"

"No, I was introduced to her when I arrived, but she excused herself in order to give us privacy. But I was greatly affected on first impression, and I think Bingley was a fool to let her get away. I was fortunate enough to be able to meet her afterwards at the park where she had taken the Gardiner children to play. After some conversation, I asked whether I might call on her today, and she agreed."

Richard looked Darcy directly in the eye as he continued. "Make no mistake about the lengths to which I was willing to go to clear up this problem with Wickham. I did not have to tell Miss Elizabeth about Georgiana in order to convince her of Wickham's perfidy, but I would have done so had it been necessary. Fortunately, my account was convincing and her trust in me sufficient to assure her of the truth of my story, especially when I told her I could provide witnesses to the truth. She came to realize that Wickham had built his structure of lies on just enough truth to make them plausible. But I was determined that this matter would be *resolved* so it could no longer cloud the air."

"Without asking my permission?" Darcy said, his anger flaring anew.

"Yes, without asking your permission. I share the responsibility for Georgiana, you know, so the decision would not have been yours alone."

"But she is my sister. And you have been gone these five years."

"During which time you have changed, and not for the better. I have spoken of it before, but that is neither here nor there. Of paramount importance is that Georgiana's near elopement could happen to other young ladies, and all because you would not trouble yourself to counter the lies Wickham told about you."

Darcy began to make a rejoinder, but he realized he would only be repeating what he had said earlier about depending on his actions as testimony of his character. After seeing that Darcy did not intend to comment, Richard continued.

"It also appears that, when you first met Miss Elizabeth, you did not conduct yourself in a manner that would have made her or anyone else reject Wickham's lies. Instead, you made them believable, and I am tired of your behaviour of excluding everyone outside your intimate circle. You have so circumscribed yourself that you could not even change when you met a woman with whom you wanted to share the rest of your life. Look at what it has cost you."

Both cousins glared at each other, but Darcy's glare was pro forma and quickly dissipated, especially as he felt a stab of grief from what his cousin had said about his loss.

"Perhaps you are right," he said at last. "I am certain no one could have handled matters any more disastrously than I have done."

Richard nodded in agreement, staring at the smoke rising off his cigar. "I went further," he said quietly. "I have been thinking much on this, and I have come to the conclusion that your selection of Miss Elizabeth Bennet was an admirable one. I think your characters complement each other, and I think you could have a satisfying life together. So I explained my coming to live at Pemberley, your mother arranging for my commission, and your being saddled with the responsibility for all the family affairs after your mother died. In short, I tried to rehabilitate your character with Miss Elizabeth. Unfortunately, I was unsuccessful in getting her to reconsider her answer to your proposal."

Darcy was no happier to hear this information than he had been to hear the earlier information, but he received it in a dark moodiness that matched that of his cousin, and his only response was a nod of acceptance.

"I believe my information was not simply rejected, but Miss Elizabeth's opinion was so fixed that she was not inclined to change her mind."

Silence reigned in the study for several long minutes as both cousins continued to smoke their cigars and ponder the unsolvable problem that confronted them.

Eventually, Darcy asked, "What shall you do now about Miss Bennet? I cannot help but wonder what Miss Elizabeth thinks of your intentions towards her sister given the ferocity with which she confronted me about Bingley."

"Miss Bennet appeared to welcome my attentions today, but I cannot return until Thursday. As for her sister, I do not think she is entirely pleased with me. I suppose she considers Bingley a better match for her sister. He certainly has a more substantial fortune, and you have told me of his amiability."

Darcy began to rummage through one of the stacks of papers on his desk until he retrieved a stack of cards with a grunt of satisfaction. He untied the ribbon around them and searched until he found one of the cards. Taking his pen, he wrote a short message on the back and blotted it.

"Here," he said, holding it out. "Use this and take your Miss Bennet to the theatre on Friday. I shall not be attending anytime soon, so someone should have use of the box."

Richard took the card and found it was a voucher from the Covent Garden Theatre where he knew Darcy rented a private box. On the back of the card, Darcy had written: "Col. R. Fitzwilliam & party will use my box for opening perf. of 'J. Caesar,' 1 May. F. Darcy."

"I thank you, Darce, but are you sure about this? I know you were looking forward to this performance."

Darcy waved off Richard's protests. "I am not in the mood for it any longer. No—go yourself and take whoever might want to attend."

"Perhaps I might convince Miss Elizabeth to attend, then you could meet us at your box—"

"No!" Darcy exclaimed. "Definitely not. I could not...would not... no. Thank you for your efforts, but it would only offend her. In fact, do not even mention my name. Just go and have a pleasant evening. And now, I still have a number of business matters with which to contend, so I beg you to excuse me so I can continue to do battle with them."

Richard nodded and silently left the study. As he looked back from the door, Darcy was seemingly immersed in examining the contents of one of the documents on his desk.

But I would wager his eyes are not focused on it, Richard thought. *Though I am not a betting man, I would definitely place that wager.*

CHAPTER 8

He is not a lover who does not love forever.
— Euripides, writer of classical Greek tragedies

Friday, May 1, 1812
Covent Garden, London

Jane looked out the window in surprise as her uncle's carriage slowed and came to a halt. Shoppers still thronged the pedestrian walkways to either side of the street since many of the shops along Bow Street stayed open until ten o'clock or even later. But there was no sign of the theatre.

"Why have we stopped, Uncle?" Elizabeth asked, leaning out of the window for a better look. A series of dividers separated the pedestrians from the streets, and she was surprised to see a line of carriages ahead of their coach with several more stopping just behind.

"Covent Garden is the largest theatre in town, Lizzy, and it is usually considered to be the leading theatre of the English-speaking world. Only Drury Lane came close, but the rebuilding likely will not be completed until the fall. Even then, it is uncertain whether it will be able to open since the management is said to have been virtually bankrupted by the cost of the renewal."

"I thought a new company had been formed to cover the cost of rebuilding by subscription," Mrs. Gardiner said.

"Quite correct, dear, but subscriptions have proven barely able to keep up with costs. Whitbread and his fellow investors are said to have little left in their purse. In any case, Lizzy, there is always a line of coaches, carriages, and hacks waiting to drop their passengers in front of the theatre. We shall simply have to wait our turn."

Both Jane and Elizabeth settled back to look out at the shops on either side of the street, and there was much to see. Streams of people strolled along the street, pausing occasionally to inspect the various offerings in the fine, high windows. There were drapers, stationers, booksellers, china sellers, and many more, all close to each other and without any break between shops. The shoppers were dressed well but not opulently. Covent Garden and similar shopping areas such as Leicester Square and the Strand were not in the most fashionable areas, but the shops were still genteel and respectable.

The girls had shopped often with their aunt in Cheapside, which was not so very different from the scene they saw here, but everything was significantly altered at night as the streets were lit by a multiplicity of lamps and lanterns of all different colours and brightness. Jane pointed out a dressmaker's establishment that showed women's materials—silks, chintzes, muslins, and more—many of them visible behind the windows lit by carefully placed lamps to pique the interest of those passing by.

Just then, their coach lurched into motion again, and they moved up a coach-length before again halting.

"We could get out and walk," Elizabeth commented, "and then we could inspect the shops more easily."

"Ah, but it is not done that way," responded her uncle with a smile. "The theatre employs people who will stop the pedestrians when we alight from our coach, forming a line so we may enter the theatre. If we walked up to the entrance, we would be simply more pedestrians, either forced to enter with those buying tickets or directed away from the arriving coaches. In addition, I should not like to try escorting three ladies past all these merchants' windows and still arrive in time for the beginning of the play."

Elizabeth sniffed audibly to show her opinion of this last comment and returned to inspecting the businesses on her side of the coach while her uncle and aunt shared a soft laugh at her expense.

"It is too bad Miss Lucas declined to attend, dear," Mr. Gardiner said to his wife. "She might have enjoyed the shops even if she does not care for Shakespeare."

"I believe she would have liked to come, if only to be able to say she had attended the theatre and seen all of the finest society in London. Why, I understand the Prince Regent will be attending tonight," responded his wife. "But Maria must have eaten some bad meat when we were at the market yesterday. I especially suspect that beef pie she purchased from the gypsy."

How Maria would have loved to boast that she dined nine times at Rosings with her ladyship, drank tea there twice, AND attended the theatre when the Prince Regent was in attendance, Elizabeth thought sardonically. *Silly girl. I TOLD her not to buy that pie.*

Gradually, their coach moved up position by position, and Elizabeth happened to be looking at Jane when she saw her sister's expression change. Jane had been idly looking at the shops on her side of the coach when her head suddenly swivelled and stopped. Her eyes seemed to sharpen and focus, and her whole expression softened even as her lips curved into a smile.

"There is Colonel Fitzwilliam waiting for us," she said.

"I daresay he is *waiting*, Jane," Mr. Gardiner commented dryly, "but I believe I am correct when I say he is *not* waiting for your aunt and me."

"And as amiable as I find the gentleman, I am certain he is not waiting for me either," Elizabeth said teasingly.

Jane's cheeks grew a little pinker, and she lowered her eyes, but Elizabeth was sure she was not displeased. However, she could not help feeling a pang of regret when she thought of Mr. Bingley.

Had it not been for Mr. Darcy's arrogant interference, that might be Mr. Bingley waiting, she thought angrily. *No matter how Colonel Fitzwilliam might try to change my mind, I do not believe I can ever forgive Mr. Darcy for that.*

As soon as their carriage stopped in front of the theatre, two servants in Covent Garden livery quickly opened the door and pulled down the step. Mr. Gardiner would normally have exited first in order to assist his wife and nieces, but he waved Jane ahead since the colonel was already stepping forward to do the honours.

Richard's breath caught in his throat as Jane stepped through the door of the coach, bent over slightly to duck under the top of the door frame. She thus presented to him a most enchanting view down the front of her fashionably low-cut evening gown.

Her aunt had ordered the gown prepared early in Jane's visit in order to show off her niece's figure to best advantage though Jane had never had occasion to wear it until her aunt suggested she do so tonight. Mrs. Gardiner's suggestion certainly achieved the intended result. Richard was not able to keep his eyes from dropping to Jane's bodice and the view of her neckline as her breasts swelled against the constraints of her gown. He was at least able to make himself wrench his eyes away after a moment so he could accept Jane's hand as she straightened and stepped to the ground.

Does she know just how enticing she looks? he wondered in numb confusion. *Does she have any idea of the effect she is having on me—and on any other man looking this way?*

Only manners strengthened by rigid self-control allowed him to exchange greetings with her, though he really wished to simply step back and stare. He did not think he had ever seen a young lady more beautiful in her person or more attractively attired, though he knew enough about women's fashion to realize that Jane's gown was nothing extraordinary. It was quite in keeping with the fashion of the day, heavily influenced by the move towards the more simplified and classical styles of Greece and Rome. The waistline was high, and the material was an inner layer of fine white linen with an outer layer of sheer white silk. Gone were the heavy brocades of the previous century, replaced by the clean lines that fell from the high waist just under her bosom all the way to her hem. The sleeves were short, hardly more than straps across the shoulder to support the dress while allowing a low, square-cut neckline to show off the snow-white perfection of a lady's bosom.

It is a beautiful gown that many a high-society daughter could not wear with more credit, Richard thought. *They might pick elaborate gowns with more embroidery and a much higher price, but they could not look as beautiful as this country lass before me—or as desirable.*

The addition of physical desirability to his already fixed admiration for this striking young woman only firmed his already expressed intentions, and the soft smile she gave him sent a tingling sensation down his spine and made his blood seem to sing in his veins. He believed he would never forget this moment, his varied emotions twisting, turning, and melting together until no single strand could be untangled from the others.

My intentions are already declared, at least to her uncle, but tonight makes me absolutely determined that nothing—absolutely nothing—shall sway me from winning her and making her my bride.

"Colonel Fitzwilliam?"

The note of query in Elizabeth Bennet's voice brought Richard's attention back to the present as he realized that, despite his attempt at self-control, he had clearly been staring too long at her sister. He was quick to turn back to the coach and assist Miss Elizabeth to the ground. The expression on her face was clear: she knew it was the sight of Jane's exposed bosom that had paralysed him.

And it was clear that *she* did not approve.

Richard was correct in his supposition since Elizabeth had heartily disagreed with her aunt's suggestion for Jane's gown earlier that day, believing it was much too revealing.

"Lizzy, you are in London, the largest and most cosmopolitan city in the world," Mrs. Gardiner had said with a smile. "Every woman attending the theatre for this opening performance will be dressed in her absolute best evening wear with considerable shoulder and bosom on display."

At Elizabeth's disbelieving look, her aunt had continued. "It is not customary or proper to wear a low-cut or short-sleeved gown to an afternoon event, even in London, but it is quite appropriate for the evening. Trust me, all the younger women tonight—both married and unmarried—will be showing considerable bosom. Jane will be much admired by all the men—and envied by all the women."

"Especially one young man," Elizabeth had grumbled under her breath.

"Well, I certainly hope so," her aunt had replied merrily. "After all, we women have to use whatever assets God has given us."

Elizabeth was well aware that her aunt was more sophisticated than either Jane or herself, but it was still startling to accept her aunt's intention to make the best use of the impact Jane's innocent but nevertheless undoubted sexuality would have on a healthy young man, even one as urbane as the son of an earl. Then she had a further thought.

"Will you be wearing…that is…"

"Will I be wearing anything similar to Jane, even at my ancient age?"

Mrs. Gardiner had laughed delightedly as Elizabeth turned bright red in embarrassment. "Yes, Lizzy, I have something in mind for myself also. After all, I have a man in my life to entice, even if we have had four children. I just wish I had had time to have something as alluring made for you, especially if your Mr. Darcy decides to accompany his cousin."

"He is *not* my Mr. Darcy," Elizabeth had said instantly, startled and upset. But her aunt had simply given her a sly smile, which had left Elizabeth feeling decidedly unsettled.

ELIZABETH WAS EASILY ABLE TO DISCERN THAT FITZWILLIAM WAS having difficulty breaking away from the vision of her sister though he did manage to straighten and mumble a greeting to her. But Elizabeth was inwardly certain that he had little awareness of what he said, and he looked distinctly relieved as he saw Mr. Gardiner step next into the doorway. That meant her uncle could assist his wife, which allowed the colonel to turn back to Jane and offer his arm. Elizabeth was warmed and disturbed at the same time as she saw the animation of her sister's smile when she took the proffered arm.

But Fitzwilliam appeared more in control of himself as he offered his other arm to Elizabeth, and she lost little time in taking it. She had managed to quell her irritation by now, and her expression was one of careful calm. She knew it would do no good to poison the relationship between Fitzwilliam and herself. Even if she thought Bingley would have been a better match for Jane, it was obvious that Jane was captivated by the colonel. If he did as he had told her uncle and managed to marry Jane, it would be disastrous not to be able to visit her beloved sister because of the disapproval of her husband.

Two uniformed doormen opened the theatre doors as they approached, giving them all a bow. Elizabeth looked around in interest once they were inside, and she quickly realized her aunt had been correct about the evening wear of the ladies. All the fashionable women walking about on the arms of their escorts or waiting to go to their seats were elaborately coifed and gowned, many in attire even more revealing than Jane's.

Several of them should have exerted a bit more common sense and self-control, considering they no longer have Jane's or even my aunt's figure, Elizabeth thought puckishly, her usual nature beginning to reassert itself. She also apprehended that Aunt Gardiner had been right about Jane's effect on the men.

The contortions some of these gentlemen are going through in trying to get a closer look at her without offending their present partners would be quite entertaining if it were not so necessary to maintain my composure.

For a moment, Elizabeth felt a brief flash of jealousy that *she* was not the cause of so many men trying to get a better look, but she easily repressed it. She had deliberately dressed in an understated gown that would have been appropriate for visiting but was rather out of place tonight. However, she felt little desire to attract the attention of other men. Having so unwittingly attracted the attention of Mr. Darcy, she had no desire for further interest along those lines.

The noise level had increased remarkably once they were inside the foyer, and Jane had to lean towards Richard as she said, "There are more people here tonight than I had expected. Is it very expensive to attend this theatre, Colonel Fitzwilliam?"

"Not unduly so, Miss Bennet. The ground level boxes go for six shillings, and a great number of people from all walks of life attend every week. It appears they will be playing to a full house tonight."

"Where shall we be sitting?"

"We have the good fortune to have the loan of a private box, so we should have an excellent view. We go up these stairs just ahead," Richard said, nodding towards the stairway. An employee in evening dress was passing parties up the stairs and, when their turn came, Richard handed him the card Darcy had given him. The man took only a cursory look at it since Richard had taken the precaution of presenting the card prior to the arrival of the Gardiner party.

The man snapped his fingers, and one of several uniformed boys sprang to his side.

"Enjoy the performance, Colonel Fitzwilliam," the man said as he handed the card to the boy.

"Thank you, Logan, we shall," responded Richard politely.

"After me, if you please." The boy, who appeared to be about twelve or thirteen, led the party up the stairs and down a long, narrow hallway.

"Here you are, ladies, gentlemen." He opened a door towards the end that led into a box. "Enjoy the play."

"Thank you," Richard said, giving the boy a shilling. Mr. Gardiner gave him another, and the boy grinned widely at his good fortune.

"Thank *you*, sirs!" he exclaimed before he scampered down the narrow hall, expertly squeezing past the next party being led to their box by one of his fellows.

"Now we know why they employ boys," Mr. Gardiner said. "They are small enough to get past parties coming this way."

The box had seats for six, three in front and three behind, with the chairs in front on a lower step so the view from the rear was unimpeded. The chairs were comfortably made with cushions on the seat and back as well as upholstered arms.

"Would you and Mrs. Gardiner care for the lower seats, sir?" Richard asked. "Or perhaps we could let the ladies sit in front while we sit behind."

"No, no, you young people sit down front. I only need my spectacles to read—my vision is otherwise quite excellent. Mrs. Gardiner and I shall make ourselves comfortable in the rear.

And you will also be able to keep an eye on your two nieces, thought Richard with amusement as he recognised Mr. Gardiner's ploy. *Who knows what might happen with Jane dressed as she is.*

Richard made sure that Elizabeth did not manage to separate him from Jane, and before she realized what was happening, he had offered her the left hand seat. She had no choice but to take it, which allowed Richard to seat Jane in the middle seat. He took the remaining seat on the right while Mr. and Mrs. Gardiner settled down in the two seats on the right directly behind Jane and him.

Richard saw Elizabeth looking at him in a speculative fashion, and he arched an interrogative eyebrow. The interior of the box was only dimly lit, but their eyes were rapidly growing used it.

"Yes, Miss Elizabeth? Did you have a question?"

"Not a question, sir, a compliment on the skilful way you arranged the seating."

"Tactics—my soldier's training, you know. But I do want to offer you a compliment on your diligence in attending your sister. No ne'er-do-well shall get close to her with *you* providing protection."

"Surely you are not suggesting you fall into that category." Elizabeth gave him her sweetest smile but with the light of deviltry dancing in her eyes. She might prefer Bingley as a husband to her sister, but she *did* very much like Fitzwilliam. "Yet I do note with dismay that you have reverted to your beloved uniform again. And just when Jane and I had reason to believe your wardrobe of fashionable attire was rather extensive."

"I am afraid your sister has caught me out, Miss Bennet," Richard remarked, turning now to Jane. "Either your assessment of my indifference to fashion was correct, or I have exhausted the only two pieces of gentlemanly attire I own."

"Ignore her, Colonel," replied Jane with a smile. "She and I often tease our younger sisters about swooning over a red coat, but I think your uniform suits you perfectly."

"I hope I might be introduced to your other sisters soon," Richard said quietly, his nerves tingling as he awaited an answer to this probe.

Jane was conscious of a sudden constriction in her throat at this indication that Richard's interest would not be limited to her tenure in London. She had to swallow several times before she could finally say, "If…if you visit our home in Hertfordshire, I shall be glad…very glad…to introduce you."

"Excellent," Richard said, feeling a weight lift off his shoulders.

"Perhaps I might pay your family a visit Saturday week? I know you travel home tomorrow."

"I...I shall look forward to seeing you again," Jane said quietly, and the softness in her eyes as she looked at him made Richard feel about six inches taller.

However, he caught the expression on her sister's face, and he was not at all sure what to make of it. Not disapproval, exactly, just... assessing. But assessing what?

"I am not at all familiar with this play," Jane said as they waited for the theatre to fill. "Lizzy and I were usually more interested in the comedies and the tragedies."

"The tragedies, Miss Bennet?" Richard asked, arching his eyebrows. "I am dreadfully sorry, but I have great difficulty picturing you delving into King Lear."

"Well, perhaps my interest did lie more towards the comedies," admitted Jane sheepishly.

Richard fixed his eyes on Elizabeth. "And does that mean you were more interested in the tragedies?"

"Actually, it was the histories rather than the tragedies, though I admit a partiality to *Romeo and Juliet* and *Macbeth*."

"I cannot remember hearing of a production of *Julius Caesar* here in London," Mrs. Gardiner said. "I read the play many years ago, but it does not seem too popular any more."

"It used to be popular some fifty years ago," her husband said. "And I hear it is very popular in America these days. Evidently, they read it in the spirit of republican patriotism, and whenever it is performed, the part of Caesar is invariably played by an actor with a most distinguished upper-class British accent."

The last sentence was stated in such a droll manner that it inspired a general round of laughter, tinged with some apprehension since relations between America and England gave every appearance of degenerating into dangerous territories.

"In any case," Richard said, not wishing to dwell on such sombre matters, "it seems this resurrection of *Julius Caesar* is the work of John Kemble, who manages the theatre and is the brother of Mrs. Sarah Siddons, the famous actress. He will play Brutus, and his brother Charles will play Marc Antony. I have heard they plan a completely different interpretation of the play. Evidently, they intend it to be more of a 'noble drama,' with great attention paid to 'accurate costuming' and 'scenic splendour.' Or, at least that was the way it was described in *The Times*."

Richard had noted that Elizabeth was looking around the theatre as he talked, and he guessed that she had just realized how favourably their box was placed, close to the left side of the stage and at a slightly higher level, where they would be able to look down on the actors from a point only slightly above their heads. Suddenly, when she twisted around to look at the empty seat behind her, he was not surprised to see a sudden look of anger on her face.

"Uncle," she announced, clearly trying to keep her voice calm, "do these not appear to be very nicely located seats? Compared to what I can see, ours would seem to be among the very best."

"Of course, Lizzy. This is a third level box, a private box. It can only be rented yearly, and the seating is thus very desirable."

Elizabeth nodded tautly, before turning to Richard. "You mentioned you had the good fortune to have the loan of a private box, Colonel Fitzwilliam. Would it be possible this box belongs to your cousin Mr. Darcy?"

Richard's expression as he looked at Elizabeth was one of calm composure though he could see embarrassed looks on the faces of her aunt and uncle out of the corner of his eye. He knew Mr. and Mrs. Gardiner had to be distressed at the unseemly anger their niece was displaying.

They, of course, must have immediately deduced what has only now occurred to their niece, he thought, *but they had too much tact to comment on it; whereas, Miss Elizabeth, with her usual forthright manner, simply plunges in and speaks her mind.*

"It is indeed Mr. Darcy's box. He was kind enough to offer it to me for our use tonight."

"I do hate to be so uncharitable since we are your guests tonight, Colonel," Elizabeth said, her anger now openly displayed, "but I remember your original reason for visiting my uncle's house. I cannot help wondering whether Mr. Darcy might coincidentally be joining us tonight."

"No, he will not," Richard said flatly. He locked stares with Elizabeth, and he saw the surprise on her face at his blunt statement and his cold, dispassionate tone. She could not long maintain her glare in light of such a refutation of her suspicions, and he could see her anger fading away.

"Then why did he give these seats to you?"

"Because he knew he would not be attending. When I mentioned my intention to attend tonight, he offered the box to me, saying someone might as well have the use of a box for which he had already paid."

Fitzwilliam's last words had been stated in an emotionless tone, and Elizabeth flushed in embarrassment as she realized how rude her comments had been.

"I might also mention," Fitzwilliam continued, "that my cousin has always favoured Shakespeare's histories, and he had shown the greatest interest in attending this revival of *Julius Caesar*. I was thus surprised when he made his offer. In addition, this is not the first time he has allowed me and others of his friends to make use of his box. He has always been most generous, even when we were boys together."

Elizabeth was now stricken at how she had converted the convivial atmosphere to one of cold formality, and she realized Fitzwilliam had just thrown in her face the knowledge that Mr. Darcy had *not* put her out of his mind but was instead avoiding his usual activities because of the blow to his spirits. She felt especially dreadful as she remembered commenting so lightly to Jane that she was sure he had other feelings that would soon drive away any thought of her. Obviously, such a change in his opinion had not taken place, and she suddenly realized just how spiteful and malicious her behaviour must appear to her companions. A great wash of embarrassment and shame swept over her, and her cheeks flamed red as other remembrances flashed across her mind.

"I am sorry," she said in a strained voice. "I spoke very much out of turn. I beg everyone's forgiveness for my careless and thoughtless words."

WITH THESE WORDS OF APOLOGY, ELIZABETH TURNED AWAY FROM everyone and stared fixedly down at the empty stage. Her mind was in turmoil, inspired by her most unusual behaviour, and she could not stop the most absurd thoughts from suggesting themselves to her.

What is making me behave so badly tonight? she thought in anguish. *In fact, what is making me act so unlike myself all the time? Since returning from Hunsford, I have been rude and angry beyond anything I can remember. And now, I have embarrassed my aunt and uncle in a manner such as I have never done before. I have been acting more like Lydia than like myself. Whatever can explain what is happening to me?*

She sat wrapped in the deepest gloom, and she made herself consider each instance in which she had exhibited such peculiar behaviour. Gradually, as she forced herself to confront her own faults and errors, her innate self-honesty came to the fore, and she began to pierce through the swirling mists that had clouded her mind. As her inner vision grew clearer, she was able to look upon herself and her conduct these past days with brutal clarity. Eventually, she thought she had isolated the probable source of her ill humour even though she was not at all pleased with the result of her examination.

Until this very moment, she thought in anguish, *I thought I had drawn the correct conclusions when Colonel Fitzwilliam first visited us and related his story. But I now see that I was entirely mistaken, and my fault has been more than just mistaken vanity in my ability to discern the character of others. An overweening pride and a haughty disdain as great as Mr. Darcy's have also been my errors, and these have led me to ascribe his behaviour to the basest possible motives. And, even as it kept me from examining his motives, it also kept me from examining my own. Time after time, I refused to listen to those who questioned how such a man as Mr. Darcy could be the scoundrel I thought him to be even as he earned the approbation of people I valued—people such as Charlotte and Mr. Bingley. I was too certain of my own judgment, and I simply dismissed all contradictory evidence as being of no consequence.*

With the likely cause of her uncharacteristic conduct identified, Elizabeth could also see a possible solution even though such a course of action would have been unthinkable before tonight. And she also saw a way to resolve her parallel worries about Jane and this breakneck campaign being conducted by Fitzwilliam to win her sister's heart.

Jane ought to be able to make the best choice for her own happiness, she vowed silently. *She should not have her options circumscribed by the actions of Mr. Darcy.*

With her decisions made, it was only a matter of minutes before she had determined what action she would need to take. Finally, with everything settled in her mind, she could contemplate the totality, and the drastic nature and unpredictable consequences of her plans were enough to make her quail in apprehension.

Gradually, despite the chill that Elizabeth's ill humour had injected, conversation resumed, and by the time the actors and the audience rose to sing the national anthem, everyone's spirits except Elizabeth's were restored. And even she began to regain her normal disposition after she had wrestled her inner turmoil into submission and come to a decision. Thus, soon after the play began, she felt her morose mood begin to lift as the quality of the actors as well as the sterling excellence of the stage and sets engaged her attention. She was soon enjoying herself immensely despite continuing misgivings concerning her decision.

MEANWHILE, JANE WAS ACTUALLY HAVING THE OPPOSITE EXPErience: as the play progressed, she found herself becoming more and more distracted, unable to concentrate on the actors, the dialogue, or the sets. Instead, she was disturbed by something much closer—the presence of Colonel Fitzwilliam beside her.

The feeling was completely unknown to her, and she had no idea what was causing it. But the longer she sat beside him in the semi-dark box, the more aware she became of his presence. She heard his soft breathing, which somehow seemed to be louder than the piercing voices of the actors on the stage. She could smell the clean scent of starched cloth, oiled leather, and an underlying scent that must be all his own. She felt as if she were running a fever, and she recalled the look on his face after she descended from the coach. She knew he had been looking at the displayed upper slopes of her breasts, and the thought pleased her and confused her at the same time.

She had the most absurd compulsion to reach out, to touch him, to feel at least that he was something other than a disembodied presence beside her. Seated within inches and yet separated from her by an impassable barrier of custom and propriety, she wished to put her hand on his arm, to knead the hard muscle she had felt through his coat when he had escorted her earlier. She knew she could not...yet she wanted to so badly.

In the previous autumn, when she was expecting Mr. Bingley to declare himself at almost any time, she had thought she would be married by now. During that time, she had thought long about the intimacies that were shared between husband and wife, and she had looked forward to discovering and exploring them with a man whom she loved. Instead, he had abandoned her, leaving her stranded between girlhood and womanhood, her soul wounded while her physical body yearned for the release denied her by society's rigid rules of conduct. Now, another man—a greatly different kind of man—attended her, and those frustrations, which had found no release with Mr. Bingley, were seeking a new outlet.

Even worse, she wanted *him* to touch *her*, and that was new and even more forbidden territory than her yearnings to put her hand on his arm. She wished she could take his hand and lay it on her thigh. Just to rest there, nothing more. She did not seek forbidden gratifications, she just wished to feel comforted...to feel wanted...and desired.

And so, driven by her yearnings, even knowing her aunt and uncle were sitting just behind her, she at last carefully moved her right arm to the upholstered arm of her chair. She could see, out of the lower corner of her eye, Richard's left arm in almost the same position on his chair a scant inch away, and he gave no appearance of having noticed her move. After several moments, having listened carefully for any signs from her aunt and uncle, she at last, greatly daring, moved her arm just enough to the side so her forearm touched his.

She felt him stiffen slightly at her touch, but her watchful eye noted that he otherwise gave no evidence of it. His head did not move, his breathing continued deep and easy, but she knew he was aware of what she had done. She wondered whether he felt she was being forward, but he made no move as she gradually moulded her arm against his until she finally felt...comfortable.

Any doubts she had about whether Richard had noticed what she had done disappeared as she felt his left knee touch hers. A shivery, delightful feeling ran down her spine, and she carefully pressed her knee back against his as acknowledgement and acceptance of his touch.

Neither Richard nor she made any further movements after that, and Jane felt a great calmness sweep through her. She settled back in her chair, and she had to restrain herself from uttering a deep sigh of contentment as she felt her concentration return.

Now she could enjoy the play.

RICHARD HAD BEEN QUITE SURPRISED WHEN HE FELT THE TOUCH of Jane's arm against his. He briefly considered that it might have been accidental, but, as he felt her arm nestle close to his and then subside, he dismissed that thought.

This is a woman who is feeling the need for consolation, he concluded after a few moments' thought. *From what Darcy told me of her mother and father, it is doubtful that she has ever received it from them. That is probably why she and Miss Elizabeth are so close: there is no other form of comfort or support to be found in their household from either a silly mother or a detached father. And, if comforting is necessary to win this woman, then comfort her I shall.*

But he still wondered whether the touching of their forearms was not purely accidental, so he went just a step further. Casually, he let his left leg lean over slightly, just enough so his knee lightly touched hers. The uncertainty was quickly resolved since Jane did not move her knee away. Instead, she pressed back, gently but firmly, and he had his answer. At least a part of her was not averse to physical contact, and he had difficulty restraining the sudden surge of joy that swept through him. He believed he was a step closer to his ultimate goal. How long it would take, he did not know. Miss Jane Bennet had been wounded—sorely wounded—and she would heal in her own time. And, when she did, he would be there.

THOUGH NEITHER JANE NOR FITZWILLIAM WAS AWARE OF IT, MR. Gardiner saw what Jane had done when she first touched him, and he laid a hand on his wife's arm and nodded towards the pair. Mrs. Gardiner's eyes narrowed as she examined what had happened, assessing the body language of both Fitzwilliam and her niece. She worried a bit as she saw them touch their knees together, but, since nothing further happened, she eventually turned to her husband and shook her head, indicating it should be ignored.

Mr. Gardiner was inclined to disagree somewhat with his wife, but he now saw Jane relax and sit back more comfortably in her chair, so he relaxed also. It had been her agitation, which she had not even realized she was displaying, that had first drawn his attention, and now that agitation appeared to have gone. So he shrugged, content to leave any further action to the discretion of his wife.

At the intermission, Elizabeth asked Richard whether she might borrow his programme, and shortly afterwards, she and Jane excused themselves. She returned it to him after they resumed their seats, and Richard was surprised to see she had folded it in half. He was more surprised by a peculiar intensity in her eyes when she handed it back to him, and after waiting for a couple of minutes, he discreetly unfolded it to see that she had written a message on the back. He returned the programme to his pocket since there was no way to read what she had written without informing the rest of the party, and Elizabeth's manner was such that he was certain her message was a private one.

The remainder of the play passed with considerable enjoyment by all, and the reception of the performance by the audience was so great that they rose at the end and continued to applaud and shout their acclaim for a considerable time.

As the party made their way out of the theatre and waited for their carriage to be brought around, Mr. and Mrs. Gardiner again thanked Richard for an excellent evening while he in turn promised both Jane and Elizabeth that he would call on them on the morrow to bid them goodbye before they left for Longbourn at ten. It was only when he had handed both of the sisters into the carriage and exchanged handshakes with Mr. Gardiner and a bow to his wife that he was able to step back into the lamplight in order to inspect the note Jane's sister had written.

Opening the programme, he found, apparently written in charcoal and in large letters due to the inadequacy of the writing implement: "Please meet at park near Uncle's house at 7:30 in morn. Jane & I leave at 10 & I wish to speak of your cousin."

Richard considered the message for several long minutes, wondering what could have inspired it. There would be time enough to find out tomorrow without losing sleep tonight, so he shrugged before stepping out to hire a hack.

CHAPTER 9

There is no surprise more magical than the surprise of being loved.
It is God's finger on man's shoulder
— Charles Morgan

Friday, May 1, 1812
Gracechurch Street, London

After returning to her aunt and uncle's home and going to their shared bedroom, Elizabeth prepared to have a frank and honest discussion with her sister on the topic of Colonel Fitzwilliam. She knew Jane was finding his attentions pleasant, but—perhaps because the topic of Mr. Bingley was so fresh in each of their minds—neither of them had talked of the colonel in any detail.

Now, given the decisions Elizabeth had made at the theatre, she needed to know just what Jane truly thought of this man. After all, if Jane's opinion of him was anything close to what Elizabeth thought it was, Fitzwilliam might well become Elizabeth's brother in the not-too-distant future. Since her own plans would be affected if she was not correct in her assessment of her sister's thoughts, firm answers were needed.

And to make sure that Jane did not go to sleep before they had a chance to talk, Elizabeth seized the first moment they were alone in their rooms to broach the subject. They still wore the gowns in which they had attended the play, and Jane did not even have a chance to dress for bed before her sister began the conversation.

"Jane, we must speak of Colonel Fitzwilliam."

Jane raised her eyebrows but said nothing, so Elizabeth continued. "We both know he is beginning to court you. His attentions have been too direct to be interpreted otherwise. Now, what I want to know— what I *need* to know—is whether you feel in any way similarly inclined?"

Jane did not respond for a moment, busying herself with removing her jewellery and placing it in her small jewellery box. Finally, she spoke softly. "I am not sure. I am not sure I want to or can even talk of my feelings yet."

"Though you tried not to show it, we both know you were terribly hurt when Mr. Bingley left and did not return."

"I cannot deny that," Jane said so quietly that Elizabeth had to strain to hear her. "My heart ached as I never thought it could."

"And it could not have been improved when Caroline Bingley snubbed you so cruelly."

Jane did not say anything for several moments as she removed her gloves and busied herself folding them. "I cannot hide that from you either. I never suspected she could deceive me in such a fashion. That did hurt but in a different way."

"I was happy—at least insofar as the word could be applied to such a malicious event—that you at last were able to see beyond her insincerity. I know she will never dupe you again. But now Mr. Darcy's cousin has made an appearance, and he gives every indication of having been completely smitten over you in a single afternoon."

Jane looked up with a tremulous smile. "Do you really think so, Lizzy?"

"More than that, I know so. He said as much to Uncle Gardiner when they talked that first day."

"It is so strange. I still feel all the pain from Mr. Bingley—so much so that I hardly dare let myself hope something might lighten that burden. But I cannot deny my heart is cheered by his attentions. But I do not know whether I want to allow myself to hope."

"Did you not hear him tonight? He promised he would call on you at Longbourn, and I am certain he will do exactly as he says."

Jane nodded gravely. "Now that you say it aloud, I realize I do not doubt he will come. But I once thought Mr. Bingley would come back, and he did not. I simply do not know whether I can trust my feelings any more."

"Colonel Fitzwilliam is not at all like Mr. Bingley."

"No, he is not. Yet I thought Mr. Bingley was quite the most amiable man I had ever known."

"The colonel is also amiable, but it is a different kind of amiability. You and Mr. Bingley have similar natures, and I always felt you could be very happy with him because you both were so much alike."

"That is true—very true. You have often said I always see too much good in other people, and that is why I seldom get angry. Mr. Bingley was also like that."

"I agree. I have a difficult time picturing Mr. Bingley getting angry, no matter the circumstances. But I could see Colonel Fitzwilliam getting angry. He was angry with me tonight, and I deserved it. I acted abominably, and I feel completely ashamed of myself."

"Oh, Lizzy, I do not think he was angry with you. He was just…just…"

"Stern? As Uncle Gardiner sometimes becomes?" responded Elizabeth with a rueful smile. "Perhaps that is more nearly correct. I made several rather foolish, rather *childish* statements tonight, and Colonel Fitzwilliam simply told me how the situation would look to an adult. I was devastated when I realized how disgracefully I had been behaving."

Jane said nothing to this, and after a period of silence, Elizabeth continued. "It is somewhat disturbing to consider this—for I do like

Colonel Fitzwilliam—but if he could be upset with me, perhaps he could get angry with you. And that is not pleasing to think of."

"I really cannot believe he would ever do that. He is far too well mannered to do such a thing. Besides, that presumes he...well, that he..."

"If you allow him to continue to call on you, I am certain he will make you an offer of marriage, and probably sooner rather than later."

Jane blushed at this statement. Elizabeth could see she was grappling with the idea, and it was a few moments before she spoke. "I cannot deny that the thought has been flitting about my mind since the afternoon he first called, but I just do not know whether I can allow myself to hope. I keep thinking—what if he acts as Mr. Bingley did? Could I stand two such disappointments? But answer this: How can you be certain he would make me an offer of marriage? No one can know the heart of another person in such a short time."

"They can when the other person is as direct as this colonel was when he talked to Uncle Gardiner. Not only did he say that he was smitten, even though he had never before believed in love at first sight, but he plainly stated his objective to our uncle, saying it was his intention to win your affections and to make you his wife."

"He said that?"

"Yes, he said exactly that. But I want you to think on this: it is most assuredly *not* Mr. Bingley we are discussing. There is a fiery, passionate man beneath his excellent manners and smooth conversation. This is a man who has been to war—a professional soldier, a man who has almost certainly killed other men in battle. Have you even thought about whether you could be happy with such a man?"

At length Jane said, "Perhaps such a man would look for something else in a wife. I certainly am not an Amazon, but would a soldier...a warrior...want such a woman for a wife? Or would he want a woman who represents the more tender side of life?"

Elizabeth shook her head in amused frustration. "You seem able to see only a good side to people, even when they do not have one."

"That is not fair. I am sure Colonel Fitzwilliam has many good qualities."

"I was not referring to him, for I quite agree with you. I was thinking of Caroline Bingley."

"Oh."

"I want you to consider what will happen if Colonel Fitzwilliam continues to call. To his credit, he knows you are still troubled in the aftermath of Mr. Bingley's disappearance, so he told my uncle he would wait until you were ready. But if he continues to call on you at Longbourn for any period of time, it will be accepted by one and all that marriage is as good as settled. If he makes an offer after a period of time, and then you decide you cannot accept, the pain he suffers will be the same that Mr.—"

At her sister's suddenly stricken look, Jane finished her thought. "That Mr. Darcy is suffering? Is that what you were going to say?"

"Yes," Elizabeth agreed in a small voice.

"I see. You have certainly given me much to think on tonight. And while I do not think I shall be forced to make any decisions right away, there is one thought I would like to share with you."

"And what is that?"

"I believe we both agree that Mr. Bingley is the very essence of amiability, even though Colonel Fitzwilliam would have to be considered by any fair judge as being extremely amiable himself. But based on those soldierly qualities you described and the way he has acted since I have known him, the colonel would have to be described as bold. Would you not agree?"

"I would. Perhaps *overbold* might be more appropriate."

"Perhaps," Jane said agreeably. "But I am finding I quite like 'bold.' I like it very much."

"I see," Elizabeth said, looking at her sister speculatively before she continued. "Well, based on the look he gave you when you descended from Uncle's coach with that low neckline, I just hope he will not be overbold. He was looking right down the front of your dress, you know."

"Yes," Jane said with a soft smile. "I know."

"Jane!" Elizabeth exclaimed in surprise. She looked her sister carefully up and down. "I am amazed, simply amazed—though perhaps I should not be since you allowed Aunt Gardiner to talk you into wearing that extremely revealing gown. However, did you know at the time that he was looking down the front of it?"

"I did. And before you returned from your bath, when we were dressing, Aunt Gardiner told Mary Alice to pull my corset extremely tight so it would push my bosom up, which was the effect we wanted."

"We? You were a part of it?"

"Of course. Aunt Gardiner may have suggested it, but she did not have to talk me into anything. I may not know yet whether Colonel Fitzwilliam is the man for me, but since Mr. Bingley left Netherfield, I have often thought of what Charlotte told you: that a young lady should show more affection than she felt. This time, I was determined not to conceal my interest. I wanted a man who was attracted to me to know I shared a similar attraction to him."

Elizabeth was absolutely open-mouthed in astonishment at this.

"I see I have shocked you," Jane said quietly. "I am sorry. I thought you would understand."

Elizabeth shook herself before leaning over to grab Jane's hand.

"The fault is mine, dearest," she said earnestly. "Now that you have explained your reasoning, it is clear that you and our aunt were thinking more deeply than I was. I should at least have considered that you might feel an attraction to this man, but I did not, so I was completely surprised by the gown you wore and your reaction to him. So much for my vaunted powers of observation!"

"And I am always so reserved. You have mentioned it before. But this time, perhaps I borrowed a bit of Colonel Fitzwilliam's boldness, for I was agreeable with everything Aunt Gardiner suggested. When I stepped down from the coach, I knew he was looking at my bosom, and I felt all fluttery when I saw the impact it had on him. I know I should feel guilty for having such shameless feelings, but I confess I feel no such thing."

"I begin to wonder whom I should be protecting from whom. When he first saw you tonight, I thought he might well start running in circles and baying at the moon."

Both sisters laughed delightedly at the idea; then Elizabeth squeezed Jane's hand firmly before they began preparing for bed. Elizabeth did not tarry long before falling asleep since she had to meet the colonel in the morning. But, after listening to what her sister had to say tonight, she was still bewildered. Was the decision she had made at the theatre for the best?

But she had no solution to that question and could only hope that time would reveal the answers she sought.

CHAPTER 10

Permanence, perseverance, and persistence in spite of all obstacles,
discouragement, and impossibilities: It is this that in all things
distinguishes the strong soul from the weak.

— Thomas Carlyle

Saturday, May 2, 1812
Gracechurch Street, London

The air was chill due to the early hour, and clouds obscured the sun as Richard approached the park. He saw Elizabeth walking back and forth alongside the roadway as he approached, and from the purposefulness of her strides, she appeared more than slightly agitated.

He understood her agitation since he was consumed with curiosity to determine why she had asked to see him. He could not believe she had changed her mind about Darcy. Nothing had happened that might have occasioned such a change of opinion, yet he could still think of nothing else of which she might wish to speak. He saw her stop walking as she saw him, and she waited while he dismounted and tethered his horse.

Her greeting was perfectly polite as always, for her manners were most excellent. *Except,* he thought in sardonic amusement, *when it comes to Darcy. There, she is apt to display an anger that she otherwise manages to conceal.*

"Thank you for coming at such a beastly hour, Colonel," she said. "You are undoubtedly wondering why I desired to speak to you before we left."

"I am, Miss Elizabeth. In fact, I am consumed with curiosity since you mentioned the matter concerned my cousin."

"Yes. Mr. Darcy."

They walked on in silence for several minutes. It seemed to Richard that she was having difficulty finding a way to begin the conversation, so he decided to help her somewhat, even if it was in a teasing manner.

"Surely you have not changed your mind concerning his declarations, have you? Your mind appeared to be so firmly fixed that I cannot think of anything that might have changed it."

Elizabeth managed a rather weak smile to his jibe. "I cannot seem to be able to restrain myself when discussing your cousin, can I?"

She stopped abruptly and faced Richard. "I must apologize for my ungenerous statements last night. I let my anger carry me away, and I am heartily ashamed of myself."

Richard nodded gravely. "Think nothing of it. As I mentioned, I am not satisfied with certain aspects of my cousin's behaviour, and your anger with him is not completely unreasonable. But you are forgiven nonetheless, for I know it is not your usual manner."

"I felt dreadful at the time, but it did lead me to think on what could have caused me to express myself so intemperately. I came to the conclusion that much of my anger is towards myself. I finally realized last night that my continuing dislike of your cousin is wildly out of proportion to what I learned of his character during your visit on Monday."

Richard nodded again at this statement, and she continued. "It

129

should not have taken me so long to reach that conclusion, but it seemed I was determined to maintain my mistaken opinions in spite of your moving description of the relationship between the two of you. It took my mortification last night to force me to face the fact that the cause of my dreadful behaviour was the conflict between what I *knew* and what I *felt* about your cousin. And in that moment of revelation, I was seized with a feeling of revulsion at the extent to which my dislike of your cousin was affecting me."

She grimaced in reaction to *that* unkind thought and continued. "So, the answer to your question about changing my mind is—not exactly."

"Not exactly? I trust you will elaborate on that?"

"It came to me last night, after your civility in the face of my uncalled-for anger, that I was not at all happy in the grip of such anger even if it was wholly deserved. Which, in this case, it was not. It was most unlike me, or at least, it was unlike the way I believed I should act. I was especially concerned with being unable to reconcile that I could like you so much and simultaneously dislike the man who was closer to you than your own brothers."

She stopped for a moment, looking down at the ground, before she drew a deep breath and continued. "So I came to a decision. Not quite a decision to change what I told you earlier about your cousin but rather to…determine…whether there was more to his character than I had previously realised. Consequently, I would like you to give your cousin a message. I cannot promise to change my mind, but if he desires to…to call on me…then I promise to receive him…and to assess him fairly to the best of my ability."

Richard looked at Elizabeth narrowly while he thought furiously. At length he said, "So, would it be correct to say that you still feel indisposed towards Darcy?"

Elizabeth agreed with a silent nod.

"But you are also saying that you are willing to give him a chance to prove you wrong. But to do so, he must be willing to come to

Hertfordshire and call on you openly. Correct?"

Another silent nod.

"In essence, he must court you like a man ought to court a woman he desires to marry, which, in Darcy's case, would mean he must be willing to put aside his prideful arrogance and reserve—in short, to show a little humility."

Richard pondered silently for a few moments. Then his white teeth gleamed in a huge smile. "I like it. Excellent."

"You do?" Elizabeth's confusion was plain to see.

"Of course. It essentially says to Darcy: 'Here is another chance, but there are no guarantees. It is up to *you* to prove yourself worthy of *me.*' Oh, that will do most excellently."

"You really think so?"

"I do. Darcy needed a jolt, which you gave him when you refused him...as was only just after he had acted so arrogantly. Thus, his suffering has been the result of his own errors. But now you have offered him a way out of his distress. I believe it may be exactly the medicine he needs to lead him to correct his bad habits. I certainly hope so, for I believe he remains the friend of my youth despite this prideful armour he has fashioned for himself."

Elizabeth drew a deep breath. "There is one other item I ought to mention though I am sure it will not be to your liking. If your cousin does call on me, I plan to ask him to repair his error with Mr. Bingley—to confess his fault and inform him of how he was unjustified in his advice."

That was an unexpected and unwelcome surprise, and Richard's expression must have indicated as much since Elizabeth's face stiffened. Richard was quick to quell his anger, however, and his voice was controlled as he asked, "Now, why should you want to do that, Miss Elizabeth? I thought we were friends."

"We are—or I hope we are. I know you want to marry my sister—"

Richard's eyebrows rose at the certainty in this statement, but she quickly added, "You said as much to my uncle, who then informed me. So you wish to marry Jane, but there remains the fact she would likely be married to Mr. Bingley by now if it were not for Mr. Darcy's interference. It is not that I want to thwart *your* intentions, but I wish Mr. Darcy to rectify his mistake and allow Jane to make up her mind without further deceit. Jane is my dearest sister, and it is my opinion that she and Mr. Bingley are alike in almost all respects. Even though I like you, you and she are dissimilar in many ways."

"Similarity is not a good predictor of happiness in marriage. I could point out any number of marriages where the couple has been excellently matched, yet their marriage has been a constant source of pain to both of them."

"And I could point out many more where a man and woman with almost nothing in common between them basically live their lives almost completely separated from their partner. But perhaps I should not even have mentioned that point because it was not a factor in my decision at all. What *is* a primary factor is that I have a responsibility to my sister above all else, even my own possible happiness. I must do the right thing to make sure she has an opportunity to make her *own* choice for her future happiness."

"And why exactly would her choosing to accept my suit not give your sister the greatest chance for future happiness? I happen to believe I *will* do a better job of making her happy than Bingley would."

"I did not say Jane might not be quite happy married to you, and you may well be right about Mr. Bingley. But do you not see? If I do nothing, then her only choice will be whether to accept *you*. In fact, I am certain that, if I do nothing, you will be successful in your suit and the two of you will be married. If, however, Jane is unhappy in that marriage, never having had the possibility of choosing between you and Mr. Bingley, then the fact that Darcy intervened would always be a point of contention between Mr. Darcy and me, probably too great to overcome."

"And what if my cousin refuses—even if he does everything else you ask? You spoke clearly when you said you might well be throwing away *your* chance for future happiness."

"Then I do not see how his suit could ever be successful with me. I could not secure my own happiness at the expense of my sister."

"I see," Richard said, and then he gave a fierce grin. "The question that comes to mind is this: Why should I cooperate with this scheme of yours? If what you say is true, and I shall be successful sooner or later with my suit, why should I not continue as I am and refuse to carry your message to my cousin? That way, Bingley would never know what Darcy has done, and I shall gain what I desire most in the world. I do not want to chance losing her, especially to a man who has previously abandoned her."

Elizabeth winced at this last charge, but she still faced Richard forthrightly. "I do not believe you would do that, sir. I believe I can safely trust your honour in this matter."

"I would not be so sure. I have already done more than Darcy knows on his behalf."

Richard's face was like graven iron, and Elizabeth sighed deeply. "Colonel, please believe me when I say that, in many ways, I would prefer *you* as a future brother-in-law to a man who, as you charge, has already abandoned my sister once. But I simply have to do what is right and best to allow Jane to make her own choice."

"Even when such a desire bears an uncanny resemblance to what my cousin tried to do in regard to his friend Bingley and your sister? He did not bear your sister any ill will in that endeavour, you will remember. He was only trying to do the best for his friend as he saw it, and you found his interference officious and unwarranted."

Elizabeth winced again, but she straightened her shoulders and looked Richard in the eye.

"The same thought had occurred to me, sir, and I assure you I gave it full consideration. I cannot say it was a decisive factor in my reasoning this morning, but it did play a part. I have a clearer understanding of the reason Mr. Darcy acted as he did, and my animosity regarding that decision is almost completely dissipated. But still, he was erroneous, even if sincere, and I must take this opportunity to attempt to right a wrong that was committed."

The two of them stood, silently looking at each other for several minutes—Richard's mind busily mulling possibilities as Elizabeth struggled to control her anxiety. At last, he sighed and looked away.

"And I have just discovered I cannot sacrifice my cousin's possible happiness in order to secure my own. You know me too well."

Elizabeth winced at the bitterness in his voice, but she did not relent, and Richard sighed heavily again. "You were right in one regard, you know. As the son of an earl, I have never wanted for anything, but not the way you thought. I have often wanted for physical needs. I have been hungry and wet and tired, and for some years after I became a soldier, I had barely enough money to cover my expenses. But none of those really bothered me. I had enough, and I was alive, so I took life as it came. It was not as if I had some lifelong dream of being a soldier, you know. I simply knew I was not meant for the church, and either the army or the navy would have sufficed. I might have sought a midshipman's berth, for example, but I had begun too late."

Richard's eyes were blazing as he looked back at Elizabeth, and his gaze was so intense that she had to step back from him as he went on. "But until I met your sister, I never truly wanted anything so badly that nothing else mattered. I have never wanted something so badly that I was willing to do whatever was necessary to attain it."

He looked away, staring into the distance before he said softly, "I would do anything, that is, except betray my cousin."

His face was bleak and hard as he straightened his shoulders. "Very well, I shall take your message to Darcy—both of your messages. If I can, I shall see him before I bid your sister farewell at nine. I may or may not have an answer by then."

He began to turn away and then turned to face Elizabeth one last time.

"But mark my words. I shall not fail in this quest of mine. I also have a duty to your sister, and I shall *not* allow an unworthy man to marry her. Good day."

With that, he turned briskly and strode back to his horse. His strides were long and determined, and his heels thudded into the ground. He loosed the reins, grasped the front edge of the saddle, and heaved himself astride his horse without touching the stirrups. He tipped his Tarleton helmet to Elizabeth in cold formality, turned his horse, and spurred him on his way. He was already at a gallop before he turned the first corner.

Elizabeth stared after him in some consternation. Colonel Fitzwilliam was quite a fearsome individual when he was intent on something, and she wondered anxiously what she might have started.

CHAPTER 11

'Tis sweet to know there is an eye will mark our coming, and look brighter when we come.

— Lord Byron

Saturday, May 2, 1812
Darcy House, London

When Richard reached Darcy's house, he saw that the knocker was not mounted on his door, an indication that either he was absent or was not receiving visitors. Since he knew Darcy was not planning a return to Pemberley for another month, he did not bother to stop. Instead, he went around the corner to the rear gate, which led to the stables. It was also closed. That, however, meant little to him at the present time, and he vented at least some of his spleen by pounding at the gate from horseback until he saw the head groom run out of the stables.

"Sawyer! I need to see my cousin immediately. Get this gate open for the love of Heaven."

"Colonel Fitzwilliam," the older man exclaimed, skidding to a halt in amazement to find the uproar being caused by his master's cousin. He

136

had known Fitzwilliam for years, so he took for granted that his reason for seeing Darcy was valid and quickly retrieved the key to the lock.

Seconds later, the door swung open, and Richard quickly spurred his horse inside. He lost little time before vaulting from the saddle and throwing the reins to one of the stable boys who had run up.

"Has anyone seen my cousin this morning?"

"No, sir, not this morning," Sawyer said, bustling up after having closed the gate. "But I can send one of the lads to find Williams…"

"No, do not bother. I have no time to waste. I shall find him myself."

"Sir, sir," Sawyer called behind him, but Richard was already heading for the house in long strides that would have required the head groom to run after him to catch up.

Richard did not see anyone as he came in the back door, and no one answered his rap at Darcy's study.

"Darcy!" he bellowed as he headed for the library. Darcy was not there either, and Richard again bellowed his name.

The door to the small dining room was jerked open, and Darcy stuck his head out. "Richard, just what do you think you are doing, shouting like that in my house?" he snarled angrily.

"I am doing what you should have done right the first time and at considerable cost to myself," Richard snapped. "I need to see you in your study immediately."

"I am having breakfast with Georgiana," Darcy said icily, "and I do not intend to have it interrupted. Try to exert a little control, will you, and I shall join you in half an hour."

"In half an hour, I have an assignation to bid farewell to a woman dearer to me than life itself, and if you will not see me now, then you can make your own attempt to repair the disaster you have made of your private life!" Richard said. He had a smile on his face, but Darcy recognised there was little humour in it.

Darcy glared angrily at his cousin for several moments, but Richard just stood looking at him with that sardonic smile on his face. He was unyielding though his toe tapped impatiently, and Darcy finally stepped back into the room.

"Dearest," Richard heard him say to Georgiana, "please forgive me, but I have to find out what has driven our cousin to forget his manners. I shall return as soon as I discover what has deranged him."

Richard could not hear Georgiana's soft reply, but Darcy reappeared in the hall quickly. "Very well, then," he said coldly. "This had better be extremely important."

"It is, and not just to you," Richard responded, ignoring his cousin's anger.

But, just as he began to follow Darcy, he turned back to the dining room and put his head inside. Georgiana looked up in surprise and gave him a tentative smile. Richard gave her a broad wink. "Do not worry your little head, Georgiana. I just have to beat some sense into your brother so he does not spend the rest of his life as a crotchety old bachelor."

He was gone instantly, and Georgiana heard his heels pounding the floor as he followed her brother down the hall.

Now what could he have meant by that? she thought in confusion. *Is he really going to beat William? And what is that about staying a bachelor? William has been acting even more strangely since returning from Rosings. What does it all mean?*

It took her several minutes to work up her courage, for Georgiana was really quite a meek and shy girl, but the questions kept echoing through her mind until she could stand it no longer. She stood and left the room, walking down the hall towards her brother's study.

In her soft slippers, her passage was all but silent.

"Now, if I might ask, just what is it that has you behaving in this beastly fashion?" Darcy snapped as soon as the door was closed.

Richard wasted no time as he asked in blunt directness, "Darcy, do you love Elizabeth Bennet?"

Darcy looked at Richard in stunned amazement and could not answer for several moments.

"Well, what is your answer?" repeated Richard. "Do you love her or not?"

"You know the answer to that. I made her an offer of marriage. Does that not indicate my feelings?"

"No, it does not," Richard said harshly. "It might indicate an infatuation or a fascination you could not withstand. If she had accepted you, your wealth and position would have prevented anyone outside your circle from criticising her openly, and she is polite and well mannered enough to charm those inside your circle. So, I want to know, do you love her enough to make a sacrifice for her? Will you endure emotional pain and probably a good portion of open humiliation in order to try to win her?"

Darcy collapsed into his chair and stared at Richard. "The questions you ask make no sense. There must be some point to this conversation, but I will be dashed if I can determine what it is."

"Just this"—Richard leaned over Darcy's desk with his fists on the top of it—"Miss Elizabeth Bennet has had a *slight* change of heart, and she has offered you an opportunity to start over. No, that is not correct. What she suggested is the possibility of *beginning*. As far as anyone else knows, you never made her an offer, and she never rejected it. The rest of the world knows nothing of your feelings for her—though I am afraid the locals might have some idea of how she feels about *you*."

Richard grinned as a cavalcade of emotions flowed across Darcy's face: surprise, hope, confusion, distaste.

Too bad, old stick, Richard thought pitilessly, *you should have done it the right way the first time.*

"Miss Elizabeth said to me, just this morning, that if you desired to call on her at her home, she will receive you. Note the choice of words, Cousin. It is important—she *will* receive you. She will not reject your visit, which will afford you the opportunity to call on her openly and to court her, all in public view. She offers to assess you fairly, but that offer only means that *you* will have to convince her there is another side to you than the one she has seen so far. Of course, from what you have told me of her mother, your arrival at her front door just might send the woman into apoplexy."

Darcy grimaced, and Richard remembered his cousin's description of Mrs. Bennet's behaviour at the Netherfield ball.

"I know, I know. It would be a blow to your pride, but pride is what has put you in your present position. Miss Elizabeth offers you the possibility of winning her affection, and she commented that one of the reasons for changing her mind even this much was my telling her I have been closer to you than I have been to my own brothers. She said if that were true, she was at least willing to entertain the possibility that there were redeeming facets to your character she has not yet seen."

Richard threw himself into a chair and sat waiting while Darcy pondered what he had said. Several times Darcy opened his mouth and tried to talk, but his emotions robbed him of the ability to speak.

Finally, he said huskily, "I do not know what to say. Of course I accept. Yes, I do love her, and I shall willingly do as she asks. I would do anything rather than face the possibility of never seeing her again. But I...I cannot find the words to express my gratitude to you."

Richard waved away his thanks and then leaned forward again. "Just do not waste this opportunity. Quite frankly, I was shocked to my core by her proposal, but that is not the end. She told me—and this was hard for *me* to accept—she said that, if you did call, she was going to demand that you inform Bingley of the error you made with respect to her sister."

This last comment shocked Darcy as much as the previous one had, and he looked at Richard in dumbfounded amazement.

"I was not at all pleased by *that* proposal, as you can imagine, but Miss Elizabeth and her sister Jane are very close, and she believes failing to correct this error would always stand between you and her."

"But you...what about your..."

"What about my suit? Well, it advances, and I believe Miss Bennet and I are making progress, but we have known each other less than a week. I know it is too early to declare myself. She is the most trusting and innocent creature you can imagine, and she was hurt cruelly by Bingley's abandonment. More time is needed, but Miss Elizabeth wants her sister to have the opportunity to make her choice between us."

"You could not have received that suggestion with equanimity," Darcy said quietly.

"Indeed not. I was quite angry with her, and we parted in cold formality. But I do not intend to allow that to sway me. Jane Bennet is expecting me to call on Saturday next, and I shall not disappoint her. That would also, I believe, be an appropriate time for you to make your call."

"I see," Darcy said, but his brow was furrowed. "It occurs to me that you did not have to tell me of this. If you had never mentioned it, I never should have known—and I should not then have been tempted to tell Bingley."

"True, but Miss Elizabeth said she would trust my honour in this, and it appears she knows me better than I knew myself. I blustered about not telling you, but she just waited until I realized I had no choice but to do as she asked."

"Then I shall not tell Bingley," Darcy said firmly. "I shall not have your chance of happiness sacrificed because of my blundering. I should have known better than to interfere in the first place."

Richard shook his head. "No, it will not do. I know Miss Elizabeth was quite sincere when she said she did not see how your suit could ever be successful if you refused this. And, despite my anger, I begin to see she may be right. If I am ultimately successful in my own quest, there should not be any misgivings on either side that might lead to future feelings of missed opportunities. Besides, you cannot shoulder all the blame. Bingley allowed himself to be persuaded after all. What do you think your chances of dissuading me in my quest would be?"

"Effectively zero, if not less," Darcy said, smiling. "I have never seen you like this, and I should not care to stand in your way."

"You see? How can I fail in my pursuit if—"

A look of shock appeared on Darcy's face as he stared over his cousin's shoulder. Twisting around, Richard saw Georgiana standing just inside the door. She looked completely confused and rather anxious as both men gazed at her in an intense manner.

"Please," she said timidly, "will someone tell me what is going on? What suit are you talking about, William? And what is this about Mr. Bingley?"

Richard rolled his eyes and gave Darcy a look of compassion. "I believe you have some very interesting topics for conversation, but I must get back to the Gardiner house before Jane leaves for Hertfordshire."

He jumped to his feet and made for the door, pausing only to give Georgiana a quick embrace.

"Do not be too hard on him, Georgiana, for he has had some difficult times lately," Richard said in a whisper. "But do not, under any circumstances, allow him to leave the room until he has told you everything!"

With that, Richard strode from the room, whistling as he pulled his watch from his pocket.

"Blazes," he said to himself in sudden urgency. "It is already a quarter past nine."

Saturday, May 2, 1812
Gracechurch Street, London

ELIZABETH LOOKED UP FROM HER BOOK AS SHE SAW JANE GO TO the window again, and she sighed deeply. She was not really reading. She was using the book as a screen to hide her own lingering feelings of stress and anxiety from the tense meeting with Fitzwilliam. She looked over at the clock on the mantel, which showed it was a quarter after nine. The colonel had not yet arrived, and he had told them the night before that he would stop by at nine to bid them farewell. Since he had never been as much as a minute late for any previous appointment, she could understand Jane's anxiety. And, since Elizabeth was certain she was the reason for it, she needed to explain to Jane what had delayed Fitzwilliam.

"You must stop worrying. There is no cause for alarm. I am sure Colonel Fitzwilliam will be here as soon as he is able. I have already spoken to Uncle Gardiner, and he will delay the coach until the colonel arrives." Elizabeth hoped to reassure her sister without having to mention the reason for the colonel's tardiness.

But Jane was not in a mood to be reassured. It seemed as if the slightest delay or disruption brought on the dread that a desertion similar to Bingley's from Netherfield was about to recur. She rubbed her hands together fretfully and rose from the window seat to pace the room restlessly. Elizabeth sighed again. This was not the best time for it, but she knew she had to explain what had happened earlier in the morning before Jane became even more distressed.

"Colonel Fitzwilliam would have been here at nine if he could—he told me so this morning. But he needed to visit his cousin immediately after he met with me, and he has obviously been delayed. Believe me— *nothing* less important could have kept him from being here on time."

Jane looked at her sister in open-mouthed amazement. "You met with him this morning? I...I do not understand."

"Come, sit down, and I shall tell you quickly, but please save your questions until after we arrive at Longbourn because I believe he will be here directly. It began last night when I made such a fool of myself at the theatre..."

"... AND THAT IS WHY HE IS LATE," ELIZABETH CONCLUDED TO A still incredulous Jane. "So you see, sister dear, you have nothing to worry about. In fact, I do not believe anything could possibly affect his regard for you. You have no reason to believe he could possibly treat you as Mr. Bingley did."

"But I still do not understand," Jane said plaintively. "Why would you say what you did about Mr. Bingley? I promise you, I am completely over him—completely. Oh, poor Colonel Fitzwilliam."

"So that you will be able to make your own choices and not have them thrust upon you. I know you well, Jane. If Colonel Fitzwilliam continues to call on you—and I know he will—and if he then, after a period of time, makes you an offer of marriage—as I am certain he will—then I believe you would not be able to do anything other than accept him. You would say what you just did: 'Poor Colonel Fitzwilliam. How could I possibly disappoint him so?'"

"That is unfair. I would do no such thing. Besides, what could lead you to interfere so? I would never do the same to you."

"Jane, Jane," Elizabeth said, laughing though Jane's last charge stung sharply. "I know you. You could not help yourself. But that is all we can say for the moment, for I believe I see the very man himself galloping up the street right now. Come, we can at least meet him downstairs even though he may well refuse to speak to *me*."

Both girls arrived at the courtyard behind the house just as Fitzwilliam was vaulting from the saddle. His horse was blowing heavily, and his coat shone with sweat. A stable boy was waiting to accept the reins, and even though he knew Jane was there, Richard was instructing the boy to walk him for at least a quarter hour before letting him drink. He well knew he had overtaxed the valiant fellow, and proper care was most necessary at these times.

"And only a little water then, Johnny. He will try to drink his fill if you let him. But he needs to cool down completely before he drinks. Here is a copper, and there will be another when I leave."

"Thank *you*, sir," piped the stable boy before leading the horse away.

Only then could Fitzwilliam turn to the ladies awaiting him. "Miss Bennet, Miss Elizabeth, my apologies for being so dreadfully late."

"Do not worry, Colonel," Jane said with a warm smile. "Lizzy asked Uncle Gardiner to delay our departure until you arrived, so there is ample time. Please, come inside and take tea with us. My uncle and aunt would also like to see you, and they are waiting upstairs, so there is no need to hurry."

With the colonel's arrival, all of Jane's anxiety had fled. And in light of what Elizabeth had told her, she believed he must feel a little uncertainty. She, therefore, was determined to reassure *him*, so she had stepped close and laid her hand on his arm in a familiar manner as she spoke. Now, having invited him up the back stairs, she threaded her arm through his and began to guide him towards the rear door, talking gaily as she walked.

Richard was pleased but somewhat stunned by the warmth of his reception. He had expected he might have to mollify Jane's apprehensions due to his late arrival, but her greeting had put his worries to rest. Knowing her normal reserved manner, he wondered what had occasioned this reception, and then he suddenly realized Jane and Elizabeth must have talked. He looked quickly over his shoulder to see Elizabeth trailing behind them, shaking her head with a wry smile on her face as she comprehended that her efforts to give her sister a choice had actually had the opposite effect and caused her to take one more step closer to Fitzwilliam.

Seeing that smile, Richard understood the same thing, and he gave her a broad smile of, if not triumph, then at least of satisfaction. Elizabeth stuck her tongue out at him, and he responded with a broad wink before disappearing up the stairs with Jane still clinging possessively to his arm.

Elizabeth rolled her eyes at this response, but she also could not repress her smile. Fitzwilliam might not be as *safe* a future brother when compared to Mr. Bingley, but he would certainly be immensely more entertaining.

Saturday, May 2, 1812
Darcy House, London

DARCY'S NERVES WERE STILL JANGLING AS HE FINALLY SAT DOWN at his desk after the intense conversation with Georgiana following Richard's visit. She had been rather excited to learn of his interest in a young lady, especially since it relieved her nagging worry that he might someday settle on Caroline Bingley. But she had not been at all happy to hear of his time in Hertfordshire and later in Kent, and she had openly wept to discover that he had deliberately concealed virtually everything from her.

Obviously, I have some bridges to mend with my sister as well as Elizabeth Bennet, he thought morosely as he pulled out several sheets of paper and trimmed a quill in preparation for his letter writing.

I shall do the straightforward task first, the one to the housekeeper at Netherfield, he thought, as he bent over his desk. *Even if Bingley sends an express immediately, there is too little time for it to arrive from Scarborough and still leave time to prepare the place. Now, what was the name of that housekeeper? Ah, yes. Nicholls.*

Darcy House, London. May 2, 1812

Dear Mrs. Nicholls,

I trust you remember my extended visit to Netherfield in the autumn. I also trust you remember that your employer, Mr. Charles Bingley, informed you that I might have the privilege of abiding there if I so chose. Please prepare the house and stable for occupancy no later than this coming Friday, May 8. It is likely that Mr. Bingley may join me within a few days, as well as a possibility for several more guests.

Thank you for your efforts, and I shall see you on Friday, arriving by coach.

Yours,
Fitzwilliam Darcy

Darcy quickly read through the brief note, nodded in satisfaction, and sanded and blotted the missive before folding and addressing it.

Now for the hard part, he thought, bending over his desk again. *Writing and sending this express will be easy; composing it will be the hard part. But, as Richard has said before: if in doubt, just tell the truth, no matter how painful it might be. And this letter will be terribly painful to write. But it will not write itself, so the sooner begun—the sooner completed.*

With the memory of Elizabeth Bennet's face flickering in and out of his mind, Darcy dipped his quill in the inkwell and began.

Darcy House, London. May 2, 1812

Dear Bingley,

Pray forgive me for interrupting your visit with your relations, but a number of events have made it necessary for me to inform you of some information that has come to my attention that concerns you in the most personal and private manner. The urgency and importance of this information makes this letter essential, and I find it necessary to presume on our friendship in order to make you aware of some distressing facts.

The first topic I need to address relates to our visit to your estate in Hertfordshire last autumn. I am sure you will remember the rather stressful conversation in which Miss Jane Bennet of Longbourn was discussed and the dispassionate assessment I gave that your attachment to the lady was not commensurate with hers for you. I believed I was advising you in your own best interests, but during my visit with my aunt in Kent, I was surprised to find Miss Elizabeth Bennet visiting her friend Mrs. Charlotte Collins, who married my aunt's parson. During the course of my visit, I was uncomfortably made aware that my assessment of Miss Bennet's feelings towards you had been in error. The encounter between Miss Elizabeth and me in which she imparted this information was difficult and confrontational, and I —

Darcy put his quill down and read what he had written so far, and his brow knuckled with displeasure. He knew that the manner in which he made his arguments to Bingley would be as important as the information itself, but this was not the way he wanted to say it. Angrily, he crumpled up his sheet of paper and tossed it into his waste receptacle.

With a sigh at the unpleasant task before him, Darcy took a fresh sheet of paper and began again…

A DOZEN SHEETS OF PAPER HAD BEEN FILLED WITH TEXT, AND that text had been heavily scratched through and altered to the point that it was next to unreadable before Darcy could say he had completed his task. And his energetic writing had broken one quill beyond any possibility of repair.

As he read through the fair copy of the letter he had put together from his many efforts, he could not say he was totally and absolutely satisfied with what he had crafted. But he also believed he had done the best he could do; this communication was simply too critical and too unpleasant to be accomplished to perfection since he did not have days in which to labour over writing it.

He knew a goodly part of his dissatisfaction was due to the importance to him of the message, coupled with his unhappiness at having to confess his mistakes to a good friend in such a critical affair. That included the last paragraph in which he mentioned having sent a message to have Netherfield prepared for guests as Bingley had offered in one of several idle discussions about whether to keep the lease at the place or let it go.

"So, the house will be ready in case you are persuaded by my arguments and wish to join me there in an attempt to repair your acquaintance with Miss Bennet," he had written at the end of his express.

Darcy hoped that he had convinced Bingley to consider his arguments with an open and forgiving heart, but he was unsure of his friend's reaction to everything he had been forced to divulge. Among these revelations was his own growing attraction to Miss Elizabeth Bennet that had culminated in his proposal of marriage in Kent, her subsequent and angry rejection of it, and his opportunity and hope to assuage her antagonistic attitude towards him and change her mind. He had winced as he wrote of his cousin's sudden and unexpected attraction to her sister and also his intention to visit Longbourn on an errand similar to his own, though not fraught with any ill feeling on the part of Miss Bennet.

What a hash I have made of this whole matter, he thought as he folded and addressed his second letter before sealing both with warm wax and an impression of his signet ring. *Richard is certainly correct about THAT.*

Darcy rang for his butler and instructed him to arrange immediately for a pair of express riders to deliver them. The older man nodded his understanding as Darcy told him to make sure he engaged a rider for the Scarborough missive who was aware of the need for the quickest possible delivery, even though that meant a higher cost.

"Speed of delivery for this one is more important than quibbling over a few shillings," Darcy said, waving the sealed square of paper.

"I understand completely, sir," Williams said with a nod. "I know just the individual to make sure it happens."

Darcy pulled his watch from its pocket as Williams departed, and he was surprised to see that it was almost four o'clock. He had totally lost track of the time while he wrote, but now, with that task completed, the discontent that had gripped him while he grappled with the express was dissipating with every passing second. His spirits rose as he contemplated being able to travel to Hertfordshire and call at Longbourn.

And see Elizabeth! he thought gaily. *Finally, to talk to her without all the subterfuge and carefully oblique comments that were all I could manage at Rosings. There is time to visit Richard and discuss the details of just how and when he will visit Longbourn. What Richard has accomplished on my behalf is near to unbelievable, considering the disaster I made of the whole affair with the Bennet sisters. I believe I must give serious consideration to his arguments about my having changed for the worse. An opinion from a close friend and relation who could do what Richard has done deserves true soul-searching on my part.*

One thought that did worry him, however, was the conflict that would almost certainly arise in Hertfordshire if Bingley acted on the express he was sending. *If Charles decides to return to Netherfield, then he and Richard will be contesting for the hand of Jane Bennet, and I shall be the person who set that confrontation in motion.*

But what else could I do? he thought uncomfortably. *With Elizabeth demanding this in return for seeing me again and giving me the chance to change her mind, the answer is that I could do nothing else. In addition, I truly did advise Bingley incorrectly when I counselled him against an attachment to Jane Bennet, and I need to set that situation aright. But if both Bingley and Richard find themselves courting the same lady, one of them will likely succeed and the other will fail. These two men are the closest friends I have in this world, and either possibility will grieve me. Of course, I now realize that Richard will need to stay at the inn in Meryton until I know for certain that Bingley will not come, but that is a trifle.*

To a certain degree, I almost hope Charles is unconvinced by my arguments; it would make the situation easier. Otherwise, with Elizabeth urging her sister to consider how well matched she is with Bingley while Richard proceeds with that single-minded determination of his, who knows what will transpire?

A sudden, alarming thought occurred to him, and a thrill of dread shot through him as he considered the possibility that something more dreadful, such as a duel, might ensue from that competition.

But that could not happen, could it? Of course not! Or could it? Richard would naturally prevail, but such an event would be devastating even if he did not kill Bingley. Of course, Bingley is not the duelling sort; it is not in his nature.

Or is it?

As Darcy strode towards his stable for the ride to Richard's town house, such worries put a damper on his earlier euphoric enthusiasm. But his apprehension about friction between Richard and Bingley was only a possibility, while his chance to see Elizabeth again was a certainty. He firmly forced such concerns from his mind as he waited for his horse to be saddled.

CHAPTER 12

Love is a condition in which the happiness of another person is essential to your own.

— Robert Heinlein

Saturday, May 2, 1812
Coaching inn on the road to Hertfordshire

Elizabeth was just stepping down from her uncle's carriage when she heard a familiar voice calling to her. Surprised, she looked up to see Kitty and Lydia leaning out of an upstairs window in the inn where their father's carriage was to meet them.

"Up here, Lizzy!" Lydia called out again, waving happily.

"We have been waiting for you for more than an hour!" Kitty said. "We did not want to be late to meet you. Papa lent us the coach for the journey."

That was not a pleasant thought to Elizabeth, remembering Lady Catherine's shock that the younger girls had been allowed out in society so young. And it was not at all wise to allow them to travel even a score of miles without adult supervision.

"Come on up and join us," Lydia added. "We have visited the milliner across the street and have dressed a salad and cucumber while we waited. There are so many things that have happened at home while you three were gone."

Elizabeth and Jane shared a look and a shrug. There was nothing else to be done, it appeared, and in any case, their conversation would be better conducted somewhere other than the courtyard of a coaching inn.

When their party had climbed the stairs of the inn, they found their sisters waiting for them in a dining room set out with such cold meats as such an inn usually afforded, crowing about how the two of them had arranged everything and would treat the travellers but then blithely saying that they must borrow the money since they had spent theirs. This drew another glance and a shake of the head between the two elder sisters, but they held their tongues since Maria Lucas was in the room, as was the waiter from the inn.

But before Elizabeth could dismiss the man, Lydia informed them with complete unconcern that she had bought a hat that was not at all handsome but that it did not matter. "The regiment is leaving Meryton in a fortnight, and afterwards who will care what one wears?"

"Are they indeed?" Elizabeth said with the greatest satisfaction. "That is excellent news."

"How can you be so callous, Lizzy?" Kitty said.

"Yes, indeed!" Lydia said in energetic agreement. "The regiment is moving to summer quarters near Brighton, and I have come up with an excellent idea for Papa to take the whole family there for the summer. Is that not a delicious scheme?"

"And it would hardly cost a thing more than staying at home all summer, which would be misery. Mama agrees with us that it is a wonderful plan."

Elizabeth looked at Jane and could see that both of them were thinking the same thing. Such a misbegotten idea would truly upset their family, which had already been upset enough by a single regiment of militia and the monthly balls at Meryton. She knew other soldiers—regulars as well as militia—were located in the area, and a full camp of red-coated soldiers and an even greater social whirl would truly set their family on its ear.

When Lydia announced that she had other news, excellent news, about one of their favourite persons, Elizabeth finally managed to break in and inform the waiter that he need not stay. As he closed the door behind him, Lydia laughed and mocked her sister's formality and discretion.

"As if he was going to hear something worse than what he usually hears around here. But it is no matter: he is an ugly fellow, and I am glad he is gone. But now for my news, and it is about dear Wickham. There is no danger of him marrying Mary King. She is gone down to stay with her uncle at Liverpool. Gone for good, and Wickham is safe."

"It might be better said that Mary King is safe," Elizabeth said irritably. "Safe from an imprudent marriage to a man with no fortune who could not support her."

"She is a great fool for going away if she liked him."

"I do hope there is no strong attachment on either side," Jane said with her usual desire to see no one suffer angst because of such an event.

"How could there be any real attachment on Wickham's part?" Lydia said with conviction. "I am certain he never cared three straws about her. Who could truly care about such a nasty little freckled thing?"

Hearing these words from her sister's lips somehow shocked Elizabeth to her core. It was not that Lydia had never said such things previously and on many occasions, but to hear such coarseness of expression coupled with a cold unconcern for another young lady of her acquaintance reminded her of some of her own inner assessments of others. Even if Elizabeth had never expressed herself in such a coarse manner, she would have inwardly agreed with many such sentiments and fancied herself liberal simply for her restraint of expression. Now, just the thought of what Lydia had said made her wince at its cruelty as well as the vulgar manner in which it was expressed.

It did not occur to her to wonder what changes had already been wrought to make her aware of her previous errors, but then the process of maturation was not one that was much noticed by the object of such evolution.

As soon as everyone had eaten and the elder sisters had paid for the fare, their father's carriage was sent for, and all the luggage and parcels were tied in place or placed inside, including the unwelcome purchases of the two youngest sisters. This necessitated the seating being cramped, and there was no escaping Lydia's conversation about the absent sisters and their experiences in London and elsewhere along with her own desires to be the first sister married so she could chaperone them to all the balls.

Elizabeth listened to her sisters' recitations of their attendance at parties and the jokes they had heard as little as she could, but she could not escape hearing Wickham's name on numerous occasions.

Saturday, May 2, 1812
Longbourn, Hertfordshire

THE ARRIVAL OF JANE AND ELIZABETH AT LONGBOURN WAS MOST happily received. The Lucases were there to meet Maria and hear the news of her visit, and fortunately for the peace of mind of the two sisters, Maria's recitations were almost totally concerned with having dined at Rosings nine times and having drunk tea twice. She failed to mention Colonel Fitzwilliam's visits in town at all, for she had not understood the reason for them, and she mentioned the theatre only to lament that stomach cramps had compelled her to miss that opportunity. For her part, Mrs. Bennet rejoiced to see Jane in undiminished beauty, and Mr. Bennet several times spoke to Elizabeth to tell her how glad he was she had come back.

Maria and her parents did not stay long and soon departed for their home. The heightened activity occasioned by Elizabeth and Jane's arrival soon diminished, and in the afternoon, Lydia suggested that all of the girls should walk to Meryton.

"It would be a chance for you and Jane to see how everybody has gotten on while you were gone," she said to Elizabeth.

"You should be more forthcoming, Lydia," Elizabeth responded. "What you really wish to do is to continue your pursuit of officers while there are still officers to pursue. I, for one, have no intention of lending credence to the opinion throughout the neighbourhood that the Miss Bennets could not be home half a day before they were chasing after officers."

Lydia was irate at having her intentions pointed out so forthrightly and responded vigorously, but Elizabeth and Jane ignored her and ascended to their room. Both of them were unhappy to hear Lydia and Kitty appealing to their mother for permission to go even if the older girls stayed at Longbourn.

"I imagine Lydia will get her way, as usual," Elizabeth said grumpily as she and Jane entered their room and applied themselves to unpacking their trunks and putting their belongings away.

"Perhaps we should have gone," Jane said thoughtfully. "Lydia seems even wilder now than she did when I departed with my aunt and uncle. Perhaps I have forgotten what she was like, but she appears more impulsive than ever. Perhaps we could have exerted a measure of guidance over her."

"When has our guidance ever done any good? But I believe you are correct: she is more uncontrolled than before either of us left. But I had another reason for declining her suggestion: I dread seeing Wickham again after learning what we did from Colonel Fitzwilliam. I am determined to avoid it as long as possible. It is comforting that the regiment's approaching departure in a fortnight will take Wickham out of our sphere and there will be nothing more to plague us on his account."

Jane looked uncomfortable at hearing of Wickham, for she still found Fitzwilliam's information difficult to believe, and her discomfort deepened as another thought occurred to her.

"I was rather surprised to hear Lydia's Brighton scheme mentioned so often, even before the Lucases left for home. I would have thought it had already been rejected, but Mama spoke openly of it several times to Papa."

"But it is clear that our father has not the smallest intention of yielding to Lydia's arguments, no matter how often repeated."

"Perhaps so, but I would have been happier if he had been more forthright in rejecting the plan."

"I know, but it is his usual manner to give answers that are vague and equivocal. He finds it amusing to see the family unable to guess his inner thoughts."

"But it also keeps my mother continuing her arguments, even if she is disheartened a small amount."

"True, but that is our mother and father," Elizabeth said sadly, a statement with which Jane could only agree.

But Elizabeth's relief concerning Mr. Wickham proved to be short-lived.

In Meryton, Wickham and several fellow officers encountered Kitty and Lydia Bennet who insisted they be escorted home. Mrs. Bennet seemed pleased to see them and invited everyone for dinner. When the two eldest sisters came downstairs, Wickham noticed them immediately and made a beeline in Elizabeth's direction, quite pleased to see his former favourite despite the initial look of dismay on her face.

But her first reaction did not perturb him unduly. He was confident that he could successfully charm and flatter Elizabeth into the same acceptance that had marked the early part of their acquaintance, though his intentions this time were more malign than previously when he had engaged her mostly to damage Darcy's reputation. He freely admitted to himself that his object this time had a more base motive, that of simple lechery.

She is more beautiful than ever, he thought. With a renewal of gallantry, *I am certain I can soon gratify her vanity and secure her preference in time for a little dalliance before the regiment departs. That will be in a fortnight, which should be enough time to achieve success and then be gone. It would be quite exciting to peel her out of that dress and lay her down on a picnic blanket to show her a thing or two and have her squealing in excitement! Later, even if I got her with child, I will have disappeared from the regiment—along with some pleasing memories!*

Wickham was certain that such coarse thoughts did not show in his expression, even to her admittedly practised eye, but perhaps he deluded himself, obsessed as he was by the pleasant prospect of seeing just what the lovely Elizabeth looked like bereft of clothing.

"I WAS SORRY TO HEAR THAT YOUR ENGAGEMENT TO MISS KING had ended," Elizabeth said, smiling sweetly, hoping to pierce his confident demeanour despite her considerable agitation. "I hope the disappointment of both parties is not too extreme."

"Her uncle demanded the return of Miss King and her mother to Liverpool," Wickham said with a shrug. "I believe he desires a more advantageous match than a penniless officer, even if the officer in question should have been a clergyman with a secure future."

As Wickham continued in his amiable and gentle manner to speak and listen with even more attention than before, Elizabeth was disgusted to remember the extent to which his manner had once delighted her. It was unbelievable that he could believe his renewed attentions could secure a reanimated preference on her part, but she could not deny the evidence of her own eyes and ears. And she was confounded when her several attempts to break away from his presence were deftly foiled with even more skill than she remembered. The result was that Wickham remained at her side through dinner and the rest of the evening, though she was pleased that he wore a look of badly concealed dissatisfaction on his face when he departed that evening.

IN THE WEEK THAT FOLLOWED, THE TUMULT THAT GRIPPED ELIZ-
abeth's mind was extreme. Hardly a day passed without Lydia and
Kitty making the journey to Meryton, though both Elizabeth and Jane
declined to accompany them, having other matters on their minds.
But their sisters' journeys invariably resulted in officers from the regiment accompanying them back to Longbourn since both parties were
engaged in extended farewells for the regiment's impending departure.
Those parties included many of the girls' favourites, such as Mr. Denny
and Captain Carter. But they also included Mr. Wickham, which kept
Elizabeth's distress level at a peak, both because her mother would
invariably invite the officers to stay for the afternoon and to dinner
and because Mr. Wickham's attentions to her continued unabated. In
fact, she grew increasingly uncomfortable at certain sly intentions she
thought she detected in the handsome and quite persuasive young man.

*I can now see what Colonel Fitzwilliam meant about Wickham seduc-
ing or attempting to seduce the daughters of servants or tradesmen,* she
thought in concern. *Is that what he is attempting with ME? It is difficult
to be sure since he is so very subtle and smooth in his speech and actions,
but it is both worrisome and…and insulting!*

That thought led Elizabeth to worry about Saturday, which promised
the visit from Mr. Darcy in company with his cousin. She had not
dared mention the subject to her mother; she knew the reaction was
sure to be unpleasant, and she felt herself too unsettled to be able to
deal with it at the present time.

Perhaps I shall be able to inform my mother soon, she thought. *But
not right now. Perhaps tomorrow.*

She also struggled with a degree of uncertainty regarding the date
of the cousins' visit. Colonel Fitzwilliam had contrived to inform her
in a discreet and cryptic sentence that Mr. Darcy had agreed to her
conditions, but there had not been a chance to confirm the details.
However, she tried to tell herself repeatedly to stop worrying about
the time of the visit. Fitzwilliam had said "Saturday week" according

to Jane, and she was sure he would come.

Even so, several times she had to stop herself from sharing her worries with Jane, which could do no good. Adding to her troubled state was a visit from their aunt Philips on Monday, which again made her wonder what had ever possessed her to make such a forward and ill-advised suggestion regarding Mr. Darcy.

Mrs. Philips, Mrs. Bennet's sister, usually visited several times each week and, on this occasion, brought news of especial interest.

"I have just been informed that the housekeeper at Netherfield has received orders to prepare the house for occupancy," she said. "Is it not exciting?"

"Well, well," Mrs. Bennet said, thrown into fidgets by the news though she made a half-hearted attempt at appearing uninterested. "So, Mr. Bingley is coming down. Of course, it is nothing to us, Sister, since we long since agreed never to mention it again. But it appears he still maintains the lease, so he is certainly welcome to come to Netherfield if he wishes."

"Mama, Aunt Philips's news is only that Netherfield is being prepared for occupancy," Elizabeth said, suddenly wishing she and Jane had managed to be elsewhere along with their two youngest sisters when their aunt called. "She did not mention whether Mr. Bingley would be in residence."

And he may well not be coming down as my mother assumes, she thought. *It may only be Mr. Darcy and Colonel Fitzwilliam if Mr. Bingley was not persuaded by the information Mr. Darcy sent him.*

"That is true, Lizzy," agreed her aunt. "The housekeeper, Mrs. Nicholls, was in Meryton this morning and mentioned it to the butcher, but I did not talk to her myself. The butcher told me that the house will be open on Friday, and he is supposed to deliver some meat there Thursday. But Mrs. Nicholls did not say Mr. Bingley would be staying there. He may have loaned the place to some friends or relatives."

"Nonsense, Lizzy," Mrs. Bennet said briskly. "Of course Mr. Bingley will be coming. Who else could it be? I declare, I do not know where you get some of your ideas!"

Jane had not been able to hear Mr. Bingley's name without changing colour slightly, but she and Elizabeth only shared a glance. They could make no further attempt to correct their mother without being compelled to explain how they had come by their information.

So certain was Mrs. Bennet that Bingley was returning to Netherfield that she immediately charged her husband with calling on him as soon as he arrived. Mr. Bennet, however, was of no mind to do so, and he forcefully declared that nothing had come of Bingley's previous visit and he would not be sent on another fool's errand. From this position, no expostulations of his wife would move him, and Mrs. Bennet was quite distraught in consequence.

Despite her own turmoil, Elizabeth marvelled at how calm and composed her sister was about Fitzwilliam's forthcoming visit. She had no trouble whatever ascertaining Jane's spirits now that they were at home and did not have to find the odd corner or brief moment alone in which to talk. While Jane easily confessed her anticipation of the colonel's arrival, she gave no indication of any anxiety whatever.

Perhaps his straightforward approach alleviates any anxiety Jane might feel about the matter, she thought. *Or else her own nature does not lead her to the kind of worry afflicting me. I wonder whether Mr. Bingley is actually going to come to Netherfield. I am sure Mr. Darcy has done as I asked...which is looking more and more ill-advised. Having both Colonel Fitzwilliam and Mr. Bingley paying court to Jane could be...well, exciting is not exactly the word I would choose, but perhaps it might describe the situation that might ensue. How will Jane react if that is what happens? I never thought of that when I spoke with Colonel Fitzwilliam! And then there is my decision to allow Mr. Darcy a chance to redeem himself...*

Somewhat offsetting her worry regarding Mr. Bingley, a midnight talk the previous evening had revealed that Jane still cherished at least some tender feelings towards her former suitor. Since Elizabeth knew her sister had never fancied herself in love before she met Mr. Bingley, she was cognizant that Jane's regard for him could not help but be tinged with all the warmth of a first attachment. Her sister still valued the memory of Mr. Bingley's interest in her as well as his manners and amiability and, though difficult to believe, bore him no bitterness for the abruptness of his departure.

The upshot was that Elizabeth was now quite uncertain where Jane's preferences lay since she clearly felt a certain attraction for both men—or at least the memory of an attraction to one of them, while the other one was real and recent in a most dramatic manner. Elizabeth had to believe Jane's feelings for that most determined man were different from those she had borne for Bingley, even before he departed. Yet it was a fact that, after Jane had learned what her sister had requested of Fitzwilliam, she had become strangely reticent about the exact manner and intensity of her feelings for him. It was all most perplexing.

Jane told me in town that she was finding that she quite liked "bold," Elizabeth thought, and she also remembered the way her sister had put her hand on Fitzwilliam's arm in her uncle's courtyard. That had been the familiar touch a sister might have for a brother—or a wife for a husband—and it had stunned her to see her reserved sister act in such a forward manner. Not improper really, but it was not the way a maiden was supposed to act towards a man outside her immediate family.

It surprised him too, she thought dryly, *but based on the smile he gave me—and his wink, the rascal—he did not mind in the least.*

Her mother, of course, had noticed nothing of the inner machinations of her two elder daughters and had been in a high state of excitement since learning that Netherfield was being opened again. But she still had doubts, which she expressed on one occasion when she managed to get Elizabeth alone

"Despite the news my sister brought," Mrs. Bennet said fretfully, "I am still concerned about this sad business of Jane's tenure in London. Jane will not speak of it directly, but it seems that she never met Bingley during the whole time she visited in town. That is past understanding! In town at the same time and never met?"

Elizabeth was rather amused that her mother had previously professed her determination not to speak of the subject again, yet she was now proceeding to do exactly that.

"London is very large, Mama, and Mr. Bingley and my aunt and uncle live in very different parts of town. But why do you worry? Surely you are confident he will come down to Netherfield."

"I have misgivings about you being correct about his not coming. In any case, he is a very undeserving young man, and even if he does come, I cannot tell whether Jane has any chance at all of getting him now."

"I would not worry so much, Mama," Elizabeth said carefully since she had information her mother did not. "Besides, there has been no news of the lease being terminated, has there?"

"No, I have heard nothing on that matter."

"Yet Mr. Bingley surely would have done so if he never intended to live there again."

"That is true," Mrs. Bennet agreed, brightening at the thought. "I do not remember my sister ever mentioning it, but I shall visit her immediately to refresh my memory. There is reason to hope even if he does not come down this time."

Elizabeth watched her mother bustle upstairs, restored to cheerfulness and humming a tune as she went. But a sudden thought about her mother's reaction when Darcy came to call reversed her satisfaction and sent a chill down her spine.

Perhaps I should have mentioned the matter to my father, she thought. *But no—he would have found the subject highly amusing and would undoubtedly have mentioned it to Mama. It will be bad enough to endure her joys and excitement when it happens without having to listen to it for an entire week.*

Wednesday, May 6, 1812
Longbourn, Hertfordshire

THE FIRST WEEK OF JANE AND ELIZABETH'S RETURN CONTINUED, and it was also the next-to-last week of the regiment's stay in Meryton. The impending departure had most of the young ladies in the neighbourhood sunk into dejection, especially Kitty and Lydia, and they frequently reproached Jane and Elizabeth for their insensibility to this impending calamity. Their affectionate mother provided no barrier to all their grief and in fact shared it as she remembered aloud what she herself had endured on a similar occasion a quarter century previously.

"I am sure I cried for two days together when Colonel Millar's regiment went away five and twenty years ago. I thought my heart would break," she reminisced in the Longbourn front parlour.

"I am sure mine shall," Lydia said.

"If we could but go to Brighton," observed Mrs. Bennet.

"Oh yes, if we could but go to Brighton. But Father is so disagreeable!"

"A little sea-bathing would set me up forever," her mother said.

"And my aunt Philips is sure it would do me a great deal of good," added Kitty.

Such lamentations resounded through Longbourn every day and joined recurring pleas made to their father about taking the family to Brighton. Those latter appeals met with the same firm refusal as had all previous petitions, though Elizabeth could not be certain her father's refusals derived from the sheer lunacy of such a plan or were more rooted in his own disinclination to exert himself. She would normally have found a certain diversion at such ridiculous plaints, but her own anxiety on this occasion drained any humour from the situation. Instead, she felt only embarrassment, especially when she considered they might well be repeated when the two cousins visited. For the first time, she realized that one of the reasons for Darcy's interference might have been his observation of her family's improprieties, especially at the Netherfield ball. It did not excuse what he had done—not completely—but Elizabeth was observing the foolishness of her mother and younger sisters through new eyes.

Nor could she receive any relief from her aunt Philips's daily visits, each of which provided additional details on the deliveries to Netherfield, which servants had returned to their previous employment and which had found other situations, and other such mundane and, to Elizabeth at least, uninteresting minutiae.

"But is it known whether Mr. Bingley is coming down?" her mother asked during each conversation.

"Mrs. Nichols professes no such knowledge," was the invariable response from Mrs. Philips. This was a slight exaggeration of that worthy housekeeper's actual response to such questions since her firm determination not to share information private to her employer caused her to maintain her silence and bustle away on her business. But Mrs. Bennet's sister was too fervent a talebearer to feel herself limited to the strict truth. A certain degree of embellishment was to be expected after all.

The result was that only Jane and Elizabeth had enough knowledge to make any guesses, and they were keeping their own counsel. Until Saturday, at least.

Thursday, May 6, 1812
Scarborough, North Yorkshire

CHARLES BINGLEY WAS NOT IN A PARTICULARLY GOOD MOOD AS he cantered into the stable yard behind his cousin's estate. A good part of his discontent was the thought of going into the house for breakfast. Despite the fact that he had worked up a good appetite with his brisk morning ride, he could depend on Caroline arriving at the breakfast table as soon as the meal was announced, and he found it wearing to have to listen to her incessant complaints: Scarborough was a boring town, there was nothing to do, and why could they not return to London?

As he swung down from the saddle and handed the reins to a stable boy, he shook his head in irritation with his sister. He knew that he should not allow her to spoil what ought to be a relaxing visit with their many relatives in the area, but he did not seem able to ignore her as he used to. He had tried to inform her that there was no reason for her dissatisfaction since Scarborough was believed to be England's first seaside resort and was a popular destination for the wealthy of London. But she had ignored him, and he knew why. She wanted to return to London in order to continue her useless pursuit of Darcy, hoping for an invitation to spend the summer months at Pemberley away from the unhealthy streets of London. That would be pleasant enough, but Caroline could not accept that Darcy was simply not interested in her beyond her relationship as a sister to his good friend—certainly not as a wife despite her beauty, wealth, and supercilious manners cultivated and honed by the elite school she and Louisa had both attended.

I am not sure just what kind of woman Darcy is looking for, he thought, *but it is certainly not Caroline. When Darcy made that comment at Netherfield about a woman not being truly accomplished unless she could improve her mind by extensive reading, she did not realize he was describing her. Caroline might read, but her book selections do nothing to broaden her horizons.*

He was at times tempted to respond with one of his late mother's favourite sayings when Caroline was young that "boring people are the first to be bored. Are you a boring person, Caroline?"

He smiled at the thought as he walked into the house. He knew he could not be so cold as to repeat his mother's words, but it was tempting. Very tempting.

The butler must have heard his footsteps as he went down the hall towards the stairs since he stepped out of his little cubby. "An express arrived for you while you were out, sir. From what the express rider said, it appears to be rather important." He gestured to a silver salver on a small table. Bingley thanked him and picked up the letter, noting it was from Darcy.

I wonder what of importance Darcy has to relate, he thought idly. *He, of course, knows that we planned to stay several more weeks before returning to London. And that we shall do, no matter how much Caroline complains. Perhaps it is about that town house I have been interested in buying. In any case, I am sure it concerns nothing of real importance.*

However, despite what the butler had said about the importance of Darcy's express, Bingley was too hungry to read it just now and instead hurried to the breakfast room.

It was almost an hour later before Bingley climbed the stairs and stalked down the hallway to his room. His breakfast sat like a lump of lead in his stomach after barely being able to restrain his temper as Caroline launched into her usual litany of complaints, and he threw Darcy's express onto the writing desk while he went to the sideboard and filled a glass from the decanter of port. He was so upset that it took a valiant effort to pass by the brandy in favour of the lesser-strength beverage, and it was almost a quarter hour more before he retrieved the express.

He noted the date and time written in the corner and shook his head. *Darcy wrote this on Saturday and it is just now arriving,* he thought in disgust. *That is almost five days! It only takes about three days by coach. Depending on the roads, of course.*

Still, he was not that surprised. A postal rider travelled only about three miles in an hour, and even the usual express rider could only manage to increase that to four miles. And they could not travel by day and night; the roads were safer now that so many turnpikes had been opened, but travelling at night was still a risky business. He knew Darcy must have paid extra for even a five-day delivery.

But Bingley was not an overly introspective man, so he shrugged and opened the express.

THREE QUARTERS OF AN HOUR AND ANOTHER GLASS OF PORT LATER, Bingley was vaguely conscious of a knock at his door, but he ignored it as he concentrated on trying to make both his message and his penmanship intelligible. The knock came again, and again he ignored it as his quill scratched over the paper.

"Charles?"

His sister's voice became more strident as she repeated his name. It was only after two more repetitions that Bingley looked up from his letter.

"Go away, Caroline," he said as he saw his sister. "I am busy. I have several expresses to write and dispatch. But make yourself useful. Ring for the butler."

Caroline's lips were compressed in anger as she went to several bell cords hanging from the ceiling and pulled one before turning back to her brother.

"Charles, stop that writing! I want to talk to you."

"I care little what you want. I am busy."

"I have just talked with Louisa, and we are both agreed that we want to load up your coach and return to London."

"You do, do you? Hah!" Bingley concluded his second express and finished addressing it when the butler knocked at the door and entered.

"Ah, Smith! I have several things that I need to get done immediately. First, send word to the stables to have my coach prepared. Then summon my valet to pack my trunk. I want to be on my way in half an hour."

The butler was taken aback to hear that their visitors were leaving, but he had received surprising instructions many times during his service, so he merely said, "Very good, sir," and stepped over to pull another bell cord.

"Next—and this is just as important—here are two expresses that I need to send, one to my estate in Hertfordshire and the other to a friend in London. Please summon a pair of riders—good ones, like the one who delivered my express this morning."

"Perhaps you might consider using just one express rider, sir? If I am not mistaken, both destinations are nearly in line with each other."

Bingley thought that over for a moment before shaking his head. "No, I shall pay the extra cost to make sure each one is delivered as fast as possible. And pack some food and drink for myself and the drivers for the road. It is going to be a hard journey in any case, but I hope to shorten it to four days."

"Very well, sir. Is there anything else?"

"No, I believe that will be all for now. Thank you."

Bingley waited until the butler left before swivelling about in his chair to face Caroline, who wore a huge, satisfied smile.

"You have nothing to smile about like that, Caroline. We are not returning to London. I am going to Netherfield instead. One of my expresses was for the housekeeper to arrange to have the house prepared for occupancy."

Caroline looked at her brother in shock. "Whatever for, Charles?"

"To try to rectify a horrible mistake if at all possible."

"Talk sense! What are you speaking of?"

"I am speaking of the conspiracy that you and my best friend engaged in to convince me not to return to Netherfield because Miss Jane Bennet was not suitable to be my wife and did not even care for me. Do you perhaps recall that little conversation the four of us had? You, me, Louisa, and Darcy?

"Well, of course, but that was in your best—"

"Do not tell me that was in my best interest!" Bingley said icily as he surged to his feet to confront his sister. He picked up Darcy's express and waved it furiously at his sister.

"Darcy confessed everything—what he did in convincing me of Jane Bennet's indifference to me and what he thought when he considered how Mrs. Bennet would order her daughter to accept any offer of marriage I made."

Caroline went dead white in shock and mortification, taking a step backwards away from her brother's anger.

"He also writes that you concealed from me that Miss Bennet was visiting her aunt and uncle in London. Also, that you coldly severed the acquaintance with a young lady you had been pretending was a friend! How could you be so callous and cruel? Is that what they taught you at that expensive school?"

"How...how can you even know of this?" Caroline stammered in mortification.

"Because he developed an interest in Miss Bennet's sister, Miss Elizabeth—so much so that he made her an offer of marriage! What do you think of that, Caroline?"

Caroline was so dumbstruck that she could make no comment at all, her mouth open wide in dismay at the shattering of all her hopes and dreams.

After several moments, she managed to say weakly, "Then... Mr. Darcy is going to marry...to marry..." Her voice went silent. Caroline Bingley simply could not say the words.

"It is not that simple," Bingley said derisively. "Miss Elizabeth proved herself no more a fortune hunter than her sister would have been. She refused Darcy's offer, and angry words were exchanged. It was she who informed him of all the particulars of your deception regarding Miss Bennet. But at least Darcy has confessed his errors to me, and now both of us have an opportunity to achieve our dreams: he with Miss Elizabeth and me with her sister. *That* is why I am going to Netherfield."

Caroline opened and closed her mouth several times over the next several seconds, trying to say something but unable to make the words come. Finally, she managed to say, her voice almost like the croaking of a frog, "I...I will not go to Netherfield! I...I refuse to have any... any part in such an unseemly scheme! I will not—"

"That is quite all right," Bingley said with a smile. "Because, you see, you are not invited. You will remain here in Scarborough—you and your sister and your sister's husband."

"But...but you are taking your coach! How will...we cannot...how...

how will we get home?" Her voice had risen almost to a screech, and the expression that twisted her lovely features was one of pure desperation and panic.

"You could hire a coach, I suppose," Bingley said with a careless shrug. "You have your own fortune, you know, unless you have overspent your income again. But if the three of you pool your funds, you should be able to manage something. Or you could always travel by post. In any case, it is not my concern. I must be on my way."

Bingley left his sister standing motionless, her mouth open in shock and dismay, stepping around her to give instructions to his valet about preparations for his journey.

CHAPTER 13

She walks in beauty,
Like the night of cloudless climes and starry skies;
And all that's best of dark and bright
Meet in her aspect and her eyes.

— Lord Byron

Saturday, May 9, 1812
Netherfield, Hertfordshire

D arcy was just preparing to mount his horse when his cousin cantered into the stable yard at Netherfield. He was in full uniform as Darcy had expected, including that incredibly ugly headgear of which the Sixth Dragoons were so proud. He personally thought it belonged to the days before knights attired themselves in metal to provide a modicum of protection on the battlefield. Good, solid iron seemed a much better idea to turn an enemy sabre than horsehair, in his opinion. But it was not his area of expertise, so he kept his silence on that topic and restrained himself to greeting his cousin.

"Good morning, Richard," he said as he swung easily into the saddle while Richard pulled his horse to a halt beside him. "Nervous?"

He thought his cousin looked at him a bit oddly at the remark, but his voice was calm as he replied, "Of course. And you?"

Darcy gave an uncomfortable shrug. "More than I care to admit. I am a bit surprised to hear you admit to feeling what I am feeling at the moment. I do not really have any idea what to expect this morning."

"When I first visited Jane, my stomach was churning to such an extent that I wanted to turn around and return home. I told myself such feelings were ridiculous and not worthy of a man of my experience and character."

"And did that help?"

"Of course not."

Both cousins had to laugh at this statement that so accurately described their own situation at the moment.

"I was thinking last night that Elizabeth and I have not had any real conversations before today. It was all the contrived small talk that passes for polite discourse—sounds that carry no real information or meaning."

"I am somewhat better off than that. Jane is so amiable that we did not have to go through a process of subterfuge and evasion before we just began...well, talking."

"Yes, exactly," Darcy said worriedly. "That is all I have experience with myself—"

"Except in private, at home with good friends and relatives," Richard interrupted. "That is how you should talk to Miss Elizabeth. As a good friend and hopefully a future relative."

Darcy gave this some thought before nodding. "Good advice, Cousin. Very good advice. I hope I can follow it. How was your evening at the inn in Meryton?"

"It was adequate. Clean, at least, though the bed was rather uncomfortable. But perhaps that was because I was tossing and turning so much."

That brought another laugh of shared emotions, and they turned their horses towards the road.

"Have you had any response from Bingley to your express," Richard asked. He was uncomfortable asking it, but he really wanted to know whether the other man was going to suddenly appear and try to repair his transgressions against Jane.

"No, but I did not expect one. An express rider is faster than the post, but I would be vastly surprised if he received it before Wednesday. He will likely send one if he decides not to come, but I would not expect to receive it before Monday or Tuesday."

"But he could arrive by coach sooner than that, correct?"

"Yes, though it would take a miracle if he arrived sooner than late Saturday evening. Sunday is more likely, and even Monday might be believable. The rains can make travel difficult at this time of year."

"Saturday or Sunday. Well, that is why I did not accept your invitation to stay at Netherfield with you."

"Well, at least the inn is clean," Darcy said benignly, which drew a snort of laughter from his cousin.

Saturday, May 9, 1812
Longbourn, Hertfordshire

IN CONSEQUENCE OF HER HUSBAND'S REFUSAL TO CALL ON MR. Bingley, Mrs. Bennet lost no time on Saturday morning in assuming her prayers had been answered and in calling on her daughters to partake of her joy when she saw two gentlemen enter the paddock and ride towards the house.

Jane, however, resolutely kept her place at the small table in the parlour though Elizabeth could not stop herself from going to the window. She saw, as she expected, the colonel and Mr. Darcy riding towards the house, and she sat down beside her sister. Gravely, she gave Jane a nod and was pleased at the sudden joy that blossomed behind her sister's eyes.

Obviously, Jane has not lost interest in Colonel Fitzwilliam, whatever happens with Mr. Bingley, thought Elizabeth with a degree of agitation. *Mr. Bingley may come or he may not come, but the die is cast, and it is now up to those two men to attend Jane. But now my own affairs demand my attention. What will happen between me and Mr. Darcy? I do not feel at all welcoming, but he definitely did as I asked with respect to his friend. Is it possible that Colonel Fitzwilliam is right about his cousin? Have I been guilty of errors in judgement similar to his. Oh, my heart must be going hundreds of beats a minute!*

"It is not Mr. Bingley, Mama," she heard Kitty say excitedly, having replaced Elizabeth at the window. "And one of them is an officer."

"Really?" exclaimed Lydia, who instantly joined her sister.

"What do you mean, it is not Mr. Bingley?" Mrs. Bennet asked in agitation. "It *must* be Mr. Bingley."

"There is another man with the officer, Mama," Kitty said, shading her eyes from the morning sun. "But he is definitely not Mr. Bingley."

"But who can it be?" Mrs. Bennet cried in despair.

"La! It looks like that man who was Mr. Bingley's friend," Kitty said. "Mr. what's-his-name. That tall, proud man."

"Good gracious!" Mrs. Bennet exclaimed as she pushed Kitty aside to look out the window. "Mr. Darcy. Can it be him? It *is* him, I vow. But why does he come? And who is the man with him?"

"Look, Kitty," exclaimed Lydia. "This officer is not in the militia. See? The uniform is different. The coat is a different red than the militia officers, and look at all the gold piping. Also, he is wearing one of those hats with the horse hair on top. Who can it be?"

"What does it matter?" Mrs. Bennet said crossly. "It is Mr. Darcy and not Mr. Bingley. Why is he visiting us? And who cares who his friend is? Even though Mr. Darcy was a friend of Mr. Bingley's and any friend of Mr. Bingley's will always be welcome here, still I must say I hate the very sight of him."

"That is unfortunate, Mama," Elizabeth said calmly, "since Mr. Darcy has come to call on me. But perhaps you should have Father refuse him entrance to the house since you object to him so greatly." Jane looked at her in surprise, but she saw the saucy look in Elizabeth's eye and realized she was teasing their mother.

"Mr. Darcy?" Mrs. Bennet said in shock. "Calling on you?"

"Yes, Mama. He was visiting his aunt Lady Catherine at Rosings when I was there. Later, in town, I gave him permission to call on me after I returned home."

Jane hid a smile of admiration at the way her sister had told their mother the exact truth—and managed to conceal almost everything worthwhile!

RICHARD WAS AMUSED BY THE CONTINUING SIGNS OF UNEASE exhibited by Darcy as the two of them drew up in front of Longbourn. Darcy had told him the house was rather modest, and that certainly seemed true from what he could see of the exterior. But Richard also noted that the structure and the grounds appeared to be in good repair and well tended. The staff also appeared alert, as exemplified by the two boys who raced over from the stables as he and Darcy walked their horses up the drive. Both boys appeared to be cheerful enough and readily accepted the reins along with instructions on the care of both animals.

The front door of the house was opened quickly to admit them, and they were shown in to the parlour and announced. Richard looked around as he entered the room, and he felt his heart jump when he saw Jane Bennet and discerned the shy look she gave him as she and her sisters made their curtseys.

Richard forced himself to look away as Elizabeth made the introductions. "Colonel Fitzwilliam, please allow me to introduce my mother, Mrs. Bennet. Jane you already know, of course, but these are my other sisters—Mary, Catherine, and Lydia. Mama, this is Mr. Darcy's cousin Colonel Fitzwilliam, the son of the Earl of Matlock. A *younger* son, as he so often avows."

This last comment was made in Elizabeth's wry tone of voice, and Richard smiled and nodded at her sally. He was amused by the incredulous and ecstatic expression Mrs. Bennet was trying to hide as she kept looking at Darcy. Judging from her complete lack of success, Richard guessed Elizabeth had not mentioned Darcy's interest until just now.

"Mr. Darcy, Colonel Fitzwilliam, you are both most welcome," Mrs. Bennet bubbled after she and her daughters had curtseyed in acknowledgement of the gentlemen's bows. She was quick to bid them to take a seat. Conspicuously, though she had just been informed of Darcy's intention to call on her least favourite daughter, the chair next to Elizabeth had been left vacant. Darcy wasted no time in claiming that seat as Mrs. Bennet responded by beaming at him.

Then she turned to Fitzwilliam. "Colonel, there is a chair over here by my younger daughters..."

Mrs. Bennet's face fell as she found that Richard was no longer standing where he had been. He had seated himself while she attended Darcy, and instead of sitting in the chair she had strategically placed between Kitty and Lydia, he had acquired one of the chairs she had moved to the corner of the room, and he had seated himself beside Jane.

"Oh, I *am* sorry, Mrs. Bennet," Richard said smoothly, as he patted his leg, which he held straight out in front of him. "I felt an immediate need to sit where I can stretch my leg out. Old injury, you know. It stiffens up when I ride."

After being informed of Darcy's intention to visit Elizabeth, Mrs. Bennet's attention was almost completely on him and only peripherally on his cousin. She had intended him only as company for her two youngest daughters, so her disappointment at the dexterity of Richard's manoeuvre was not as great as that of Lydia and Kitty, who had been atwitter with anticipation at having an officer of such elevated rank at their disposal. But she tried to put on the best face she could.

"Certainly, certainly, my dear Colonel, you must take care of yourself, having been wounded in the service of the King. But Lydia and Kitty were…well…" Her words dribbled to a halt, and Richard saw Darcy and Elizabeth lean towards each other and exchange some inaudible, whispered comments.

"Did you say something, Lizzy?" Mrs. Bennet asked sharply.

"No, Mama, I was clearing my throat," her daughter responded calmly. Richard was somewhat doubtful that Elizabeth was speaking the literal truth though her expression was perfectly placid. But he could see that Darcy was having difficulty suppressing a laugh, and Darcy was well acquainted with the origin and severity of Richard's injury. He suspected Mrs. Bennet had her doubts also from the suspicion on her face, but the expression quickly vanished as he watched. He knew she had put her irritation aside in the exhilaration of her daughter's astonishing opportunity with a gentleman of ten thousand a year.

Satisfied that Darcy and Elizabeth were well situated with Mrs. Bennet in fawning attendance, Richard was free to turn his attention to Jane.

"You are certainly looking well, Miss Bennet. I trust your trip home was not unduly fatiguing."

"No trip can be fatiguing with Elizabeth along, Colonel. But we are both glad to be returned home. But tell me, sir, is this trouble with your leg a continuing problem, or are you newly injured? I could see no signs of it in town."

Richard looked at her sharply and was delighted to see a spark of mischief in her eyes rather than the sadness that had been there when he first met her.

"I can see that little escapes your eye, Miss Bennet, and I admit myself fairly caught. I do indeed bear the scar of an old injury, but it occurred some years ago. And while it resulted from a battle of sorts and still hurts on occasion, it was not suffered in the service of the King. In fact, the circumstances are far too embarrassing for me to relate at this time."

Jane looked at him speculatively but finally nodded. "Very well, then, I shall not press you, but I am not sure you have completely convinced my mother. She had every intention of placing you at the disposal of my younger sisters."

Richard nodded wryly. "I did see that, but I confess Darcy provided a little warning. And he is not the only one who has managed to avoid being trapped by the London marriage mart these many years. Even the younger son of an earl must develop a flair for tactics and manoeuvres or else fall prey to a clever society mother."

"Ah, I see. So you cleverly used your tactical skills to avoid the youngest Bennet sisters. Very well done, sir."

Jane glanced over at Lydia and Kitty, who both still wore a look of disappointment as Richard continued. "But I did not avoid all the Bennet sisters, you know. I made sure I found a seat by the eldest and the most beautiful of all of them."

Jane coloured at the flattering remark, but Richard was surprised to see she had not heard it with pleasure since she suddenly could not meet his eyes. "You are very kind, sir," she said demurely, but Richard could tell her former cheerfulness had fled.

Undoubtedly, Bingley must have given her a similar compliment before he disappeared, Richard realised, *and now I have innocently brought back those memories. She cannot help but wonder whether I shall prove to be as insincere as he was. Well, I had decided, even after Darcy agreed to write Bingley, that I would not slow my pursuit, and I shall not let this pass. It is never too early to draw further distinctions between that idiot and myself.*

"Miss Bennet, please believe me when I tell you that I understand how you have been hurt." Richard spoke in a quiet, serious voice that could not be overheard by Jane's sisters. "It is not my intention to intrude into your private affairs, but the whole episode with your sister and my cousin has made me aware of relations between you and Mr. Bingley that I never would have learned otherwise. So I do understand, and I want you to know I do not make idle compliments, nor do

I toy with a lady's emotions. I meant neither more nor less than exactly what I have said...at this time. We are still only newly acquainted, but when the time is right, I shall have more to say. But depend on this, Miss Bennet—I shall not disappear unless I am banished, so you may rest assured that your future choices rest in your own hands."

Jane looked up at this statement, which was similar to what Elizabeth had reported of her conversation with their uncle in London. It was a forthright statement of his intentions, and hearing such from another was different from hearing it declared by the person himself. She saw sincerity in Fitzwilliam's eyes, and they looked at each other for several seconds before she had to look away.

Does he really mean it? she thought in confusion. *Elizabeth and Uncle Gardiner were certain of it, and looking at him at this moment, I cannot disbelieve him. But do I dare hope for it? His attentions are pleasing, and he is certainly amiable, knowledgeable, and well mannered. But even if he means what he says about his constancy—that he will not disappear—is he the man with whom I want to spend the rest of my life? And suppose Mr. Bingley comes to Netherfield after all? What do I do then?*

That question could not have a definitive answer at the present time—she needed to get to know this man better, and Mr. Bingley might never come—but she firmly told herself to stop worrying about the colonel's sincerity. If the opinions of both her uncle Gardiner and her dear sister agreed with her own, then the matter was settled.

As my aunt told me several times in town, it is an unusual woman who is not disappointed in love at least once before settling on a husband. So I shall stop making myself sad and despondent about what IS NOT and simply enjoy what IS, and let the future take care of itself.

"That is much better," Richard said lightly when Jane looked up with her usual cheerful smile. "Your face is made for smiles, not for frowns or worried looks."

"If you say so, then it must be true," she responded with equal lightness. "The same should also be said of my sister, but I do not think she is finding much enjoyment in her conversation."

A graceful movement of her head indicated Darcy and Elizabeth, who sat together but appeared to be having difficulty making conversation.

"Ah, I see what you mean. But I suppose it is difficult to easily converse with the mistress of the house hovering like a mare watching her colt take his first awkward steps."

Jane had to lower her head and bring her handkerchief to her lips to stifle her amusement because Richard had described the scene perfectly.

"Yes, you make a good point, sir. The atmosphere cannot be to the liking of either Mr. Darcy or Lizzy."

"Nor, now that I think about it, is it especially pleasing to the two of us. But an experienced military man like me should be able to devise a tactical solution to this problem."

"Ah. I shall watch with great curiosity."

Richard's teeth gleamed as he smiled broadly before turning towards the other couple.

"Darcy, old man," he said in a carrying voice. "It is a glorious day, is it not? An excellent day for a walk, at which we know Miss Elizabeth excels. And Miss Bennet just mentioned that she and her sister had been considering shopping for some ribbon this afternoon. What do you say to walking out with them and taking advantage of this welcome sunshine?"

Richard's suggestion met with rather more acclamation than he had intended since the glum looks fell from the faces of both Kitty and Lydia as they immediately jumped to their feet.

"Oh yes, a walk sounds wonderful. Let me get my shawl and bonnet," cried Lydia.

"What a cheerful idea, Colonel Fitzwilliam," added Kitty. "I shall be back directly."

Lydia was immediately gone from the room with Kitty close on her heels, both of them mesmerized by the thought of monopolizing the attentions of this intriguing and aristocratic officer—once they had separated him from their dull elder sister, of course. That would be simplicity itself since Jane had never shown a single iota of interest in officers. What did she care for such an opportunity? And while he might not be as handsome as some, he was certainly impressive in stature with his red coat and his imposing helmet. And he was the son of an earl besides!

Their feet could be heard clattering on the stairs before Darcy had fully comprehended Richard's unexpected suggestion.

Elizabeth rolled her eyes in mortification at such a commonplace but still embarrassing demonstration by her younger sisters. She was greatly pleased, however, at the opportunity to escape the overly attentive presence of her mother. Mrs. Bennet was not a walker, and she would definitely remain in the house. So, after a quick word with Darcy, Elizabeth also departed.

Jane, however, was still in her seat when Richard looked around, and she now looked at him with a considering expression on her face.

"It is the strangest thing, but I had not known I needed more ribbon," she said calmly. "Was this an example of the tactics you were speaking of, sir?"

"Well, yes, but these were not as successful as some," Richard said sheepishly, giving an exaggerated shrug. "But, no matter. At least it gets Darcy and your sister outside, and that was my main object—or at least *one* of my main objects. And, as you undoubtedly know, tactics are those moves taken for short-term advantage, and I am more interested in long-term strategic objectives."

"Indeed," Jane said quietly, rising to her feet. "Then I shall get my shawl and bonnet, Colonel Fitzwilliam."

Though she spoke calmly, a pretty blush belied her calm demeanour.

CHAPTER 14

Then indecision brings its own delays,
And days are lost lamenting o'er lost days.
Are you in earnest? Seize this very minute;
What you can do, or dream you can, begin it;
Boldness has genius, power, and magic in it.
— Johann Wolfgang von Goethe

Saturday, May 9, 1812
Meryton, Hertfordshire

The first part of the walk to Meryton passed predictably with Lydia and Kitty seeking in vain to manoeuvre themselves between Jane and the tall, red-coated officer who carefully controlled his pace so he remained steadfastly beside Jane.

"Colonel Fitzwilliam, do tell us all about London society," Lydia said excitedly. "Is it really as magnificent as everyone says?" It was perhaps her tenth question so far, and Kitty had offered a dozen of her own.

"I would not know, Miss Lydia," Richard said patiently, maintaining a careful grip on his exasperation while Jane carefully refrained from smiling at his discomfiture. "My regiment has been gone from England for several years and only returned six months ago. In any case, I am far too busy to have much time for the frivolities of high society."

Trying to find replacements for so many empty saddles, he thought bleakly. *Do these two even know their country is in a war to the death with the Corsican madman? Do they think that my fellows and I exist solely for their amusement?*

"But you are the son of an earl," Lydia said effervescently. "Having you at a ball or a dinner would be the object of every hostess, I am sure."

"I am only a younger son and a very dull one at that. My elder brother, George, will inherit my father's titles and estates. I am just a simple soldier."

"And already a colonel while still so young," Kitty exclaimed, ignoring Richard's response.

"I have been a serving officer for more than twelve years, Miss Catherine."

"So long?" Lydia said. "But you are much younger than Colonel Forster. And he is newly married, you know. His wife is a friend of mine, and she is only seventeen years old."

"Colonel Forster is a militia officer, and he was undoubtedly appointed to his position because he is a landowner in his home county. It is different in the regulars where commissions below the rank of colonel have to be purchased. Promotions, however, usually occur slowly, whether by merit or seniority, and only when there is a vacancy in the regiment. Unfortunately, there are many more vacancies these days since we are at war."

"I know little about such military matters," Jane said. "About all I know is what Lizzy mentioned: that you were a captain five years ago when you left for Egypt."

"Exactly right, and my promotions were due to the many vacancies during those five years. That was how I inherited the regiment, but my acting rank still had to be confirmed by the War Office when I returned."

Richard saw the expression on Jane's face, and he knew he had allowed remembrances of unpleasant events to darken his expression. He shook his head sharply, firmly attempting to put the memory of violence, horror, and lost friends from his mind, and his smile was as warm as ever as he looked at her.

"Actually, a commission as a lieutenant was purchased for me by Darcy's mother when I was just seventeen, and even then I had to wait for a vacancy to occur. It is one of many reasons I was so close to his parents: I never could have afforded even the price of a cornet's commission, which is the lowest cavalry officer."

"I was not aware that your commission was purchased. I thought that, as an earl's son..."

Her voice trailed off in confusion, and Richard read her confusion in her eyes. "Many people outside my sphere are not aware that commissions have to be purchased," he said, his smile intentionally warm to relieve her distress. "You were not present when I explained that part of my history to your aunt and sister, but I believe you are aware that I spent much of my boyhood with the Darcy family."

At Jane's nod, he continued. "When I was twelve, my father and I had a...disagreement about my profession. He banished me to the stables, and I left his home, going to live with Lady Anne and Uncle Darcy until I was seventeen."

"And your father?"

"We have not spoken since," Richard replied simply.

"Oh dear, that is terrible."

"It causes me little pain, Miss Bennet, and my father did not do worse. He did not deny me the rest of my family, for example. I visit my mother when I am able, and we exchange letters. Also with my sister. We are quite close, and she was just a babe when I left home."

He gave a sudden smile, his eyes unfocused in memory. "I remember that young man of seventeen and his adolescent ideas on soldiering as if it were yesterday. I was so naïve when I first put on the uniform.

It makes me squirm when I remember how much I thought I knew and how little of it turned out to be valid."

"I believe that is often the case," Jane said reassuringly.

"You are correct. I still see it every time a young man joins the regiment and we have to teach him the error of his ways."

Neither Lydia nor Kitty was pleased at the direction the conversation had taken. They had never doubted they would be able to monopolize the exchange with this very eligible young officer. He may be less handsome than Mr. Wickham, but he was certainly quite manly and sturdy in appearance—and he was the son of nobility.

However, for some inexplicable reason, he appeared far more interested in the company of their elder sister than themselves. Both of the thoughtless girls were baffled by Fitzwilliam's disinterest; in fact, it took most of the walk to Meryton before they finally comprehended that they simply could not hold his interest. He would answer their questions as economically as possible and then return his attention to Jane.

Finally, in a huff at their lack of success, the two girls skipped on ahead and soon caught up with and passed Elizabeth and Mr. Darcy. Their thoughts had now settled on the possibilities of meeting officers in town. Even the sadness due to the coming departure of the militia was forgotten momentarily at the prospect of immediate diversion.

Richard heaved an audible sigh of relief as Lydia and Kitty's incessant chatter faded. Jane laughed softly at his relief from the fluttering antics of her two younger sisters, and he looked over at her ruefully.

"I should be better at containing my temper, but it is hard to believe they are related to you and Miss Elizabeth."

"Lizzy would agree with you wholeheartedly. She and I have tried to restrain them from chasing after officers but, as you can see, not very successfully." She turned to look at her sister and Darcy. "That was why I was so saddened to hear of your having to leave your home. I do not know how I could possibly exist without Lizzy. I love my other sisters, of course, but Lizzy is the one who understands me. We can talk to each other about anything. I missed her dreadfully these past months."

Richard merely nodded, not wishing to pursue a topic with so many unhappy aspects. Instead, he gestured towards the pair in front of them. They had been conversing together with gradually increasing animation since escaping from Longbourn and had grown even more demonstrative since Lydia and Kitty walked ahead.

"I would wager my cousin and your sister still have some areas of disagreement, but at least they are talking. I think that is an encouraging step for Darcy though I hope you will forgive my bias in his favour. But I think they would make a good match once they get past the disagreements from their previous history and grow to know each other."

"I believe you may be correct. I do not know your cousin very well, but he is obviously quick and well-informed. And while I love Lizzy, she is much smarter than I, and sometimes I do not understand her."

Richard smiled broadly. "That is almost the exact way I would have described my relationship with Darcy, Miss Bennet. He thinks so quickly that he often meditates himself into the blackest of moods. Your sister is much more lively, and I think she would tease him out of such states. That is one of the reasons I think the two of them would do well together…eventually."

"I agree, but then I never held the same ill feelings towards Mr. Darcy that Elizabeth did. But I do wish she was not so determined to take my side against him."

Richard looked at her in some confusion, and Jane continued. "I do not want Lizzy to throw away a chance of happiness because of me. I asked her not to dwell on what he may have done to separate Mr. Bingley and me, but she will not desist."

"Darcy has already resolved to try to make amends on that subject," Richard said slowly, noting that Elizabeth was doing most of the talking while Darcy listened intently. "He has written to Bingley and informed him of his mistake."

Even though I think Bingley has already proved himself unworthy of this woman, he thought gloomily, *he will soon be in residence at Netherfield…and able to visit Jane. I sometimes think Darcy's mother did too good a job of instilling a sense of fair play and justice in both of us. I would much rather never have told him of Miss Elizabeth's demands about Bingley since I would prefer that Bingley stayed as far away from Jane Bennet as possible.*

"I was rather upset with Lizzy when she told me what she had done," Jane said, a hint of sharpness in her tone. "Mr. Bingley was the one who allowed himself to be convinced. He must share part of the blame."

Exactly, thought Richard. *Except I would make that "all of" rather than "part of."*

"But Elizabeth had already requested it of you, and you had already talked to your cousin, so there was nothing I could do," Jane said fretfully.

Richard nodded absently and said to himself, *Leaving this woman is one mistake I will NOT make.*

He walked on for several paces before he noticed that Jane was no longer beside him. He looked back to find she had stopped suddenly in the road. Her cheeks were bright red, and she stared at him with an expression he could not decipher.

"Is something the matter, Miss Bennet?" he asked in sudden concern.

Her lovely violet eyes were wide as she looked at him unblinkingly for a moment, and Richard realized he must have done something to incite this response.

"What you just said," Jane whispered.

Richard wrinkled his forehead in confusion. "What? What did I just say?"

Jane looked at him for a moment before again whispering, "About leaving. Or not leaving. What did you mean?"

Richard immediately struck his forehead in mortification. "Did I just speak aloud?" he said, and Jane nodded silently.

"I was not aware I had done so. I was deep in thought."

Jane did not say anything at first, just continued to look at him with that same inscrutable expression.

"Then you did not mean what you said?" she asked finally.

He shook his head. "I meant every word, Miss Bennet. But I had no plan of giving voice to my intentions until the time was right. The words must have slipped out while I was distracted."

"Your intentions?" Jane said weakly.

"Yes, my intentions," Richard said firmly. "You have undoubtedly talked with your sister, and I cannot believe she has not shared what I told your uncle. I had not meant to blurt out those intentions in such an unplanned way, but now, since it appears my mouth is living its own life, I cannot wait for the perfect moment. So, as I told your uncle on the first day I called on you—and as I am sure your sister has related—I have fallen deeply in love with you, no matter that we have only known each other a week. I fully intend to do whatever it takes, for as long as it takes, to convince you to accept my hand in marriage."

Jane could only stand and look at Richard while he gazed at her with a serious, meaningful regard. That was exactly what Elizabeth had told her he had said to Uncle Gardiner. She had not *disbelieved* exactly, but it had just seemed so incredible that he would make such a statement so soon after they met. It had simply not seemed possible... until this moment.

"Oh," she said eventually, and Richard smiled slightly at her simple comment.

"As I said before, I know you have been hurt, partly due to my cousin's interference and partly due to Mr. Bingley's lack of resolve. Accordingly, I had intended to wait until a future time to state my intentions openly though I knew you must have been informed of them by your sister. I understood it would sound incredible—it sounds incredible to *me*, even now—and I had planned to be more deliberate. When I said what I did about not disappearing when we were at Longbourn, I considered being less forthright. But I was distressed that my attempt to pay you a compliment had obviously reawakened the memory of disappointed hopes, so I decided it was necessary to draw a distinction between me and your previous beau. I have my faults, Miss Bennet, but lack of resolve is not one of them. And, while my mistake just now has accelerated my plan—my strategic objectives, if you will—you may depend on this. When *you* are ready, you may *refuse* my addresses, but you shall not have to worry about their being *made.*"

Again, after a few seconds, Jane uttered another, "Oh."

"Yes, Miss Bennet, 'Oh,'" Richard said wryly, and his jibe shook her out of her stunned silence.

Jane's realisation of what he had just said and her reaction to it made her suddenly turn bright red, and she lowered her eyes.

"And now, perhaps we should continue on," Richard said with more calmness than he felt. "Darcy and your sister have already passed around the next bend, and we are delinquent in our duty to provide chaperonage to such ardent suitors."

She could not help but giggle at his teasing comment. "Yes, we should, sir," she said softly. Her eyes were still downcast, but she felt the warmth of her cheeks fading as they resumed walking.

Jane kept glancing over at the tall, sturdy man walking beside her. She wanted to say something about what he had just said to her, to ask that he state his intentions in the formal manner that would constitute a proposal of marriage. But he had made his intent as clear as was possible at this time, given the fact that he recognised the need to avoid pressing her until she was ready.

She sighed inwardly, knowing that his perception had been accurate. Despite wishing Elizabeth had not demanded that Darcy inform Bingley of his mistakes, she was simultaneously aware that she was not yet fully reconciled to Mr. Bingley's sudden departure. That had to be resolved as she had already told her sister of her lingering thoughts about her former suitor. But Fitzwilliam had been so direct regarding his own desires that a part of her wanted simply to surrender herself to someone who was not afraid to make decisions. She felt the pull to yield to him and allow him to lead her along a path he chose rather than to wander the sad pathways she had trodden for this last half year.

Finally, trying to keep her tone light, she said, "Is it a family compulsion to be so direct when it comes to these matters, Colonel?"

"I would not have said so until today, Miss Bennet," Richard responded, a twinkle in his dark eyes, "but now I am more understanding of Darcy's desire to blurt out his disastrous proposal at Hunsford."

Jane glanced over at him and then away, wanting desperately to observe him at length and, at the same time, distressed at her boldness.

But he is so tall, she thought to herself. *And, while I do not share my sisters' admiration for red coats, I have to admit he does present an admirable appearance in his uniform. He is, all in all, quite…impressive.*

Her cheeks flamed red again as she felt a sudden desire to have those strong arms fold around her, pulling her into an embrace that she would not and could not resist.

Her own thoughts on this matter so fully obsessed her that she was not aware of his eyes flickering to her continually. She had no way of knowing that he had been drowning in the beauty of her wide, violet eyes during those moments they had been fixed on him. In fact, they had so affected him that he had been forced to sternly repress and control his desire to take her firmly in his arms and kiss those lovely, soft lips that had been slightly parted in astonishment.

CHAPTER 15

My lord cardinal [Richelieu], there is one fact which you seem to have entirely forgotten. God is a sure paymaster. He may not pay at the end of every week or month or year; but I charge you, remember that He pays in the end.

— Anne of Austria

Saturday, May 9, 1812
Meryton, Hertfordshire

Despite their attempt to walk faster, it was a simple fact that Jane was not nearly as accomplished a walker as Elizabeth. And while Richard could easily have increased his own pace, he could only have done so by forging ahead by himself, a thought that never crossed his mind. So it was that Elizabeth and Darcy were still about thirty yards ahead when, as they reached the outskirts of Meryton, George Wickham stepped out of a shop in company with three other officers.

Richard was close enough to hear Wickham utter an exclamation of surprise as he caught sight of the two walkers who were just passing the shop, which caused both Elizabeth and Darcy to stop in the

192

middle of the road and turn towards Wickham and his friends. Richard could see from the piping and the cut of their uniforms that all four red-coated men were lieutenants from the same regiment, undoubtedly the local militia of which he had heard. The regiment had spent the winter months in Meryton and were being sent to summer quarters on the southern coast.

But such mundane thoughts were inconsequential to the cold, savage fury that swept through him at the thought of finally being in the presence of the scoundrel who had nearly ruined the life of his dear Georgiana.

Because Wickham and his friends had stepped out in the road to face Darcy and Elizabeth, they did not see Richard and Jane, who were walking up the road behind the officers. But Richard was close enough to hear the familiar voice of Wickham. That sneering tone, which had merely been objectionable when he had known him at Pemberley as a young man, now served to increase his already smouldering anger to the seething point.

"Ho, Miss Elizabeth," Wickham called loudly. "And Mr. Darcy walking out with her. Such a fine couple, eh, lads?"

A titter of amusement went through the other three, which must have encouraged Wickham, for he stepped closer.

"I *am* disappointed, Miss Bennet, to find that you have been enticed by the Darcy fortune and consequence. I thought better of you—I really did—even though you and your sisters have no dowry and your father's estate is entailed to another. But who can account for desperation—right, lads?"

Richard saw Darcy step forward, his jaws clenched in rage, which caused Wickham's companions to step forward also. This threatening manner caused Darcy to stop since it was clear that, if he confronted Wickham physically, the other three would likely come to his aid.

"I know you would love to thrash me, Darce old man," Wickham said mockingly, "but all your fortune will not help you if you raise a hand against me and my friends. And, since you yourself have no friends hereabouts, I would recommend that you be on your way like a good little boy. After all, everyone here is well aware of all your offences against me."

"Still the bully, I see," Darcy said icily, and Richard was now close enough to see the contemptuous expression on Elizabeth's face. It was clear that whatever lingering doubts she might have held regarding Wickham had long since been dispelled and in the most thorough fashion.

Darcy's contemptuous comment had evidently infuriated Wickham; he put a hand on his sword and stepped towards Darcy, who showed no inclination to retreat but rather stepped in front of Elizabeth to shield her.

"I do not have to take that kind of abuse any longer..." Wickham began.

Richard was still ten yards behind Wickham and his fellows, but he knew he could delay no further; the situation gave every appearance of getting out of control very quickly. He knew he had to do something immediately.

"Well, if it is not Lieutenant George Wickham," he boomed in a voice shaped by innumerable shouted commands to mounted troops at drill and on the battlefield. "I never expected to come upon you in this place—and wearing the King's uniform. Will wonders never cease?"

The unexpected nature of the shout from behind them, as well as its strength, broke the concentration the four officers had trained on Darcy, and they whirled about instantly.

"Please remain here, Miss Bennet," Richard said quietly but firmly before stepping towards the four officers, all of whom were staring at him in surprise and even alarm. That alarm was undoubtedly the reason their hands had gone to their sword hilts at his unexpected comment. They had reacted to the harsh overtones of the statement even if the words themselves had been quite benign. Beyond them, further up the road, Lydia and Kitty had turned around and now stared at the scene in open-mouthed wonder and confusion.

"Where the devil did you come from, Fitzwilliam?" Wickham blustered loudly, and Richard shook his head in mock disappointment.

"Now, that is not a very respectful comment, Lieutenant, especially when speaking to a superior officer," Richard said easily as he came to a stop several yards away. His speech was calm and collected, but it ought to have woken alarms in the mind of the other men, had they the experience and wit to know they had just wandered into treacherous waters. "I have to wonder whether your training in military courtesy has been sadly neglected. Or perhaps you were just asleep when that topic was taught? But it is not at all what I would have expected from four officers such as yourselves—even if your regiment is of the militia."

While the other men now were expectant and alert, if a bit confused, Richard appeared totally relaxed, standing with his arms behind his back. Despite his size, he hardly presented a formidable picture, especially since his comments had been spoken so mildly. Wickham ought to have known better from their years together at Pemberley, but his blood was up, and he had friends to stand with him.

JANE HAD STOPPED IN THE ROADWAY AS COLONEL FITZWILLIAM had ordered her to do, responding instinctively in the manner of a maiden when her protector steps forward in her defence. She was now about ten yards from the group of red-coated men, but she clearly recognised something the militia officers had not perceived. The colonel was *not* standing in an unconcerned manner—not at all. His hands were behind his back, true, but he had turned his sword belt around so that his sheathed sabre hung behind his leg and out of sight of the four who confronted him. One of his hands—*huge* hands, Jane now realised—held the scabbard of boiled leather while the other gripped the wire-wound hilt of his heavy cavalry weapon. She felt prickling along the back of her neck and down her back.

This is NOT a trivial affair—this is REAL. There is danger, real danger, in this situation, and I have never encountered anything like it. Does Mr. Wickham see that? Does he understand his peril? Certainly, Colonel Fitzwilliam is prepared for anything. I can see it in the tension of his shoulders even if these four fools cannot. He is prepared to draw that sword instantly if events force him to do so.

The thought brought her eyes back to the hilt of his sabre, and a single glance revealed its well-worn appearance.

That is not a dress sword, she realized with a jolt of wonder. *Why did I not see it before? I have seen the swords these militia officers wear, shining and adorned with gold gilt about the hilt and scabbard. This sword is weathered and worn. Not dirty, certainly, but stained and well-used.*

She had no idea from what those stains might originate, but she did know that some stains did not wash out. Her neck prickled again as her racing mind pictured Colonel Fitzwilliam holding that sabre in one of his huge hands on the drill field or on the field of battle. Instinctively, she knew he had seen life and death situations completely foreign to her experience, all with that fearsome weapon in his massive hand, and she was deathly afraid of any impending confrontation.

However, it did not seem that the colonel was worried. Except for the tension in his shoulders—visible to her but not to Wickham and his friends—she could see no other signs of concern on his part. Instead, he seemed composed and confident despite facing possible odds of four to one.

"In fact, young sirs," Fitzwilliam continued in the same mild tones, "as I stand here, a colonel in the regular army of His Majesty, commanding a regiment of his dragoons, I am quite surprised to see four hands on the hilts of four swords, all belonging to four mere lieutenants of militia."

A number of people from the village had gathered around the tableau in the street by this time, and several shopkeepers stood just outside the doors to their shops to see what was happening.

"I have to wonder," Fitzwilliam said softly, the mildness gone from his voice as he bared his teeth in the rictus of a smile, "whether you four lads understand that, if even half an inch of sword shows out of one of your scabbards, I shall kill you, one and all, right in this street." His words fell into the stillness with the impact of heavy weights hitting the ground from a great height.

"And I have to wonder whether you pups are aware that, by merely putting your hands on your sword hilts, you have all made yourselves guilty of the capital crimes of mutiny and threatening a superior officer, His Majesty's realm now being in a state of war. I could have all four of you miserable excuses for King's officers in front of a court before the afternoon is over and dangling from a rope before tomorrow's sun is fully over the horizon."

Not a sound could be heard in the street as all those around, including the four officers in front of the colonel, realized the truth of what they had just heard. No one moved a muscle, and Fitzwilliam's grin grew wider though no less mirthless.

"Those of you who do not desire to be killed in this street had best assume a less threatening posture," he said quietly.

The four officers had never seen anything as fast as the sudden blur of the colonel's sword leaving his scabbard. Before they could take a breath, they found themselves facing their adversary, who stood easily with sabre in hand, balanced on the balls of his feet and ready for anything. The tip of his heavy, dull-gleaming sabre was downward, but the face of each of the four red-coated officers was pale as they saw death look them in the eye.

As if the drawing of that sabre had restored their minds to consciousness, all four men immediately took their hands off the hilts of their dress swords. Jane was not surprised to see that all of those swords, even Wickham's, were decorated much more lavishly than Colonel Fitzwilliam's, but not one of them wanted to pit their blades against that of the frightening figure before them.

"Ah, much better but still not adequate, lads," Fitzwilliam said coldly. "The custom we have in the King's service is that junior officers are at the position of attention when in the presence of a superior officer."

The other three officers instantly braced to attention, followed somewhat belatedly by Wickham.

"Now that the formalities are complete, Lieutenant Wickham," Fitzwilliam continued, his voice mild again, "perhaps you could tell me why I just heard a lieutenant of His Majesty's militia foully slander my cousin Darcy in public—preparatory, it seemed to me, to what looked suspiciously like the intent of administering a beating to said cousin?"

Wickham said nothing, but his eyes were dark pools of hate as he stared at Fitzwilliam.

"Nothing to say, eh? I suppose that is not too surprising since I feel certain no one here is aware that most everything you have told them about my cousin has been a complete and absolute fabrication—in short, Wickham, a series of outright, bald-faced lies."

There was a rustle and whispering among the onlookers at this statement.

"These ordinary people are probably not aware that you were given a legacy of a full thousand pounds upon the death of old Mr. Darcy, the father of my slandered cousin."

A spate of whispering broke out but was instantly hushed as Colonel Fitzwilliam continued. "Nor, I am sure, are they aware that the present Mr. Darcy made a bargain in which he gave you three thousand pounds in return for your relinquishing any claim to a living in the church. I daresay my cousin Darcy should have known better, but he was obviously indulging more in wishful thinking than cold logic."

These statements, delivered in a matter-of-fact voice that carried to the back of the now-larger crowd, brought about renewed whispering, and Wickham's expression was that of a trapped man.

"Four thousand pounds, Wickham. Many of these people will not see that much money in their whole lives, and you had it in your hands before you were four and twenty—put into your hands by the man you have foully slandered in this neighbourhood. Of course, that figure does not include the several times Darcy paid off the debts you left behind. And now, I daresay, you have none of that fortune left."

Fitzwilliam looked around at the crowd, and he could see the suspicious looks being directed towards Wickham by several of the shopkeepers. Then he looked back at the oldest of Wickham's three companions.

"You appear to be the senior, Lieutenant. What is your name?"

"Denny, sir."

"Well, Lieutenant Denny, then be aware of this. I have known George Wickham since I was twelve years old, and I have personal knowledge that what I say is true. My parents, the Earl and Countess of Matlock, are also aware of it. If, as I suspect, Lieutenant Wickham owes money to the officers of the regiment, might you have any idea how he intends to pay off those debts?"

The glance Denny gave Wickham had little of friendship in it.

"No, sir, I do not know. And yes, sir, he does have a number of debts of honour."

"Gambling debts. Well, George never was as good at any of the games of chance as he thought he was. But now, I believe you three have things you should be doing—such as taking a fellow officer before your colonel, perhaps? In fact, I shall make that an order. Do you understand me, Lieutenant Denny?"

"Yes, sir," Denny said, beads of sweat now visible on his brow.

"And I would advise you to take care as you escort him to Colonel Forster, for I give you fair warning that George Wickham is quite accomplished at running out on debts. I hope that also is clear, Lieutenant."

"Yes, sir. Completely clear."

"Very good. Well, that seems to be all. That being so, you gentlemen—if I may use the term loosely—are dismissed to your duties."

Wickham was not close to being quick enough to flee. He was still gaping at Fitzwilliam when two of his erstwhile friends had him by the elbow and were urging him down the street, followed by Denny. Jeers and catcalls sounded behind him, drowning out his sudden protests at the manner in which he was forcibly marched on his way.

Lydia and Kitty appeared not to know what to do at first, standing stock still, their heads swivelling back and forth between Colonel Fitzwilliam and their former favourite, who had just taken a drastic fall from grace. Finally, after whispering together for a moment, both girls ran up the street to catch up with the red-coated quartet.

Jane was not nearly as bewildered, and she now noted several shop-keepers exiting their shops with notes and receipts in hand as they made haste to catch up with the men surrounding Wickham.

Fitzwilliam turned back towards Jane, and he looked quite satisfied as he did some kind of complicated pirouette with his sword before smoothly sliding it into his sheath, a movement so rapid and fluid that Jane knew it must be the result of thousands of repetitions.

"Well, *that* was certainly exciting," Darcy drawled wryly as he and Elizabeth joined his cousin and the four continued their inter-rupted walk.

"Yes, it was," the colonel said, and Jane was surprised at the harshness in his voice. "And it need not have happened if you had not become so distant and reserved. You should have exposed Wickham the first time you met him here in Hertfordshire. Then he could not have cheated these shopkeepers and his fellow officers. And that does not even take into account the probability that he has been dallying with the daughters of these simple folk."

Darcy stiffened at Fitzwilliam's cold, slicing voice, his anger plain to see. "I was trying to protect Georgiana—"

"I never mentioned Georgiana when I related my story to Miss Elizabeth and her aunt, so there is no reason you could not have done similarly."

Elizabeth's eyes were on Darcy now, and Jane could read the question in them.

"Tell her, Darce," Fitzwilliam said forcefully. "If she is worth marrying, she has to be worth trusting with the Darcy family secrets. But it is best that you explain yourself. I have no idea what transpired while I was gone these five years, but the Darcy I grew up with never would have allowed things to get so bad. I suspect Miss Elizabeth would find that man much easier to understand."

Darcy looked at his cousin angrily for a moment, but as Fitzwilliam watched his cousin's anger visibly fade, his own stern visage softened accordingly. But when Darcy nodded in agreement and turned towards Elizabeth, he stopped him with an upraised hand.

"That subject should be discussed later and more privately, especially since Miss Elizabeth's sisters appear to have decided to rejoin us."

Again, Darcy nodded in agreement as the two girls came running up to them and skidded to a stop.

"Colonel Fitzwilliam, Colonel Fitzwilliam," Kitty burst out, panting breathless either from bewilderment or exercise. "What just happened?"

"Why are Mr. Wickham's friends taking him away like that?" Lydia said, glancing up the street as the quartet of militia officers turned aside from the road towards their encampment. "They did not look very friendly when we ran up to them. And they would not even stop to talk though Mr. Wickham was pleading with them to let him go."

"What you just observed, my dear ladies," Fitzwilliam said, "is justice being done."

"Justice?" Lydia said in protest. "But Mr. Wickham—"

"—is going to get what he deserves," Jane said firmly. "You saw all those shopkeepers hurrying after the officers, did you not?"

"Well, yes, but why does that matter?" Lydia cried.

"Because they just learned that your Mr. Wickham is never going to pay what he owes them. He has no money to do so, and he leaves debts wherever he goes. I watched Mr. Wickham as Colonel Fitzwilliam

201

said as much, and I recognised the truth of what he said. In fact, I have been castigating myself for being so gullible as to be taken in by Mr. Wickham's well-spoken and amiable nature. And Mr. Darcy could also give testimony to that, because the colonel says his cousin has assumed Mr. Wickham's debts several times previously."

"And I have just decided that I shall do so one more time," Darcy interrupted harshly. "My cousin Fitzwilliam is right: this is my fault because I did not make Wickham's true nature known to everyone, and I cannot allow these tradesmen to suffer because I did not do what was right."

"And Colonel Fitzwilliam revealed that Mr. Wickham is not only a gamester but never had any intention of making good his losses to his fellow officers," Jane said, looking sternly at both Lydia and Kitty.

"That is the primary reason those officers are taking Wickham to their colonel," Fitzwilliam said coldly. "An officer's honour is highly important to him even though he be only a lieutenant in a militia regiment rather than being in the regulars like me. That is why gambling debts are referred to as 'debts of honour' since an officer is honour-bound to repay them. But Wickham has no money, and I daresay he was exceedingly anxious to be away from this country town. He always has an instinct when his string is about to run out. Doubtless he would have found it necessary to flee the regiment at some point. This encounter today just accelerated that moment."

From the looks on her younger sisters' faces, Jane had her doubts that they truly comprehended much of these explanations. But she also saw their expressions change to craftiness, and she did not need to read their mind to know they had just realized that they possessed pearls of gossip they could relate to all their friends. Without even a goodbye, both girls turned and scurried off up the street.

"I suppose I should try to stop those two," Elizabeth said in mortification, "but I am feeling so drained that I simply cannot summon the willpower."

She looked at Fitzwilliam with an indecipherable expression. "I thought I was going to see blood in the street just now, Colonel. I always looked at those swords the militia officers wore as simply an adornment, somewhat like a woman's necklace."

"My cousin can be somewhat formidable," Darcy said with obvious fondness. "He usually manages to maintain a semblance of politeness and good manners to keep it concealed, but he has lived much of his life in a different world than the three of us."

"Look," Elizabeth exclaimed in amusement. "You have made him flush in embarrassment, Mr. Darcy."

Only then did she notice that Darcy had rather tentatively offered his arm preparatory to continuing their walk up the street. She looked at him for only a moment and then took it, tucking her hand around his forearm.

As they walked slowly away rather stiffly, Jane, her violet eyes shining, said softly, "Bravo, sir."

Fitzwilliam only shrugged then offered his own arm before they began to follow Darcy and Elizabeth.

"Well, someone had to do something," he said, a trifle apologetically.

Jane nodded in agreement. *But you stepped forward to do that something,* she thought, *while everyone else just stood about looking at what was happening without any idea what to do. I certainly had no idea things like this could happen, and I had no more clue than everyone else about what to do. Colonel Fitzwilliam may be fair spoken, but he is a man used to action and getting things done.*

This led to another, more disturbing thought. *And he has said he intends to make me his wife. After witnessing what just transpired, I find myself wondering how I could possibly doubt that he will fail in his intent—Mr. Bingley or no.*

With these thoughts in mind and after walking past several shops, Jane shook her head firmly. "I cannot allow you to dismiss what you did so casually. It was like nothing I have ever witnessed before, and

I suddenly understood how sheltered my life has been. That was a real situation, completely outside my experience. As Lizzy said: men could have died."

"Possibly, I suppose, but I hope I am not indulging in false modesty when I say that it was not likely. None of those four, especially Wickham, had the stomach for a fight with someone who knew what he was about. I have been in dangerous situations before, unlike any of those four, and I was confident all of them would back away if I pushed hard."

Jane looked at him a long moment. "I hope you will not take this amiss, Colonel, because it is not meant as a criticism. It is a mere statement of fact when I say you are totally unlike anyone I have known before."

Colonel Fitzwilliam's teeth gleamed as he looked down at her cheerfully. "No offence taken, Miss Bennet. Such an assessment bodes well for the ultimate success of my endeavours, I believe."

Jane felt her cheeks warm at again hearing this…this rather unsettling man…so forthrightly state his desires. She cast about desperately for a way to change the subject.

"Another thing I found fascinating," she finally said, a bit lamely, "is the way your speech seemed to change so easily. At one moment, you were taunting those men in gentlemanly tones, and then the next your speech sounded more like it came from the…the…"

"From the docks?" Fitzwilliam asked cheerfully.

"Well, I have no way of knowing, really, but it seems likely."

"I command a regiment that was originally raised in Wales, but we have added a mixture of odds and ends from just about everywhere over the years. When things get a bit exciting, I sometimes talk like old Sergeant Jones, the grizzled veteran who first taught a very, very young Lieutenant Richard Fitzwilliam how to be a soldier."

"I see," Jane said, smiling slightly as she glanced over at the sturdy man with the sun-darkened face and the gleaming teeth. Then her eyes swung back to Darcy and Elizabeth walking rather slowly ahead of them, and her smile grew warmer. It certainly seemed as if Darcy and Elizabeth were talking more easily. She certainly hoped so because she thought he could make her sister happy if Lizzy would just give him a chance.

But, as concerning as Lizzy's situation was, Jane's thoughts kept returning to the tension-packed encounter just concluded. As she had commented, the danger had seemed paramount at the time, but she was not remembering the danger right now as much as some odd little snippets about Fitzwilliam himself. For example, she had been shocked at the size of his wrists when he put his hands behind his back, one hand on his sword and the other on his scabbard. The curl of his arms had pulled the cuffs of his uniform jacket upward revealing wrists of a more impressive thickness than she had ever before seen on a man, even the blacksmith in Meryton. And then she had realized that his hands had been equally large with fingers thick and wide. She had already seen how his hand could swallow her own when he raised it to his lips previously, but seeing those fingers curl around the hilt of his sword had brought home the power in those hands.

And in his arms and shoulders also. She had previously thought his uniform coat had been badly tailored, but seeing the fabric strain as he jerked his sword from the scabbard had shown her to be in error. His uniform had been tailored to allow the necessary freedom of his shoulders, chest, and arms. She was certain she had *never* seen a gentleman with shoulders like *that*. From their first meeting, she had recognised he was a much *wider* man than his cousin was, but she had not realized the true extent of the difference until she had seen him uncoil and set himself, ready to move if Wickham or his friends had drawn their swords.

She remembered the slender hands and fingers of Mr. Bingley, which were, in her experience, the rule for most gentlemen. She supposed she ought to feel disdain that Colonel Fitzwilliam's wrists and arms were more like those of a farmer or labourer than of a gentleman, but she felt nothing of the kind. She actually felt a thrill at the thought of his large hand holding her own on the dance floor. And as for the thought of those strong fingers on her waist…or elsewhere…

An exciting tingle ran up and then down her spine, and Jane carefully looked away at the shop windows as they walked, hoping she was thus able to hide the blush she felt warming her cheeks.

CHAPTER 16

While we are free to choose our actions, we are not free to choose the consequences of our actions

— Stephen R. Covey

Saturday, May 9, 1812
Meryton, Hertfordshire

Jane and Richard caught up with Elizabeth and Darcy, who had stepped into a millinery shop where she and her sisters often shopped. Elizabeth glanced at them as they entered.

"It seemed we ought to at least pretend to look for new ribbons since it was the reason for our escape from Longbourn."

"Of course," Richard said cheerfully. "One cannot have too many ribbons, I always say."

To this, Elizabeth only arched one eyebrow in disbelief just as the shopkeeper bustled over to join them. He was well familiar with both sisters, but seeing them enter on the arms of two such fine-looking gentlemen excited both his curiosity and his instinct for a possible sale.

"Good day to ye, Miss Bennet, Miss Elizabeth. Are ye lookin' fer somethin' special today?"

"Nothing special, Mr. Milliken," Elizabeth said. "Perhaps some ribbon for Jane or even Colonel Fitzwilliam. Mr. Darcy and I are just looking."

"Of course, of course, Miss Elizabeth," Mr. Milliken said, beaming. He recognised Darcy's name, and while he had heard it disparaged by several of his customers, he cared nothing for any opinions the gentry might hold. He knew the man was wealthy and could pay his bills… unlike some he could name.

Several of the local ladies were in the shop, including Mrs. Goulding, and had looked up as the quartet entered. Mrs. Goulding's senses had pricked up as soon as she saw Darcy with Elizabeth on his arm. She had previously been introduced to him and did not need the repetition of his name to jump to the obvious—at least to her—conclusions. She immediately came over to greet Darcy, presuming on their previous introduction to assuage her curiosity. For his part, though Darcy looked somewhat uncomfortable, he greeted her politely enough, conscious of Elizabeth watching him closely. He also gave every evidence of civility as Mrs. Goulding introduced the other ladies of her acquaintance to him.

During the exchange of civilities, Darcy went so far as to introduce Richard and to volunteer the information that both of them were visiting Longbourn for the day. He himself was residing at Netherfield for the nonce and might be joined by the tenant of the estate, Mr. Bingley, during the following week. The impact of this additional titbit of news, in addition to Darcy's attendance on Elizabeth, clearly added to the visible excitement of the ladies, and they soon found reason to be on their way.

Richard watched all this closely, and though he knew none of the departing ladies, he had only to watch them hurry up the street while speaking in animated tones to draw the obvious conclusions.

"Well, they do say gossip is the only news that spreads faster than an express post, Darce," he said cheerfully. "The fact that you have been seen escorting Miss Elizabeth around Meryton—and will be staying at Netherfield for a time—will soon be known far and wide."

Darcy only shrugged at this. He had been aware of that his would likely happen before he made his comments, but he also knew such gossip could not hurt his desired intention. Elizabeth, however, had been watching Darcy closely to detect whether he would display his usual reserve and arrogance and had not anticipated the actions of Mrs. Goulding and her friends. Now she did so, and a look of consternation came and went on her face as she struggled to control her expression.

"I am very much afraid," Richard continued blandly, "that as soon as this news is well established, an expectation will arise throughout the neighbourhood that an understanding has been reached between you and Miss Elizabeth. That is the way gossip spreads. Soon it will bear little resemblance to fact but will be accepted as proven beyond a doubt by all who hear it."

"You are likely correct," Darcy said with what Richard recognised as blandness equal to his own. He heard Jane stifle a laugh beside him as a renewed look of alarm appeared on her sister's face in response to what Richard had said while the slow smile on Darcy's face grew into a grin of satisfaction. Elizabeth tried to glare reproachfully at Richard as she grasped the full impact of what had just happened, but he only returned her glare with a smug smile. Jane's smothered laughter changed to open delight as different expressions flickered across her sister's face as she was forced to desist from her unsuccessful attempt to intimidate either gentleman.

"Shall we continue with our shopping, Miss Elizabeth?" Darcy asked, offering his arm, and Elizabeth looked at it for a moment as if it was a source of infection, but she finally shrugged and accepted it with a rueful smile.

"Do not think this changes anything, Mr. Darcy," she said with an attempt at severity.

"Of course not. I would not dare such a presumption," he said in a calm voice, but his eyes danced with amusement.

"There is a peculiar satiric light in your eyes, sir."

"Nonsense—Richard used to say such a satiric light in my eyes was more usual than peculiar. Perhaps he may one day be able to say the same again."

Elizabeth looked at him rather warily, not knowing whether he was being serious. "Perhaps," she said finally before they moved off to look at a table of hats.

Jane laughed softly again, watching her sister with an affectionate smile. "It is seldom that anyone gets the better of Lizzy in such a verbal exchange."

"I am well aware of that," said Richard, "and I plan to long savour this moment."

Jane looked at his satisfied smile quizzically, but he only smiled more broadly and offered his arm.

I DO plan on remembering and savouring the moment, he thought smugly, *but I plan to do so at the expense of a future sister, not at the expense of a mere acquaintance.*

BY THE TIME THEIR PARTY FINISHED WALKING ALONG THE SHOP fronts and reached the edge of Meryton, Lydia and Kitty had not reappeared from their errand to spread gossip while it was still fresh. Though irritated by such behaviour, Elizabeth and Jane could only shrug; the two girls knew the way back to Longbourn as well as they did, and the embarrassment of having such a pair of foolish sisters was a familiar burden. In any case, neither Darcy nor Richard seemed to notice, and their conversation was much more cheerful and open than when they walked to town. As they arrived at Longbourn, Mrs. Bennet was just returning in the carriage while the housekeeper, Mrs. Hill, waited for her at the front door.

"Lizzy! Lizzy!" Mrs. Bennet exclaimed as she stepped down from the carriage. "I have just visited with my sister, and she is absolutely exhilarated by the wonderful news I brought her. Please, Mr. Darcy, come into our front room. Hill! We need tea and cakes immediately in the front room."

"At once, ma'am," Hill said before turning away into the house.

"What news are you talking of, Mama?" Elizabeth asked in trepidation as all of them walked into the house.

"Why, that you have had a gentleman caller, Lizzy! Whatever other news would there be?"

Elizabeth rolled her eyes in mortification at her mother's dual lack of propriety—first, in aiding in the spread of even more gossip and, second, of boasting of it in front of Darcy.

However, when she cast a swift glance his way, Elizabeth did not see the revulsion on Darcy's face she had expected at this new evidence of her mother's lack of proper manners. Instead, he was having difficulty suppressing a smile, and Elizabeth suddenly apprehended that his lack of offence was due to her mother unwittingly aiding his cause by thwarting her daughter's intention to keep him at arm's length.

Frustrated in her wish to remain aloof and detached, Elizabeth could not, however, repress her playfulness. So, when her mother turned away and could not see her, she gave in to temptation and stuck her tongue out at Darcy. She was disappointed that it not only did not offend him but seemed to increase his amusement. His only difficulty appeared to be that he was struggling to conceal his smile.

Shortly after they took their seats, Mr. Bennet came into the parlour. He was holding Richard's helmet, looking at it in confusion.

"Mrs. Bennet, do you have any idea about the source of this incredible headpiece?"

He was startled as he looked up and saw the visitors. "Oh, excuse me, gentlemen," he said in embarrassment as both Darcy and Richard stood. "I was not aware we had visitors."

"Father, you remember Mr. Darcy, do you not?" Elizabeth said, remembering her manners.

"Oh, certainly, certainly. Ah, yes...that is, pleased to see you,

Mr. Darcy. Ah…welcome to Longbourn."

"And this is his cousin Colonel Fitzwilliam, a son of the Earl of Matlock."

"And you also, sir…welcome, welcome."

"Thank you, sir. And that incredible headpiece is indeed mine. Incredibly cumbersome it is, too, and not even very useful in action. But, as you know, tradition often rules in the military."

Mr. Bennet's interest in the silver helmet with black horsehair aided in his recovery of at least a little of his composure. "Dragoon helmet, is it not?"

"It is, sir. Sixth Dragoons."

"Colonel, eh?" he said, peering more closely at Fitzwilliam. "I apologize for my impertinence, but I have grown accustomed to the shakos worn by the militia who have been quartering here for the winter. When I saw this helmet, my curiosity got the better of me. Sixth Dragoons, you say? My memory may be false, but I remember reading they were in Egypt some years back."

"That is correct, sir—Egypt and then later Italy and Sicily."

Mrs. Bennet had been growing more and more bored by this useless discussion, and she burst out, "Mr. Bennet! You will not believe what I have just learned from my sister. She is now convinced that Mr. Bingley will soon return to Netherfield. Will that not be a wonderful thing for our Jane?"

Mr. Bennet was not pleased to have his conversation interrupted, nor was he overly pleased by what his wife said. He could see that Darcy's cousin was seated next to Jane, and he could also see that his eldest daughter was embarrassed by her mother's indiscreet enthusiasm over Bingley. He had no idea how it had come about, but it was blindingly obvious that this officer had a personal interest in his eldest daughter and she in him. In exasperation, he wondered how his wife could not have seen it.

"That is a subject for later discussion, Mrs. Bennet," he said, attempting to restrain his irritation. "For now, you have guests who require your attendance. Have you asked them to dine with us? Well, please do so. Now, I must return to my…study. I have some…papers that need seeing to. Mr. Darcy, Colonel Fitzwilliam. I hope to talk with you later."

Soon after Mr. Bennet left, his two younger daughters made their reappearance with the front door slamming as usual before both girls burst into the room.

"Mama, you will never believe what has happened in town," Lydia cried.

"It is Mr. Wickham, Mama," added Kitty. "He has been arrested."

"Yes, he has. Mr. Denny told me Colonel Forster ordered him arrested and is sending to the War Office to have officers sent down for a…a…court-manual."

"Court-*martial*, Lydia," Elizabeth said irritably. "Not court-manual."

"Mr. Wickham?" cried Mrs. Bennet. "Why, whatever for?"

"Mr. Wickham and his friends almost started a sword fight right in the streets," Lydia said. "We saw that, and then his friends took him off to Colonel Forster. But Mr. Denny says that is not the reason he was arrested. It is because of all the money he owes the other officers as well as shopkeepers in town. Denny said Wickham has no money and cannot pay."

"Yes, that is what they were saying, Mama," Kitty agreed. "All the officers were so excited about that as well as the fight Mr. Wickham almost had in the street with Colonel Fitzwilliam. The colonel pulled his sword, but Mr. Wickham would have certainly won if they had fought. But Mr. Denny and his other friends pulled him away to see Colonel Forster."

"Mr. Denny said something about 'debts of honour,' whatever those are," Lydia said, pouting, "but I hardly listened when he tried to explain because all I could think of was poor Mr. Wickham being treated so unfairly."

Elizabeth had been quite disturbed during the entire walk to Meryton—from worry over Colonel Fitzwilliam and Jane to Mr. Darcy's fumbling attempts at conversation, culminating in the alarming confrontation between Wickham and Colonel Fitzwilliam. This last comment was so outrageous and yet so typical of the extreme foolish ignorance of her younger sisters that her self-control was shattered, and a surge of rage swept through her. She instantly sprang to her feet in mortification and fury, taking several steps forward to confront her youngest sisters with her hands clenched into fists at her side.

"You are two of the most foolish ninnies I have ever seen," she cried, her voice harsh. "Do you not realize that Mr. Wickham almost *died* today? If he had so much as reached for his sword, he would have died immediately, right before your eyes. Colonel Fitzwilliam is a *real* soldier! He is not a fake, pretend officer like those you two have been swooning over, and the two of you are too witless to see what is so indisputable."

"That is not true—" Lydia burst out, but Elizabeth's outrage was too great, and she overrode Lydia brutally in a way she had never before done.

"It *is* true," she exclaimed, cutting off her sister and leaving her with her mouth open in shock. "What you foolish children witnessed today was not an amusing game put on for your enjoyment. It was *real*. Mr. Wickham is lucky that he was merely taken to his colonel instead of having his blood soak into the dirt of the street."

"But it was not fair," Kitty wailed, horrified at being so sternly put in her place before visitors, one of whom wore a red coat.

"Did you not see most of the shopkeepers running after Mr. Wickham, waving their promissory notes in the air? Mr. Wickham owed money he could not pay, and people are put in jail if they cannot pay their debts—debtor's prison. And he also owed money to his fellow officers, which is even worse. Ask Colonel Fitzwilliam."

The look she gave both Darcy and Fitzwilliam was one of anguished chagrin, but she was surprised that neither showed any condemnation of her outburst. Instead, they were smiling at each other in satisfaction.

"Court-martial," Darcy said with a slow, hungry smile.

"And if this colonel is sending to the War Office for a board of officers, he is already measuring Wickham for a jail cell," Richard responded with a thin smile of his own.

"Oh, how wonderful. Excellent."

"Indeed, Darce. Wonderful indeed."

"I do not understand," Kitty said in confusion.

"That is because you are too silly to comprehend what took place before your very eyes," Elizabeth said. "We have been completely wrong about Mr. Wickham, Mama. *I* have been completely wrong. He is a scoundrel beyond measure."

"And just how could you know that, Lizzy?" asked Lydia angrily.

"Foolish girl! Did you not listen to what Colonel Fitzwilliam said in Meryton? He has known Mr. Wickham for most of his life, Mama, and he told all the townspeople how Mr. Wickham has wasted *thousands* of pounds that he got from the Darcy family—"

"Four thousand pounds," Richard said mildly, the corners of his mouth still curled into a smile. Elizabeth could see he was taking pleasure in seeing her defend his cousin, but she could do nothing else in this situation.

"—and the colonel related how Mr. Wickham always runs up debts and then vanishes, leaving Mr. Darcy to make those debts good because his father had such an attachment to Mr. Wickham. It made me ashamed, thoroughly ashamed, for every kind word I ever said about Mr. Wickham. I know now that everything I said was foolish and childish and misinformed and...just terrible.

And, she thought, as she finally sat down, *there is that cryptic comment the colonel made about Darcy's sister. What did he mean by that? What did Wickham do to her?*

There was a strained silence for a few minutes, and even Kitty and

Lydia belatedly appeared to realize the impropriety of what they had said. Finally, Richard cleared his throat and changed the subject.

"Perhaps I might ask for some enlightenment about this assembly you mentioned on our walk, Miss Elizabeth?"

Even Mrs. Bennet was glad to discuss another subject, and the conversation soon moved on to less embarrassing topics, though it was some time before the party began to feel more cheerful.

Kitty and Lydia, of course, quickly found such bland subjects completely without interest, but not wishing to be further admonished so severely by their sister, they settled for quietly excusing themselves from the room.

THE TWO VISITORS HAD TO DEPART SHORTLY AFTER DINNER SINCE the colonel needed to return to London. Jane and Elizabeth accompanied them outside while their mounts were brought to the front door. Elizabeth saw her mother watching Darcy and her from the parlour window with a satisfied expression, but Mrs. Bennet gave no indication of even being aware of Jane and Fitzwilliam standing together.

"It was thoughtful of you to call on us, Mr. Darcy," Elizabeth said, as he took the reins from the stable boy.

"Thank you for the opportunity to do so."

Elizabeth coloured at the sincerity infusing his simple statement. "It was…enlightening."

"Might I take it from your comment that a return visit might be possible?"

Elizabeth looked up at him seriously for a moment. "Yes, Mr. Darcy, you may," she said softly.

"Thank you." If there was the slightest catch in his throat, Elizabeth gave no sign of noticing it, only nodding gravely.

"For my part, my duties make it impossible for me to return until Saturday next," Richard said to Jane. "I wish it were otherwise, but we have many new lads and also many replacement mounts. All have to be trained and exercised together before the regiment can be deemed fit for action again. The squadrons could train independently to this point, but now the regiment needs to relearn how to work together as a whole. I shall not be free until after Saturday Morning Parade."

"I quite understand," Jane said, "though I confess I feel a bit chilled by the way you casually mention going to war. Until today, I had not truly comprehended just how different is the kind of life you have led compared to my own life. So much more…dangerous."

This last statement was made so softly that only Richard heard her, and he responded with a shrug. "Do not disparage the part played by the female half of our island race. You are the reason people like me do what we do. Otherwise, we soldiers should go mad if there was nothing to our lives but war and death. You keep us sane."

He visibly shook himself and smiled broadly. "But let that be an end of morbid thoughts for today. My thoughts are going to be about dancing, and I shall return in good time for this assembly. It has been years since I danced, but I plan to practice assiduously in the hope of not embarrassing myself."

"I am sure you will do quite well, Colonel, and I shall save two sets for you."

Elizabeth noted the expressions that flickered across Richard and Jane's faces, and she felt a sinking sensation in her stomach. Fitzwilliam was obviously cheered by Jane's simple affirmation of her interest, but the oblique reference to the sets she might be saving for *others* could not help but provide a measure of anxiety for both of them.

Why did I demand that Mr. Darcy inform Mr. Bingley of what he did to separate Jane and his friend? she thought. *I wanted to do what was best for Jane since Mr. Bingley had been the cause of the heartache that afflicted her for so many months. I wanted her to be able to make a choice, but now I wonder whether I am not doing exactly as Colonel Fitzwilliam said: interfering in Jane's life much as Mr. Darcy did when he convinced his friend to stay in town and not return. Am I making everything worse?*

Almost as if both Jane and the colonel were reading her mind, they gave her a single quick but searching look, and she wanted to blurt out that she was just trying to protect her sister. But she could not do that, and she was grateful when they looked back at each other.

Richard nodded solemnly. "I believe it is time that we were on our way, Darcy," he said. "I have to ride to London, and the ladies need to get out of this cool spring air before they catch a chill."

Easily, he swung himself up into the saddle. "So I shall bid you farewell, Miss Bennet, until Saturday."

"Goodbye, Colonel Fitzwilliam," Jane called. And Elizabeth's feeling of discomfort returned because she could see that Jane wished she could say more.

CHAPTER 17

If I am not worth the wooing, I am surely not worth the winning.

— Henry Wadsworth Longfellow

Saturday, May 9, 1812
Longbourn, Hertfordshire

"A re you sure you have to ride back to camp tonight?" Darcy asked. "Can you not spend the night at the inn in Meryton? Or you could stay at Netherfield. I assure you Bingley would not mind even if he did show up unexpectedly."

"Possibly not, if he is as amiable as you describe him, but I would feel deucedly awkward to be staying at his house when I am trying my best to secure Miss Bennet's hand for myself. As for your first question, I really should ride back to camp tonight. I have many things to do, starting early in the morning. It will be a busy week if I am to make it back here for that assembly."

"I have no idea whether Bingley still has an interest in Miss Bennet. Even if he does and actually comes to Netherfield, it may make no difference. In fact, from the way she looked at you today, I wonder whether she may have been more indifferent towards Bingley than her sister believes."

"I am afraid I have to disagree with you on that point. I definitely perceived sadness in her, especially when I first met her. I very much hope I have lifted some of that sadness, and what you say brings me cheer. But, when I first met her, she did grieve for something she believed she had lost—of that I am certain."

Darcy was silent for a few moments as he visibly digested what Richard said. At last, he heaved a sigh. "If you are correct, then I made a grievous mistake as Elizabeth charged. But she did not look today as if she is troubled by what she may have lost. And she has to be moved by your blatant imitation of a man totally smitten by love. It is so overwhelming that I am sometimes moved to nausea."

"Now, now, no hard feelings, old sport. Besides, I thought you were making real progress with Miss Elizabeth today."

"Progress, yes, and for that I am grateful. But it was painful—very painful. I made the point that certain of her judgments were based on misconceptions, and we resolved some of those. But often I was forced to admit her assessments were all too accurate—painfully so."

"Well, when a man falls into bad habits, it is usually uncomfortable to change. But I trust you think the effort worthwhile?"

"Oh, without doubt. It may be painful, but I would rather suffer at the hands of Elizabeth Bennet than sit in my study, brooding and dulling my despair with brandy."

"Then it was a good day for both of us. And with the cheerful thought of Wickham sitting under guard and possibly in irons, I shall bid you good night and be on my way."

"Take care. I would not think a single brigand would pose a threat, but sometimes jackals hunt in packs."

"Of that I am aware, and I have a brace of loaded pistols in my saddlebags and another pair for my boots. Two of them are the ones you gave me, the ones with primers that never misfire."

"Be watchful then. I shall see you at the assembly."

ELIZABETH OPENED HER DOOR TO SEE WHAT WAS DELAYING JANE, only to find her sister coming to their room, towelling the last of the moisture from her hair as she returned from bathing. Elizabeth put a finger to her lips and pointed inside the room, and Jane nodded her understanding. Neither of them said anything until Elizabeth had closed and bolted the door.

"For what we have to discuss, the hallway is not the place to speak," Elizabeth said. "Mary has already retired to her room next door, which will prevent Lydia from trying to eavesdrop on our conversation. I have discovered her several times sneaking into Mary's room so she could listen in on our conversations. She uses a wine glass pressed against the wall and puts her ear to the stem."

"Really?" Jane asked in surprise.

"Really. I tried it myself, and it works. I was able to listen to Kitty and Lydia giggle and carry on as if I was concealed in the closet."

"I have never heard of such a thing."

"Nor had I, and I have no idea where *she* learned it. In fact, I am probably better off not knowing how she came by this particular piece of mischief."

"No doubt." Jane sat on her bed, making herself comfortable with her back against the wall while Elizabeth sat as she usually did, on the foot of her bed with her legs tucked underneath her. "So tell me, sister dear, what did you think of the day? Besides it being quite enlightening, that is."

"Eavesdropper," Elizabeth said in challenge, but she smiled as she said it. Then she sobered. "It truly was a day of discoveries for Mr. Darcy and for me. I can say this without fear of contradiction: he is a very *complex* man."

"You are not exactly a simple person. As much as I love you, many times I do not understand you."

Elizabeth looked at Jane in wonder. "You know—Mr. Darcy said that Colonel Fitzwilliam often says the same about him. His Christian name is Richard, by the way. I am not sure whether you knew that."

"Richard," Jane said, rolling the sound on her tongue. "I thought that was his name, but it is good to get it confirmed. It is a name that fits him quite well. I cannot think of him with an unusual type of name. He is so straightforward that he should have a straightforward name."

"He should, should he?" Elizabeth said, eyeing Jane appraisingly.

"No, no, Lizzy. Do not attempt to change the subject. Continue with what you were saying about Mr. Darcy."

Elizabeth looked at her for a moment before shrugging. "He really does not like to talk about himself. He had to exert himself to avoid changing the subject whenever he had to talk of anything of a personal nature. He even admitted as much. I think that is one of the bad habits the colonel spoke of."

Jane nodded, and Elizabeth continued, "He did not know how to begin the conversation, so I suggested we return to the time we first met and continue from there. It seems that my early perceptions and his own were wildly different—and both of us may have been only partly right. For example, I mentioned that Sir William Lucas spends all his time being civil to everyone. From Mr. Darcy's view, he concedes that Sir William probably means well, but he also related that Sir William asked whether he had a house in town and whether he often danced at St. James's. From Mr. Darcy's point of view, he thought the questions rather intrusive from a person with whom he was only casually acquainted."

"That does seem true, I suppose."

"I found myself agreeing, especially when Mr. Darcy talked about his first impression on entering the assembly. He said he must have heard 'ten thousand a year' being whispered back and forth at least half a dozen times. I remember the colonel describing Mr. Darcy's being pursued by so many young ladies and their mothers, and I can understand his distaste at finding that his fortune was the first thing everyone knew of him. Jane, do you remember Mama saying that he sat next to Mrs. Long for half an hour without speaking? Well, Mr. Darcy looked rather hurt when I mentioned that to him. He said he had considered Mrs. Long to be the most polite person he met all night. He thought she obviously did not have anything pressing to say and, except for a single question about Netherfield, maintained a polite silence, leaving him to his thoughts."

"Oh my. That *is* another way of looking at it, I suppose."

"But he was unable to refute a number of points I brought up. For example, I told him about overhearing him say I was 'tolerable but not handsome enough to tempt' him and he could not 'give consequence to young ladies who are slighted by other men.'"

"Oh my. So what was his reply to that?"

Elizabeth shrugged. "I wanted to see what he could possibly have to say about it since it quite fixed my opinion of him from our very first meeting. But he absolutely blanched with horror when I repeated it. Then he told me he really had not meant it, he never dreamed I had heard it, and he had only said it because he was desperate to get Bingley to cease his efforts to get him to dance. But he did not try to evade his responsibility. 'I said it,' he told me, 'and it was inexcusable to have done so.' Then he apologized at length and stated he could only ask for a chance to prove he was not in the habit of making such cruel and thoughtless statements."

"And are you inclined to give him that opportunity?"

"Oh, I suppose I must after having so neatly mouse-trapped myself," Elizabeth said ruefully.

"And that was before Mama and Aunt Philips had begun to spread the news about Mr. Darcy calling on you today. Added to what Mrs. Goulding will be telling everyone, you and Mr. Darcy will be a big topic of conversation for the next week, if not longer."

"You are probably right," Elizabeth agreed gloomily. But, after only a few seconds, she shrugged. "Well, there is nothing to be done about it. But I am not happy that our mother only seemed to notice Mr. Darcy and paid no attention to your Richard."

"It was not that bad, Lizzy. She did seem pleased that he visited."

"But only because of the prestige of his being an earl's son. I cannot believe she is not aware of his interest in you, but she ignores it if she does. The only thing she cares about is Mr. Bingley's return to Netherfield. Oh, I wish I had kept my lips sealed."

To that, Jane only shrugged. "You only wished to do what was best for me. Do not trouble yourself about it. Colonel...that is, Richard... does not seem overly worried about what you did."

"Yes, he does not lack for confidence, does he? I daresay he could just walk right through a brick wall if it got in his way, leaving a very large hole and a pile of masonry."

Both sisters shared a soft laugh at their mental image of the red-coated Fitzwilliam dusting the brick dust off his uniform before continuing on his way. After a few moments, Elizabeth added, "Mr. Darcy told me that we were correct in our guess about the things Colonel Fitzwilliam would not say about Mr. Wickham. The man tried to get Mr. Darcy's sister to elope with him last summer when she was only fifteen."

"Fifteen? That is horrible."

"Mr. Darcy said it was only luck that allowed him to foil the plot. Evidently, Wickham and his sister's companion conspired after her fortune of thirty thousand pounds."

"My goodness."

"Indeed. That is a sum to truly excite a scoundrel like Wickham, and it would exact considerable revenge on Mr. Darcy. Wickham evidently blames Mr. Darcy for his own lack of success in life."

"So what do you think, Lizzy? It certainly seemed as though you and Mr. Darcy were more comfortable after that terrible business in Meryton."

"Was that not the most terrifying thing you have ever seen? When I saw how fast the colonel pulled out his sword and stood ready and poised to strike, he looked truly dangerous—deadly, to be honest. I suspect he was somewhat disappointed when Wickham would not pull his own sword. But, yes—Mr. Darcy and I did get on better after that. Though I wished I had brought my parasol when Colonel Fitzwilliam made the remark about everybody in the neighbourhood soon believing that Mr. Darcy and I had an 'understanding.' When Mr. Darcy gave him that huge, satisfied grin, I would have poked the colonel in the side."

"Oh, that was truly delightful, Lizzy. Richard said he will treasure the memory always."

"'Always,' is it? Perhaps I shall have to think up something special for Colonel Fitzwilliam. But now let us talk about you, Jane—you and your Richard."

Jane blushed at her sister's remark, but she knew better than to try to evade Elizabeth when she was seriously interested in finding out about something or other. So she said simply, "Richard said he plans to make me an offer of marriage sooner or later, when I am settled about Mr. Bingley. He said I might refuse it, but I did not have to worry about it being made."

"Oh my," breathed Elizabeth, "that *is* direct. I had thought he would wait longer."

"I believe he intended to, but he was thinking to himself and absent-mindedly spoke without realising it."

"What did he say?"

"Well, he was not aware he had spoken aloud when he said leaving me was one mistake *he* would never make. I stopped suddenly, catching him by surprise, and only when I demanded to know what he meant did he understand that he had put his thoughts into words. It was then that he explained himself more fully, saying he would be making his 'assurances' sooner or later."

"Which is much the same as he told our uncle Gardiner. And they spoke only the day after he met you. Your Richard is not a man who suffers from an indecisive nature."

"Unlike Mr. Bingley," Jane said quietly.

"Me and my mouth," Elizabeth said, wincing at the thought.

"No, I think it is best this way. It may not be exactly as you considered it, but I do need to resolve the question about Mr. Bingley before I can finally understand what I truly feel about Colonel Fitzwilliam. I have avoided thinking about Mr. Bingley for so long that I was surprised to find myself remembering so many pleasant things about him. If he does come down and shows any interest in me, I shall have some serious thinking to do."

"How do you *think* you feel about the two men?"

Jane looked at Elizabeth calmly. "About Mr. Bingley? I simply do not know. If he does not come, that is an answer in itself. If he does come, I shall have to see what happens."

She was silent for a few moments, her eyes focused somewhere else before she finally said, "As for Colonel Fitzwilliam, I am definitely attracted to him. I might easily find myself in love with him at some point though I cannot be certain that my feelings are that strong at the present moment. Of course, it is difficult to sort everything out when he makes it so crystal clear that *he* loves *me*. That is…breathtaking."

"Really," Elizabeth said softly.

"Really. But I do need to settle my mind about Mr. Bingley. Did I truly love him earlier? If so, why am I now attracted to Richard? Or was it just that Mr. Bingley was so amiable and charming and gentle that he touched my heart? I do not know, but perhaps, if I do see him again, I may be able to find some answers. But is Aunt Philips right about it being definite that he will soon be at Netherfield?"

"I am sorry to say that our dear aunt has not a clue, Jane. As Mr. Darcy explained: it is impossible to know for certain since his coach would travel faster than an express rider if Bingley could afford the expense of changing horses often. But his own estimate is that the earliest he could arrive is late tomorrow or possibly Monday."

After a moment's thought, Elizabeth said wryly, "Mr. Darcy said he has been visiting relatives in Scarborough with his two sisters, so I suppose they may also arrive when he does. You ought to think that through, remembering the way Miss Bingley deceived you, so that you can meet her calmly and dispassionately."

"If they have learned of Mr. Darcy's intentions towards you, they might want to stay away."

"Likely so, but only time will tell. However, Mr. Darcy did ask whether I would consent to meet his sister. It appears she overheard him and the colonel engaged in some rather intense conversation concerning the two of us, and Miss Darcy demanded to know what was being discussed. So Mr. Darcy told her everything, and now she is wild to meet me. But, while he can now allow her to come since Mr. Wickham has been arrested, he will not send for her unless I agree."

"That shows significant consideration for your wishes, Lizzy."

"Yes, I know. And it is an honour to have his sister desiring so much to meet me, but I would rather she did not. I believe if I do agree to meet her, I shall have passed the point beyond which there will truly be no going back."

"Lizzy, you ninny. Richard is right: you are already *past* that point, even if you struggle against the realisation." Jane sobered suddenly. "And so, possibly, am I. I remember Mr. Bingley, but it is hard to see him when I think of Richard. It is almost like my memory of Mr. Bingley is pale and faded, while Richard is large and vibrant and colourful."

"Colourful, certainly," Elizabeth said with a smile. "Well, the coming week should be quite entertaining."

"For you, perhaps, but I am not so sure about myself. Mr. Bingley may arrive or he may not, and Richard cannot visit until the assembly. To borrow a phrase from our dear mother, I feel as if I might go distracted!"

Both sisters laughed delightedly at the mental image Jane had painted. They shared a quick embrace, and Elizabeth gave Jane a kiss on her forehead before they got in their beds and blew out the candles.

CHAPTER 18

Love is a sweet tyranny, because the lover endureth his torments willingly.

— Proverb

Sunday, May 10, 1812
Longbourn, Hertfordshire

I t took only until the next morning for Elizabeth to realize how close to the mark Jane had been when she said matters were probably past the point of no return for her and Mr. Darcy. When she walked to church with her family, Mr. Darcy stood waiting at the door of the chapel. Elizabeth was fairly certain he had only been lingering to wish them all a good morning, but her mother was quick to nudge Elizabeth close so that Darcy could offer his arm. She had no choice but to take it, with the result that he then escorted Elizabeth inside. She indicated the pew where she and her family usually sat, and Darcy appeared ready to hand her into the pew and sit in the empty pew just behind. However, Mrs. Bennet was too quick for him and ushered her four other daughters into that empty pew. That left Mr. Bennet and Mr. Darcy standing in the aisle, looking at each other as they realized they had been outmanoeuvred. Despite her lack of sensibility in many other areas, Mrs. Bennet possessed a highly refined sense of cunning in the hunt for a husband for one of her brood.

The two men could only shrug and accept the accomplished fact, and Darcy took the seat beside Elizabeth while Mr. Bennet sat beside his wife. Elizabeth's cheeks were pink and her eyes downcast as Darcy sat stiffly beside her, and she was certain everyone in the chapel must be looking at her and jumping straight to an obvious, if premature, conclusion.

Even when she was young, Elizabeth had never resisted attending religious services, and she had always enjoyed the singing that was part of it. While she was singing a hymn, she had always felt a little closer to her Lord and Maker, and the fact that she was the possessor of a lovely soprano singing voice aided her enjoyment. She was, however, rather surprised to find Mr. Darcy adding a strong, melodious baritone to join her and the rest of the congregation. In addition, he appeared to know the words to the hymns by heart and had no more need to consult his prayer book than she did.

After the service concluded, Mrs. Bennet was quick to tender an invitation to Darcy to dine with them, and it was accepted with similar rapidity. In this matter, his objectives and Mrs. Bennet's were identical, and he responded to Elizabeth's stern look with a smile of such absolute innocence that she could not be angry with him for long. Instead, she made the best of the situation when they returned to Longbourn by announcing her intention to take a walk after dinner and inviting Darcy to accompany her. He was as quick to accept this invitation as he had accepted the previous one.

Sunday, May 10, 1812
Netherfield, Hertfordshire

DARCY WAS SITTING IN THE FRONT PARLOUR READING A BOOK when he heard the sound of horses' hooves and iron-shod wheels on gravel. As he looked out the window, the low-lying sun illuminated Charles Bingley's unbelievably mud-spattered carriage coming to a halt in front of the entrance to Netherfield. He immediately marked the place in his book and stood, pulling his coat down in place before going to the front door and stepping outside.

Bingley was just stepping down from the carriage, and he looked up cheerfully at Darcy's hail of greeting even as he moved somewhat gingerly.

"You look a little stiff and sore, old friend," Darcy said, bounding down the steps to grasp Bingley's hand. "Hard trip?"

"Quite," Bingley said with a wry smile and a wave of his hand at his carriage and the equally mud-spattered horses. "We didn't get beyond the rain until yesterday, and the roads are a mess. Not as bad as in previous years, of course, but bad enough."

"Well, come inside and warm your bones. Ah, here come the servants to collect the luggage. Uh…it does not appear that your sisters accompanied you."

"No, and that is a story in and of itself, Darcy. It happened like this after I received your express on Thursday…"

Darcy had made certain that a good, solid meal would be ready for his friend if he arrived since he suspected Bingley would be famished after a hard day of travelling. Conversation since the two of them sat down at the small table had been scant as his estimate had proven correct, and Bingley had rather single-mindedly applied himself to the meat, potatoes, and bread set before him.

Now Bingley sat back with a sigh and patted his lips with a napkin. "Now I feel at least half-human again. After a long, hot soak in the tub and a good night's sleep in a good bed, I shall feel completely restored.'

"The housekeeper has made sure there is all the hot water you would need whenever you are ready," Darcy said.

"Excellent." But Bingley did not spring up to rush to his room as

Darcy expected and instead looked at him speculatively.

"First, Darcy, I think we need to speak of the reason I made this hasty and unplanned journey. Your express explained much, but I still have a multitude of questions."

"Which I shall answer to the best of my ability. But first, I need to make my apologies for having dared to give you such mistaken opinions regarding you and Miss Bennet. It was arrogant of me to do so, and I am heartily sorry."

"Your apology is all well and good though I am not sure you have to seek forgiveness for all that much. After all, you did it for the best of reasons, trying to take care of me as you have so often done. But it is past astonishing that Miss Elizabeth came to tell you so much private information about her sister. You say you are interested in her and have been even before we departed Hertfordshire? Romantically so? I never had a hint of it!"

"I think Caroline was the only one who did, and it was likely her jealousy that inspired her guesses. I suppose you remember her jests about my admiration of a pair of 'fine eyes'?"

"I do remember, but I had no idea what she was talking about. I simply ignored her as I usually do, especially when she was in one of her 'stalking' moods. That is something for which I ought to apologize. I simply could not get her to see reason and desist from her pursuit of you."

Darcy waved off the apology. "It is just the way she is. We shall probably never know what drove her to waste so much time on a forlorn quest, but it caused me no real pain. But yes, I am interested—romantically interested—in Elizabeth Bennet. So much so that I made her a rather badly delivered proposal of marriage, which she rejected. It was when she charged me with ruining the chance for happiness of her sister that I had the first intimations of my mistakes in advising you as I did."

He paused for a moment, collecting his thoughts.

"It was when she went on to accuse me of having similarly thwarted the hopes of George Wickham that my cousin Fitzwilliam inserted himself into the affair. As you know, he and I share the guardianship of my sister, and in addition to having taken advantage of my family to the tune of some thousands of pounds over the years, Wickham also contrived..."

Bingley listened to Darcy's recitation of the whole history of Wickham's involvement with the Darcy family with an open mouth and a sense of shock at his friend openly speaking of so many private family affairs to him. It was unprecedented in his experience since Darcy had always been so reserved and private about such things, but he believed this sudden loss of reticence was due to what it had almost cost his friend. Now Darcy seemed determined to lay out—at least to those close to him—the unknown facts that had been driving him for so long.

"It is unbelievable that you were able to thwart Wickham at Ramsgate," he said finally, shaking his head in dismay at the hairsbreadth closeness by which utter disaster had been avoided. "I remember how shaken you seemed when you brought Georgiana back to town, but you obviously did not wish to discuss the subject, so I did not inquire. So that is how your cousin came to meet Miss Bennet."

"And instantly be smitten with her, which is exceedingly worrisome to me, for I now find two of the closest men in my whole world in an intense competition for the hand of the same young lady."

"*Possibly* in competition for her hand," Bingley said uncomfortably. "I am not at all certain just how I feel about the young lady. Everything is all mixed together in my mind: her serene acceptance of my obvious interest in her, the things you argued, the way Caroline and Louisa behaved—which was really despicable, you know, as I informed Caroline before I left Scarborough."

"Stranding both sisters and Mr. Hurst on their own," Darcy said with a smile. "What shall they ever do without you to manipulate? Or, rather, attempt to manipulate. They did not seem a bit aware of the deft manner in which you ignored their advice and pleas and did as you thought best, did they?"

Bingley gave a snort of derisive laughter. "I remember that both of them argued against the ball at Netherfield—"

"—to which you had already agreed, ignoring their pleas!"

"—and seemed to think it was their arguments against Miss Bennet that were the reason I did not return…"

"No, that was my doing, I am sorry to say."

"So now they will have to get back to town somehow. I do not know whether they have enough money between them to rent a carriage, but as I suggested, they can travel by post!"

Both men got a good chuckle out of that thought before Bingley turned again to why he had come back to Netherfield.

"So I must see Miss Bennet again and try to settle my feelings about her then and now. It is not unknown for people to be in love and then fall out of love for reasons unknown. But you say your cousin's interest in her is considerable?"

"Unwavering. He told me that he plans to make her an offer of marriage when the time is right, for which reason I characterized the competition between the two of you to be worrisome."

"Well, I shall not fight a duel with him," Bingley said amusedly. "I do not know him that well, but he always seemed a man I should not like to cross, no matter how polite and genteel he seemed."

"A duel would be a very bad idea, Bingley. Let me tell you what happened in Meryton just yesterday when Fitzwilliam finally confronted George Wickham. He was gone from the country when Wickham made his attempt with Georgiana, but he is a very direct sort. If he had been able to find Wickham at the time…well, let me tell you about yesterday…"

Monday, May 11, 1812
Longbourn, Hertfordshire

"MAMA, COME QUICK!" LYDIA SAID FROM THE WINDOW. "MR. DARCY is turning into the drive, and I believe he has Mr. Bingley with him."

Mrs. Bennet could not stop herself from rushing to the window though she tried to tell herself not to be as hasty as she had been on Saturday. But, to her utter joy, it was clear that the second rider turning off the road was not that earl's son, Colonel Fitz…Fitzwarrant? Fitzsimmons?

Whatever, she told herself. *THIS must be Mr. Bingley. He is come, just as my sister predicted.*

"Kitty," she said over her shoulder, "rush upstairs and tell Jane to come down immediately. Mr. Bingley has come to visit."

"And Mr. Darcy?" Kitty asked, trying to get a look through the window with her mother and Lydia in the way.

"Yes, yes! Of course. Now hurry upstairs, girl."

Jane and Elizabeth were talking in their room, wondering whether Mr. Darcy was going to visit, when Kitty ran into the room and passed on her mother's command.

"Ah, but is it really Mr. Bingley?" Elizabeth asked slyly. "Mama was certain it had to be Mr. Bingley on Saturday but it was not, you know."

"Mama says it is," Kitty answered.

"But are you yourself positive?"

"Well, I could not see for myself…but Mama says for you to come down immediately, Jane."

"I think we must go, Lizzy," Jane said, trying to quell the sudden fluttery feeling in her stomach. "Even if it is only Mr. Darcy, you will need me to chaperone the two of you, especially if you entice him into a brisk morning walk."

The two of them barely had time to seat themselves in the parlour— their mother trying to direct each of her daughters into the chairs she thought would provide the most advantageous placement in her never-ceasing roll of fostering marriages for all her brood—before Mrs. Hill opened the door.

"Mr. Darcy and Mr. Bingley," she announced, and Jane looked up briefly, instantly recognised Bingley, and promptly had to lower her gaze as his eyes swivelled in her direction.

However, the amenities had to be observed, so the ladies rose to give their curtseys in response to the bows of the gentlemen. That done, Mrs. Bennet tried to direct the gentlemen to the chairs she had prepared for them so they would be placed close to but not directly beside the young lady of their choice and in a position where she could see everyone that mattered.

Instead, Darcy strode over, grabbing a vacant chair on the way, and seated himself by Elizabeth while Bingley followed his lead to sit by Jane, leaving Mrs. Bennet no choice but to sit where she had planned, though she could no longer see the gentlemen's faces as directly as she would have liked.

"Miss Bennet," said Bingley, turning towards her slightly more and thwarting her mother again. "I trust I find you and your family in good health."

"Yes, indeed, sir. All of us have passed the winter with no real illnesses except a few colds."

"Except the one that afflicted you when you came to visit my sisters," Bingley said with the slightest of smiles.

"That is true, I must admit. But how are your sisters, sir? And Mr. Hurst?"

"Still in Scarborough, though I suppose they will manage to get back to London sooner or later."

Jane had no idea how to interpret such a cryptic remark, but she was pleased that she would not have to meet his two sisters. Comprehension of how false they had been was not in her gentle nature, and nothing in her nature told her how to deal with such failures of friendship. In her mind, she could only assume that one's friends were her friends forever. Unfortunately, that had not proven to be the case, and she was pleased that she would not have to face either Caroline or Louisa just yet.

Elizabeth had begun surreptitiously to watch both Jane and Bingley as soon he sat down, and she was surprised that there were so few awkward moments between them. In fact, they soon seemed to be conversing much as they had the previous autumn. Bingley was as attentive as ever, and Jane responded with similar openness and good humour. She looked over at Darcy, who watched as closely as she did, arching her eyebrows in silent enquiry, to which he responded with a shrug of his shoulders. Clearly, Jane and Bingley needed more time and conversation before any real assessment of their feelings was possible.

In the meantime, Elizabeth still had more to learn about the enigmatic man who was looking more and more likely to be successful in his suit on this second attempt, so she left her sister and Bingley to their own discourse and turned her attention to Darcy.

The morning passed very pleasantly with Elizabeth suggesting a walk. This was received with enthusiasm by all four since they would prefer to be out from under the close inspection of Mrs. Bennet, who treasured every smile and laugh, adding them to the running total in her internal ledger. She was growing absolutely certain that she would soon have two daughters, at least, who were well married and might provide a modicum of security to all her family.

Elizabeth could not remember spending a more pleasant time with Darcy during their entire acquaintance, so she had much to speak of after the gentlemen departed. She was not as certain about her sister and Bingley, though Jane seemed animated enough to make her wonder whether Bingley was not awakening long-dormant emotions in her. So, after she and Jane managed to gain the privacy of their room, she was the first to speak.

"What is your verdict on this first day of Mr. Bingley's return?

He seemed to give every indication of being as smitten as he did last autumn, but what are your thoughts?"

Jane had sat down and begun to unpin and brush out her lustrous hair, and Elizabeth knew she was using such familiar activities to gather her thoughts. So she forced herself to keep her silence and just sat on the end of her bed until her sister was ready to speak.

It was several minutes before Jane paused in her work and twisted around to face Elizabeth.

"It was indeed an enjoyable day, Lizzy, and I could not help but be reminded of what I first thought when I met Mr. Bingley, that he is everything a young man ought to be—a perfect gentleman."

"Sensible and well mannered," Elizabeth said, casting her mind back to that long-ago conversation. "Also handsome and, most important for Mama, wealthy."

"Elizabeth!" Jane said in surprise before she saw the glint of humour in her sister's eye.

"Well, it does not hurt, you know. One of us girls has to marry well, after all."

"But you appear to be getting on admirably with Mr. Darcy."

"He does grow on one, I am finding. But he also appears somewhat... restrained...as though he has been severe for so long that he cannot fully relax."

"I am sure that time will take care of that. I am absolutely certain that he could never think of any other young lady as he thinks of you."

"Perhaps. And if he did blurt out another proposal of marriage, I might have to consider it for a period, but I cannot think of a reason to deny him. I wonder whether the first time did not wound him so much that he is still rather tentative. But let us talk about you—about two gentlemen who appear quite interested in you—though Colonel Fitzwilliam's attitude might be more aptly described as 'total captivation' than merely 'interested.'"

"They are so very different, and I am struggling with that."

"But which would make you happy? Remember, marriage is for life. One cannot take a husband back to the chapel and trade him in for a new one."

"Of course, but I am definitely unsure of my feelings. Today may be too quick and recent, but I remember what I thought earlier when I pondered what it would be like to be married to Mr. Bingley. I was certain that our life together would be satisfying and amiable. I know Mr. Bingley would not treat me badly and would be very agreeable."

"But Colonel Fitzwilliam?"

"He…he excites me, Lizzy," Jane said, after thinking on the question. "I get all tingly inside when I think about being married to him."

"And he will ask for your hand, of course. He said as much, and I think the good colonel is very dependable when he says something. Of course, he is not exactly handsome. Even Mr. Darcy admits that."

"He is not ugly, Lizzy!" Jane said loyally. "He is just…just Colonel Fitzwilliam!"

"So which one will you accept, assuming both of them make an offer?"

Jane threw up her hands in dismay, her brow furrowing as she tried to collect her thoughts. "I do not *know*! It is so perplexing to be faced with such disparate choices. How do I balance which is the more attractive gentleman? Mr. Bingley is so good-humoured, for example, but then I remember that intense smile that…that Richard has when he looks right into my eyes as if there is no one else in the world except the two of us. How do I choose between such men? At least you only have the one gentleman pursuing you."

"If what Mr. Darcy is doing can be called 'pursuit.'" Elizabeth said thoughtfully. "At this moment, I wish he would give me one of those smiles like your Richard does and take me in his arms right in the front parlour so I would have to marry him! I wish he had the…the impetuosity that your Richard has."

"Then I suppose we shall just have to let time take its course," Jane said, turning back to her mirror and picking up her brush.

THAT DAY SET THE PATTERN FOR THE REST OF THE WEEK. DARCY and Bingley called every morning after breakfast, usually accompanying the girls on a walk through the countryside or perhaps strolling in the Longbourn garden or walking into Meryton. Invitations to dinner were always forthcoming from Mrs. Bennet and, after Mr. Bennet found out that Darcy played chess, were often followed by a match between the two. At such times, Bingley often took the opportunity to invite Jane for another walk through the gardens.

It was not an understatement to say that the popularity of Longbourn took a dramatic upswing after the local families learned that both Darcy and Bingley were paying court to the Miss Bennets. Bingley had always been popular in the neighbourhood while Darcy's stature among the tradesmen in Meryton had risen rapidly after he began paying off Wickham's debts. The shocking revelations about the way Wickham had deceived everyone caused the neighbourhood gentry to look at Darcy anew, and his rectifying of Wickham's larcenies with the local tradesmen had been noted with surprise and approval.

It was a rare day that at least two or three carriages were not parked in front of the house while the ladies drank tea with Mrs. Bennet, waiting for a glimpse of the gentlemen passing by the window with Elizabeth and Jane as they returned from their morning walk. All of Mrs. Bennet's friends joined with her, outwardly at least, in celebrating the excellent fortune of the Bennet family in general and Mrs. Bennet in particular. Not even the fast-approaching departure of the regiment and the consequent wailing of Lydia and Kitty were enough to shake their mother from her appointed mission, and she counted the hours that Darcy spent with Elizabeth as a moneylender would count his payments.

During the week, Lydia's plight became even more extreme. She was special friends with Mrs Forster, a young woman who had married the colonel of the regiment in February, and Lydia had received a most exciting invitation to accompany her to Brighton when the regiment moved to their summer camp. Her excitement could scarce be believed, but all was brought crashing down after Mrs. Bennet had a talk with her husband. She insisted that both Elizabeth and Jane would soon be married and Lydia should not be gone to Brighton and miss those events. Mr. Bennet took her point and accordingly refused to allow Lydia to leave. The resulting wails briefly resounded through the halls of Longbourn until Mr. Bennet, upset at having his chess match with Darcy interrupted, sent her to her room with orders to stay there until she could control her emotions.

By Wednesday, Elizabeth was almost ready to cease her resistance to what appeared to be her appointed fate, and she gave Mr. Darcy permission to have his sister join him at Netherfield. It was not that all their differences had been resolved. In fact, by unspoken but mutual agreement, they had not revisited those topics since that first intense and eventful Saturday. Instead, they concentrated on determining whether they could get on well enough to make a future life together a possibility.

It was these daily contacts that were bringing Elizabeth into a growing realisation that, whatever her unresolved doubts might be, Mr. Darcy was, in disposition and talents, far more matched to her own quick-witted character than she ever would have believed. It was a most surprising revelation to find themselves perceiving things in the same manner when most other people appeared to find those topics quite bewildering. And it was flattering that his affection for her was so strong that he would undertake to change those habits of character that concerned his cousin on returning to England. She had changed her mind enough to believe their union might well be to the advantage of both of them.

By her ease and liveliness, his mind and manner would certainly be softened—some of that had already occurred—and she was certain she would benefit from his judgment, information, and knowledge of the world. She had considered herself well read, and it was surprising to find his command of most areas far surpassed her own. It was this dawning understanding that had caused her to agree at last to his request to allow his sister to visit and be introduced to her. While they still needed additional time to allow some of the wounds they had inflicted on each other to heal, she was increasingly certain that she had found a companion for the rest of her life.

Similar understanding did not appear to have blossomed in Darcy, however, even as her own opinions changed. She found him still tentative in his manner, retaining an excessive caution towards her that was undoubtedly the result of his memory of past offences. Elizabeth was thus somewhat frustrated when he seemed prepared for a much lengthier period of contrition than she now believed was required. However, since she found herself enjoying his company more as the days passed, the situation was not one that called for dramatic measures; she would simply let matters take their course unless more determined action was called for at some point in the future.

JANE'S WEEK, ON THE OTHER HAND, HAD BEEN A MIXTURE OF PLEAS-ant days with Mr. Bingley combined with evenings marked by considerable anxiety. Her anxiety was stimulated whenever her mother paused from extolling the virtues of Mr. Darcy and the good fortune of her Lizzy in order to wax eloquent in anticipation of an offer of marriage from Mr. Bingley. Mrs. Bennet seemed completely oblivious to Colonel Fitzwilliam's reasons for calling on her elder daughter and Jane's unresolved quandary regarding the two men.

"Mr. Bingley has been so very attentive to my Jane since returning to Netherfield," Mrs. Bennet said more than once to her many visitors. "Oh, what a fine thing it would be to have two daughters so well settled in marriage. It would make all I have suffered worthwhile at last."

Previously, Jane simply would have ignored such foolish comments. Now, she was dismayed to find her mother's inane utterances inspiring a most unusual inner anger that she struggled to contain. And, because she was the person she was, Jane reacted not by confronting her mother, as Elizabeth would have, but by fleeing to their room. By the time Saturday afternoon arrived, she was a bundle of nerves, and even Elizabeth was hard put to alleviate her anxiety as they dressed for the assembly.

"My eyes look red and puffy," Jane declared, staring fretfully at her reflection in the mirror. Elizabeth rolled her eyes in frustration, for Jane had already said as much before this.

"Nonsense," Elizabeth said, twisting her sister around so they faced each other. She peered carefully into Jane's eyes before shaking her head. "Your imagination is playing you false. Look for yourself—your eyes are as clear and fresh as ever, and they are not puffy at all. That is just a shadow from the sun slanting through the window."

Jane looked at herself again, and she was forced to admit the possibility though she was not sure she was convinced. Of course, if Lizzy said it, then she had to believe it. Still…

Jane looked over at her gown laid out on her bed. It was brand new, sent as a special gift from London by her aunt Gardiner, and had only been delivered on Thursday. It was most elegant and fashionable, high-waisted and graceful in the current fashion with a "V" neckline and puffy, short sleeves. It was easily the finest dress she had ever owned… and also the most revealing.

Jane had tried it on in her room the previous day with just Elizabeth present, and she had been taken aback by its daring. The dress was of fine white lawn muslin, very sheer and embroidered in silver-gilt thread. Like all soft muslin dresses, it had clung to her figure, highlighting her natural silhouette. The bodice was especially enticing, even more than the gown she had worn to the theatre. Like that gown, it concealed her shoulders though it exposed much of her bosom. If her aunt Gardiner was to be believed, it was fashionable to expose most of the wearer's breasts but not her shoulders. Some of the French gowns of previous years had even gone as far as to expose the wearer's nipples.

English fashions had never been that daring, and neither was this gift from her aunt. But both Jane and Elizabeth had been surprised at how low the "V" bodice dipped and how much of Jane's full breasts had been revealed. Because of the sheerness of the fabric, several petticoats had been included to make the dress flare out at the hem, but even then, Jane had been uncomfortably aware of the way the dress swayed and moulded to her legs as she moved.

The note with the dress was written in her aunt's distinctive handwriting and sat before her on her dressing table. As Jane looked at it again, she fancied her cheeks were growing warmer as it said: "The dress is French in origin and is meant to be worn without stays unless a lady's figure demands them. I can assure you, dear Jane, that your figure definitely does not need stays."

Elizabeth now looked at the gown with a judicious eye. "I can well imagine what Colonel Fitzwilliam's response will be, based on the stunned expression on his face at the theatre. And Mr. Bingley is certain to be similarly affected if he has any red blood at all in his veins. But do you think you can really wear this? It is *extremely* daring."

Jane had already given that question considerable thought, remembering her enjoyment of the way Richard had looked at her at the theatre. She had thus already decided to wear the gown, which was why it was on her bed. She would not put it on until right before leaving in order to avoid any chance of marring the pristine whiteness of the fabric of either the gown or the matching long gloves.

As she sat before her dressing mirror, she wore a white, slippery silk petticoat that reached to just below her breasts. The petticoat would help keep her dress silhouette smooth and provide a little support for her bosom, which was otherwise unrestrained. A small bustle pad had been included with the dress, and she wore it just below the small of her back as directed by her aunt. It was intended to lift the dress back and support extra skirt fullness. She had already donned sheer silk stockings and garters with the aid of a maid, and new, white evening slippers were on her feet.

"Oh, I do wish Mama was not attending tonight," Jane said mournfully, her nerves once again making her stomach roil. "She is going to push me at Mr. Bingley the way she pushed you at Mr. Darcy, and that will hurt Colonel Fitzwilliam."

"So it is 'Colonel Fitzwilliam' now, is it? What happened to 'Richard this' and 'Richard that'? No doubt, if you do not go tonight you might avoid some embarrassment at the hands of our mother, but you will also miss seeing your Colonel Fitzwilliam."

"I wish he had called during the week. Surely, he could have managed to call at least once."

"He could not call because he has duties to perform, and you well know it. If you want a man who has nothing to do but idle his time away, pick Mr. Bingley. But if you want a man who excites you, as you mentioned, even if he is not a rich man, then you will have to be satisfied with Richard Fitzwilliam."

"But Mr. Bingley…"

"…was my idea, and if I could unmake it, I would. In any case, your Richard did send you two letters through Mr. Darcy—two letters, by the way, that you would not permit me to read."

Jane blushed again. "There was nothing improper in what he wrote me. It was just…he was just very…forthright."

"By which I assume that he kept repeating 'I love you' over and over."

"Well, not repeating…at least, not exactly in those words…"

Lydia suddenly burst into their bedroom without knocking, which brought her a quick rebuke from both her sisters, but as usual she just ignored them, being under her mother's protection for the evening.

"Jane, Mama said you are to wear your chemisette under your new gown," Lydia said, trying…and failing…to imitate a commanding tone. "She says Aunt Gardiner does not know country society, and your new gown is too revealing. She does not want you to frighten off Mr. Bingley."

"Lydia, leave so Jane can finish dressing," Elizabeth said firmly.

"Well, I am just telling Jane what Mama said, so you have no call to be so haughty with me," Lydia said with a flounce. "Anyway, since Jane will be dancing all night with Mr. Bingley, perhaps Colonel Fitzwilliam will ask *me* for a set."

"Lydia!" Elizabeth said sternly, getting to her feet. Lydia quickly fled the room, slamming the door after her.

"That girl will come to a bad end if Father allows Mama to continue to coddle her," Elizabeth groused as she resumed her seat. "At least the regiment will be gone by mid-week—without Lydia—and life should become a bit calmer. However, I do not see you standing up to get your chemisette."

"No," Jane said simply with a slight smile. The chemisette was usually worn more during the day for modesty's sake, and Jane had no intention of wearing it tonight.

"And, as we both know, your new gown is cut even more daringly than the gown you wore to the theatre."

"Yes, that is certainly true," Jane said, suddenly leaning forward towards her mirror as if to detect a shiny nose or forehead.

"You will fall out of the top of it," Elizabeth said, casting a calculating eye at the neckline of the gown.

"I hope not," Jane said blushingly. "At least, not tonight."

"I do wish I had your figure," Elizabeth grumbled, "so I could wear a dress like yours. Maybe that would force Mr. Darcy to stop treating me like I was a soap bubble about to burst."

"Elizabeth!" Jane said in mock horror.

"Well, when he was impulsive and I was totally ignorant of how he felt, he was willing to blurt out all manner of assurances. Now that I agree he is not completely repulsive and might even be a tolerable companion in marriage, he is peculiarly unwilling to make any commitments at all. And I do not have the figure to wear a dress like yours so I can fall out of the top of it and compromise him into marrying me."

"Elizabeth Bennet!"

CHAPTER 19

Then indecision brings its own delays,
And days are lost lamenting o'er lost days.
Are you in earnest? Seize this very minute;
What you can do, or dream you can, begin it;
Boldness has genius, power and magic in it.
— Johann Wolfgang von Goethe

Saturday, May 16, 1812
Meryton, Hertfordshire

Richard had just pulled his second boot up and tucked his trouser leg into it so no wrinkles were showing when Sergeant Bascomb returned from his errand downstairs.

"Here you are, sir," his orderly said as he entered after a quick knock. "I asked downstairs, and this man says he can tie one of those fancy knots for you."

"Excellent work, Sergeant. I was afraid I was going to have to wear my uniform after all," Richard said cheerfully, gratefully handing the neck cloth to the man who followed Bascomb into the room.

The man took the cloth and examined Richard's high, stiff collar before nodding approvingly. Quickly, he folded the cloth several times before winding it around his neck.

"If ye would keep your chin up, sir," he said as he began to expertly flip and tuck the cravat, working so fast that Richard could not follow the man's motions. Sergeant Bascomb only rolled his eyes in disdain for the dictates of current fashion. The man, who was employed by the innkeeper, was finished in only a few minutes.

"There ye are, sir. As good as any fancy gentleman could desire, I would warrant," he said with satisfaction.

"I am no fancy anything, but it certainly appears satisfactory," Richard said absently as he examined the result critically in the mirror. "Fetch the man a florin from my purse, will you, Sergeant? He has certainly earned it tonight."

"Thank 'ee, thank 'ee, sir," the servant said as he gleefully pocketed his money and bowed his way out of the room. He had expected a shilling at best for his efforts, for this officer did not appear wealthy at all, what with no carriage and only an ordinary soldier to help with his dressing. But the servant was certainly not a man to look askance at good fortune, and he was already whistling as he clattered back downstairs to share his good fortune with his wife, who was busy in the kitchen.

After he left, Sergeant Bascomb helped him with his dark maroon tailcoat, grumbling, "Much too generous for the likes of him, if I do say so, sir."

"Then you shall just have to learn to tie a cravat. I can have Darcy's man teach you."

"As you wish, sir," Bascomb said gloomily. He had worn the King's uniform since running off to the army from his father's small, rented farm, and he did not see why it should not be perfectly good for any occasion. But he had reconciled himself to the fact that his colonel was deadly serious about the young lady he was to meet tonight, and it appeared that nothing less than a trip to the pastor would satisfy him.

"I should not need you for the rest of the evening, but mind that

247

you keep your celebrations within bounds. No upset daughters of the townspeople and especially no fighting with the local folk."

"Yes, sir," Bascomb said morosely, for he considered a barroom brawl as nothing more than good entertainment and an excuse to buy drinks for the house. He could not see why officers did not see it as he did.

Richard only grinned, placed his top hat jauntily on his head, and proceeded downstairs and then out to the street. The last edge of the sun was just disappearing, and candles in the lanterns up and down the street were being lit. He continued to whistle a cheerful Irish tune as he crossed the street to the assembly rooms where the first carriages were just beginning to arrive.

As he entered, he saw there were only a few people present, none of whom he could remember meeting. He had wanted to make sure he arrived before Jane and her sisters, and he had obviously accomplished his purpose. He took the opportunity to explore the rooms around the perimeter of the large hall where the dancing would take place. Several of the musicians had already arrived, and they were just beginning to tune their instruments on the balcony overlooking the centre of the long hall.

Even though Meryton was a modest-sized town, Richard was not surprised at the size of the hall since most towns with a merchant class took pains to have a suitable set of assembly rooms. It could not compare, he knew, with the balls that might be held at a grand estate like his father's. Such events would include an abundant supper and a professional troupe of musicians with a wide repertoire of dances. But this hall was perfectly adequate to his taste since he had learned at an early age to do without the luxuries with which his brothers were accustomed.

Gradually, the rooms filled up as the local families arrived with their sons and daughters, some of whom looked about with anticipation and others—undoubtedly with an excess of shyness—with trepidation.

"Ah, Colonel Fitzwilliam, good evening. My daughter pointed you out to me, and I could not wait to introduce myself."

Richard turned around to see a spare, grey-haired gentleman whom he did not recognise with a plumpish, somewhat younger woman on his arm. Their identity was obvious since they were also accompanied by Maria Lucas, whom he remembered from Rosings and London.

"Good evening, sir. You are presumably Sir William Lucas, Miss Lucas's father, and the beautiful woman on your arm must be your wife, Lady Lucas."

"See, Father? Did I not tell you he was charming?" Maria Lucas giggled. She blushed as he looked her way, but he appeared so cheerful that she giggled again and gave him a quick curtsey.

"You did indeed, Maria. And you are correct, sir, in your surmise. We are neighbours to the Bennet family, with whom I understand you are also acquainted."

"Indeed, sir, as is my cousin Darcy who is hoping to become more closely acquainted with one of the Bennet daughters."

"So we understand, Colonel," Lady Lucas said. "It has been, as you might imagine, a favourite topic of conversation all week."

"I daresay," Richard said dryly, and Sir William beamed at him, pleased to meet such an amiable young man who was also the son of the Earl of Matlock.

"I am sure the local young ladies will be most pleased to have you in attendance tonight," Lady Lucas said. "In fact, I have seen more than a few admiring glances cast your way just in the last minute."

"Alas, I am afraid most of the local young ladies are doomed to disappointment tonight, Lady Lucas," Richard said, his eyes brightening as he espied Mrs. Bennet entering the hall with all five daughters in tow.

"Why, whatever do you mean, sir?" Sir William asked in dismay as he suddenly wondered whether this colonel was as averse to dancing as his cousin.

"Just this, sir—and it is no slur upon the young ladies in attendance," Richard said. "I am certain they are as well-mannered as they are beautiful, but you see, I am on a mission similar to my cousin's."

He nodded his head in the direction of Mrs. Bennet as she proceeded down the side of the hall. "I, too, intend to further my acquaintance with one of Mrs. Bennet's daughters. Now, if you will please excuse me—"

With a quick bow, Richard moved away, leaving Sir William and his wife momentarily nonplussed.

"What did he mean, William?" Lady Lucas asked in puzzlement.

Since her husband saw that the arrow-straight path of Fitzwilliam would intersect with the progress of the Bennet females, he was able to answer. "Evidently, he meant he is in pursuit of another of the Bennet sisters, my dear, and that almost certainly means Jane Bennet. Surely, the son of an earl would never consider an attachment with one of the others."

"But what about Mr. Bingley? All my friends have talked of nothing else but his return to Netherfield and the resumption of his attentions to Jane."

"It appears, my dear, that the wealthy Mr. Bingley has some competition in that area. Judging by the way Jane is receiving him, there can be no doubt of her interest in return."

"But what if both are pursuing her hand? How would she choose in that case?"

"Well, Mr. Bingley has an advantage as far as wealth, from what I hear, but it looks as if the colonel might have an advantage as far as emotion. It should make a most lively contest."

"Oh my. Everyone assumed both Lizzy and Jane would soon be married, but this new possibility is simply marvellous. Come, sir! There is Mrs. Goulding and Mrs. Long. They must know of this startling news immediately."

Jane had noticed Richard as soon as she entered the hall behind her mother, and she saw him immediately excuse himself from

250

the Lucases and angle towards her. She also saw the way he seemed to stand up even taller as he got a good look at her dress, and she did not believe she was mistaken when she saw his stride falter. But he quickly gathered himself and continued towards her.

She could see her mother looking around, trying to find the objects of her desire, Mr. Darcy and Mr. Bingley. Mrs. Bennet was paying no attention to the sturdy man coming towards Jane, and it was not until he stepped in front of them, barring their way, that her mother stopped searching about and looked up at him in surprise.

"Mrs. Bennet, it is a pleasure to see you again. I trust you and your family are doing well this fine night?" Richard said smoothly, giving her a quick bow. Mrs. Bennet gave him an instinctive curtsey, as did her daughters, but it was obvious she had been completely caught off guard.

"Well…ah…yes, I am…that is, we are…"

"That is splendid, ma'am. Splendid. Miss Bennet, Miss Elizabeth, you and your sisters appear to be in fine health as well tonight. I assume you are looking forward to the dancing?"

Richard had firm control of his emotions, forcing himself to ignore the vision of Jane in that magnificent dress. Still, he was aware of the smile she struggled to hide, and he knew she, at least, was completely aware of the effect she was having on him. His heartbeat increased at the realisation that she had again clearly dressed with the intention of making herself desirable, and he had to force himself to pay the proper attention to his manners.

"Well, some of us are," Elizabeth said, eying him closely, "though I am afraid my sister Mary has brought a book. I do not believe you have met Mary, Colonel. Allow me to introduce my next younger sister, who is older than Kitty and Lydia, whom you already know. Mary, this is Colonel Richard Fitzwilliam, who is Mr. Darcy's cousin and the son of the Earl of Matlock."

Mary quickly stepped forward and did her curtsey, but she appeared to have been taken aback. As soon as the courtesy was completed, she stepped back behind her younger sisters, who were gazing at Richard with what looked like a mixture of irritation and confusion.

I would wager they still cannot understand why I would be interested in their eldest sister instead of themselves, he thought in amusement. *I wonder whether they will ever be capable of seeing themselves as I see them.*

"Very nice to meet you, Miss Mary. Now, is that all, Miss Elizabeth? You are confident you have no other sisters tucked away somewhere?"

"No, sir, I give you my pledge. This is all of us."

"Excellent," Richard said with a smile. Then he turned to Jane, and his polite expression faded as he was finally able to devote his full attention to her. It would not be a misstatement to say that his eyes swam as he drank in the full measure of her and her attire. He knew she had to be aware of the way his eyes had dropped to her very revealing neckline, but her slight smile demonstrated perfectly that she did not find his interest offensive.

Richard had to clear his throat before he could speak naturally. "Miss Bennet," he said with an intensity that was meaningful only to the two of them and perhaps Elizabeth, "if I may be so bold, I must say you are looking surpassingly beautiful tonight."

Jane gave him another curtsey, unable to stop the smile of pleasure generated by his heartfelt comment.

"Thank you, sir," she said demurely, but Richard could see her eyes looking up at him through her lashes as she bent slightly in her curtsey to give him a better view of her breasts. All of a sudden, the cravat at his throat seemed to be choking him.

"No thanks are necessary, Miss Bennet," he said after a moment, "for it is a mere statement of fact. But I do crave a boon from you. Is it possible there is an unreserved set on your card tonight?"

"Oh, dear me," she said, pulling out her dance card. "It appears that every available spot is already taken." But she smiled as she said it, and mischief danced in her eyes.

"See for yourself, sir," she said, holding out her card to him. Richard took it and quickly inspected it. The first set was marked "Richard," as was the third. Two other sets were marked "Mr. Bingley."

He felt a surge of warmth at her use of his first name, and he had been expecting the inclusion of Bingley's name since Darcy had informed him in an express of Bingley's arrival and the fact that he was calling daily at Longbourn.

And being received—and received most graciously from what Darcy wrote, he thought with more than a little disappointment. But he restrained himself from dwelling on that emotion since he knew he could have expected nothing else. He was well aware that Jane needed to resolve that issue in her own mind before the two of them could proceed further.

"I see," he said, handing her card back, forcing himself to suppress the smile that wanted to bubble up from below. "It appears you will have a very full evening, Miss Bennet. I wish you the greatest enjoyment from it."

"I have already had more enjoyment than I deserve, sir," she said simply, and Richard's heart lurched again at the way her smile was reflected in her sparkling violet eyes.

MRS. BENNET, HOWEVER, OBSERVED THE PROCEEDINGS WITH confusion and exasperation.

What is that silly girl playing at? she thought irritably. *She has obviously disoriented the man with that daring gown my sister Gardiner sent her. Where ARE Mr. Bingley and Mr. Darcy?*

"Ah, I see my cousin has arrived," Richard said. "I am sure he will wish to pay his respects immediately, so I shall leave you for the moment. I hope we may talk further later in the evening, Miss Bennet."

"I believe you may rely on that, sir," Jane said with a warm smile. Richard returned her smile and gave her a bow before excusing himself and moving off.

"Well," Elizabeth said with a sly smile. "Is it my imagination, or has it become rather warm all of a sudden?"

"I am sure it is just your imagination, Lizzy," Jane said, turning to her sister.

Both she and Elizabeth shared a giggle behind gloved hands, and this was finally too much for Mrs. Bennet.

"What are you two about?" she demanded in exasperation. "Here, let me see that dance card."

After Jane handed her the card, her mother looked at it in confusion. "Why are all the spaces filled, Jane? We only just arrived, and no one has asked for a dance except this Colonel Fitzwilliam, and you refused him. All the spaces are filled with either Mr. Bingley or this 'Richard.' Just who is he?"

"Yes, what are you talking about, Jane?" Lydia said, pressing up beside her mother to look over her shoulder with Kitty close in her wake.

"You were not listening to Lizzy's introduction of the colonel to Mary," Jane said quietly, reclaiming her card deftly before her mother was aware it was gone. "I did not refuse Colonel Fitzwilliam at all. I simply said my card was full. And it is."

"Richard is Colonel Fitzwilliam's Christian name," Elizabeth said mildly.

"But what of Mr. Bingley?" Mrs. Bennet asked, her vexation making the question sound more like a wail.

"I believe Mr. Bingley has the even numbered sets, Mama," Jane said quietly, returning the card to the small, beaded reticule dangling from a cord looped about her wrist.

"But this means you will be keeping Colonel Fitzwilliam all to yourself for at least half the evening, Jane," Lydia said unhappily.

"And look!" Kitty exclaimed. "He has gone back to the Lucases and appears to be asking Maria for a dance. How can he dance with either of us if you selfishly possess him for so long?"

"I am sorry to have to be the bearer of bad tidings, sisters, but the two of you had best come with me," Elizabeth said, taking both Lydia and Kitty by their arms and leading them away. "Since neither of you appear capable of using either eyes or heads for anything other than decoration, I must explain it with complete clarity so you will understand..."

Mrs. Bennet's mouth was agape as Elizabeth led her daughters away, and now she whirled back on Jane.

"Just what is the meaning of all this, Jane Bennet? Mr. Bingley is here. I can see him coming this way with Mr. Darcy. And now you have given half of your dances away to this...this officer! Of what are you thinking?"

"Mama," Jane sighed, "I am sorry to have to tell you this, but you have seen everything and understood nothing. Did you not wonder why Colonel Fitzwilliam called with his cousin last Saturday? Did you not read the letter I brought from Uncle Gardiner? In plain fact, Colonel Fitzwilliam was calling on me in town before Elizabeth ever gave Mr. Darcy permission to call on *her*."

Mrs. Bennet stood with her mouth agape, wondering to herself where she had placed her brother's letter. She had intended to read it sometime, but there had been so many other things to do when the girls returned from town.

"But Mr. Bingley..." she sputtered.

"Is quite a nice gentleman who has been most attentive," Jane said calmly. "Now he is almost upon us, so I suggest you regain your composure immediately."

Despite the serenity she exhibited, Jane had to keep tight control of her emotions as Mr. Darcy approached with Mr. Bingley behind him. She hoped she was succeeding, but she had no such confidence in her mother.

She noted that the approaching men were the centre of considerable attention with many observers following their progress and whispering to each other.

"Mrs. Bennet, ladies," Darcy said formally as he and Bingley arrived.

"I trust I find you and your family in good health and cheer tonight? It is a lovely evening, is it not?"

"Indeed it is, Mr. Darcy," Mrs. Bennet bubbled. "Good evening, Mr. Bingley. It is good to see you again."

Jane almost rolled her eyes in mortification at the fawning tone of her mother's voice, but it was not a great surprise after the past week. She shook her head internally as she recognised that attempting to explain the situation that existed between Richard and her had been a waste of time. Quite plainly, her mother had not listened to a single word she said regarding Richard's interest in her and hers in him. Either that or she was deliberately ignoring that information and proceeding with her own agenda, which was to promote a marriage to the wealthy Mr. Bingley with her usual single-mindedness. Non-essential questions, no matter how perplexing, could be saved for another time.

Mr. Bingley's greeting was perfectly polite and civil, but Jane could see that it took considerable self-control. He clearly was as affected as Richard had been by her attire, and she wondered whether she was being vain to enjoy the pleasant emotion of being so admired by two such admirable gentlemen. Yet, despite the fact that his eyes dipped downward as Richard's had, he seemed somewhat distant to Jane— as if he had pressing matters on his mind perhaps. She wondered whether the fact that Richard was also in attendance tonight might be responsible. She was certain that his demeanour was not what it had been all week.

Oh, where is Lizzy? she thought frantically. *I need her powers of observation. Mine appear all jumbled and untrustworthy.*

One thing was perfectly apparent, however: not only had both gentlemen's steps faltered when they beheld her wearing this daring gown, Mr. Darcy had had much the same reaction. In fact, the eyes of every male within sight seemed to keep whirling in her direction.

I did not plan on THIS much attention, Jane thought anxiously, but she was distracted from that worrying thought as she noted Mr. Darcy's anxiety. He seemed to have recovered from his first sight of her daring attire and now kept an eye on Bingley while he looked about the hall.

Obviously, he is wondering where Lizzy is, Jane thought as Bingley seemed to have an uncharacteristically difficult time making idle conversation. *I shall have to inform him that she will be back directly...*

But she never got the chance. Mrs. Bennet could not abide silence when in the throes of The Hunt. If no one else would talk, *she* would!

"It has been most pleasant to have you back in residence at Netherfield, Mr. Bingley. Do you know how long you plan to stay? It is some months before the shooting season begins, but the families who have been in town for the winter are starting to return. I am sure there will be plenty of social events to attract a gentleman like you."

"I...I am not certain how long I shall stay," Bingley said with an undecipherable expression. "It was much the same when I left for town. I never reached a decision on not returning, but I had...pressing business in town that prevented my return."

"People did wonder whether you meant to quit the place entirely, but I am glad to see they were wrong. There has been one change while you were gone that I am not sure Jane mentioned to you: Lizzy's friend Miss Lucas was married early in the year, and she is settled in Kent."

"No, Miss Bennet did not mention it, but Darcy did tell me that she married his aunt's parson. He met her there when he visited his aunt, and it was also the occasion for renewing his acquaintance with Miss Elizabeth."

"Yes, I am sure Lady Lucas is well pleased to have her settled so nicely. Charlotte and Lizzy were always such good friends, you know."

"So I have been told, ma'am."

"You have become quite a regular at our table this past week, and I hope to see you dine with us at Longbourn many more times."

"I am not certain how long my stay will be, Mrs. Bennet. But if I stay for any length of time, I am sure I shall again dine at Longbourn."

Jane saw that Mr. Bingley was in considerable discomfort at this question, but her mother never noticed. "Excellent, excellent, my dear Mr. Bingley," she gushed.

Elizabeth now joined their group, and Jane had to suppress a smile at the look of relief on Darcy's face. He made a motion with his head, and he and Elizabeth stepped away. The two of them spoke together for a few moments, but general conversation in the hall had increased to the point that Jane could not hear what was said. However, Elizabeth handed him her dance card from her reticule, and Darcy looked startled as he inspected it. Elizabeth waited calmly, though a slightly mischievous smile curved her lips, and Darcy bore a rather dazed smile as he returned her card.

In the meantime, Mrs. Bennet had been maintaining a soliloquy with Mr. Bingley as her object, but finally he managed to break the flow of words when she paused for breath.

"Miss Bennet, I hope you have some sets open."

Jane nodded her agreement while she forced herself to ignore the inner turmoil that roiled her midsection. "Indeed I do, sir. Four sets are open."

"Then I would be pleased if you would reserve a pair of sets for me." Bingley's smile was civil and polite, but it was also somewhat strained since he had to be aware that she was reserving a pair of sets for Colonel Fitzwilliam.

But Jane gave no hint of her thoughts as she applied her pencil to her dance card before looking up at Bingley. "There. It is done, Mr. Bingley. Sets two and four are reserved for you."

Bingley gave a nod and a bow before thanking her and excusing himself. But if the couple had maintained a measure of composure, the same could not be said for Mrs. Bennet. She was clearly so irate that her emotions were almost out of control, and she barely managed to restrain herself until Darcy and Bingley turned away.

To find the punchbowl, they said, Jane thought. *But it appears as if Mr. Bingley would prefer something stronger.*

The thought did not give rise to the amusement Elizabeth would have felt because Jane was unhappy to cause anyone pain. But her turmoil disappeared as Richard appeared at that moment to lead her onto the dance floor. He arrived in such good time that Mrs. Bennet had no more than formed the angry words intended for her elder daughter before he stood before them, ensuring the diatribe remained unspoken.

Jane's relief at his presence spread a wave of calm contentment through her. He was such a strong man to lean on with his blunt features and cheerful demeanour, and she felt comforted and safe in his presence. Her earlier discontentment vanished like a wisp of fog dissolved by the sun. She knew she would probably enjoy her dances with Mr. Bingley, with the possibility of a few anxious moments, but those thoughts could not worry her now. She gloried in the warm smile Richard wore as they began moving to the intricate patterns of one of the popular contradances. She just enjoyed looking into his dark eyes, never imagining what the clear gaze of her sparkling, violet eyes was doing to her partner.

Nor, of course, was she aware of the way the soft muslin of her dress moulded to her curves and outlined her long legs as she moved gracefully through the complicated steps. Even though Richard was aware of it all—the daring dress she wore and the enticing movements of her body beneath the folds of materials—he could not take his eyes off Jane's, a fact noticed by Mr. Bingley with a sinking sensation and by Mrs. Bennet with growing anger.

So many eyes followed Jane and Richard as they moved about the dance floor that none of the principals and few of the onlookers so much as noticed the ease and clear enjoyment of Darcy and Elizabeth together. Only Sir William Lucas took more than a casual glance in their direction, and he derived considerable amusement and pleasure from seeing Darcy go through the motions that he once so disparaged.

"Every savage can dance," Sir William remembered him saying and turned about to find his wife and share his thoughts with her.

CHAPTER 20

Here is my heart and I give it to you
Take me with you across this land
These are my dreams, so simple and few
Dreams we hold in the palm of our hands.

— Loreena Mckennitt,
"Never-Ending Road (Amhrán Duit)"

Saturday, May 16, 1812
Meryton, Hertfordshire

Bingley's sudden stop caught Jane by surprise, for she had been concentrating on the steps of the dance in a way that was unnecessary during her earlier sets with Richard. She halted when Bingley did and looked at him quizzically. Certainly, his manners and temperament had been without fault all evening, and she easily understood how he had affected her when she first knew him and then again when he returned to Netherfield. To be noticed by a gentleman of such style and elegance was complimentary in the extreme, but the question of the moment was the intensity of her feelings for him at the present time, especially when compared to the openly expressed attraction of Colonel Richard Fitzwilliam.

She was certain that Bingley's feelings were much the same as those of Richard, even if Bingley had not expressed them candidly. She knew she had felt much the same the previous autumn before he abruptly left Netherfield, but there simply was no other explanation for his return to the neighbourhood and his marked attention to her. He was courting her, and she was confident that this time he would make an offer of marriage.

The only question in her mind was her response to that offer, especially when Richard had firmly stated that he would make his own addresses after she had time to resolve her hurt and disappointment of the past half year. She had thought of little else in the whirlwind that had swirled since Richard first asked to call on her, but she had not been able to come to any decision. If Bingley had not returned, she was confident that she would have accepted Richard when he acted.

But that did not matter since Bingley *had* returned, and she was still completely at sea in this critical matter. On Bingley's part, she believed now—as she had last autumn—that the two of them could be quite happy in marriage. They were so similar in temperament and manner that she could not imagine having occasion to quarrel. Bingley was handsome and wealthy, which a young lady like herself had to consider since she would bring no fortune to the marriage. It might be considered rather churlish in the increasingly popular romantic novels of recent years, but she knew she was too steady and realistic simply to ignore such matters.

But it did not signify in this case since Bingley was more than wealthy enough to support a wife and family in luxury while Richard had an income that was adequate to the same purpose even if it was not as extensive as Bingley's. So the question came down to affection on her part for these two men, and she could not answer that question at the present time. It was too soon; events were moving too rapidly. She wanted more time, but she was aware that time was the one item in short supply in her situation. What would she do if one or the other of these two men forced her hand?

And that might be occurring at the present moment as Bingley said awkwardly, "Miss Bennet, I would very much like to have a few words with you in private. Might you consider accompanying me outside to the terrace?"

"Certainly, Mr. Bingley," Jane said cautiously, taking the arm he offered her even as her inner self was crying, *Stop! Stop! It is all happening too fast! I am not ready!*

But she could not say such things out loud, so she allowed him to escort her through the open doors to the more comfortable air outside where other couples stood about, cooling themselves after the exertion of a dance set lasting a good half an hour. Bingley guided her to a bench in the far corner, partially screened by several rosebushes.

He evidently found this secluded area while I was dancing with Richard, Jane thought, mentally steeling herself for what she believed would follow.

Once he had seated Jane, Bingley stood silent for a space while she simply waited since it was evident he was having difficulty in finding words. It took him more than a minute before he was able to begin in an emotion-choked voice.

"Miss Bennet, I come to you as a man who realises he has treated you in an unforgivable manner. When I left for town last fall, I fully intended to return in a few days. However, I was…I allowed myself… to be convinced that I had been deceiving myself about the affection I thought you felt for me. I was…persuaded…that you actually regarded me only with friendship and not the affection I held for you. The result was that I did not return to Netherfield and instead tried to forget you."

Bingley had begun to pace as he bared his soul in this manner, and Jane felt embarrassment for the inner turmoil driving him to reveal such intensely private thoughts and feelings. She also felt a sense of loss at their missed opportunity last autumn. She knew she deserved a share of the blame; she had grown so adept at hiding her feelings that it was not surprising that Mr. Bingley had been unaware of her feelings. At the present time, as Bingley struggled with his emotions, she was not certain whether that missed opportunity was gone forever or was, in fact, retrievable. All she knew was that she was torn in different directions and had not made a decision.

"But I could not forget you, Miss Bennet. I went to parties and dinners and attended the theatre, but I could not make myself forget you. Only when Darcy wrote to me saying he had come to believe that his assurances of your indifference had been in error did I have any expectation that I was not the only one who was feeling the pain of thwarted hopes. From what Darcy has told me of his confrontation with you sister in Kent, you undoubtedly know how this came about. But if he made a mistake in trying to persuade me of your indifference, I cannot avoid bearing the blame for acceding to his advice. The fault is mine."

Bingley dropped to one knee and looked up at her, and Jane could see the depth of emotion in his eyes before he continued. "Miss Bennet, I do not know how I shall be able to make up for the pain you have suffered—that I caused you to suffer—but I assure you I am willing—nay, eager—to spend the rest of my life trying. I love you most dearly, and I shall always love you. You would make me the happiest man alive if you would consent to accept my hand in marriage."

Jane had to pull her handkerchief out to dab at the corner of her eyes as Mr. Bingley finished. She felt the despair he must have felt as he at last realized his error after being informed by Darcy at Elizabeth's request, and she could sense the desperation that had driven him to make this offer after having only returned to Netherfield the previous Sunday.

She knew the reason he must have felt compelled to act now—tonight—instead of searching for just the right moment. He had seen her dancing with Richard, and she knew he must have sensed some part of the enjoyment she had derived from being with that rough-hewn man. But above all, she felt a strong compulsion to avoid hurting the man on his knee before her. She wanted desperately to accept him or at least find some way to alleviate his suffering. The thought of inflicting still more pain by refusing his offer was almost more than she could bear.

Almost.

Despite her quandary over the past week and especially tonight, this moment suddenly caused the cobwebs of uncertainty to dissolve. She had walked into this garden filled with dismay at the indecision that gripped her, and now it was gone as if it never existed. But she forced herself to concentrate since she had to give Mr. Bingley an answer.

Asking for time to consider his proposal might lessen his pain in the short term, but it would be deceitful, she thought. *It is a sad fact, but nevertheless a true one, that some opportunities, if not taken, truly are lost forever. What was the line in Julius Caesar? Ah, yes—"There is a tide in the affairs of men which, taken at the flood, leads on to fortune. Omitted, all the voyage of their life is bound in shallows and in miseries."*

That is what happened to Mr. Bingley and me. Our tide came, and for reasons good or bad, we did not take it, and now it is gone forever, even if I did not realize it before this moment. If I shy away from telling this man the truth and hurting him tonight, then I shall only hurt another man who is dear to me. Unfortunately, I know what I must do, and no matter how much it may hurt Mr. Bingley at this time, he MUST have the truth. The truth at the right time might have made everything turn out differently last autumn, and it is essential now. Concealment will only make everything worse—and might even cause unpredictable harm to Richard—and to myself.

Bingley had been growing more and more agitated as Jane sat silently thinking, but finally, when she had her thoughts marshalled, she began.

"I must thank you, sir, for the effort and the pain it must have cost you to make these revelations to me. It is never easy to speak of our innermost thoughts and feelings, and I wish I could reward such courage and forthrightness by giving you the answer you seek. But

I cannot. I would go to almost any lengths to avoid causing another person pain, but I have come to know that, if I try to lessen your pain now, I shall likely only make it worse later—for you, for myself, and...for others.

"You see, Mr. Bingley, I have just realized that my heart belongs to another. And I could never forgive myself if I yield to my weakness and cause that person pain because I am unwilling to tell you the truth. So, I am sorry, sir, but I must decline your kind offer."

Bingley looked crushed as she had known he would, and Jane felt the remorse tear at her heart.

Finally, Bingley was able to speak, and he said flatly, "Colonel Fitzwilliam. Darcy's cousin."

Jane looked him calmly in the eye and nodded her head. Bingley's head dropped to his chest, and he groaned as he heaved himself upright.

Looking away, Bingley said in a voice full of pain, "Was it really my departure and failure to return? If I had stayed, would my offer have received a different answer?"

Jane looked up at him and waited until he could meet her eye before she answered. "That is unfair, sir," she replied gravely. "We can only deal with the life we have to live, not the one we would like to have lived. Only the Lord above could answer the question you just asked, and I am convinced that we have to live our lives from this moment forward. I believe it does no good to look back too much at what might have been."

Now Jane stood up. "In any case, sir, I must beg leave to return inside, for I am chilled and need to return to the warmth."

And to Richard, she thought.

As they moved away, neither Jane nor Mr. Bingley saw Maria Lucas and one of her friends as the two girls stood up from behind the waist-high hedge that framed the terrace, holding on to each other's arms at their excitement and eagerness to rejoin the assembly and pass on the news they had just overheard.

Richard saw Bingley escort Jane back inside, and it was undeniable that things had not gone well for him. He was distinctly pale, and his face looked pinched as he bowed and left Jane's side. She stood alone, watching him walk off, holding his head high in what looked to be a desperate attempt to assuage his pride.

When Jane looked around, Richard was already making his way towards her. When he reached her, she said, "Richard, would you wait while I get my shawl? I need to talk to you, and it is quite chilly on the terrace."

"Certainly, but I would be willing to loan you my coat."

"I think not," Jane said with a wan smile. "It looks too handsome on you to think of removing it. Stay here, please. I shall only be a minute."

Richard watched Jane as she walked to where her mother was sitting and picked up her shawl. Mrs. Bennet grabbed Jane's arm and said something to her that made Jane shake her head. Mrs. Bennet spoke more forcefully, and Jane shook her head again, jerking her arm loose. She walked away even as her mother was calling after her, but Richard could discern no words over the combination of music and conversation in the room.

When Jane reached him, he offered his arm and she hung on it gratefully. "My mother is displeased with me tonight," she said as they walked towards the doors.

"And why is that, if I might ask?"

"I would rather wait until we can find some place with a modicum of privacy."

Elizabeth was standing with Darcy, catching her breath after three sets with him, when she noticed Maria Lucas enter from the garden and almost run to her mother. Several other gentlemen had approached Elizabeth earlier and requested a dance or a set, but she had informed them that that her card was full. She did not really believe that this would set tongues wagging since virtually everyone in the neighbourhood had become aware of Darcy's attentions over the past week.

"I wonder what that might mean," she said softly, nodding her head in Maria's direction. Darcy looked at her questioningly, and she went on. "Jane and Mr. Bingley just returned from the garden looking rather distressed."

"I know," Darcy said with a nod. "I had the feeling he might feel compelled to speak with your sister, but neither of them looks particularly happy."

"Maria Lucas was almost on their heels, and it seems she has something urgent to tell her mother. And now Lady Lucas is heading towards my mother. Come—let us join them. I want to hear what she says."

"Mrs. Bennet," Lady Lucas exclaimed as Darcy and Elizabeth joined her mother. "You will never guess what Maria just related."

Mrs. Bennet's eyes lit up as Lady Lucas informed her, almost word for word, of Bingley's emotional proposal of marriage in the garden.

"Oh, I am so happy to hear that, Lady Lucas. I knew how it would be since I always told Jane she could not be so beautiful for nothing. Ever since Mr. Bingley came into Hertfordshire, I was convinced they would come together. Is he not the handsomest young man that ever was seen?" Darcy and Elizabeth were now forgotten, and Jane was beyond competition her favourite child. At that moment, she cared for no other.

"Do not be so hasty, Mrs. Bennet," Lady Lucas said. "It seems, from what Maria told me, that Jane refused him. She said her heart was given to another."

Elizabeth was certain that she saw a hint of malicious pleasure in Lady Lucas's eyes as her mother stood open-mouthed in shock. The competition between these two ladies for neighbourhood gossip was beyond measure, and Lady Lucas had just scored a dramatic point in their rivalry.

Mrs. Bennet could say nothing for a full two minutes, during which she stared at Lady Lucas with a look of unutterable horror on her face as if she were confronting some demonic creature from the depths of the ocean who was about to rip her to shreds.

Then a shriek of mingled rage and mortification resounded throughout the assembly hall, drawing every eye her way. As if her scream had galvanized her into action, she immediately sped away, crying out for her carriage and demanding her other daughters attend her.

Darcy and Elizabeth looked at each other before Elizabeth said, "I suppose we ought to find Jane and the colonel. I saw them leave the hall some minutes ago."

"You had better get your shawl," Darcy said. "It is somewhat chilly outside right now."

When Richard and Jane got to the terrace, it was less crowded than previously, for people were moving inside to prepare for the next set.

"The next set is ours, you know," he said mildly.

"Please, I have quite lost my desire for dancing. I need to talk to you, and I find I cannot wait. Look, over there—that bench is deserted."

And it is not the one where I sat while Bingley proposed, Jane thought. *I do NOT want to sit there when I talk to Richard.*

When they reached the bench, Jane sat down while Richard initially remained standing, only sitting down at her urging.

Now that they were alone, Jane wanted desperately to have Richard hold her, to provide some warmth to her heart, which felt like a cold lump in her chest. But, while there was some privacy here for conversation, they were in plain sight of everyone who was outside for the cooler air. Therefore, that particular need could not be assuaged. Instead, she slipped her arm under his and reached for his gloved hand. She drew a shuddering breath as she felt his strong hand and fingers close over her hand, giving her a measure of the comfort she desired so badly.

"It would appear that Mr. Bingley has had a rather dramatic impact on you, Miss Bennet," he said in his deep voice. "Did he do anything unseemly?"

"Oh no, nothing like that. He…proposed marriage, and I found it…difficult…no, not difficult because I knew what I had to do. I found it *painful* to refuse him."

"Ah. That explains his pale demeanour when he escorted you inside. Painful—yes, that would be it. You would never want to hurt anyone, would you?"

"And he did not deserve to be hurt, for he had merely made a mistake instead of setting out to inflict pain on me. But I could not draw it out. I needed to answer him straightaway."

"Which is usually the best policy. Rip the thorn out quickly—trying to ease it out only prolongs the pain. But now you are rather depressed for having done the right thing."

"I told him my heart was given to another, Richard," Jane said in a small voice because now doubts were beginning to afflict her.

"You did, did you? And might I hope the other person is my unworthy self?"

"You know it is." She looked up at Richard again. "If you remember, you once said you would wait until you could tell I was ready. You do not have to discern my emotions any longer since I can assure you that I am ready."

"Ah, so it's ready that you are, my fine lass? Then it's to be making my assurances that I'm to be doing."

Jane laughed in relief as Richard's rolling brogue made her bleakness depart.

"You shall slip up one of these days, sir, and fall into that uncouth accent in front of someone important, like the King or a general."

"Then you shall be there to see it, Jane Bennet, for I love you more than I believed I could ever love anyone, and I shall not rest until we are married. In fact, I was not even sure whether I *believed* in love before I met you. But now you hold my heart in your possession, and nothing I have in life is worth a farthing if you are not at my side."

Jane felt contentment sweep through her again as the words were said at last, and now the two of them could get on with the rest of their lives.

"I wore this dress for you tonight," she said softly, looking into his dark, deep eyes. "My aunt Gardiner purchased it and sent it to me, but my mother told me not to wear it tonight because it was too daring. But I wanted you to want me, Richard."

"I have wanted you since I first saw you, you little minx," Richard growled, "but not until that night at the theatre did I realize how much."

"Yes, I know. When you looked down my dress."

"You knew? I almost could not *breathe* when you stepped down from that coach."

"We women always know. We do not have many weapons, but those we have, we prefer to keep very sharp."

"That is a startling thought." Richard looked at her rather dubiously, and Jane laughed in delight.

"I shall take care to give you more startling thoughts in the years to come," she said with a mischievous smile.

"The years to come, is it? And I suppose we are to live in sin all those years, for my question is unanswered."

"Yes," Jane said with a smile so lovely Richard wished he could freeze it and keep it with him always. "Yes, I will marry you. I will live with you and love you and keep you and bear your children. Yes, my love, yes!"

"*Now* I am content. But this is a momentous occasion. Perhaps we should seal this bargain of ours with a kiss."

"Perhaps we should, sir, but I have to inform you: I have never been kissed. You will have to instruct me."

"I do not believe instruction is really necessary," he said, standing and pulling her to her feet. "I think with a little *demonstration*, you will pick up the elements rather quickly. But there is little privacy on this terrace."

"I care not. No one appears to be even looking our way, and what could happen in any case? That my father should demand we marry?"

"I suppose that is true, my dearest love. And your wish is my command."

Jane found herself holding her breath, for Richard's face had been getting nearer as he talked. Her soft lips parted, and she instinctively closed her eyes as his mouth came down on hers. She felt a thrill run down her spine as his arm went around her back and pulled her to him. She melted against him, returning his kiss with artless fervour, glorying in this heretofore-inexperienced act of love.

It was more than a minute before they separated, looking at each other in mutual wonder.

"I think—" Jane began, but the rest of her thought was lost as a shrill shriek sounded from inside the assembly hall. Richard was on his feet without even realising it, already in a fighting crouch and pawing for the sword that was not there. The other couples on the terrace were making for the door to find out what had happened.

"Perhaps we should—" Richard began, but Jane put a hand on his arm to forestall him.

"I have a ghastly feeling that I know what has happened because I have heard that sound before. And I am unwilling to lose this moment because of the foibles of a mother with a weak mind." Her hand reached up to clasp the back of his head.

"You were saying?" she said softly, pulling his head to hers.

This time, Jane embraced him as they kissed, and she thrilled as he held her. He had his arms all the way around her, and she tried to pull him closer, wishing she could mould herself to him while his lips pressed deliciously into hers. As his tongue touched her lips, she sucked in a breath. She had never dreamed of such a thing, but it felt both exquisite and natural.

When they broke apart this time, both of them were breathing deeply. She sighed as she laid her head against his shoulder. She was taller than her sister, and the top of her head came up to Richard's chin, where Elizabeth's would barely have reached his shoulder. It seemed to Jane that they were made for each other, for it felt like the most natural thing in the world to be held like this. His arms were still around her when they heard Darcy clear his throat behind them.

"Does this mean you have some news for me, Richard?" he asked drolly.

Richard began to move away from Jane, but she would not have it. She clutched his lapels fiercely and pulled herself against him, refusing to let him go. She turned her head but kept it on Richard's chest as she saw that Darcy and her sister had come out on the otherwise-deserted terrace.

"You may have heard a screech a few minutes ago, Jane," Elizabeth said. "That was Mama after Lady Lucas informed her that Mr. Bingley had made an offer of marriage to you, which you refused."

"Oh dear," Jane said, but she did not leave her cocoon within the safe haven of Richard's arms. "We did hear something, Lizzy, but I am afraid we were reluctant to go and see what it was. In any case, I was quite sure I recognised that screech."

"She also had me to advise her," Richard added. "A good officer knows when to advance and when to retreat. An *excellent* officer knows when not to even stick his head up and take a look."

"And I suppose that means you consider yourself an 'excellent' officer," Darcy said wryly. "A less generous person than I am might say it more resembled cowardice in the face of the enemy."

"Nonsense—Mrs. Bennet is destined to be my mother-in-law, so she, by definition, cannot be classed as an enemy."

"Which, I suppose, accounts for our finding you and Miss Bennet in this compromising embrace. It would appear you have some news to add to what Mrs. Bennet just heard."

"At least, you will not have to worry about the reaction of our mother when she learns of it," Elizabeth said. "When Mama heard what Lady Lucas had to tell, she let out the cry you heard and then sped off to collect the younger girls before ordering the carriage brought around to take everyone back to Longbourn immediately, even though Kitty and Lydia cried at being forced to leave. I stayed well away so she could not order me to accompany her. I hope she will send the carriage back for us, but I am sure of nothing."

Elizabeth looked directly at Jane. "I am afraid our homecoming tonight will not be very pleasant."

"It does not matter," Jane said, looking up at Richard. "I already have everything in the world I need to make me happy."

CHAPTER 21

He either fears his fate too much, Or his desserts are small,
Who dares not put it to the touch, To win or lose it all.

— Montrose's Toast

Saturday, May 16, 1812
Longbourn, Hertfordshire

It was near midnight before Jane and Elizabeth arrived back at Longbourn. Their mother had not remembered—or perhaps had deliberately forgotten—to send the carriage back for them. Fortunately, Darcy and Bingley had arrived at the assembly in Bingley's coach, so the sisters did not have to walk back to Longbourn. Richard watched them leave with mixed feelings about having to depend on Bingley after the high emotions during the evening.

The journey had progressed mostly in silence since the drama of Jane having refused Bingley's proposal hung in the air as an unspoken damper to casual conversation. So Elizabeth was already in a foul mood before she reached for the front door, which seemingly opened of its own accord, leaving both girls facing the glowering visage of their mother.

"So you have finally deigned to return home, have you?" she said venomously. "Well, both of you get inside this instant!"

"Mama, you took the carriage and never sent it back for us," Elizabeth said. "You could hardly expect us to walk home in the dark and with just evening slippers on our feet." Her voice was mild, but inwardly she was irritated and struggled to control her temper.

"Never mind that, Miss Lizzy. I am not prepared to put up with your sharp tongue tonight when I have been so bitterly disappointed by Jane! You get upstairs to your bedroom. Jane and I have some matters that must be set aright instantly. Follow me, Jane."

Mrs. Bennet led the way down the hall to her husband's library and opened the door.

"Inside, Jane," she commanded, and Jane silently entered the library. Elizabeth was on Jane's heels, and her mother hissed to see her order had not been obeyed. She attempted to block the way into the room, but Elizabeth nimbly slipped past.

Mr. Bennet was sitting behind his desk reading as this occurred, and he put down his book and rolled his eyes in exasperation.

"What is this, Mrs. Bennet? Why am I disturbed in such an unseemly manner and at such a late hour? And without even the courtesy of a knock?"

Mrs. Bennet ignored his query and pointed to Jane, who was standing silently by Elizabeth.

"It is your daughter, Mr. Bennet. She has defied me in the most mortifying manner, and I demand that you command her to follow my instructions. Already I have been so badly humiliated that I do not know how I shall ever be able to hold my head up in public."

"Is this Jane you are referring to?" Mr. Bennet asked dubiously. "Whatever could the girl have done to prompt such a display on your part?"

"How can you be so tiresome? It is Mr. Bingley, of course. He has just this evening made her an extremely generous offer of marriage, and your ungrateful daughter has defied me by refusing him. It is intolerable, sir. Intolerable!"

Mr. Bennet sighed and removed his reading glasses, pinching and massaging the bridge of his nose to ease away the soreness.

"I believe we have had a similar conversation, except it involved Lizzy and my foolish cousin. You were not able to carry the day at that time. Whatever makes you think you will be more successful now?"

"Is it not obvious?" cried his wife. "You must *command* her to do her duty. Jane is not a sharpish, ungrateful girl like some I might name. *She* will do as she is told if you will but command her."

"I think you assume too much. Young people are often apt to fall in love and marry those they please with little or no help from their elders. In addition, I have a suspicion that Jane's heart may already have been leading her in another direction well before this proposal from Mr. Bingley."

Turning to Jane, he asked gently, "Is that not so, child?"

"It is true, Father. It is Colonel Fitzwilliam whom I love, and he loves me. Tonight, after Mr. Bingley's proposal, he made me an offer of marriage, and I have accepted it."

Mrs. Bennet let out another screech of rage on hearing this, but her husband merely chuckled.

"I thought as much when I saw him in our front room last week. He appeared particularly attentive, even if your mother did not seem to notice it."

He turned back to his wife. "Do you not see how amazing this is, Mrs. Bennet? Our eldest daughter has received two offers of marriage in a single night. You have caused all this turmoil for nothing."

But Mrs. Bennet was not of the same mind. "It is not to be borne! This penniless colonel is nothing beside Mr. Bingley. Nothing! Mr. Bingley has five thousand a year, and this...this officer...has been disowned by his own father. Thrown out of his house. Lydia told me he admitted as much himself. No, Mr. Bennet, it will not do.

You must make your daughter do her duty!"

"Colonel Fitzwilliam is not penniless," Jane said, "and he was not—"

But Mrs. Bennet shouted her down. "I was *thrilled* when Lady Lucas told me her daughter overheard Mr. Bingley make Jane an offer of marriage. But I could not believe my ears when she went on to say that Jane *refused him*. My nerves completely collapsed, sir. Completely. I almost fainted dead away."

"And you took the carriage home and could not even be bothered to send it back for us, Mama," Elizabeth said with cold fury. "If not for the efforts of Mr. Darcy and Mr. Bingley, we should have been obliged to walk home in the dark. Luckily, we rode home in Mr. Bingley's coach."

"What?" roared Mr. Bennet. "Is this true, madam? You did not send the carriage to fetch my daughters back to their home?"

But Mrs. Bennet was not to be deterred by her husband's anger as she continued to rail at her daughter.

"How could you treat me so, Jane? You know my nerves are not up to it. You have done nothing but talk all week of how exciting it was to have Mr. Bingley returning."

"*I* never talked about Mr. Bingley at all, Mama," Jane said fiercely, her ire raised at last. "That was *you* boasting to all your friends about the wonderful opportunity to have two daughters married to rich men. But I love Richard, and I *will* marry him,"

"And you defy me over this pauper of a colonel? Why, he could not even buy his own army commission! Lydia told me he was fortunate to receive the charity of Mr. Darcy's parents—else he should have had to take employment in the stables. Now you *shall* listen to me, young lady. You *shall* marry Mr. Bingley. You must send him a message in the morning and tell him you have reconsidered,"

"I shall do nothing of the kind, Mama. I have already accepted Richard, and he will call on Father in the morning."

"He is nothing in comparison to Mr. Bingley. I shall tell Hill to refuse to allow him in the house!"

"Silence!" roared Mr. Bennet again. This time he surged to his feet and leaned over his desk so his face was inches from that of his wife. "You will either be quiet, Mrs. Bennet, or I shall order you to your room!"

Both Jane and Elizabeth were taken aback by their father's never-before-exhibited anger, something completely new to their experience. But their mother was even more affected and actually recoiled from the fury she had engendered in her usually compliant husband.

"How could you speak to me in such a manner, Thomas?" she whimpered.

But Mr. Bennet was not to be influenced by such obvious wiles, and he said coldly, "No one except *me*, the master of this house, determines who will be allowed to enter and who will be refused, madam. And I will *never* abide one of my daughters being abandoned in such a thoughtless manner as I am told was done tonight. Such behaviour as this is completely inexcusable and is *not* to be repeated. Is that clearly understood, madam?"

His shaken wife, truly frightened of her husband's wrath, could only nod in acceptance.

"Very well, then," he said, resuming his seat. "I will ask some questions, and I will receive some answers without any more argument. Now, Jane, I am not saying that the man's fortune is the only factor to consider, but I must know whether your colonel can support you. From his note, your uncle did not see a problem, but he gave no details. Can you add anything to answer that question?"

"I am not certain of the details, Father. Richard and I did not speak of it, but I am confident he is able to support me. I cannot believe he would have declared himself if he had insufficient income to support a wife."

Mr. Bennet rolled his eyes at hearing this, but Elizabeth broke in. "I know some of the details, Papa. As my uncle's note says, he talked with Colonel Fitzwilliam when he called on Jane. I have to confess that I told Uncle Gardiner the colonel had little money, which naturally concerned him, and he and the colonel discussed the matter. When my uncle and I talked afterwards, he was quite confident that the colonel is not a pauper, as I had thought, even if he is not as wealthy as Mr. Bingley. He owns a house in town near to my uncle's house, though it is a bit smaller. And he and a neighbour share a stable."

Mr. Bennet nodded his head at this last point, because it gave him a benchmark. A gentleman could not afford a stable with horses, a carriage, and grooms to care for them if he did not have an income of at least four or five hundred pounds a year.

"And Colonel Fitzwilliam received a bequest from Mr. Darcy's father when he died," Elizabeth said. "The colonel used that bequest to purchase his house and invested the remainder in the Funds. He has also saved a portion of his pay, especially when he was gone from England, and also received rents of his house during that time. I do not know whether he is aware that Jane has no fortune, but it does not appear to concern him. Even if he goes on half-pay when the war ends, he convinced Uncle Gardiner that he could support a wife and family on his income."

Mr. Bennet again nodded his head. It was normal practice for a gentleman to invest his fortune in the government funds and live off the five percent income.

"Well, possessing a house *and* a share of a stable is quite commendable, Lizzy. Now why did you not know these facts, Jane? I would think you would have made sure your young man could support you before you blithely gave him your acceptance."

Jane turned beet red and opened her mouth to say something, but Elizabeth was quick to come to her rescue. "That is not fair, Father. You have only recently been introduced to Colonel Fitzwilliam, but I know from many weeks' acquaintance that he is an honourable man who never would have courted Jane unless he knew he could support her. He just…well, he *inspires* confidence, is the only way I can phrase it."

"He does, does he?" Mr. Bennet said musingly, cocking an eyebrow at Jane, who nodded vigorously. "Very well then, Jane. I shall speak to your young man in the morning to delve into these matters in more detail, but unless I find surprises, I can see no reason not to give him my permission."

"But Mr. Bingley..." moaned Mrs. Bennet.

"Mr. Bingley will have to put some salve on his wounds," said her husband coldly. "After all, have you forgotten that he deserted our daughter and left her to tend her own wounds in silence and solitude? I shall not spend overmuch time weeping for Mr. Bingley *or* his five thousand a year. This colonel looks to have almost half of my own income, and I have supported a household and five daughters for these twenty years, so I do not see a problem."

"Thank you, Father," Jane said, as she leaned over to kiss his forehead. She and Elizabeth left the room in good cheer, leaving their mother wringing her hands in misery.

"Mrs. Bennet," they heard their father say sternly as they started up the stairs, "you will please take your whining and complaining to your room and give me some peace and solitude. Have you forgotten that Mr. Darcy will likely call tomorrow in addition to Jane's Colonel Fitzwilliam? Will you run Mr. Darcy off because of your displeasure?"

As the two girls approached their room, Jane leaned close and whispered, "Would you delay dressing for bed, Lizzy? I am distressed, and I desperately need to talk."

Elizabeth looked at her sister rather quizzically but nodded her assent. Thus, when they entered their room, Jane immediately assumed her usual position: sitting in her bed with her back against the headboard.

Elizabeth lost little time in joining her. "Are you still troubled by what our mother said? You should just ignore her. She is being even more silly than usual, and she cannot stand being shown to be wrong at the best of times."

"I know that, but what worries me is that she makes me far angrier than I should be. I have been subject to similar fits of irritation and even rage virtually all week. I cannot remember feeling anything similar before this, and I am quite disturbed by it."

"I noticed your agitation, but I thought it was just because Mr. Bingley was calling every day and you were eager to see Richard."

"You are correct, but it was more than that. I was worried because I did not know what I would do with two gentlemen calling on me. It was only when Mr. Bingley openly proposed that my mind cleared. But during the week, whenever our mother would say something about how attentive Mr. Bingley was or how it would be so wonderful to have two daughters well settled, I would get so angry I wanted to scream at her. Really, I did."

"Scream at her? That is remarkable for you. But you did not do so."

"But I had to flee to my room immediately, or else I cannot say what might have happened. And then tonight—when she said what she did about Richard—I was even angrier, if that is possible. If our father had not shown the firmness he did, I truly believe I would have been screaming back at my mother while she screamed at me."

"And it worries you," Elizabeth said, not asking a question but making a simple statement of fact.

"Desperately so. I am so afraid something has become terribly wrong with me, and I am afraid I shall disappoint Richard by being subject to similar fits of anger."

"Oh, I think that is unlikely since I believe I understand what is happening. All I can say is, 'Welcome to the same imperfect world in which the rest of us mortals dwell.'"

"What do you mean? I do not understand you."

"Jane, Jane, it is just that you have been so unbelievably gentle and mild all your life. It has been positively *unearthly*. Why, the emotions you experienced tonight are no different than most people feel when things are going badly. But *we* have to learn to control ourselves while you were never plagued by those feelings and, thus, never learned to deal with them."

Elizabeth smiled at her sister, who looked at her in confusion, her brow wrinkled.

"Well, actually that is not quite right, Jane. You did deal with your feelings since, in fact, you did not scream at our mother though she richly deserved it. But you are not used to having to exert that type of control, so it feels strange and wrong to you."

"Perhaps you are right," Jane said slowly, her agitation beginning to dwindle as she grappled with her problem. "But why should it occur now?"

"Because now you want something badly—very badly indeed. You want to marry Richard, and our mother has tried to thwart your wishes. First, she failed to notice your interest in Richard or his in you, and then she kept interjecting Mr. Bingley into the conversations. And tonight she quite literally tried to wrest Richard away by seeking to have Father order you to marry Mr. Bingley. She was counting on your usual mild and obedient nature to carry the day, but luckily, Father stood up to her in much the same way he did after I refused Mr. Collins, though he was much angrier on this occasion—much more so than I have ever seen before."

"I am sure you are right," Jane said quietly. "But I would not have allowed either Mama or Papa to change my mind."

"I know, dear heart, I know. But I was still proud of Papa."

Jane nodded in agreement while she pondered Lizzy's comments. "I think you may have the right of it—as far as it goes."

"As far as it goes?" Elizabeth's eyebrows went up in query, but she said nothing else as Jane thought a bit longer. The more she thought, the more anxious she became until her agitation eventually overcame her natural reserve.

"My anger is not...the only matter causing me concern. I have other...other...oh, this is so embarrassing!"

"If you do not wish to discuss what concerns you, I shall not press you," Elizabeth said, putting her hand on Jane's arm and squeezing it comfortingly. "But you know you are always assured of my silence."

Jane nodded, for she was well aware of Elizabeth's discretion without it being said. However, though it was difficult, she decided she had to talk to *someone*...

"It is just that I keep remembering how Mama has said so often that we must be prepared to endure the beastly urges of our husbands. Yet I am feeling...dreaming things...that are so...so..."

"I believe you would be better advised to listen to Aunt Gardiner in matters such as these, Jane."

"I know, I know! Yet I did not expect what I felt tonight when Richard kissed me. It felt wonderful when he put his hands around my back, but I wanted...I wanted more..."

Elizabeth smiled her understanding and took Jane's hand. "Jane, do you not remember Aunt Gardiner talking to us in London? She made it clear that women often feel far more physical attraction for their husbands than our mother would have us believe. Since I am certain you have entertained thoughts of being married to Richard, I am not surprised to hear what you say."

Jane looked at her sister for a moment before nodding slowly in agreement as she remembered her aunt's earnest words. Finally, she admitted, "I do remember that conversation, Lizzy. However, when Richard formally made his proposal tonight, I had this sudden... *impulse* is the best word I can think of. I wanted to be alone with him...completely alone. I thought of asking him to take me to Gretna Green this very night, but I would have gone to his room if he had suggested it. He is far too honourable to have done so, of course, but it is probably well that you and Mr. Darcy were with us, lest I might have made the suggestion myself."

"That is a bit surprising...but only a bit, I suppose. Remember something else our aunt said: that it is not the urge that is sinful but rather the giving in to that urge. Nevertheless, I would recommend you not wait very long before making the union official."

"I know," Jane said with a wan smile. "I would like nothing better than to get married tomorrow."

"And that would *truly* excite our mother's wrath!"

"I suppose so, but I find the thought of our mother's anger no longer moves me. She has already gone to great lengths to tarnish what should have been a most happy occasion, and she has ridiculed and belittled Richard unmercifully. So I believe the wishes of my mother will not receive much consideration regarding the date for the wedding or anything else. All that matters is what Richard wants."

Elizabeth laughed aloud at this comment. "If the date for marrying you were only based on the way he looked at you tonight—and he possessed a special license—tomorrow would likely be a most eventful day!"

CHAPTER 22

Your eyes kissed mine; I saw the love in them shine;
You brought me heaven right then, When your eyes kissed mine.
— "Plaisir d'Amour," folk song originally composed
by Martini il Tedesco for the French court

Sunday, May 17, 1812
Longbourn, Hertfordshire

J ane arose and dressed early on Sunday morning before taking up a position by the window to watch for Richard's arrival. Based on what he had said as he handed her into Bingley's coach the evening before, she expected him to arrive early in order to talk to her father. Elizabeth looked out from under her blanket as her sister dressed, but such early activity held little attraction for her, so she pulled the blanket over her head and went back to sleep.

As soon as Richard came into view, Jane ran downstairs to the door. Her mother was just coming out of the parlour, and she glared at Jane as she ran past, opening her mouth to say something. Jane ignored her completely, opening the door just as Richard was giving the reins of his horse to a stable boy.

"Good morning, Jane," Richard said with a smile, turning towards her. He was rather surprised to see her running eagerly to greet him with both hands outstretched since he was familiar with her natural reserve. However, he could see from the look on her face that she was in the grip of a powerful emotion. He reached his own hands out to hers, but he was further surprised as she eagerly threw herself into his embrace.

"Oh, Richard, Richard, it seems an eternity since last night," Jane said fervently, pressing her head into his shoulder. "I know it is silly, but I have missed you dreadfully all night. All I want is for you to hold me like this forever."

"I am certainly not complaining, love. But are you not concerned that your mother will disapprove of our embracing right outside the front door?"

"I care nothing for what she says—nothing at all. She was simply horrible last night, and while I shall miss my father, I should be happy to never spend another night under her roof."

"It appears the homecoming your sister termed 'difficult' was even worse than she feared," Richard said with concern. He was confident that only an extremely dreadful experience could have moved Jane to express herself in such harsh terms towards any member of her family.

"It was bad enough when she was haranguing me for not accepting Mr. Bingley, but then she began to insult and castigate you because you were 'penniless' and 'disowned' by your father. I have never been so angry in my life, and I do not like myself when I get that angry."

"I can well understand, love, especially since I can see your mother glaring at us through a window. It does appear I am not one of her favourites."

"Never you mind. Lizzy stood up for you and told my father what you and Uncle Gardiner discussed. Papa said he would want to speak of the same things when you called, but he essentially already approves of you."

"So perhaps I should go in and see him so I can escort you to church?"

"I wish I could stay like this forever, but you are certainly right. But remember what I said: I do not desire to stay here a single night more than I must, so you and Father must set a date for our wedding just as soon as may be. Today would be best, but I would settle for tomorrow."

"I should not oppose either possibility, but unfortunately neither of them is likely. After I secure your father's permission, there is the matter of a license, which requires a wait of seven days. I trust we shall not have to wait that long—I have made certain preparations, you see—but I still need to speak with your parson. I am not known to him, of course, so he may be stubborn and try to make us wait the full period. But even if he is reasonable, a wait of a few days in unavoidable. However, if remaining under your mother's roof is too burdensome, I am sure you could go to your uncle's home and we could be married in my parish in town. But that is a drastic step. Your father and I must talk."

Jane sighed in disappointment, but she realized she was probably not being reasonable. She knew there were certain formalities that had to be observed, but she had tossed and turned well after Elizabeth fell asleep the previous night, unable to force the events of the evening and the previous week from her mind. She was furious with her mother for turning what should have been one of the happiest days of her life into one of the worst, and she was determined to wait no longer than required. She finally pushed back from Richard's embrace though she still clung to his arm as she took him inside to meet her father.

JANE WENT TO SIT IN THE FRONT ROOM WHILE RICHARD AND HER father talked, ignoring her mother and her attempt at conversation until she got up and left the room in irritation. It was no more than ten minutes after that before she heard her father's library door open, and Richard immediately appeared in the doorway.

"Would you care to join us, Jane? Your father and I have settled everything except for the date and place, and I believe you should be involved in those decisions."

"Thank you, Richard. That is very considerate." In truth, she was pleased by the speed with which the two men settled affairs and somewhat surprised to be consulted so explicitly. Everything she had ever heard had the bride's father and the future husband settling on a date and then informing everyone else, so she was happy at this thoughtfulness.

Her father looked up at her cheerfully from the papers on his desk as she entered his library. "Well, Jane, you will be glad to know that certain charges about your future husband's lack of fortune turned out to be a trifle on the pessimistic side. Your prospects will be just as Lizzie told me—comfortable, though not luxurious—and I have given my blessing for the two of you to marry."

"I am pleased to hear that, Papa." Jane was still clinging to Richard's arm, and she felt a wave of relief sweep through her.

"Now, your gentleman tells me you have some rather forceful ideas about getting married at the earliest possible date." Jane's relief faltered somewhat at this reminder of the other issues still to be resolved.

"Today was my preferred choice," Jane said firmly.

"So he told me, but you must know that is just not possible. Now, you do not specifically need my permission since you are of legal age, but I have given it anyway. The usual way is to have the banns read in church on three Sundays prior to the wedding…"

"I will ask Richard to take me to Gretna Green this instant if there is no other choice," Jane said firmly. "I will not wait an hour longer than absolutely necessary."

"Now, do not get overwrought," Mr. Bennet said mildly. "I just said that was the *usual* way. The other way is to purchase what is called a common license, which forgoes the banns and only imposes a seven-day wait instead of two weeks with the banns. Interestingly, Colonel Fitzwilliam seems to have done some preliminary planning and is already in possession of just such a license."

Richard patted his coat pocket and smiled. "It may have been a bit presumptuous on my part, but as I told your uncle, I was determined to eventually win your affection and make you my wife. That being the case, I secured a common license after returning to London. It is dated May 12, so we may be married as soon as the twentieth, which is Wednesday, either at your parish or at mine in London."

"Not a special license, young man?" Mr. Bennet asked slyly, and Richard laughed.

"Not that Jane is not worth it, sir, but I hope I know not to spend twenty guineas when, with proper planning, a few shillings will produce the same result. It would be better spent on her wardrobe than on gaining the consent of the archbishop."

"I can do nothing other than agree with such a sensible statement even though this house will be a far less sensible place once you take Jane away. But we still have to settle on a firm date and place."

Jane sighed and looked at Richard. "You already know my wishes, but I shall abide by whatever you think is best."

"We both know there are certain people on both sides of our family who would want to attend and need to travel to Hertfordshire, my love," he said. "Your aunt and uncle Gardiner, for certain. I need to inform my mother and sister, though I believe Darcy's sister will arrive tomorrow. She would not forgive me if I married without her attendance. I should also inform my aunt Lady Catherine, little though I believe she will attend. If we send expresses promptly to all concerned, I believe we may safely schedule the ceremony for Wednesday, though we should consult with your pastor immediately."

"I have already sent him a message and asked him to call as soon after church services as possible," Mr. Bennet said.

Though disappointed at not being able to marry this very day, Jane now understood the reasons it was not possible. Her smile was a bit wistful, but she felt content at having things settled. "I also believe

Wednesday will do nicely, Richard. But no longer."

She looked directly at her father. "No matter how much my mother wails her displeasure, I will not wait a day longer. I would rather travel to London and be married in Richard's parish. She has already done her very best to ruin what should be the happiest event in my life."

Mr. Bennet nodded agreement, grieved that this daughter who deserved the very best had been so ill served by her own mother. "I shall speak with her. She will cause no further problems, including complaining that you must be wed with new clothes. If she cannot hold her tongue or conceal her displeasure, she will spend the next three days in her room."

Jane nodded in agreement, unhappy at having forced her father to act so uncharacteristically, but she was not sorry for having said what she did. Her concern now was for the most important person in her life, her future husband, and she was not going to tolerate having her mother affront him further.

As she and Richard left, she stopped him for a moment, rising on tiptoe to whisper in his ear, "Please forgive me, but my mother's opposition is not the only reason for my impatience. It may be forward of me, but I am exceedingly anxious to be away with you."

Richard smiled and whispered back, "I feel exactly as you do, my love. Knowing you wish to be alone with me as much as I wish to be alone with you is a treasure I shall always remember."

As soon as they entered the hall, they saw Elizabeth waiting by the front door. Since she held shawls, bonnets, and gloves for both of them, her desire to depart the house could not be mistaken. Since Jane felt similarly, she and Richard lost no time in joining her.

"Did everything go well?" Elizabeth asked as the two of them pulled on gloves and tied each other's bonnets.

"As well as could be expected once I finally accepted that an immediate ceremony was not possible. But my esteemed future husband had events well in hand as usual and already possesses the required license. My father sent a note to the parson asking him to call, so we shall be married on Wednesday."

"The parson was not the only person summoned," Elizabeth said, almost herding her sister and Richard through the front door. "I heard Hill telling my mother that our father wanted to talk to her immediately. Mama tried to evade him, but Hill informed her that Papa would accept no excuses. I had planned to walk to church with Mr. Darcy, but I hurriedly dressed and came downstairs with our things. I can meet Mr. Darcy at the chapel."

"I am a bit surprised at my father summoning my mother," Jane said. "He told me he was going to speak with her about her treatment of Richard, but I was somewhat sceptical since he seldom exerts himself. Perhaps he believed me about Gretna Green if my mother continued to insult my future husband."

"Really, my skin is thicker than that, my love" Richard said mildly. "Since you accepted the offer of my hand, what else matters?"

"Perhaps so, but mine is not, and I cannot abide her denigrating you any longer. I may have been more patient before we met, but now you are too important to me. I will not tolerate any further attempts by her to ruin this happy time."

The sun and the open air soon had its usual effect on Elizabeth, whose normally cheerful spirit seemed to blossom in the sunlight, and she was joined on this day by her sister, who was not nearly as fond of walking. Jane felt her gloom lifting, however, as Richard and Elizabeth talked playfully about the wedding on Wednesday, making light of her mother. Elizabeth professed that Mrs. Bennet would soon change her attitude and would then utter nothing but the most laudatory descriptions of Richard. The real threat, as she saw it, was that their mother would then enthusiastically try to delay the ceremony, saying that all manner of preparations were absolutely required. Richard laughed that off, saying that Darcy had already promised the use of his coach if a journey to Gretna Green proved necessary. Soon, Jane could not help but join the conversation, and the sun was warm on their shoulders as the three of them walked, talked, and laughed.

The sound of an approaching carriage was heard as they neared the chapel, and they moved to the side of the road to allow it to pass. Instead, they heard Darcy's distinctive voice call out, "Pull up, Stewart!" as it drew near.

The three of them turned to see Darcy jumping down before the coach finished rocking on its springs. He held up a hand to stop his footmen from descending and pulled down the step himself. A gloved feminine hand took his extended one, and a young lady descended gracefully. She was tall—taller even than Jane—and, despite her womanly and graceful carriage, evidently no more than fifteen or sixteen years of age.

This must be Darcy's sister, Jane thought instantly, and the two siblings approached just as Elizabeth leaned closer to impart the same information.

"Georgiana," Darcy said with evident pride, "please allow me to introduce Miss Elizabeth Bennet, of whom we have spoken. And this is her elder sister, Miss Jane Bennet, who will soon be our new cousin since she has rashly accepted an offer of marriage from our wayward military relation. Ladies, Miss Georgiana Darcy, my sister."

Miss Darcy's curtsey was graceful, but her eyes were downcast and her colour was heightened. Jane at first wondered whether the girl was reluctant to meet the two of them, but a quick upward glance of Miss Darcy's eyes banished that supposition even as it formed.

I remember seeing that look in the eyes of a newly born farm animal, she thought. *That is a wary, timid look or one of extreme shyness. It is certainly not the pride Wickham described to Elizabeth.*

Miss Darcy's words as they exchanged greetings and Darcy waxed eloquent about Georgiana's accomplishments buttressed Jane's guess, for the young girl could hardly speak more than monosyllables.

But her frightened looks dissipated as Jane and Elizabeth easily drew Georgiana into conversation while Darcy stood by, beaming with pride and satisfaction. It was clear to Jane that Georgiana was intensely curious and interested in both sisters, one of whom was already destined to be a close relation, wife to the cousin who had virtually grown up in their home.

However, Jane could see from Miss Darcy's glances that she was possibly even more interested in Elizabeth. *I wonder whether she knows that her brother is in love with Lizzy and desperately wishes to marry her?* Jane wondered. *I wish we knew each other well enough that I could take her aside and ask why Mr. Darcy cannot seem to finalize his desires just yet after having been interested enough to be on the verge of offering marriage. Men can be so baffling.*

But, as she looked aside at Richard, she amended that thought. *Except for my Richard, that is. One never has to wonder about HIS intentions. He states them forthrightly and then follows through at the proper time and without hesitation.*

Even without Georgiana Darcy's demonstrated shyness, Wickham's lies about Darcy's supposed offences against him had already discredited the stories he told of Miss Darcy's pride and arrogance. From her modest and gentle manners and her obvious attempts to overcome her reticence, Jane was certain that she and the young girl would quickly become warm and loving cousins. It could not be otherwise, given her own nature coupled with the sense and good humour radiating from the girl's face as they talked.

Meanwhile, Bingley had descended unnoticed from the coach, and it was several minutes before Darcy belatedly realized it.

"Please excuse my atrociously ignoring the amenities," he said, putting his arm to his cousin's elbow to turn him about. "Richard, please allow me to present my good friend Charles Bingley. Charles, this is my cousin—and also a good friend—Colonel Richard Fitzwilliam, of whom we have spoken."

Richard gave Bingley a punctiliously correct bow while carefully controlling his expression. He knew the man had to be embarrassed by the situation, and he did not want to make things worse.

"I am pleased to make your acquaintance at last, sir. Darcy has often spoken of what a good friend you have been to him."

"And he has often spoken of you, Colonel, as well as informing me of your good news. May I offer my sincere congratulations on your engagement?"

"Thank you, Mr. Bingley," Richard replied with a nod, hiding his discomfort at seeing how much the effort cost the other man.

Bingley nodded with only a hint of jerkiness to indicate the awkwardness and unhappiness he felt, but he had one more task to perform. For that task, he had to wait for a break in the conversation between the Bennet sisters and Miss Darcy, and that pause came quickly as the three noticed him standing close.

"Miss Bennet," he said bravely, "Darcy has told me of your betrothal to his cousin. Please allow me to offer my congratulations and my wishes for all health and happiness for both of you in your marriage."

Jane nodded gravely, her beautiful eyes showing her understanding of his pain, but she had made her choice knowing such an uncomfortable moment as this would be a certainty.

"I thank you, sir. Both Richard and I accept your assurances in the spirit in which they were offered, and we also most sincerely hope that you will someday find the same joy and happiness we share."

Bingley tried to conceal a wince at these words, which might have seemed false and condescending from someone else. But, coming as it did from Jane Bennet, he knew she was sincere. As he bowed over her hand, he raised it to his lips and lightly brushed his lips to the fabric of her glove. Then, as he released her hand and straightened, they shared one last glance that showed they both understood how this moment had come to pass.

Bingley turned to Richard and offered his hand, which was received without hesitation. Then, with one last nod to the man who had obtained what once had been within his own grasp, he departed towards the church, leaving the group to their own conversation.

For in that group, he bitterly realised, he could henceforth never be more than an outsider.

CHAPTER 23

A man who becomes conscious of the responsibility he bears toward a human being who affectionately waits for him, or to an unfinished work, will never be able to throw away his life. He knows the 'why' for his existence, and will be able to bear almost any 'how.'

— Viktor Frankl

Sunday, May 17, 1812
Matlock Hall, London

As he turned up the drive to Matlock Hall, Richard was surprised at the memories that came unbidden to his mind. Many were good ones, for the sequence of events that led to his departure from his father's home occurred in a short span of time and thus only generated relatively few—albeit quite intense—remembrances. Prior to that cataclysmic event, his main recollection of his father was of a remote figure before whom he would be paraded at infrequent intervals. Other than those reminiscences, which were not really painful in and of themselves, he mostly remembered his mother and his older brother, George, who was about a year and a half his senior. He and George had attended the same school, but his younger brothers, Thomas and Edward, who had been five and eight years younger than he was, had not yet started school at the time he left home. Accordingly, he had enjoyed little contact with them before departing Matlock.

Thomas would be four and twenty now, and Edward three years younger still, but I have had no communication with them since leaving, Richard thought sourly. *They essentially took their cue from Father and never answered any of my letters. But it hurts that George essentially did the same and totally cut me out of his life. He even went to the trouble and expense of having my letters returned so I would know he had seen them. So all I have are Mother and Elaine.*

With a surge of anger, he reined in his imminent fall into self-pity, thrusting such maudlin thoughts aside.

It could be much worse and you know it, Fitzwilliam, he told himself forcefully. *At least my aunt and uncle Darcy welcomed me into their home, provided me with a means of supporting myself, and treated me as if I were Darcy's brother. And even Father did not forbid Mother and Elaine from corresponding or seeing me. So I have no cause to repine and must be grateful for what I have instead of whining over disappointments. Stop it.*

As he rode up the drive, he briefly—very briefly—considered stopping at the front door and knocking as the normal visitor would do. But he rather gleefully put that thought where it belonged and turned his horse towards the rear entrance and the stables.

I am still a Fitzwilliam, by God, he thought firmly, *even if a somewhat disobedient one. I will NOT beg leave to be admitted like some casual visitor desiring to view the public areas of the house.*

He was surprised to see Old Frederick come out to take his horse. He had last seen the head groom more than five years ago, before he left England, and he would have been less surprised to find him in the grave than coming out to collect his horse. But here was the same white-haired man, moving somewhat gingerly as if walking gave him pain but still able to get about. And his wrinkled, sun-browned face was split by a wide, welcoming grin.

"Master Richard, as I live and breathe. It is a wonder to see you after so many years. And look at you in your fancy uniform. Surely you must be a gen'ral by now!"

"Only a mere colonel of cavalry, Frederick." Richard laughed, both gratified and a bit embarrassed at such an effusive greeting.

He had indeed dressed in his best uniform for this visit as a somewhat defiant bit of bravado, and Sergeant Bascomb had been completely in his element as he helped him dress. His red coat was his newest, the scarlet undimmed by washings or exposure to the elements. The white facings at the lapels, collar, and cuffs were spotless, as were his white crossbelt and white breeches. His high black boots came above his knee, and Bascomb had polished them to a brilliant sheen.

He also wore the regulation dragoon helmet of polished black leather with a high crest trimmed in gold and a black horsehair plume hanging down the back below his neck. He had decided against the non-regulation but much lighter and more comfortable Tarleton helmet that he usually wore in favour of the more impressive regulation helmet, and polished silver spurs adorned his boots. Only the starkly functional cavalry sabre made a discordant note, and in that area, Richard was not willing to compromise. He could act the dandy when it pleased him, but he never compromised when it came to good steel and a sharp edge.

"Well, colonel is next to gen'ral, and you not yet thirty," the old man said, his admiration and pride so evident that Richard had to laugh aloud.

"Do you happen to know whether my mother and sister are in the house, Frederick?" he asked quickly.

"Must be, sir. No one has left the house all day."

"Thank you. I do not know how long I shall be—possibly no more than half an hour. So you can leave the saddle on."

"It be no trouble to get him unsaddled and wiped down, sir. One of the lads can do it, so it be no trouble to me at all," Frederick said, giving him a conspiratorial wink.

"Very well, then. Many thanks."

Richard entered through the back entrance and walked up front to the small butler's cubby. Merideth heard the jingle of his spurs before he got close and looked around the doorjamb curiously.

"Master Richard!"

"Hullo, Merideth. How is your family keeping these days?"

"Very fine, sir, very fine indeed," Merideth beamed. "Ruthie married herself a clerk, John is working apprentice to the smithy, and Sally is helping her mother in the kitchen. The other four are still too young, you know."

"Four? You mean your brood is up to seven now? It was only four when I left, and you were not a youngling then. Should not a man of your years think of slowing down?"

Merideth beamed in pleasure at the teasing, for he had not married until he was forty, and he was rightfully proud of siring seven healthy children.

"But, sir, I am forgetting my manners." He drew himself up straight and gave Richard a courtly bow. "Welcome home, Master Richard. It is far too seldom that we see you."

"Now, none of that, Merideth. I am on an errand that cannot be delayed. Can you tell me the whereabouts of my mother and sister? I need to speak with them."

"Lady Matlock is in the front room taking tea with the master, sir. And Miss Elaine is upstairs practicing her music."

Richard made sure to keep his face impassive, for he would have vastly preferred to be able to see his mother without confronting his father. His usual course would have been to leave and come back at a time when he could see his mother and sister privately, but he could not spare the time.

"Would you please send someone to ask my sister to join us in the front room? Tell her it is important and time is pressing."

"Certainly, sir," Merideth said gravely. He was well aware of the dispute between Lord Matlock and his son, and it saddened him, for the lad had obviously turned out to be a strapping, fine young man.

"Thank you, Merideth," Richard said, turning away towards the front room. He walked with a steady stride, determined not to let the undesirability of his task deter him. He removed his helmet and held it under his left arm as he came to the front room. He paused, considering whether to go on through the door as would be normal for a member of the family, but he shrugged and knocked firmly. Bravado was one thing, but in reality, he truly was a stranger in this house, no matter how welcome the staff had made him feel.

"Enter," came clearly through the door in his mother's firm voice, and Richard opened the door and stepped inside.

"Richard!" exclaimed his mother in surprise and pleasure. The older man sitting across from her wore a look of equal surprise but considerably less pleasure.

Nevertheless, Richard forced his stride to be firm without being overly so as he walked over to the small table with the tea service. Lady Matlock gave her husband a somewhat worried look but then dismissed it. She did not get to see this son often, and she would not allow her husband's displeasure to affect her. This room was for her use as she saw fit, and if he could not be civil, then she would politely but firmly ask him to leave.

"This is a pleasant and quite unexpected surprise," she said as Richard came up and leaned over to kiss her cheek. Then he turned, clicked his heels together, and gave his father a precisely measured bow suitable to his rank.

"My lord," he said, and he was proud that his voice was both firm and as neutral as he could make it. He would *not* give in to the juvenile temptation of showing disrespect or resentment.

Lord Matlock nodded his head but said nothing. In fact, Richard was quite surprised to find his father appearing much older than he had expected, and he was disturbed to note the heavy walking stick resting by its handle over the chair arm. Lord Matlock had grown considerably bulkier as well as older, and he obviously needed the cane for walking.

"I know I did not send word that I would be visiting today, Mother, but I have some news to tell you. In fact, I asked to have Elaine join us so I can tell you both at once."

Something stirred in Lord Matlock's eyes as he noted the way his son phrased his errand to include only his mother and sister. He looked carefully to see whether there was some deliberate disrespect intended, but honesty compelled him to conclude his son had not even realized what he was saying. He did not know why it should pain him since he was the one who had made the decision that estranged the two of them, but he could not deny the sharp twinge of regret he felt.

"That sounds serious," Lady Matlock said, but her concern was in a different area. "Is your regiment being sent away again?"

Richard gave her a reassuring smile. "I cannot say what the War Office may decide, but there is no such plan I am aware of at this time."

"But there was little warning last time—only a fortnight or so before you boarded ship and were gone for five years."

"Ah, but there is a slight difference this time, Mother," Richard said with a crooked grin. "Colonel Gordon was aware of the plans for some months previously, but he was not in the habit of informing mere captains of their destiny. But now I command the regiment, and the War Office is silent thus far."

"Good. Let some other regiment go next time. Yours has already been battered enough."

Lord Matlock felt another sharp pang at the easy conversation between his wife and her son, but he knew part of his discomfort came from his knowledge of just how badly his son's regiment had been damaged. It had, in fact, been nearly broken. Despite the estrangement between them, he had avidly read every letter and communiqué concerning his son's regiment in *The Military Gazette*. He never let anyone see him do so, but he was more conversant than his wife as to how dreadful the carnage had been in Egypt and in Italy.

"Richard!"

Richard turned to see his sister running towards him, and he barely had time to turn completely around before she clasped him in a fierce embrace.

"Hello, Sprout," he said fondly. "But what is this? I believe you have grown another inch in six months. Did I not order you to stop growing?"

"Yes, you did," Elaine said gaily, giving him another hug before turning to give her mother and father a more restrained kiss on the cheek. "But you never do anything to back up your orders, so I just ignored you as I always do. But why did you not tell us you were coming? With everything Mother schedules for me, I could have been *anywhere* this afternoon."

"I had no real choice since everything is quite rushed," Richard said carefully. "You see, I have met the woman I never expected to meet, and she has consented to be my wife. We are to be married on Wednesday."

There was a brief moment of silence from his mother as she absorbed his news, but his sister had no such compunctions.

"Richard! Why did you not tell us! Oh, you are probably teasing me again. Do *not* tell me you are teasing me."

"I am not teasing you this time, Elaine," Richard said with a smile.

"Tell me everything. Is she beautiful? How did you meet her? Why have you never mentioned her? Oh, Richard, sometimes you are the most *exasperating* brother."

"Richard," his mother said more calmly, "I believe it would be best if you sat down and told us about this most surprising development. Now, tell us about this young lady and how you came to meet her. Would you care for a cup of tea?"

Richard looked around for a place to put his helmet, but his sister took it from his hands and tossed it on a nearby sofa before she pulled him down onto another sofa beside her. His spurs jingled against the floor and his sword rattled against the sofa, but he managed to take his seat without losing too much of his dignity.

"Well, to begin with, her name is Miss Jane Bennet, and she is the eldest daughter of a small landowner in Hertfordshire. I met her sister, Miss Elizabeth Bennet, when I was visiting Lady Catherine recently with Darcy, and then I met Jane when I visited her sister in London."

He looked carefully at his mother, but he also had his eye on his father as he continued. "You probably should know that Darcy has become interested in Miss Elizabeth, and he is at present courting her. I believe he will soon propose marriage, and I believe she will accept him."

"Darcy?" rumbled Lord Matlock in shock. "What about Anne? Catherine told me not two months ago that Anne was improving every month, and it would soon be possible for her to take her place at Darcy's side."

Richard now turned his head and looked his father directly in the eye. "My lord, that is a delusion of your sister, my aunt. It was heart-breaking to see Anne after an absence of five years and observe how wasted she had become. Perhaps it has happened so gradually that everyone else is used to it, but I have seen death too many times to be mistaken. My cousin is never going to take her place by *anyone's* side. She will be lucky to last another year. And she knows it. We spoke of it, and she has no self-delusions. She said she is too tired to go on. She is ready for the end to come."

Lord Matlock looked as if he was on the verge of an explosive outburst of rage, but then he looked into his son's eyes, and he read brutal honesty there mixed with deep grief. He slumped back in realisation that Richard had to be right: Anne had looked quite unwell when he saw her last, but he had allowed himself to be persuaded by his sister.

"Poor Anne," whispered Elaine. "I wondered myself, but I did not want to believe it."

"I agree with Richard, but I did not see anything to be gained by disputing my sister," Lady Matlock said gravely. "But this news about Darcy will hit her hard."

"It is time for Darcy to take a wife. He is eight and twenty, and it is time Pemberley had an heir," Richard said.

"But what about you, then, Brother?" asked his sister slyly. "You are a year older than Darcy, but you said you would not be married until you were done with active service."

"And I had no idea of it, Sprout," Richard said with a grin. "But after I met Jane, I was lost. She is indeed beautiful, but more importantly, she is also the sweetest and most loving woman I have ever met. In truth, she is an angel. I could no more have stopped myself from pursuing her than I could have ceased breathing."

"Incredible," said his sister softly, seeing the fervency in her brother's eyes.

"This is most enlightening, Richard, but I am troubled by the rapidity of what is happening," his mother said, handing him a cup of tea. "What is the rush? After all, you will be married for life. Should you not slow down and take some time to ponder whether you are making a good choice?"

Richard only grinned at her. "No, Mother, I will not risk losing her. And she is adamant about having the wedding as soon as possible. Her mother does not look on this match with favour. She wants Jane to marry another, considerably wealthier, young man. He also made her an offer, and her mother evidently used some intemperate language in trying to force Jane to accept his offer instead of mine. I believe her words describing me included 'pauper' and 'penniless' and 'he is nothing in comparison.' Jane, who is loyal to the very bone, was mortally offended by these insults and refuses to spend a day longer than necessary under her mother's roof."

"That does not sound like a family worthy of a connexion with our family," Lord Matlock grumbled, his brows beetled in disapproval.

Richard's head turned to regard his father like the head of a predator turning to regard a competitor, and his eyes were like granite. "In truth, my lord, Mrs. Bennet is one of the most foolish women I have known, but she faces an unpleasant situation: an older husband whose estate is entailed away to a cousin. When her husband dies, she and her daughters will have nothing on which to live, and desperation drives even wise people to do desperate things. And, you will pardon my impertinence, my lord, but this connexion is of no concern to you whatever."

Tension crackled in the room as both men glared fiercely at each other, but the confrontation did not last long before Lord Matlock looked away, unable to confront the son he had driven from his home.

Lady Matlock was quick to end the uncomfortable silence. "It appears your mind is quite made up on the matter."

"It is, Mother," Richard agreed though he was almost quivering with the stress of holding his temper. "I came to invite you and Elaine to attend if you so desire. Please understand that I will not be offended if you cannot be there. The journey to Hertfordshire takes several hours, I have been unable to give you adequate warning, and Elaine is in the middle of her first Season, so I completely understand if previous engagements prevent your attendance. But I did want to offer you the opportunity."

"Nonsense, of course we shall be there," his mother said.

Elaine was even more direct. "I cannot think of anything that would please me more than to miss another breakfast or ball with the latest set of chowder-headed young gentlemen in pursuit of my fortune."

"Excellent," Richard said, smiling at his sister's wry comment. He pulled out a folded piece of paper and handed it to his mother. "Here are the directions to the chapel at Longbourn. Now, I hate to depart so quickly, but I must see to the regiment's needs and request a little unexpected leave from the major general. And I still must journey to see Lady Catherine and return to Hertfordshire."

"It appears my brother cannot endure a long separation from his lady fair, Mother," his sister said with a straight face. But Richard knew her mischievous side, and he just smiled at her as he stood.

"One of these days, Sprout, some young man is going to catch *your* fancy, and then we shall see how you enjoy having the tables turned."

His sister just sniffed haughtily, but her eyes were sparkling with good humour as her brother leaned down to kiss her cheek.

Richard fetched his helmet from the sofa, and he was just preparing to give his mother a kiss when his father spoke.

"Richard…" he said, his voice suddenly old and quavery.

"Yes, my lord?"

"Would you…mind…if I also attended?"

Richard was shocked, both at the request and at the tentative tone in which it was delivered. He could see that his father expected a refusal and had persevered to make the request even though he believed it would be rejected.

But Richard could not seek vengeance in such a matter as this. In truth, he cared little whether his father attended because nothing that happened now could affect the reality of what had already occurred. So he responded by giving his father a formal bow.

"Of course, my lord. I am certain Jane would be pleased to have you attend."

Lord Matlock nodded jerkily, and then continued, "I…I believe I made a mistake many years ago, and…and I could not bear not seeing my grandchildren."

He looked at his son, standing so tall, so immensely sturdy, and so impressively accoutred. "I do not believe you would have been any good as a clergyman anyway."

"On that, my lord, I am certain we can both agree," Richard said quietly.

He and his father looked at each other before he turned to kiss his mother and sister. As he walked away, he knew this did not change anything between the two of them. There was simply nothing there. But he would not deny the old man his grandchildren just as his father had not denied him the rest of the family, though he was only close to his mother and sister. He knew his father would now make sure to provide at least some assistance to his grandchildren, and the children would be better for having a grandfather they could see on occasion rather than an embarrassing subject that could not be discussed.

It is not enough, of course, he told himself, *but it is the best that can be done. Some decisions simply foreclose alternative possibilities and cannot be undone.*

CHAPTER 24

The only way to get rid of responsibilities is to discharge them.
— Walter S. Robertson

Sunday, May 17, 1812
Rosings, Kent

As soon as Richard turned into the drive to Rosings and saw his aunt's carriage parked outside her front door with servants scampering back and forth between house and vehicle, he had a sinking sensation that this visit was going to be nothing like his visit to Matlock.

Lady Catherine is clearly planning to travel, and the frenzy of all concerned indicates the departure is hasty and unplanned. Why, the driver has not even finished harnessing the horses. What is she intending to do?

Almost immediately, he realized he had asked himself a rhetorical question since there could only be one possible explanation.

Darcy, he thought. *Somehow she got word of Darcy's interest in Miss Elizabeth, and it would be just like her ladyship to take it upon herself to do what Darcy's mother cannot do—convince him to change his mind. The news must have come to Mrs. Collins from Hertfordshire, and that lady would be duty-bound to inform her husband. He in turn would never consider not passing the information to his patroness. So here is a fine mess I shall have to untangle.*

Since it appeared his aunt might be leaving at any minute, Richard quickly dismounted in front of the stairs and tied his reins to a wheel of the coach. The servants were so busy scurrying back and forth from the house to the carriage that no one took notice of him, much less attended to his mount, so he turned to the house and bounded up the stairs.

He found his aunt just inside the door, barking instructions to her grovelling butler and a crowd of other servants, all wearing hangdog expressions. Lady Catherine reacted quickly to the sound of his jingling spurs, turning around hurriedly only to gape at him in stupefaction.

"Fitzwilliam! What are you doing here at such a distressing time?"

"I came in order to—"

"Never mind, never mind. I have no time for trivialities, just—"

"And I might well ask the reason for all this turmoil?" Richard said, waving his arm at the servants moving busily through the door.

"I have an errand of the utmost importance, and I have no time to tarry. We shall talk on another occasion, but at the moment, I have to depart in order to save your cousin from the uttermost folly."

"And which cousin is that, Aunt? I do have several, you know," he said mildly.

"Use your wits, Nephew. Your cousin Darcy! I have information that he plans a folly that will not only ruin him but which threatens to ruin the whole family. I must confront him at once and bring him to his senses."

Richard could only shake his head in amazement at his aunt's lack of perception. Lady Catherine, however, ascribed his reaction to a lack of understanding, which triggered her fury.

"Do you know what your fool of a cousin is about to do? I am informed that he is paying court to Mrs. Collins's friend, Miss Bennet. Can you believe that he would so treacherously deceive Anne? Can anyone believe it? Miss Elizabeth Bennet! She has neither fortune nor connexions, her father's estate is entailed away to Mr. Collins, and she and her sisters will be almost destitute when their father dies. That is obviously why she lured Darcy with her wiles and arts. Though it is hard to believe, my idiot of a nephew does not even realize it. He must have completely lost his senses! That is the reason for my hurried departure—I am off to Hertfordshire to bring this outlandish affair to an end."

Richard firmly repressed the curse he was on the verge of uttering at the insults offered to the Bennet family—his future relations—as well as at the presumptuous intentions of his aunt to interfere in Darcy's life. But he managed to restrain his fury, forcing his words into a semblance of calmness.

"Aunt, I have information you need to hear before you consider leaving. Might I suggest we step into your library for a private discussion?"

But Lady Catherine was determined not to be swayed from her intention and said stridently, "I told you, that I do not have time for you, Fitzwilliam. Not at this hour. I must be...awwarrkkk!"

The incoherent exclamation was forced from her as Richard's temper snapped. He stepped forward, seized her elbow, and forcibly turned her around and marched her towards her library. She was at first shocked into silence by the astounding fact that someone—anyone—would presume to lay hands on her. But she was also stricken by sudden fear, for she had never before felt such irresistible strength in another person. She had made one abortive attempt to resist her nephew, but she might as well have tried to restrain one of the huge draft horses used in the fields.

Lady Catherine was quick to gather her courage, for she was no coward, even if she had never dreamed her nephew could possibly be so strong.

"Unhand me, Fitzwilliam!" she screeched. "Immediately, do you hear?"

She tried to hit him with the parasol in her right hand, but Richard simply intercepted it with his left hand, plucking it from her grasp with little effort, and her eyes widened as he crumpled it easily with one hand before casting it aside. He quickly had her inside her library and closed the door firmly behind him.

"What is the meaning of this?" she shrieked in rage as Richard released her. Her fury was towering, for she could not remember any time in her life when her will had been so blatantly thwarted. "I shall inform my brother forthwith of this intolerable assault on my—"

"SILENCE!"

Richard's voice had been trained to bellow orders to his men on the battlefield with shot and shell screaming all about, and Lady Catherine took several steps backwards, reflexively flinching and ducking away from the sheer volume of his command.

"That is much better, your ladyship," Richard said in a more normal tone. "Now, I have some news that is related to what you were screaming about in front of all your servants and staff."

"How dare you interfere between me and my—"

"God's Teeth, Aunt!" Richard roared, interrupting her tirade as his temper slipped again. "Do you not know the harm done by talking of private family matters in front of your staff? How long do you think it will be before the entire neighbourhood is informed of every particular of what you have said?"

"That gives you no reason to put hands on me or to speak to me in such a manner," his aunt spat furiously.

"I wish there had been some other way, but you *would not listen*. You *never* listen to others. Well, you had better take a deep breath and listen to me now. You shall not depart this library until you have done so."

Lady Catherine was so angry that she wanted to do anything other than bow to his request—nay, *his demand*. But she uneasily remembered the terrifying strength of her nephew. She was uncomfortably aware that he would have little difficulty in doing exactly as he threatened.

At length, she grudgingly said in cold, clipped tones, "Very well, then. You wanted to talk—begin talking."

"Thank you. Now, the first item is a trivial one: Darcy is not courting Miss Bennet."

"But Mr. Collins—"

"However, he *is* courting her sister, Miss Elizabeth Bennet."

"What difference does that make? You know whom I meant. The impertinent young snippet who visited Mrs. Collins last month. Oh, she must have been weaving her webs about Darcy even then. And doing so right under my very nose!"

"It does make a difference, a real and very distinct difference. Because it is *I* who am courting the eldest Bennet sister, Miss Jane Bennet. Further, I have succeeded in my quest, and she has accepted my offer of marriage. We shall be married this Wednesday."

"What?"

In her shock and confusion, Lady Catherine staggered and collapsed into a stuffed chair.

"Does this mean I was misinformed about Darcy? Was it you that Mr. Collins meant when he informed me?"

Obviously, Richard thought sardonically, *the prospect of ME marrying a simple girl from the country with no fortune and no connexions is not nearly as severe as it is for DARCY to be considering such. The reason being, of course, that it is not I who am supposed to be marrying Anne. How far do her delusions stretch, I wonder?*

"But no," Lady Catherine exclaimed, sitting up straighter. "You just said he was courting Miss Elizabeth Bennet. What are you two playing at, Fitzwilliam? It is not at all humorous, that I can tell you! So you just remove that smile from your face."

"We are not playing at anything, Aunt. I am engaged to Miss Jane Bennet. I have already seen my parents and sister, and they will all be in attendance on Wednesday."

Lady Catherine heard this with the next thing to shock, for she was intimately familiar with the estrangement between father and son. But knowing what had led to this evident rapprochement held little interest for her compared to her central concern.

"And what of Darcy?" she asked coldly.

Richard shrugged. "He attends to Miss Elizabeth, but nothing is settled between them. However, I know he loves her beyond anything in his life, and he wants nothing more than to secure her acceptance of his hand."

"Do not play me for a fool, Fitzwilliam. I can understand how this fortune hunter used her arts and allurements to snare my nephew. His presence in Hertfordshire, of which I was only informed this morning, demonstrates how he has been drawn in. But hopefully he still retains at least some use of his reason and can manage to resist her until I get there."

"You are not listening again, Aunt. It is not Darcy who is preventing their union—it is Miss Elizabeth who still maintains reservations."

"What? That cannot be. It is simply beyond ludicrous. This is a young woman without family, connexions, or fortune. If Darcy had been intemperate enough to make her an offer of marriage, she would have snapped it up instantly."

"Unfortunately for your assumptions, madam, Darcy already *has* made her an offer of marriage, and Miss Elizabeth did, in fact, refuse his offer. He attends her now in an attempt to change her mind."

Richard's voice was calm, but it was as firm as steel. He looked his aunt directly in the eye, daring her to disbelieve him, and she had to look away first.

"Impossible," she mumbled uncertainly.

"Aunt, I was *there*. I *heard* her refuse him. Do not doubt me on this. I pledge the truth of what I say with my sacred honour. You *must* understand: Darcy loves her, and he will never be happy unless he wins her heart."

"But Anne," Lady Catherine whispered brokenly. "They were formed for each other, descended from magnificent families with splendid fortunes. My sister and I planned this union when they were in their cradles. Is it now to be thwarted by a young woman of inferior birth, of no importance in the world, and wholly unrelated to the family?"

"Miss Elizabeth Bennet is the woman for him. I am as certain of it as I stand here. But we must now talk of something I dreadfully wish did not have to be mentioned, and that is Anne. You must come to understand that Anne and Darcy could never marry even if they were of a mind to do so."

"Of what can you be talking?" Lady Catherine's voice was strident, and Richard closed his eyes in pain, wishing he did not have to do this.

But she must see, he thought desperately. *She must!*

"Aunt," he said gently, crossing over to kneel beside her, "please look me in the eye. You must be aware of how Anne is weakening. You keep talking of how she is growing stronger, but it is not true. She is…"

Richard paused to swallow the lump in his throat before he could force himself to continue. "She is dying, Aunt. She knows it, and Darcy knows it. As soon as I returned to England and visited, I saw it. I have seen death far too many times to be mistaken. I wager she will not last the year. I am amazed she survived the past winter."

"No, no, no…"

"I wish it were not so, but denying it is worse than facing it. She is your only daughter, and you are not even spending what time she has left with her. Instead, you continue to delude yourself with a belief that she will soon be strong enough to marry Darcy."

"It cannot be. I *will not* let it be…"

"You do remember the chill she caught at Christmas? She thought she was going to die then. Do you remember? Surely you cannot deny the evidence of your own eyes."

Richard was looking directly into her angry, disbelieving eyes when he saw it happen. The look of brittle certainty that buttressed the strong, firm lines of Lady Catherine's face wavered—wavered, dissipated, and then vanished like a mist. He saw his aunt's face do something he had never believed to see: it began to crumple as she could no longer maintain her delusions.

"Noooooooooooooooo!"

The long, low cry of rejection came from so deep within her that the older lady had almost forgotten she even possessed that kind of passion, and her eyes were suddenly brimming with tears that could not be staunched. Lady Catherine sat rigid for a moment, tears flowing down her cheeks while her lips trembled, and then she simply hunched downward, curling her neck as her hands came up to cover her eyes.

"No, no, no, no, no!" she wailed, and Richard leaned forward and pulled her towards him. She fiercely tried to push him away at first, but his strength could not be resisted, and she collapsed against him, her head tucked into his shoulder as the grief-stricken mother wept for the daughter she finally realized she was going to lose.

CHAPTER 25

It is the passion that is in a kiss that gives to it its sweetness; it is the affection in a kiss that sanctifies it.

— Christian Nevell Bovee

Sunday, May 17, 1812
Longbourn, Hertfordshire

Due to his aunt's emotional collapse, Richard could not depart Rosings until he had accomplished several tasks. First and foremost was convincing Lady Catherine and her daughter to drop their various subterfuges and speak honestly with each other. The state of Anne's health was too dire to suffer any further delay, so he had left his aunt in the library while he went to the front of the house and instructed her servants to unpack the carriage and return it to the stables. Despite the browbeaten nature of Lady Catherine's staff, none felt any desire to contradict the forceful commands of her nephew.

With that accomplished, he sought out Anne and explained the tumultuous events of the morning. She, too, was reluctant to confront her mother, but Richard convinced her to accompany him to the library. Before he left, he had the rather melancholy satisfaction of seeing mother and daughter finally speaking about subjects they had studiously avoided for so long. An unexpected benefit accruing to his efforts was that Anne was able to explain to her mother how he and Darcy had inexplicably fallen in love with two young ladies from the country. Those tasks seemed the limit of what he could accomplish at Rosings, and shortly afterwards he had taken his leave. It was apparent that neither his aunt nor cousin would be attending the wedding, but at least Lady Catherine appeared to accept the inevitability of the marriages of both nephews.

It was fully dark when he finally dismounted before Longbourn and handed the reins to a stable boy. He stretched and twisted, feeling the all-too-familiar tightness and weariness of having spent far too long in the saddle. His horse was actually more rested than he since he had changed mounts at Rosings and again at his London house. He, however, had had no such respite, and he was tired, sore, and so covered with dust that he was not fit to be seen in polite company. But he was resolved that he would not return to his rooms without having seen Jane.

All the Bennet family were in the sitting room, with the addition of Georgiana who sat talking with Elizabeth; both held books that appeared to receive little attention. With energetic motions of his hands, Richard was at least able to keep everyone from springing to their feet though Jane was already moving to greet him. Darcy and Mr. Bennet sat back down and bent over a chessboard while the others either sewed or read by the light of the many candles in the room. Jane smiled happily as she approached, and the warmth of that smile struck such a chord of happiness inside him that he felt the familiar tightening in his chest.

He put his hands out to her, drinking in the beauty of those huge, violet eyes, but when Jane appeared ready to embrace him, he stepped back.

"Please, I am too filthy for company, and I probably should not have stopped. But I wanted to at least see you before I returned to the inn."

Jane looked him up and down appraisingly. "Well, you are a trifle dusty, I admit, but perhaps there is a way to remedy that without your having to return to Meryton. You could bathe upstairs while one of the servants takes a brush to your uniform."

Darcy, who had joined him by that time, asked quietly, "How did your meetings go?"

"Rather better than I had expected. My mother and sister were both eager to come, but I was somewhat surprised that my father will also be attending."

Darcy's eyebrows rose, but he could ask more pressing questions later. "And Lady Catherine?"

"Unfortunately, neither she nor Anne will be able to make the journey, I am afraid. Anne remains rather weak, and her ladyship said she needed to remain to attend her."

Darcy nodded in seeming understanding, but Richard well knew that his simple statements would need further explanation when they attained privacy. He also noted that Elizabeth had paused in her sewing to listen. She could not be aware of the true severity of Anne's condition, but she knew the girl was not well. He could leave the task of informing her to Darcy while Georgiana, who sat beside her, sighed deeply before returning to her book. She was all too familiar with Anne's condition, and Richard knew she also feared for her cousin's life.

But evidently, Mrs. Bennet had ears like a bat, and Richard saw the look of excitement that instantly infused her face.

"Excuse me, Colonel Fitzwilliam, but did I hear that your parents will be attending?" she asked, her eagerness plain to see. Richard saw Mr. Bennet roll his eyes heavenward at his wife's interruption, and he was gratified that he was able to keep his own expression neutral.

This is one case where a deficiency in propriety might work to our advantage, at least insofar as it could lessen the tension and antagonism between Jane and her mother. Mrs. Bennet clearly has just been struck by the revelation that the attendance of a peer of the realm and his wife at our wedding will be a social triumph for her, at least in this neighbourhood, and that will likely occupy her thoughts and time.

"You are indeed correct," he said, making sure his face was under full control. "Both Lord Matlock and my mother, Lady Matlock, will be present. In addition, my sister, Lady Elaine, will be interrupting her first Season in town to attend. Lady Elaine and I are very close."

He saw Jane duck her head and bring her handkerchief to her lips to hide her smile at the stilted manner in which he had emphasised the rank and status of his family, knowing that such phrasing would appeal to her mother.

"That is very interesting news, Colonel Fitzwilliam. If you will excuse me, I believe I shall take a look at the preparations for the wedding breakfast."

She hurriedly left the room, and although she closed the door firmly, all could hear her call for her housekeeper in a loud voice that receded as she scurried down the hall towards the kitchen.

Elizabeth did not even look up from her sewing, making her comment with a straight face. "You know, it is quite strange, but I cannot remember hearing my mother mention having a wedding breakfast until this moment."

"Lizzy, I beg you to restrain your humour at the expense of your mother," Mr. Bennet said, his eyes never leaving the chess pieces. "This is likely to keep her fully entertained until Wednesday, so I do not want you to break her concentration. Mr. Darcy, if you please, your rook is still under attack, and I do not believe you can save it."

Darcy and Elizabeth both shared a quick smile, and then he returned to the game. Jane leaned over to Richard and whispered, "Papa is truly enjoying the challenge of a good opponent. He has demolished all possible players among our acquaintances so often that he has difficulty finding anyone who will sit down with him at his beloved chessboard."

"He has certainly found an adequate challenger in this case. Darcy is an excellent player—far, far better than myself."

"I believe Papa is hoping to get a win this time. They have been playing all week, but all of the games have been draws."

"I can see your father is putting Darcy to the test. My cousin has that entranced look he gets when he is deep in concentration. But I believe you mentioned something about a bath."

"Let me ring for some tea and ask for hot water for the bath. In the meantime, I would be interested in the details of your journey."

"I also stopped by my house to change horses. I had previously written my butler to have your rooms prepared, but everyone was pleased to hear the news confirmed."

At Jane's raised eyebrows, Richard smiled rather sheepishly. "There is my presumption again—"

"I do not mind your presumption when I am its object, my dear."

"Which is excellent since I am not certain I can restrain myself. As for your rooms, a number of former soldiers who can no longer take the field are in my employ, and they said preparations are virtually complete. I was *presumptuous* enough to tell them the colours I thought you would like, but the paint and wallpapers can easily be changed if they are not to your liking."

Jane gave a smile at the droll humour of Richard's comment. "I am certain everything will be quite acceptable." Her smile became coquettish as her voice dropped to a murmur. "I am certain I shall have little time for opinions about the furnishings once you have me at your mercy."

Richard had to swallow at yet another unmistakable indication that his future wife's physical desire was more striking than he had anticipated from someone of her serene disposition. She smiled at the look on his face and said, even more softly, "You know, sir, that I am the opposite of an unwilling bride."

"I could not mistake that, my love, with you demanding that I marry you immediately or take you off to Scotland. But I have much to learn of your nature..."

"And I yours—*after* you take me to your bed."

"Sans attire, Miss Bennet. Sans attire."

"I am depending on that, sir."

Both would have wished to say more, but this room was not the time or the place.

And it is fortunate that we do not have the privacy of a coaching inn, he thought, *since I do not believe this woman would hesitate to assume the title of Mrs. Fitzwilliam before it was formally awarded by the pastor.*

So he was forced to satisfy himself by simply raising her hand to lightly caress her fingers with his lips before ascending the stairs to find the blessed relief of hot, cleansing water.

JANE WAS WAITING WHEN RICHARD ALL BUT SKIPPED DOWN THE stairs after his bath. She was surprised at how such a large man could be so swift and nimble, only touching every other stair in his precipitous descent. He finished by jumping the last three steps and landed with a solid thump right in front of her.

"I feel like a new man," he said with a huge smile.

"Though I wish you were not so eager to see me. As I watched your mad descent, I worried that you might fall flat on your face as we girls so often did in past years. However, on another subject, I will say your uniform appears quite presentable."

"Much more so than I would have believed possible with just whisks and cleaning cloths. I was sure that nothing less than a full washing would get all the dust out."

"The maids have had many occasions to do similar things to our attire, especially after Lizzy has had one of her long rambles through mud and water. On a lighter note, it appears Papa was correct about my mother. She has not reappeared since you mentioned your parents. Are you hungry? We have already had our dinner, but I am sure the cook can put together something."

"Your offer is gratefully accepted."

Richard's meal was an informal affair with no one other than Jane joining him at the table. Mrs. Bennet did bustle down the hall a time or two, but she was too engrossed in her activities to enter, while Darcy and Mr. Bennet remained bent over their game.

RICHARD SAID LITTLE AS HE ATTENDED TO HIS PLATE, HAVING eaten nothing since a hurried breakfast. When he finally leaned back and blotted his lips with his napkin, he looked at Jane with a satisfied smile.

"I would like to suggest a walk in the gardens, but first, shall we take a look at how the chess combatants are getting on?"

Jane nodded her agreement, and they paused to watch the silent hostilities. It took five minutes of perusal of the board and the remaining pieces before Richard was satisfied and indicated that he was ready. Jane was more than ready since she dearly wished some private conversation, and she had her shawl to protect against the chill of the May evening. They paused for a few moments after leaving the house to allow their eyes to adjust to the moonlight.

"Your father indeed won Darcy's rook, which is a most significant accomplishment," Richard said shortly after they began to stroll. "But I am afraid he had to give up his black bishop to do so. That often occurs when pursuing an aggressive attack, but your father has the advantage of the exchange. A rook is worth more than a bishop."

"I shall take your word for it. I know little about chess other than the basic moves."

"It is not a game for everyone. I am more of a whist player myself. I would rather bury my mistakes after ten minutes of play at the card table than to sit over a losing chess position for several hours. However, despite having the advantage of the exchange of pieces, your father has a critical problem. Darcy has pushed one of his pawns to the sixth rank with his king guarding it. Your father will have to block the back rank with his remaining rook, but Darcy can attack with his white bishop. I am sure they will have to exchange pieces, which will leave nothing but pawns on the board. That part of the game is called the endgame, and it is where Darcy excels, because success usually comes down to pure calculation."

"So Mr. Darcy is a good player? I could see Father was surprised at only being able to achieve tie games so far."

Richard laughed lightly. "Getting a draw from Darcy is a signal achievement. It is something I cannot seem to manage."

"I am afraid Papa may be a bit too proud of his ability, though he does not play as much as he would like. Few in the neighbourhood will accept his challenge any longer, except on rare occasions. For many years, he has defeated everyone he has played."

"Your father is an excellent player, but Darcy is also. In fact, he is deemed one of the best players in town, and a number of gentlemen have joined his club specifically to play him."

"Oh, it would please Father immensely to learn that. If you do not mind, perhaps you can mention it to him before you leave?"

"I shall make a point of it. However, I wonder whether Darcy is doing his suit any good by contesting so strenuously with your father. He is so completely consumed by the game that he is paying little attention to your sister. I hope she does not feel neglected."

"I do not think so. Lizzy knows how much Father loves the game. Mr. Darcy's willingness to play is not going to hurt him in her eyes. In fact, I must say that I think her opinion of him is significantly better than he appears to think it is."

"I have been thinking the same thing. Of course, I have been concentrating on matters closer to my own heart and might not have been as observant as I would have been otherwise."

Jane smiled in the darkness, feeling a flush of pleasure at being reminded of his single-minded pursuit. At the same time, she could not stop a bittersweet tightness in her chest at remembering the despondency she had felt just weeks ago. So much had changed in such a short time.

Sternly, she told herself to set aside any lingering sadness about Mr. Bingley. *First of all, it is most unfair to Richard. His love for me seems so elemental and pure that dwelling on previous sadness tarnishes it by comparison. Secondly is the way I feel about HIM. The passage of time makes an impartial comparison most difficult, but I have to believe my previous feelings for Mr. Bingley are nothing in comparison my love for Richard. I suppose I might have been happy enough with Mr. Bingley had events turned out otherwise, but I never would have felt this overwhelming desire—*

Richard's sudden veer to the left caught her by surprise and broke her train of thought, but she never thought about resisting. She trusted him too much, and besides, her arm was tucked inside his. As soon as they were screened from the house, he spun her slightly so he could pull her into his embrace. She did not resist though she leaned back slightly to peer upward at his face, dimly visible in the moonlight.

"And what is this, sir?" she asked in mock severity, though her emotion might have been more believable if her own arms had not gone around his waist.

"I have had to endure most of the day without seeing you, my sweet, and I have missed you cruelly." He leaned down to kiss her forehead.

"And I have missed you," she said, standing on tiptoe so she could lightly brush her lips across his. She was somewhat surprised to feel the rasp of his growth of beard since his morning shave. It had been barely visible in the candlelight, but it was simply one more thing to learn about this man. It did not trouble her as he deepened their kiss; it was just another discovery.

Her arms barely went around Richard's waist as she pulled herself against him, trying to mould her body to his. Though he had the slim-hipped build of a horseman, he was a large man, and she felt helpless in the strength of his arms. But it was a nice, natural helplessness, that of a maiden in the arms of her warrior, and she moved against him as Richard began to plant soft, feathery light kisses down her cheek.

His kisses felt wonderful to Jane: soft, intimate indications of his passion for her. It was not at all objectionable even though somewhat improper as their marriage was not yet an accomplished fact. But she felt the same passion for him, a breathtaking thrill down her spine as his lips reached her slim neck.

"Umm, I had no idea being kissed there would feel so wonderful," she said huskily as she leaned her head to the side and lifted her chin so he had easier access to her neck.

"There are many other places that also feel nice, my love," he said, working his way back up her neck. "This one, for example…"

Jane felt another thrill as his warm breath filled her ear.

"Perhaps you see what I mean?" he whispered, his tongue tracing the convolutions of her ear. Then his strong teeth nipped gently at her ear lobe…

Jane pulled herself still more firmly against him, winding her fingers together behind his back and wishing they were already married. She knew that she ought to feel relief at having all questions answered and every obstacle to their union set aside, but an odd tension in her midriff had taken its place. She instinctively knew she was experiencing the stirrings of physical desire for her future husband, but the explanation did little to alleviate her distress.

While she was untutored in the details of intimacies between a man and a woman, she could not be totally ignorant of the basics involved in marital consummation. How could it be otherwise, having grown up on a small country estate with the livestock mating and giving birth to young? This thought made her tingle in anticipation and a little fear, but the anticipation greatly outweighed the fear, despite what her mother had said of the evils associated with the marital state. She had good reason to suspect her mother was not the best source of information on that subject, and Elizabeth shared her suspicions. Nevertheless, neither of them had any way of resolving their doubts.

I wish I could consult with my aunt Gardiner when she and Uncle arrive, but I am certain there will be no chance for such a private conversation. Still, from the way I feel now, at least SOME parts of the consummation will be enjoyable.

"I see I have much to learn from you, sir," she said huskily as Richard turned her head to nibble at her other ear and sent new thrills down that side of her neck. She turned her head into his and claimed his mouth with her own, standing on tiptoe again and thrusting her hips hard against his in a vain attempt to alleviate the unknown urges surging within her. She opened her lips and her tongue darted out to tease against his as her hips moved against him without conscious volition. She was disappointed when their kiss ended, but then she felt Richard's lips close to her ear.

"Miss Bennet," he whispered, and Jane was surprised at the strain in his voice. "I beg leave to apologize for pulling you into concealment like this. I had intended only a simple kiss rather than giving vent to my beastly urges and taking liberties with your person."

"Liberties, is it? And beastly urges?" she whispered back breathlessly. She heard the mixture of emotions in his voice—playfulness and intimacy mixed with repentance—and she was determined that he should not feel as if he needed to make his apologies when she was a willing accomplice to his desires. Richard's breath smelled fresh and clean, and she breathed in the scent of soap that lingered on his skin as he turned her head to nibble at her other ear.

"Yes, Miss Bennet. I simply forgot myself for a moment, but now I—"

"Stop, sir," she said, laughing softly at the melodramatic tone of his voice. "You have no need for apologies, for I have no wish for you to stop. Your attempt at self-control is admirable, but you must remember my lack of experience. How can I ever form an opinion about these 'liberties' until you actually take them?"

She saw his head draw back as he looked at her. "But...are you not offended?"

"If this were a simple dance and we were walking outside after first meeting, I would be offended. But after you declared yourself most forcefully and proved your sincerity, how could I be offended that my husband wishes to take all manner of liberties with my virginal body? You must understand that I wish you to take those liberties, Richard Fitzwilliam. If this were a romance and you were a knight who had just saved me from a dragon, I would be aiding you in tearing off my clothing to serve as bedding while you ravished me as many times as you wished."

She pulled his head back to hers and they kissed long and satisfyingly before he again drew back to look at her deeply.

"I see I have many things to learn about my lady love. I had not been aware that I was about to marry an adventuress! Still, I had expected you to rein in my impulsive nature instead of encouraging my explorations. This is a fine turn of events."

He nuzzled her hair, loving the freshly washed scent of it mixed with the perfume she wore. Jane again lifted her face to his, and her lips were as eager as his when he reclaimed them. Her tongue again darted against his, and her hands moved over his back, marvelling at the thick bands of muscle under his coat. Richard felt her tremble in his arms as hands, in turn, explored the curve of her body from torso to waist.

"I am not at all displeased, Richard," she said eventually, her hand firmly holding his to her right breast. "I quite enjoyed your explorations, and they do not seem excessively outrageous. Especially since, if I had had my way when we went to my father, you would have already taken every liberty imaginable with me, either at some coaching inn on the way to or from Scotland or perhaps even upstairs in the bedroom we reserve for visitors."

"But, as you say, you did not get your way—"

"There is no one I trust as I do you, Richard," she interrupted softly. "I trust you even more than I do my father. I cannot believe you would do anything that I might find objectionable—new and unexpected, perhaps, but not objectionable."

"Ah," he sighed. "I have the reputation to uphold of being a soldier with beastly urges, and yet all I do is inspire trust. I assure you, madam, I truly do have beastly urges."

"Pray continue, sir—I am curious and interested in learning, and if I find something not to my liking, I assure you I shall make my opinions known. However, as it would cause a stir in the household, I do not suppose we should rip off my clothing and consummate our marriage at just this moment—"

"Madam—"

"Yes, yes, I know—I shall stop teasing. As I was saying, I suppose we ought to return to the house."

"Likely so. It is growing somewhat cooler, and we should return while I still have some shred of my self-control left."

"I suppose you are correct, sir, even though I am possessed of a certain curiosity to see what happens when this vaunted self-control of yours slips."

"You shall soon have the opportunity, and it is doubtful whether I shall allow you to leave my chambers for a full week once we are wed."

"A full week, sir? Come now, are you not exaggerating? We should have to at least come downstairs to eat."

"I have a fine cook, and she can readily send a tray upstairs."

"But even then, we must occasionally bathe and refresh ourselves—"

"There is a large bathtub in the dressing room adjoining my bedroom. You can use it, and I shall watch as you bathe. In fact, there will be no need for a maid to assist you at all. I shall pour the water over you myself, and I shall even hold the towel and a warm robe after you finish."

"Oh my," Jane said, unconsciously pressing her hips forward at the thought.

She had imagined a few of the intimacies that must take place between husband and wife, but they had all been mysteriously shrouded in darkness. Until this moment, she had never imagined him looking on her bare body, and the thought was deliciously, almost sinfully, exciting. Finally, she gathered herself enough to attempt another protest.

"But I want my hair to look nice for you, and I shall need…"

"Your hair will be let down and undone for the whole week. It will not have a single pin in it for that entire time. Resign yourself to it, madam. You are marrying a brute of a soldier, and I intend to have my way with you."

"Then I suppose I must resign myself to the inevitable," she sighed, lifting her lips to his for another kiss.

Eventually, Jane laid her head on his chest again. "It appears it is far too late for any second thoughts, I suppose, so I shall just have to do my duty as a wife and submit to your lascivious desires with as much grace as I can maintain."

"Lascivious desires, is it?" Richard grinned.

"So my mother informs me, though I admit the possibility that she might be mistaken in the matter. But before we do so, might I ask that you come early tomorrow? Lizzy and I had not anticipated your skilful tactical move about your parents to engage my mother's thoughts, and we are desperate to escape her attentions. We thought tomorrow would be a good day for a picnic, and we would like to begin no later than eight in the morning so we can get away unnoticed."

"Eight? That is a trifle early for a picnic."

"We wanted to be gone from the house before my mother comes downstairs as she is wont to do around nine o'clock. She usually has Lizzy anchored in the front room so she may show her off to anyone who drops by and wax eloquently on the great advantages of having a daughter courted by such a wonderful young man as Mr. Darcy. And, since your parents will be attending our wedding, you have rehabilitated me in her eyes, so she might well take time away from planning the wedding breakfast to include me. But it is Lizzy who is most desperate to get away. She has even been forced several times to forgo her morning walks."

"A dire situation, indeed."

"Most dire. We have arranged for Hill to have a pair of baskets prepared for both the morning and the noon meal, and she will make sure the baskets are ready so Lizzy and I can leave by the rear door. If you and Mr. Darcy await us by the rear fence, we can be well away from the house before my mother comes downstairs. By the time she learns we have left on a picnic, she will be unable to order us to return."

"Two meals? How far is your sister planning to walk?"

"Not too far—a mile or two, I believe. She knows several places on our father's lands where we can picnic under the trees and no one will even know we are there. I would suggest you wear your uniform since it is likely to be more comfortable for walking."

"That will definitely not be a problem," Richard said, laughing somewhat self-consciously. "I am still struggling to feel at ease in more fashionable attire."

When they returned to the house, they found that her father had indeed been forced into an endgame but had managed another draw after both pushed their last pawn to the back rank and converted them to queens. Mr. Bennet had pinned Darcy's new queen against his king and forced a trade of the last pieces left on the board.

Mr. Bennet appeared somewhat disappointed at the result, but he was considerably cheered when Richard made a point of informing him of Darcy's high reputation in town.

Jane and Richard shared a glance after their attention was drawn to the contented way Elizabeth watched the game. Though neither of the combatants saw the several looks she directed their way as they discussed the crucial points of the game, both Jane and Richard saw the expression on her face. It was clear to both of them that she was viewing the two most important men in her life with obvious and almost triumphant satisfaction.

CHAPTER 26

My love loves me, and all the wonders I see;
A rainbow shines in my window; my love loves me.
— "Plaisir d'Amour," folk song originally composed
by Martini il Tedesco for the French court

Monday, May 18, 1812
Hertfordshire

It was fifteen minutes before eight o'clock the next morning when Richard arrived at Longbourn, and Darcy was already waiting, standing by the rear fence. As soon as Richard swung down, a stable boy was ready to take the reins and lead his horse away.

"It looks to be a marvellous spring day," Richard said, scanning the blue sky dotted with puffy white clouds.

"Perhaps a bit nippy for the ladies, but I imagine they will be dressed appropriately. But I have a proposition to suggest to you. You are aware, of course, that Georgiana and I are staying with Bingley at his estate."

"Indeed. So he has not departed? After I saw his face on Sunday, I was not sure he would stay."

"I daresay it crossed his mind, but I suspect he now believes Miss

Bennet must have been indifferent to him all along, despite my information to the contrary. Under the circumstances, there seemed no reason to inform him differently. In any case, when I mentioned last night that your parents and sister would be attending the wedding on Wednesday, he suggested that everyone, including you, could stay at Netherfield the day before."

"That is prodigiously civil of him, Darcy, given the events of the past weeks," Richard said after several moments' consideration of this surprising offer.

"Bingley is nothing if not civil," Darcy said, his smile bittersweet. "He is not your measure in other areas, but both of us together could scarce match him in civility and manners. I often comment that he is decent to the bone."

"Evidently. It makes me feel ashamed of certain thoughts I entertained when I learned the quality of the woman he abandoned."

"You must allow me to accept the blame for that error for reasons we both know. Oh, I suppose his sisters bear some responsibility, but I am convinced I was more instrumental than they. Bingley has such a natural modesty and dependence on my opinion that he was willing to accept my assurances of Miss Bennet's indifference and act accordingly."

"Meaning he could not make up his own mind and thus allowed himself to be directed by others."

Darcy shrugged. "I said he was not your equal in certain areas and certainly not when it comes to decisiveness and energy. When you make up your mind, nothing less than the intervention of God Almighty and all His angels could sway you, and even then I believe I could get even odds from a gamester on the matter."

Richard grinned at the image Darcy painted. "Which is the reason I had to spend my young manhood at Pemberley rather than Matlock Hall."

"I believe that was more stubbornness than determination though you may think of it as you will. But we have digressed. What of Bingley's offer?"

Richard grew thoughtful as he pondered the question. "To be honest, I had assumed everyone would come down on Wednesday by coach and then return to London. It is only a little over twenty miles after all. I suppose I could send an express and put the question to them after we return from our picnic. Of course, I myself would feel a certain awkwardness."

"I believe Bingley is attempting to put the past behind him. He said all of us would be in company in the future due to your marriage and our friendship, so it was time to come to grips with that reality."

"When you phrase it like that, it would be churlish on my part to reject such a generous offer."

He grinned suddenly and clapped Darcy on the back. "Of course, certain of my past behaviours *could* be described as being churlish as you well know. Very well, please tell him I accept with thanks, with the qualification that my family may have already made their plans. Just in case, I shall dispatch an express to my mother immediately after we return to Longbourn."

"Excellent. I told Bingley I thought you would be agreeable to his offer…after you got past your stiff-necked pride, of course."

"Of course. But do not presume too much, Cousin. It has been years since we last boxed, but I have not forgotten our lessons together."

"But I have gotten much wiser since then. I was always faster on my feet, so I doubt you could catch me. As for mounted, I do not think there is a horse alive that would bear that immense body of yours fast enough to catch Marlborough."

Richard grinned in delight, careful to leave the matter where it was. This conversation was additional evidence that his cousin of old, the boy with whom he had grown to manhood, might be re-emerging, and he was not inclined to push too hastily. Instead, he changed subjects.

"Now I have to put this to you squarely, Darce. How do you and

Miss Elizabeth get on? She gave every indication of enjoying your company at the assembly and afterwards."

Darcy's smile was now replaced with a look of concern. "I am not completely sure."

"What can you mean?" Richard said in exasperation. "I saw the way she looked at you while you played chess with her father. That was a look of contentment and ease, Darce. You are allowing yourself to be ruled by past mistakes. Miss Elizabeth loves her father dearly, despite his faults, and I am certain she was pleased that the two of you were so comfortable together."

"Perhaps," Darcy said, and his uncertainty was plain to see. "Still, we have so many areas of dispute, and—"

"—sometimes you are enough to drive a strong man to drink," Richard said, rolling his eyes in vexation. "Or to drive a man to strong drink. Or both."

Darcy looked sheepish but did not dispute his cousin, who continued: "I suppose I need not ask whether you have made any kind of attempt to ascertain whether a repetition of your proposal might bring a different response—do I?"

"Not yet. It is too soon. We both need more time."

"Jane will not come right out and say it, but she clearly thinks her beloved sister has a different opinion of you than she did previously. She did say that, when she mentioned how everyone in Meryton is speaking of an attachment between the two of you as an accepted fact, her sister only nodded but did not dispute what she had been told. Get a grip on your nerve, Darce. Push on!"

"Not...not yet. I do not want to rush too fast since I am all too aware of the disasters I barely avoided when I rushed ahead with my proposal in Kent."

There seemed to be nothing further to say, so Richard changed the subject as they waited for their ladies.

Determination

The two sisters appeared at the back door within a few minutes, carrying a pair of baskets that were clearly heavy. The two men immediately came to their aid, but even they were surprised at the weight of the baskets. Richard flipped aside the cloth covering on his basket and marvelled at the contents.

"My word, Jane, there is enough here for eight rather than just the four of us. There is ham, bread, boiled eggs, cheese, fruit and a bottle of wine with two glasses."

"I think Hill rather approves of both of you," Jane said, flexing her arm gratefully. "I am glad to be relieved of my burden. As for Hill, she especially seemed to think a big man like you would have an appetite to match."

"I daresay if Hill came to manage our house after we are married, I should soon be so fat not even the sturdiest horse could bear my weight."

Jane only raised her eyebrows at this comment as the four of them set out, and she carefully did not mention what Hill had said to her privately as she left: *Judging from the way your young man adores you, Miss Jane, you will need all your strength once you are married. So you be sure and eat your share.*

Remembering the thrill that went up and down her spine at these words, Jane rather tended to agree with the wisdom of their long-time housekeeper.

With Elizabeth's guidance, the four of them set out on one of her favourite paths, and about three-quarters of an hour of brisk walking took them to a bridge over a bubbling stream. The trees and shrubbery pressed close to the road, but Elizabeth pointed out a nearly invisible gap that led them along the tree-lined creek for another quarter of a mile before they came to a larger copse of trees where the surrounding land dipped down in a hollow. Thickets of dense bushes filled in virtually all the spaces between the tree trunks in the grove, and there was no visible way inside. However, Elizabeth pushed through several branches that looked no different from the rest of the copse but revealed a narrow passage into the grove.

Once the couples were inside the wood, the trees overhead provided complete shade and prevented bushes from growing. Underfoot was the detritus of many autumns, soft and yielding fallen leaves, and a flat area beside the creek was perfect for spreading the two picnic blankets.

Numerous birds had populated the thick branches but had flown off when the four of them pushed into the open area. However, once the couples settled onto the blankets and set out a light breakfast from one basket, many of the birds gradually returned. Soon, their chirping and calling formed a backdrop to the low conversation among the four intruders in their midst as they ate their morning meal.

RICHARD SAT COMFORTABLY, HIS BACK AGAINST A TREE, WITH Jane close beside him, her legs tucked under her. The two of them talked easily with Jane laughing delightedly at his recollections of humorous episodes from his military experiences. She was obviously very comfortable sitting so close, often touching him on the hand or arm to make a point as if she had been doing so all her life.

He was disappointed, however, that the same was not true for Elizabeth and Darcy. Elizabeth also sat with her legs tucked under her and her skirts spread, but Darcy had taken a seat on the trunk of a fallen tree several feet away. From Richard's long experience with his cousin, his assessment was that Darcy would prefer to sit closer to Elizabeth but did not dare. He wondered whether he ought to have been even more forceful in his earlier conversation with his cousin, but given the depth of Darcy's disappointment at the Parsonage, it was probably just as well that his cousin was showing a degree of caution.

In any case, it did not appear that Elizabeth was uncomfortable with Darcy's hesitancy, and his information from Jane suggesting her sister's changed attitude towards Darcy was enough to convince him that the couple would find a resolution to this matter sooner or later. And Jane's whispered information during their walk here that

Elizabeth wished to have some time alone with Darcy this morning was promising, so he put aside his worries.

Thus, he was not surprised when Elizabeth said, about a quarter of an hour later, "I would like to walk on, perhaps to Oakham Mount. Would you care to accompany me, Mr. Darcy?"

Darcy was quite agreeable and quickly arose to assist her. Richard wondered whether Jane might wish to chaperone her sister, but she remained seated. "I shall never be the walker you are, Lizzy. I would prefer to stay here with Richard. Will you be returning for the noon meal?"

"I am not sure. Perhaps we should divide the bounty and take one of the baskets. Then we might eat when we feel hungry."

"That is sensible, but take care in your selections—remember how much Hill packed. But I do suggest coming back here before returning to Longbourn so we can all return at the same time. Our mother is likely to be angry that we did not tell her of our plans."

"Trying to offer more targets and spread her fire, eh?" Richard said cheerfully. "Good military tactics, my love."

Elizabeth nodded her agreement, and she and Darcy packed a smaller, lighter basket before departing. After they left, Richard looked over at Jane and raised his eyebrows inquisitively. "I wonder if those two might need a chaperone," he said with a mischievous lift of his eyebrows.

"And if they should?" Jane said lightly before growing serious. "I know Lizzy wishes some time alone with Mr. Darcy without the press of our family and all our visitors. This morning seemed to both of us the perfect opportunity since I wished the same thing with you."

"Perhaps they should have stayed to provide a chaperone for us," Richard said teasingly.

"I suppose we could catch up with them if we hurried…"

"No, no, that would be too tiring," Richard said, never having stirred from his comfortable seat against the tree. "In any case, Darcy is eight and twenty and well aware of the bounds of propriety. If he is hesitant to do anything that might offend your sister, he is unlikely to chance liberties that she did not expressly sanction."

"Perhaps you might be surprised at what either of the Bennet sisters would expressly sanction," Jane said softly, her eyes on her hands in her lap. Richard's eyebrows went up as he wondered about this comment, but Jane waved the thought away.

"Never mind, never mind. It was a frivolous thought, not at all serious." She looked around at the trees overhead, which let only muted dapples of sunlight through the thick branches. "This is a pretty place, is it not? Very relaxing with the gurgling of the stream and the birds singing in the trees. Lizzy comes here often to be away from the chatter and noise of our sisters and our mother."

She looked at Richard solemnly for a moment. "Having such a large family has its drawbacks, you know. I believe Lizzy feels those disadvantages more sharply than I do."

Richard nodded his understanding, reaching out to squeeze her hand while he enjoyed looking into those beautiful eyes of hers. "Perhaps we should discuss other topics than a life you will be leaving behind. I asked Darcy this morning whether he had given any thought to renewing his addresses, but he still seems hesitant, not wishing to rush her into making a decision that he worries will go against him."

Jane said nothing at first, looking down at his hand. "I still marvel at how much larger your hand is than mine, and I am not a small woman. Also, the calluses on your hands are clearly the result of hard work, yet your touch is as gentle as that of a baby."

"I shall take care when sliding my hand over your skin when I have you safely in my clutches, dearest—I have learned gentleness along with strength. I should not wish to abrade your skin's delicacy."

"That is certainly a relief. I believe I would be a twig in your fingers." She smiled happily and squeezed his hand again.

"As for what you said about your cousin, I have to say this: I have been keeping Lizzy's secrets for so long, and she mine, that my first impulse was to evade your question. But that will no longer do, will it? We shall be married in just a few days, and I shall be keeping *your* secrets from that point."

"You do not have to say anything if it would cause you to betray a confidence."

Jane only smiled and shook her head, squeezing his hand again to emphasise her point. "That is not my concern. I am only saying that the changes in our lives will require some getting used to. But I do not believe Lizzy would expect me to keep such secrets from you. So, yes, she has concluded that she and Mr. Darcy would do quite well together, and while she has not said so specifically, I am sure she would give him a favourable reply if he repeated his offer. But please do not share this with him just now. Lizzy knows he is being cautious, and she will eventually say something if his hesitation continues; his desires are plain to see. But she wishes to wait until after we are married. She says our mother is difficult enough with only one daughter formally engaged."

Richard had to laugh at the image that came to his mind. "Especially since your mother will not have the objections she had to me. Very well—I am relieved for Darcy's sake, and my lips are sealed. I have no wish to worsen your relations with your mother."

"Oh, I have got over most of my anger. I am afraid my mother cannot help being the way she is."

"I never took offence at what she said, dear heart. She is trying to resolve an unpleasant situation, and her desperation drives her to foolishness. Let it go and remember that she loves you."

"She has much to keep her occupied since you so casually mentioned the social triumph she will accomplish by having an earl and his family visiting her home."

Jane shook her head in resignation, and she and Richard shared a wry smile at the foibles of both their families.

"Which brings up another matter: Darcy told me this morning that Mr. Bingley wishes to offer the hospitality of Netherfield to my family and me on the night before the wedding. I shall have to send an express to my mother when we return to Longbourn since I had assumed they would simply drive down from Matlock Hall and return the same day. In case they decide to accept Bingley's offer, it would give me the opportunity to introduce you before the ceremony."

Jane said nothing at first, but Richard could see that she was troubled.

"I am sorry if this brings up unpleasant memories, my dear, but I could not ignore such a generous offer. We shall be seeing Bingley on many occasions after Darcy marries your sister."

"Oh, do not be sorry, Richard. It is just...well...I do not regret having come to love you though I am still surprised at its rapidity. It seems if we have known each other forever. I was just remembering my discomfort at having to cause Mr. Bingley pain. Despite the necessity of acting as I did, I found it quite difficult."

"Of course you did, my sweet. How could you feel otherwise and remain true to your nature? I know many young ladies who would have taken considerable pleasure in dashing his hopes as he had previously dashed theirs, and I am incomparably blessed to have won the affection of a young lady who would never consider acting in such an understandable but unkind manner."

Jane blushed at his fervent statement and looked down for a moment in embarrassment before she asked, almost in a whisper, "Richard, I...I am feeling...very...oh, I do not know. Will you hold me? I am all..."

She had no need for further words as Richard lifted her effortlessly onto his lap with her back cradled by his right arm while his left went around her waist and pulled her tightly against him. Her head came naturally to rest on his shoulder, and he heard her sigh in relief as the tension seemed to flow out of her.

"Thank you," she said softly. "I do not want to...burden you, but I cannot tell you how comforting you are to me. I feel that nothing can go wrong when you are holding me."

"You could never be a burden, dearest one," Richard said, luxuriating in the clean, sweet smell of her dark hair under his chin. "I shall hold you as often and for as long as you wish for all of our life together."

Jane snuggled in even closer at these words. "That sounds like so long now—'for all of our life together.' Who could have thought my life would change so much and so quickly?"

"It was your eyes, you know."

"My eyes?"

"The first day I saw you. I looked into the intense violet of your eyes, and it was the most beautiful sight I had ever seen. I do believe I was lost after that."

Jane laughed softly. "Do you know what convinced *me?*"

"No, but it is a matter of considerable interest to me."

"It was your boldness—the way you stated your intentions so forthrightly to my uncle, to Lizzy, and then to me. And your pursuit was just as resolute."

"When I look back on it, I can hardly believe my effrontery at daring to seek your hand as I did," Richard said with a smile. "But I was so determined to win your affection that I never paused to consider any other course of action."

Jane snuggled down into his embrace again. "I, for one, am glad beyond measure that you dared to try. If you had not, I likely would have eventually found an acceptable person to marry, but I cannot believe I would have been able to love and respect him as I do you. My sister and I are not alike in all respects. That was why Lizzy was so adamant about Darcy speaking to Mr. Bingley: she thought he and I were well matched. But you fill a need in me that he never could—a need I was not even aware existed."

"You must stop now, my dear, or else I shall grow so prideful and arrogant you should soon have cause to regret your decision."

Jane laughed again and dug her cheek into his shoulder before relaxing again. As the minutes stretched, Richard gradually realized that she had fallen asleep. He understood perfectly why she needed sleep; the past several days had been intensely stressful to her. Though he held a lovely and desirable young woman in his arms, he was careful not to wake her, firmly restraining his impulse to slide the hand around her waist down over her hip and onto her leg.

We shall be married in just a few days, he told himself. *Besides, she just said she trusted me and felt comforted in my arms. And how would I repay her admiration? By wanting to paw her like some ordinary soldier who was trying his luck with the barkeep's daughter?*

He felt incredibly content as Jane's slow, deep breathing continued, and he laid his head back against the soft moss coating the tree trunk, which provided a wonderful pillow. He was not aware just when he fell into the same slumber as she had...

IT DID NOT TAKE LONG FOR ELIZABETH TO LEAD DARCY TO A SMALL, concealed clearing similar to but smaller than the one where she left her sister and Darcy's cousin. They spread their blankets over the same yielding ground cover of leaves and vegetation and sat in the centre, facing each other. Their eyes were serious as they contemplated one another since they knew there were still issues to resolve between them despite those they had already laid to rest.

Though Elizabeth had taken the lead to bring them here, Darcy spoke first since she somehow could not make the words come.

"I wonder whether we should have stayed to chaperone my cousin and your sister," he said with a smile twitching the corners of his lips. "When I looked back and saw the way they gazed at each other, I felt a twinge of guilt at departing."

All Elizabeth could muster was a rather weak smile at this comment. When she and Darcy had walked here, she had not bothered to rehearse what she wished to say to him. It had not seemed necessary; she had never had difficulty finding the words to express her opinions though she sometimes disguised them, depending on the cleverness of the person with whom she was speaking. As her aunt Gardiner had advised, however, she should more frequently consider whether she *ought* to speak. Being able to put her thoughts into words had never been a problem, her aunt had said with her uncle nodding his concurrence. Eloquence was a steady, dependable attribute of Elizabeth's character.

Until now. Now she could think of nothing to say.

"Of course," Darcy said thoughtfully, "Richard is as aware of the proprieties as I am, and he loves your sister too much to chance offending her."

His thoughtful look was replaced by a mischievous smile. "Then again, what does it really matter? The punishment for such impatience would be that they marry, and that will be a settled fact in two days."

He looked over at Elizabeth and was startled to see her visibly struggling with her thoughts, her mouth opening and closing as if she was having difficulty speaking.

"Miss Elizabeth!" he said in sudden worry. "Are you feeling ill? You look distinctly out of sorts…"

Somehow, Darcy's sudden worry for her cleared Elizabeth's mind— or, at least, partially so. She was motivated to speak, but her motivation was impulsive in nature rather than thoughtful.

Darcy was startled as Elizabeth suddenly grabbed his hand in both of hers and held it in a surprisingly strong grip.

"Mr. Darcy…sir," she stammered, the words so urgent that they tumbled over each other in her mind, forcing her to start over. "Mr. Darcy…you…you must allow me to say how much I…I admire you…and…and love you!"

Darcy was shocked to his core to hear words that closely paralleled his own on the disastrous evening at the Parsonage. He was even more stunned by the intensity of emotion that lay behind them. His precious Elizabeth always had the charm and wit to speak in a subtle and restrained manner in keeping with her polite conduct. To see her like this was so stunning as to take his breath away.

"You will, of course, remember when you said much the same thing, and you will also remember the intemperate manner in which I responded to your expression of love—for which I have been sorry for some weeks—and wished to find a way to apologize," she said in a rush. "But there was no opportunity. We still had problems to resolve before I could be so forthright."

She paused to catch her breath. "But in the intense days that followed, I believe we have put enough of those problems behind us that we can now move ahead. But I believe you are too fearful of antagonizing me to chance doing so without being more cautious than you were previously. But it is not necessary, sir—not at all."

Elizabeth swallowed as she looked at him intently, her eyes bright. "If…if you still wish to marry me, Mr. Darcy, then you may depend upon a more thoughtful and positive response than before."

Darcy was so anxious at hearing words such as this, words that he had never imagined hearing from this young lady, that he had difficulty speaking. Finally, all he could manage was a hoarse, "Really?"

"Really, Mr. Darcy," Elizabeth said, raising his hands to her lips and kissing his fingers. She looked at him with the most beautiful and warm smile he had ever seen from her and repeated, "Really."

He smiled suddenly and gave a soft laugh of pure joy. "You cannot know how your words, surprising and unexpected as they are, fill me with joy…Elizabeth." He smiled even more broadly at the thought of being able finally to address this wonderful lady by her Christian name, and that smile on his face unlocked something inside of her.

She had spoken words of impulse, driven by the thought that waiting for the right time to take matters into her own hands was another variation of Darcy's own hesitation. The time was now, and she had spoken. But his smile of utmost happiness caused her to follow impulsive words with impulsive actions.

Of a sudden, she threw herself into Darcy's arms, releasing his hands and flinging her arms about his neck. The impact caused him to tumble over on his back, and she was on top of him, hugging him with as much strength as she possessed while planting kisses all over his face, murmuring soft words of endearment that he had only heard in his dreams.

Their lips met and clung, and both of them threw caution to the wind. All was settled, and neither of them could wait any longer. Her hands fumbled at his clothing, having no idea what to do, and his own hands instinctively pulled the hem of her dress up so that he could feel the warm, soft, exhilarating skin of her legs and her perfect bottom.

She was not offended at all, and her soft words urged him on as they began to untangle the mysteries of each other's clothing so that they could explore other, more basic mysteries...

JANE AND RICHARD WERE STILL RELAXING AFTER THEIR LEISURELY noon meal when they heard the sound of what they presumed was Darcy and Elizabeth pushing through the underbrush. They were much as the other couple had left them with Richard leaning back against the tree and Jane sitting close beside him, the only difference that the remains of their noon meal were spread out beside them. They watched with interest as the other couple pushed past the brush and entered the clearing.

Richard was about to open his mouth to greet them in his usual manner, but he paused instead when Elizabeth, as soon as she had got past the bushes, claimed Darcy's arm in a manner that spoke volumes to Richard's practised eye. If that was not indication enough, they were so close that they were almost touching as they seated themselves on the blanket.

As a cavalry officer and a leader of men who were combative, irascible, and often more than a little resistant to instant obedience to commands, Richard had honed his skills at observing others over the years. Now he noted that, where their demeanour had been stiff and tentative during their morning meal, the two appeared quite comfortable at the moment, talking easily with each other and with Jane. They smiled and looked at each other unabashedly and often, and several times Elizabeth unconsciously laid her hand lightly on Darcy's arm. In other words, the whole manner of these two complicated individuals bore little resemblance to that of the couple who had departed earlier. And he found those differences interesting—very interesting indeed.

"Well, I can see you had a feast while we were gone," Elizabeth said cheerfully, gazing about at the wreckage from the basket.

"It does appear as if little remains from your basket, Cuz," Darcy said.

"You did have an opportunity to pack enough in your own basket," Richard said, showing not even a shred of regret or apology at his appetite. "Mrs. Hill is truly a gem of a woman and well understands how to feed a hungry, hard-working cavalryman."

"I recommend you have a word with Richard's cook once you are settled, Miss Bennet," Darcy said. "If you do not institute a certain restraint in the menu, I believe your husband will soon need to invest in new clothing. *Larger* clothing."

Jane did not rise to Darcy's teasing, only sharing a fond glance with Richard, who now noticed additional items indicative of interest. For one thing, though Elizabeth wore her bonnet, he could see that her hair looked somewhat less than perfectly arranged, which was a distinct difference from the morning. And Darcy's cravat, while tied with a degree of skill, was not knotted with the perfection that his valet always managed.

He smiled inwardly, convinced that these two had experienced some kind of epiphany that included a merging of their characters and possibly certain physical activities. A single quick glance at Jane and the miniscule raising of her eyebrows indicated she was having similar thoughts.

But his observations and suppositions, while interesting, were not a matter for open discussion, and he consigned them to the back of his mind for later and private discussion. But he anticipated some interesting developments in a few days after he and Jane were safely married.

"I believe we should be on our way, Lizzy," Jane said. "Mama is going to be furious enough at having us gone all day without our being late to dinner."

Quickly, Jane and Elizabeth repacked and arranged their depleted picnic baskets, and the four of them began to pick their way out of the thicket. When they reached Longbourn, the displeasure of Mrs. Bennet was apparent, but Mrs. Long and Lady Lucas were visiting, so she could not express herself as forcefully as she might have. She commanded Jane and Elizabeth to come in to meet her guests who had specifically stopped by to see them. Within a few minutes, however, Elizabeth begged leave to return to her room, saying she was feeling rather ill and wished to rest before dinner.

After she had gone upstairs, Richard waited until he caught Jane's eye and then nodded towards the hall. He quietly got to his feet and waited for Jane in the hall before he said very softly, "I believe you ought to look in on your sister. The housekeeper you mentioned—will she keep a confidence?"

Jane looked at him in surprise, but it was only a moment before he saw comprehension dawn in her eyes. "How very unforeseen, especially for Lizzy. But I believe you are right. I noticed some discomfort as we walked home, but I thought nothing of it."

"If you speak with your housekeeper, her advice is likely to be far superior to anything I might advise."

"I am surprised Lizzy would be so...so hasty."

"I was certain she and Darcy had reached some kind of accommodation when they returned. It appears as if they sealed it with something more than a kiss." Jane put her hand over her mouth to muffle her giggle at this comment.

"And we could have done the same," she said with a wicked glint in her eye.

"True, but we did not have the anguish your sister and Darcy have shared. We are being more hasty than they in our own way, which I prefer."

"As do I," she said, squeezing Richard's arm.

"I suspect she and Darcy will wait until after we are married to make their own announcement. But we digress. You should go to your sister."

"I shall, my love." She smiled, and Richard leaned down to brush his lips over hers before she went up the stairs.

It was nearly ten o'clock when Darcy and Richard left Longbourn. Richard had agreed to move to Netherfield the next morning, but he would be returning to the inn that night. The two of them discussed inconsequential matters as they rode through the darkness with the moon to guide them until Darcy heaved a sigh and halted his horse.

"Just a minute, Richard. We need to discuss something."

Richard walked his horse back to his cousin, but Darcy took a few moments before he spoke. "After dinner, Elizabeth told me what you recommended to Jane. So you must—"

"It is none of my business, Cousin. I only tried to help."

"I want you to know it is all my fault and no blame should be laid to Elizabeth's charge. It was entirely my fault."

Richard was silent for a moment, wondering whether to respond to this. Finally, he gave a sigh, hoping what he had to say would not adversely affect the warming of the relationship between himself and Darcy. But he simply could not allow what Darcy had said to stand.

"Pardon my bluntness, but what you just said is a load of absolute rubbish."

"What?" Darcy said blankly.

"For Heaven's sake—do you think that you and Elizabeth are the first young couple to anticipate the pastor? I say that with the assumption that you and Miss Elizabeth reached an amicable resolution of your remaining differences and agreed to marry."

Richard was barely able to make out Darcy's nod in the darkness and continued. "Of course, you should have the wedding as soon as possible. It only makes sense, now that what has happened has happened. But you are marrying the lady, are you not? So I will not listen to any wailing about blaming this person or blaming that person. Horse manure. No one is to blame, and the only means of rectifying what the two of you did today is to marry, which you both wish to do. So I will not listen to any further talk about blame."

Darcy was silent for several moments. "I thought you would be angry with me. I do want you to know that I value your good opinion of me, little though I have deserved it since you returned."

"Then let this be the last I hear of this *shouldering the blame* nonsense. Just marry the woman and make her happy. What else could I desire for a brother to do?"

"Nothing else," Darcy said after a moment's thought. He wondered whether Richard and Jane had taken the opportunity to anticipate the pastor also, but he decided the conversation had reached an appropriate ending.

CHAPTER 27

You know when you have found your prince because you not only have a smile on your face but in your heart as well.

— Author Unknown

Monday, May 18, 1812
Longbourn, Hertfordshire

After Darcy and Richard left Longbourn, Elizabeth and Jane lost no time in retiring to their room. They helped each other braid their hair for sleeping, saying little as they dressed for bed since the subject they both wished to discuss was so sensitive and private that they needed to pick their words with care.

Jane climbed into her bed, and Elizabeth took a seat at the foot of the bed, tucking her feet under her nightgown. She grimaced slightly at the soreness in her groin, but it was really much better than it had been earlier in the evening.

"I do not believe I shall be able to sleep any time soon," she finally said.

"Nor do I," Jane replied, but their conversation ground to a halt at that point.

Finally, Elizabeth gave a rueful laugh, knowing one of them had to speak. "This will not do, Jane. We know each other too well. To put it plainly, you obviously suspect what happened today between Darcy and me."

Jane shook her head in disappointment. "I thought I was better at maintaining a serene expression."

"Against everyone except your dearest sister—yes. We cannot hide much from each other."

"True. So, may I assume Mr. Darcy repeated his offer and received an answer more in keeping with his desires than he did the first time?"

"He did, but only after I asked whether he still wished to marry me."

"You said that?" Jane said delightedly.

"I did. It was an impulse. I decided it was time to act."

"Then why the worried expression, Lizzy? You said you were going to act sooner or later if Darcy continued to hesitate."

"Yes, agreeing to marry is what I wished for…but I did not plan on what happened afterwards…"

"Ah. So that troubles you."

"Well…"

"But I suspect you did not anticipate it either. I imagine you and Darcy shared a kiss or two, then one thing led to another."

Elizabeth looked Jane in the eye and nodded slowly, not bothering to explain that everything began when she threw herself into his arms.

"Oh, Lizzy, your worries are for naught. The man is going to marry you after all. So what is the harm if you anticipated the wedding ceremony by a few weeks?"

"I know, I know! I would have said exactly the same if it had been you and Richard—"

"It might have been; instead, we took a nap and talked."

"—but I was not prepared for it to happen to me."

"You have always felt things more intently than I. Richard pointed out that you and Darcy have endured considerable anguish to get to this point, which might be one reason for some…precipitate actions."

"I suppose," Elizabeth said thoughtfully.

"It is rather surprising to be speaking of such private matters, but we shall soon be married women, and the realities of married life will present us with a number of dramatic changes to our lives. We should be prepared to talk of things we can hardly anticipate now."

Elizabeth shook her head wryly. "So much for my vaunted self-control. I only intended some private conversation since I did not wish Darcy to continue doing penitence for my sake, and then…" She gave an eloquent shrug of her shoulders.

"It has been an eventful two weeks."

"It has indeed. Three weeks ago, I *knew* William was the last man in the world I could marry, and now I have not only become engaged but have lost my maidenly innocence."

"Since I can see it no longer bothers you overmuch, I shall not waste my time in worrying about you chastising yourself."

"I just realized chastising myself would do no good," Elizabeth said more cheerfully. "Hill put me right into a hot bath and attended me herself. I confided to her that William and I were engaged, and all she said was how happy she was for both of us."

"I know. Our mother will be happy for the advantages of your marrying a wealthy man, but Hill is happy because *you* are happy."

"Exactly right. I am sure she will keep my secret."

"She always has before. Have you and Darcy talked about a date for the wedding?"

"Two weeks after yours," Elizabeth said firmly. "William plans to talk with Father tomorrow, but he will also ask him to keep it a secret until after you and Richard are married. But we should not wait any longer, just in case…"

Jane nodded a silent agreement, for neither of them wanted a child born too soon after the wedding.

"Mama will be disappointed since she would wish many weeks of delightful preparations."

"Delightful for her, perhaps, but pure misery for William and me. He has already been far too patient with Mama's friends and relations—especially Aunt Philips."

Jane winced but nodded agreement. They both loved their aunt, for she had a good heart, but she seemed unable to restrain her vulgar comments. Indeed, she did not really seem aware she *was* being vulgar.

"Oh, I wish I could be married on Wednesday with you," Elizabeth exclaimed. "William talked much today of the grounds of his estate in Derbyshire. I suppose I sounded like a fortune hunter when I told him how much I would like to walk those paths in person, though he cautioned that the entire circuit is more than ten miles."

"As if that will dissuade *you*."

"Exactly!"

She looked so happy at the thought of wandering through the extensive gardens that Jane had to laugh and clap her hands.

"Whatever was that for?" Elizabeth asked in confusion.

"Only that you are who you are, Lizzy. Most real fortune hunters would be more interested in the house and furnishings than in the pathways through the woods." Jane laughed again at the thought.

Elizabeth smiled in return, but then her expression changed. "I hope Pemberley is not as ornate as Rosings," she said with a worried frown.

"I cannot say since I have seen neither, but Richard did tell me that he had never been very comfortable at Rosings and that Pemberley was much more to his liking. That should give you a ray of hope."

"I do hope so. I would not want to have to watch my tongue every moment if Pemberley were decorated in the same style as Rosings. And you know that being able to hold my tongue is not one of my distinguishing features."

"Yes, but you usually phrase your derisive comments in such a fashion that a listener cannot determine whether a comment from you is favourable or unfavourable."

"I shall have to take a vow to restrain my impertinent nature from this moment. It would not do to offend both my new husband and my new sister at one and the same time."

Jane gave a soft exclamation of surprise. At Elizabeth's look, she said, "I just realized I shall have a new sister quite soon though I shall not meet her until the wedding—or possibly tomorrow if Richard's parents come to Netherfield."

A strange look crossed Jane's face at the mention of Netherfield since it reminded her of all her mother's previous hopes that her daughter would someday be mistress there. Tonight, however, the thought, though unexpected, could not cause her any pain. Her heart was entirely in the keeping of Colonel Richard Fitzwilliam. Memories of previous disappointments seemed as ethereal as if they had occurred ages previously.

CHAPTER 28

Fortune favors the bold, but abandons the timid.

— Latin Proverb

Tuesday, May 19, 1812
Netherfield, Hertfordshire

On Tuesday, Richard stood outside the front entrance to Netherfield with Jane at his side as the large Matlock coach pulled up. He was in a distinctly rebellious frame of mind due to the fact that Jane was standing there. He knew his father would expect nothing less; he was always careful that the distinction of rank be observed, and he would expect a young lady from a family such as hers to wait upon him rather than the reverse.

Richard had argued that she should wait at Longbourn until his parents called to make her acquaintance, but that had been his stubbornness talking. Jane, Elizabeth, and Darcy had made the opposite case, pointing out that the Earl of Matlock was a prestigious man in the kingdom, and since both Darcy and Richard were well apprised of his foibles, it would be foolish to antagonize him deliberately. Their arguments had carried the day since even Richard realized he was being unreasonable. But he was still not happy about it.

For the same reason, Elizabeth stood by Darcy's side. Her father's approval had been applied for and quickly obtained earlier that morning, and Mr. Bennet had readily agreed with his daughter's suggestion to withhold a general announcement, especially to Mrs. Bennet, until after Jane and Richard's wedding. Mr. Bennet had been equally agreeable to the wedding date Elizabeth suggested though Richard knew it would have been impossible to determine whether he had any suspicions about the reason for such haste. It was, after all, well known that most young men were anxious to take their new wives to their beds. In any case, from what Darcy had told him, Mr. Bennet's only expressed thought was that the departure of Jane and Elizabeth would mean the end of any semblance of sense at Longbourn.

Though he hated to admit the possibility, Richard could not quell the faint apprehension associated with having Jane meet his family. He very much wanted his mother and sister to like her and appreciate the reasons she meant so much to him. For his father, he had significantly fewer hopes, primarily centred on desiring that the dispute between the two of them did not surface again and cause Jane any distress.

Georgiana stood beside Elizabeth, their arms intertwined. She, at least, had also been informed of the engagement of her brother, and her expressions of joy at the occasion had been bounded only by her fervent desire of being loved by her new sister. That Elizabeth had felt similarly had been an occasion for tears of joy on both their parts.

Bingley stood beside Darcy as they waited, and Richard was still rather disconcerted at the way Netherfield had been thrown open— first to him and now to his family. He was certain he could not have received a more gracious reception, and Bingley's manner could not be faulted. Richard prided himself on his civility, but he would not delude himself that he could have been as hospitable were the situation reversed.

Lord Matlock stepped down first, and Richard was somewhat

surprised to see how heavily his father leaned on his cane. Obviously, walking caused him considerable pain, but just as obviously, he refused to let it keep him from performing his duties as husband and father as he offered his hand to support both his wife and daughter when they stepped down from the coach.

Richard knew the time had come to make introductions, and he quelled his apprehensions as Darcy stepped forward. There was a prescribed order to such formalities, after all.

"Aunt, Uncle, Cousin Elaine, please permit me to introduce my good friend and our host at Netherfield, Charles Bingley. Charles, my aunt and uncle the Earl and Countess of Matlock and their daughter, Lady Elaine Fitzwilliam."

"My lord, my lady, Lady Elaine," Bingley said with a crisp bow, "I am honoured."

"Thank you, Mr. Bingley. It was most gracious of you to invite us," Lord Matlock rumbled.

"Indeed it was, sir," his wife added. "Darcy has mentioned your name to us several times, and I know he holds you in the highest regard. Thank you for your hospitality."

Now the time had come, and Richard drew a deep breath as he stepped forward with Jane on his arm.

"Father, Mother, Elaine, permit me the honour of presenting my betrothed, Miss Jane Bennet of Longbourn. Jane, my parents, Lord and Lady Matlock, and my sister, Lady Elaine."

"Lord Matlock, Lady Matlock, Lady Elaine, I am honoured to make your acquaintance," Jane said in her soft voice as she gracefully curtseyed.

"Miss Bennet, the pleasure is ours," Lord Matlock said, and his wife was equally gracious, impressed by both her appearance and her bearing. Lady Matlock caught the eye of her son as her husband turned back to Darcy, and she gave him a quick nod of approval.

"Oh my," Elaine said, stepping away from her mother and father, who lingered as Darcy introduced Elizabeth. "You said she was beautiful, and you did not exaggerate, Brother. Whatever can she see in you?"

Richard only grinned at his sister's lively remark. "Your time will come, Sprout," he promised her, "and then it shall be my turn to make humorous remarks at your expense."

"Perhaps it shall, Richard," his sister said, smiling sweetly but with a twinkle in her eye. "However, because of your elder years, it is unlikely you will survive to see it."

"Please ignore her, my dear. I believe she was dropped on her head too many times as an infant."

Jane only smiled at the other girl. "She reminds me of Lizzy and her satirical eye, Richard. They should get on famously."

Elaine looked over at Elizabeth giving a graceful curtsey to Richard's parents. "Two sisters, one who has smitten my brother and the other who appears to have done the same to my rather aloof cousin. I look forward to meeting her since she appears to have formed an agreeable attachment with Georgiana. When will she and Darcy marry, I wonder?"

"Nothing has been announced yet," Richard added quickly, his voice quiet. "But though you have the insightful eye of our mother, please do not say anything just now. She and Darcy want to wait until Jane and I are married."

"Now is probably the time to warn you about my mother, Lady Elaine," Jane said, her discomfort plain to see. "She is rather…uh, foolish, I am afraid to say, and—"

"Say no more." Elaine gaily gave a dismissive wave of a gloved hand. "Having grown up with my exceedingly foolish aunt Lady Catherine—you have heard about her, I presume?—I shall not be making any judgements about relatives."

"Thank you, Lady Elaine," Jane said gratefully.

"But I must insist you cease this 'Lady Elaine' nonsense. We shall soon be sisters—you must call me Elaine, and I shall call you Jane."

Jane smiled and was quick to assent. Meanwhile, after greeting Georgiana with an embrace and a kiss, Lady Matlock detached herself from her husband and walked over to join her son and Jane.

"I heard what my daughter said about 'Lady Elaine,' my dear, and it must be the same for me."

She smoothly removed Jane's arm from Richard's and slipped it through her own. "I shall hear no titles from your lips—I hope you will call me Mother, and you shall be my Jane. I have missed too much of my son's life already, and I am determined to rectify that calamity from this point on. Besides, since you have already proven you possess more optimism than common sense by accepting my most rebellious son, I can see we shall be great friends."

Jane smiled and agreed to Lady Matlock's request though Richard could see that she was a bit uncertain.

She is undoubtedly unsure that she could ever be so informal with a woman she regards as a great lady, he thought with amusement. *But I shall speak with her and assure her of Mother's earnestness.*

Lady Matlock now nodded her head and turned back to her son. "She is everything you said, Richard. I can see now how everything happened so fast. You would have been a fool not to pursue her."

Richard gave an internal wince as he saw a flicker of emotion momentarily pass across Bingley's face. *Obviously, despite his excellent manners and amiability, this is still a sensitive topic for him,* he thought.

"Come, dear, let us go inside and talk," his mother said, turning towards the house and still holding Jane's arm in hers. "You must tell me all about how you came to meet my son…"

LADY MATLOCK'S HUSBAND FOLLOWED HER INTO THE HOUSE, leaving Darcy and Elizabeth free to join Richard and Elaine. After a moment's hesitation, Bingley did the same, and Darcy was quick to introduce him to Richard's sister.

"It is very hospitable of you to make us welcome in your home,

Mr. Bingley," said Elaine, smiling. "Mother would have been very cross if we had travelled the morning of the wedding. She really does not like the dust of the road. I hope you have a good supply of hot water as she will need two baths before she feels presentable."

"Umm…yes…well, I…uh…" Bingley mumbled, and Richard glanced over at him curiously. While he did not know the man very well, he did know his manners were usually impeccable. He was not prone to stammering as he had just done.

"I believe there should be a good supply of hot water, Bingley," Darcy said. "I heard you ask your housekeeper to see to it."

"Excellent," Elaine said. "Mother will be so happy. And you, Miss Elizabeth, your sister said we should get along famously since you possess a satirical eye. Richard has undoubtedly warned you about me."

"Actually, Lady Elaine, Colonel Fitzwilliam seems to have forgotten to talk about you at all," Elizabeth said with a sly grin at her future brother. "What shall we do to punish him for such an oversight?"

"I cannot say immediately since it bears some thought. But I should warn you that I am averse to being called Lady Elaine more than once per day."

"And I have just met your quota. Very well, then, I shall call you Elaine, and you can call me Elizabeth. Or perhaps you might prefer Lizzy or Eliza—I respond equally well to any of them."

"I do believe we have an understanding. Now, Mr. Bingley," she said, turning to Bingley cheerfully, "perhaps you would be kind enough to show me about your house? Mother will wish to have a long talk with my future sister, and I know from experience that she will have no desire to have me present. For some unknown reason, she seems to believe I am a trifle impertinent."

"Uh…yes…that is, if you would come this way…"

Bingley had reflexively held out his arm, and he appeared rather nonplussed as Elaine casually took it, seeming almost to guide him into his own house rather than the other way round.

Richard did not quite know what to make of the rather befuddled look on Bingley's face as he and his sister proceeded down the hallway. Richard looked at Darcy, wondering at what seemed to be unusual behaviour in his friend, but Darcy had rolled his eyes upward and his lips were moving soundlessly. His eyes met those of Elizabeth, who was also looking at both Bingley and Darcy in confusion. She appeared to be as disconcerted as he was and only shrugged her shoulders in bewilderment.

The reason for Bingley's bemusement may have been mysterious to Richard and Elizabeth, but it was only too familiar to Darcy, acquainted as he was with his friend's foibles. His cousin Elaine was passably handsome though not nearly the beauty her mother was, but she was definitely a Fitzwilliam, having inherited her full measure of quirky stubbornness and sauciness. She refused to imitate the usual young ladies who were taking their first Season along with her, and she had disconcerted more than one young scion of a noble but impoverished family, who had been more interested in her fortune than her person. Bingley knew little of this though Darcy had at least given him a brief sketch of his relations before they arrived. But Darcy easily recognised the signs of what had affected his friend.

Darcy rolled his eyes heavenward for a second time as Bingley stumbled and stuttered when he tried to describe the various rooms of the house while walking with his guests. It was clear to Darcy that his friend had, as on a number of previous occasions, fallen suddenly and without warning in love.

WHILE LORD MATLOCK AND HIS WIFE TOOK THE OPPORTUNITY to bathe and refresh themselves after the journey from Matlock Hall, the rest of the party gathered in the music room where tea and cakes were already in place. Georgiana and Elizabeth immediately went to the pianoforte; they had already spent many enjoyable hours in their brief acquaintance and commenced to play at duets, though with little success since feminine giggles were heard more often than music. Elaine was more than happy to stand beside the instrument, egging the two girls on with humorous comments on their efforts, which often reduced them to helpless laughter, while Darcy sat nearby with Richard and Jane. He was content mainly to watch Elizabeth, thrilled that her easy manner and cheerful laughter with his sister answered all his hopes about their association.

Bingley stood close by, and Darcy noted that his earlier look of bemusement had faded. He was now his usual, amiable self, complimenting Georgiana and Elizabeth on their performance despite their titters, his serious tones contrasting with Elaine's more irreverent jests. For the most part, Richard and Jane ignored much of the interplay at the pianoforte, talking softly as they exchanged occasional quiet comments.

Darcy looked over at Elaine as he heard her say, in response to a question from his sister about the London Season, "Oh, it is not too terrible, Georgiana. I know you are a bit anxious about coming out, but with the right attitude, you can look on the various manoeuvrings of the impeccably attired peacocks and popinjays with considerable enjoyment."

She turned to Bingley and asked, "Have you ever taken part in any of the activities of the Season, Mr. Bingley?"

"A very few only," he answered soberly. "Darcy recommended that I do so to at least gain an impression of the activities. But I did not really enjoy myself. I felt distinctly out of place."

"That does you no discredit, sir," Elaine said gaily. "But you at least have an idea of what I speak. I think the Honourable Robert Mills Hastings and the Baronet Adrian Simpson are two of the most sterling examples of the type I mention. Neither of them has a bean between them, of course, despite their attractive appearance and languid manners, so I have to suspect that the lure of my fortune is what draws them and makes them so very attentive."

"Unfortunately, I am not acquainted with either of them...uh... Miss Elaine. But I am certain that cannot be their only motivation."

"You would likely change your mind if you knew them, Mr. Bingley," Elaine said with a laugh.

For his part, Darcy was somewhat familiar with both of the so-called gentlemen his cousin had mentioned, at least by reputation, and they were indeed as she described them—greedy, obnoxious, and stultifyingly boring. Knowing her character as he did, he was not surprised to find her comments so unfavourable. He and Richard were well-used to her often incisive, even biting, humour, which often went well beyond Elizabeth's wry comments.

That degree of tartness is not in Elizabeth's nature, he thought. *Elaine's forthrightness certainly took Bingley aback at first, but he appears to have gotten used to her quickly. Certainly, he is laughing as often at her general impressions of the London Season as everyone else.*

He did wonder why Elaine was seeking Bingley's opinions so openly when they had just met, but he gave a mental shrug and put the thought aside. He was well aware that Elaine's perceptiveness resembled her mother's, and seeking an answer to what she did was often fruitless and had to wait until she was ready to disclose her reasons.

If she ever is ready, that is, he thought with amusement. *She is almost as difficult to interpret as I used to be though she is excessively opaque rather than just reserved. Perhaps I ought to have a private word with her and warn her against the dangers of being too hard to understand?*

But that thought would have to wait for another time since Elizabeth had noted the fixation of his gaze and responded with her warm smile that made his heart swell in his chest. The emotion and knowledge of being loved was deeply new to him. It was only a few days since he had been firmly of the opinion that continued penance on his part was needed in compensation of earlier missteps. He had been stunned at the way she had thrown caution to the winds the previous day, both emotionally and physically. In the tumultuous aftermath, they had agreed that clear and forthright statements between them were needed to avoid future misunderstandings.

Darcy had been well aware that his own attraction for Elizabeth had been a mixture of both the romantic and the physical, but he had been surprised beyond measure to learn that *she* could feel similarly. The memory of the unbearable sweetness of their lovemaking was enough to make him flush dark red, and he rigidly forced his mind into safer channels. There would be time enough for such memories once they were safely married.

"Ah, there you are, Richard," his mother said as she entered the room, and everyone began to stand.

"Never mind that," Lady Matlock said, putting a hand on Richard's shoulder before taking a seat on a comfortable sofa. "It will be tiresome to have everyone jumping to their feet every time your father or I enter or leave a room."

Lord Matlock appeared a minute later and put a cup of tea and a plate with several small cakes beside her before carefully lowering himself onto the sofa.

"Thank you, my dear," Lady Matlock said before nodding towards the pianoforte. "Miss Elizabeth appears to be getting along well with your sister, Darcy. In fact, the way they are giggling together appears more like two sisters than anything else. It makes me wonder whether an announcement of some kind on your part might be imminent."

Darcy only looked inscrutable, and Richard laughed. "I hope you are not thinking to read his expression, Mother. You know as well as I that no one can tell what he is thinking when he puts his mind to it."

"Still—"

"This is Richard and Jane's time," Darcy said calmly, and Lady Matlock settled back with a look of satisfaction. Richard easily realized she had divined an answer from Darcy despite his best effort at composure.

Darcy used Jane's Christian name instead of Miss Bennet, he thought. *That is how one addresses a family member, and Mother immediately concluded that he would not have done so if he had not reached some kind of understanding with Miss Elizabeth.*

But his glance towards the scene at the pianoforte revealed more of interest than Georgiana and Elizabeth.

"To be honest, Mother," Richard said thoughtfully, "Darcy is not the only one providing some food for thought."

Lady Matlock looked rather startled at this and looked at the pianoforte more closely.

"Elaine?" she said at last.

"And Mr. Bingley," Richard said with a nod.

"I suppose you mean that the two of them are standing closer together than is usual," his mother said slowly.

"And the easy manner in which they are conversing while mostly ignoring everyone else."

"I see nothing remarkable," Lord Matlock said dismissively. "In any case, Elaine is immersed in her first Season and is sure to be courted assiduously by many young men of the most excellent pedigree."

Richard looked at his father in exasperation, but his experiences since leaving home tempered his impulse to make a harsh rejoinder to his father's thoughtless comment. However, his mother clearly saw past his years of controlling his expression and recognised his impatience. Her intervention on his behalf was considerably smoother and more deft than he could have managed.

"Dear, have you not noticed how critical Elaine has been of the young men she has met so far in the Season? And her descriptions of the social events are not at all complimentary. I am afraid she is not enjoying herself at all."

"Perhaps not, but that is just her manner. I remember how Catherine used to describe social events before she met Sir Lewis. These days, it is considered very stylish to pretend to be indifferent to such social events, and Elaine is acting in a similar fashion. She will certainly find someone who suits her at some point."

"I am not so sure, my dear," Lady Matlock said dubiously. "She already refers to the young men she has met at various social gatherings as 'prancing peacocks' and 'over-bred fortune hunters.' In fact, I should not be surprised if she soon announces that she has seen all she wishes to see of London society and refuses to attend any more events."

"She would not," Lord Matlock exclaimed. "I forbid it. Categorically!"

Richard could not withhold a comment this time though he did attempt to reduce his father's reaction by the mildness of his tone. "I should recommend against forbidding a course of action by one of your offspring again, my lord. It might possibly elicit a response you had not anticipated."

Jane looked on in alarm as Lord Matlock glared at his son, but Richard did not return his glare. His face was calm, and he simply refused to be drawn into a disagreement. Lady Matlock again intervened, attempting to bring an end to her husband's glare as she sighed in resignation.

"Dear," she said soothingly, putting a hand on her husband's arm, "you should listen to your son on this matter. Remember, Elaine is as much his sister as she is our daughter. He knows her mind well."

Lord Matlock clearly was not inclined to agree with his wife's mollifying words, but he felt a stir of alarm as he remembered how badly he had misjudged the temper of his second son. He knew instinctively that he could not bear the same thing happening with his only daughter. After several moments' thought, he unwillingly gave a grudging nod and made no further comment.

Richard knew this was as much an admission of error as his father was capable of giving, but it seemed to be enough for his mother, who turned back to him.

"So, what are your thoughts, Richard?"

"Much the same as yours, I am sure. Elaine has little patience with people she considers to be insincere or performing, and the few comments she has made would lead me to believe she will not participate much longer. We Fitzwilliams are not known for suffering fools gladly."

Lord Matlock looked as if he would have liked to dispute this but instead said nothing after his wife nodded her agreement with his son. Richard could see that Jane was rather disconcerted by this near dispute between father and son, and he could understand why.

Her mother's persistent foolishness in almost all matters and her father's dereliction in his duty to guide and control his family have prevented any real civil discourse inside her family, he thought. *This is a subject Jane and I shall have to discuss.*

Having given the matter some thought, Darcy finally offered an opinion related to Richard's original comment. "I think you may be right about an attraction on Elaine's part, Richard. I am more certain about Bingley since I know him better. He is clearly interested in Elaine. I have seen him in that state too often to be mistaken though I am not nearly as certain of the strength of that attraction."

Darcy gave Jane a guarded look, given his disastrous intervention and misjudgements in her case, but she appeared not to notice his glance, instead watching Bingley and Elaine thoughtfully.

Obviously, if she was inclined to be angry with me about Bingley, that anger has faded, he thought in relief. *Of course, it is probably more likely that her attitude is exactly as Elizabeth has said, and she is incapable of harbouring a feeling of having been wronged, much less a desire to exact vengeance. And, since the Matlocks know nothing of that history, I am going to dismiss any worries on the subject. To paraphrase my future wife, this will be the last time I shall think on it.*

CHAPTER 29

The most precious possession that ever comes
To a man in this world
Is a woman's heart.

— by Josiah G. Holland

Tuesday, May 19, 1812
Longbourn, Hertfordshire

I t was just past dusk at Longbourn, and the house was well-lit against the oncoming darkness. Because numerous visitors were expected, Mrs. Bennet had ordered the wax candles and whale-oil lamps brought out despite being more expensive. She had no intention of using the usual tallow candles with their offensive smell when visitors of such quality were expected.

The windows were a cheery, yellow blaze from the outside, and two handsome coaches were parked to the side of the house while the horses had been released and were being fed and groomed until they were needed for the return to Netherfield. Several other carriages, smaller and less imposing, were parked in front of the house as their passengers paid a short visit on the eve of the wedding.

Through the windows, a visitor could easily see that the front room and dining room were crowded with people, and Mrs. Bennet could scarcely remember a time when her prestige had stood as high as tonight. Lord and Lady Matlock had come unexpectedly to visit in the afternoon and had stayed on to partake of dinner. News of their visit had spread as if by mystical means, and it seemed that the entirety of the Bennet family's acquaintance of four and twenty families had called on them to be introduced to such eminent guests. Of course, it was Lady Matlock who actually greeted most of those who stopped by since Lord Matlock had found an unlikely ally in Mr. Bennet. They were ensconced in the library, discussing books, politics, and the virtues of a fine bottle of brandy that Mr. Bennet had been saving for a special occasion.

However, the crush of people had driven one couple to seek separation from the press of humanity, and Jane Bennet sat with her betrothed in a secluded corner of the garden. They sat on her favourite bench, one made of a dark wood polished to slick smoothness by the fabric of many a human fundament and believed to have come from India. However, the reason for that bench being her favourite tonight was that it screened them from view of both the house and the drive.

Richard sat on that bench in the comfortable darkness of a beautiful, cool spring evening, holding Jane on his lap in a close embrace with her head tucked under his chin. She had settled herself contentedly against him as soon as they sat, murmuring her thankfulness to be out of the house and away from the scrutiny and interest of all the visitors. They had talked quietly at times and sat silently at others, satisfied simply to be together.

"I wish that you and I could just go somewhere and spend the night together," she said suddenly, her voice soft. "It is not so much that I desire to make love with you, though I certainly wish to do so, but I want very much to be close beside you while we go to sleep. I do not ever want to be separated from you though I know it must happen sometimes."

"I understand completely, my love, though I am afraid it might raise a few eyebrows if we simply climbed the stairs to your room."

"Especially since Lizzy and I share a bedroom," she said with a giggle.

"Even more startling. We are not French, after all."

"Are they really so licentious? I have always wondered whether those rumours have any truth to them."

"Very little, I believe, though I know the French really do eat frog legs. Contrarily, it is likely that they whisper rumours about the stiff British and what happens in our homes when the candles are extinguished."

She gave a muffled sound of amusement and was quiet for some moments until she said, "I very much like your mother and sister. They are so very nice and kind."

"And my father?" Richard's voice was amused.

"He seems very dignified."

"That is a polite way to avoid saying that he has more than a touch of arrogance. But do not worry. Mother said that you have charmed him completely, not only with your manners but also by your character, especially when you told the story of our courtship. She said your recitation of my confrontation with Wickham brought him immense satisfaction. Neither of them ever liked George, whom they had met when they visited Pemberley. My mother didn't trust him, though I am afraid my father's opinion was based mostly on his being the son of a steward."

"I cannot help but feel sorry for Mr. Wickham," she said softly, squirming slightly in discomfort at such compliments. "I know what he did, and I know justice has been done, but I am sorry for the waste. He could have led a useful life had he not chosen so foolishly."

"George Wickham has had more chances than ever falls to most people, and I am happy that he will not have a chance to victimize any more shopkeepers or seduce their daughters."

"I know, and I agree. But still..." She sighed.

"In addition," Richard said firmly, changing the subject away from

Wickham, "Mother said that Father went on to say that, of the wives of his four sons, you will be the most beautiful. I can only commend his judgement on that matter."

"Oh, Richard, you are making me blush again."

Richard had a ready solution for that comment, and not for the first time that evening, he lowered his head to her soft lips. When they finally leaned away, Richard said huskily, "When we are finally alone, my love, do not take your hair down. That task I reserve to myself, and I shall remove every hair pin no matter how long it takes or how dangerous you keep saying it would be."

Jane laughed delightedly in response. "We shall see whether that is *really* the first thing your hands reach for. I am inclined to think you will be too busy raising the hem of my nightdress to bother with my hair."

"That is indeed an enticing choice to be sure, but you must remember that I am a disciplined soldier. I must make sure you are not stabbed by one of the multitude of sharp bits of metal in your hair before I proceed with the rest of my plan."

"My mother visited me last night and made a number of suggestions regarding what I should expect upon entering the married condition. Fortunately, my aunt Gardiner spoke with me afterwards and was able to put my mind at ease."

"From brief experience, I daresay I could hazard a guess at your mother's advice. But I hope you listened respectfully to your aunt. I have a high regard for her good sense."

"Oh, my mother went on for some time about enduring the evils of the marital state. She recommended lying back, closing my eyes, and waiting for it be over. I listened dutifully and did not even laugh."

"Oh Lord," he said feelingly.

"Do not worry, dear Richard," Jane said, tightening her arms and glorying in the comfort and security she felt in his arms. "I did not tell her that if you had not been the most stalwart of gentlemen, I would already be well aware of all the evils she mentioned. I believe she would faint dead away if she had any idea of how much I would have enjoyed you taking every possible advantage of me yesterday."

She drew back to look up at him, her voice soft and throaty as she said, "I do love you so much, Richard. I cannot wait until I have you all to myself. I shall miss Lizzy, of course, but otherwise, I am exceedingly anxious to be away from Longbourn."

Richard tucked her head beneath his chin again, unhappily aware of the way Mrs. Bennet had spoiled Jane's anticipation of their wedding. But there was nothing to be done about the matter, and they returned to sitting silently and listening to the voices and laughter coming from the house.

"I like your sister very much," Jane said suddenly. "She and Lizzy are indeed alike, though they think and talk so rapidly that I often get lost."

After several moments' thought, Richard asked quietly, "Have you noticed how often Bingley and Elaine were in company today?"

"I did after Mr. Darcy made his comment about them. I suppose they might have been talking because the rest of us were occupied, but there did appear to be a certain amount of interest on both sides."

"Darcy is a bit worried that Bingley might be rebounding from his failed offer to you. He does not want his friend to be hurt by rushing into another romantic attachment too quickly."

"I am sure your sister would not treat him badly," Jane said in alarm.

"Not on purpose, no, but Darcy fears she might do so without intending to. He thinks Bingley too easily falls in love and has developed an interest there."

"That is not surprising. Your sister is a very interesting young lady. I think she would inspire an interest in many a young man."

"Most of whom would only be interested in her fortune," Richard said grimly with the protective instinct of an older brother. "I know Elaine is as capable as I am of recognising such creatures, but I am not as worried about Bingley being hurt as I am that he might engage her heart while his own is less intensely involved. I cannot bear the thought that he might cause her such pain as he caused you. I simply could not stand it."

Jane said nothing to this, seemingly content to remain nestling close to Richard, but her thoughts were serious. While she could not think of a man she would trust more than him, she also had personal knowledge that he was a man of direct and forcible action as shown by his confrontation with Wickham.. She felt sorry for any thoughtless young man who might believe he could safely victimize Lady Elaine Fitzwilliam and not have to face a vengeful Colonel Richard Fitzwilliam with either pistol or sword in hand. She hoped Mr. Bingley would not find himself in that position, but she had no inclination to insert herself into the situation. Such a world was not hers, and she would leave those matters in the capable hands of her future husband.

Her thoughts were interrupted, however, by the sound of soft footsteps on the other side of the hedge.

"That is far enough, Elizabeth," they heard Darcy say softly.

"Why, William, whatever can you be thinking?" Elizabeth said with a quiet laugh. Her voice was suddenly cut off, and Jane and Richard were easily able to ascertain from the sound of their breathing and the soft rustle of clothing that the other couple were sharing a passionate kiss.

"That is much better," Elizabeth said softly, giving a sigh of satisfaction when they finally broke apart. "I cannot believe how mistaken my opinions of you once were. Now, I cannot think of another man in the entire world whom I could possibly consider marrying."

"Many of your opinions were justified..."

"But many of them were not. I was a child, a selfish, thoughtless—"

Again, Elizabeth's voice was replaced by the sound of cloth against cloth, and Richard and Jane squirmed uncomfortably at the dilemma they faced. They were terribly uneasy about overhearing such a private moment, but what could they do? If they revealed their presence now,

Darcy and Elizabeth would be terribly embarrassed. But if they did not make themselves known, what else might transpire?

Jane and Richard's choice to remain silent was soon tested as they heard Elizabeth give a soft laugh that was almost a purr of delight.

"I love how you hold me, just as I adore you in every other way. You are truly the best man I have ever known."

"Even when I do this?"

"Especially when you do that, my love. I do not think I shall ever get enough of that."

"And this?"

Elizabeth laughed throatily, "You are a very naughty boy, William. But you know you must stop that and soon, very soon…"

"I wish I could disagree," Darcy said resignedly, "but you are right. We shall soon be missed, and it would not do for your mother to discover me taking liberties when she does not yet know of our engagement."

"Oh, I don't suppose anyone will miss us for a while yet," Elizabeth said archly. "In fact, I believe my mother would be exhilarated rather than offended since she would then be certain that we would marry, while now she only has hopes."

Jane and Richard sat rigid in mortification as Darcy and Elizabeth murmured endearments to each other, punctuated by the sounds of their kisses, but there was nothing they could do now.

Suddenly, Elizabeth giggled. "I have had a sudden thought. Come, darling, there is a bench on the other side of this hedge that is screened from both the house and the road."

A sudden stab of horror shot through Richard and Jane, and they were about to flee into the night when Mrs. Bennet won their undying gratitude as they heard her call loudly from the front door.

"Lizzy! Lizzy! Come inside immediately before you catch your death of cold! And your aunt Philips wants to see you before she leaves."

Darcy groaned, and Elizabeth muttered in irritation at the impeccable timing of her mother.

"Well, there's nothing for it, my love, but to return inside," Darcy said ruefully.

"True," grumbled Elizabeth, but then she laughed softly. "Never mind. I know you are disappointed, but we shall have an afternoon picnic as soon as Jane and Richard have departed. We can use the glen where Jane and your cousin stayed, and there is complete privacy there. But come inside now and rest, content with my promise of a picnic in a few days."

"Do not entice me, wench. You know I cannot think when I am alone with you."

"That is good, Mr. Darcy. That is very, very good."

"Lizzy! Come inside this instant!"

"Come, my dear," Darcy said resignedly. "It is time for the play to begin."

Richard and Jane were silent as Darcy and Elizabeth walked away, and they both gave a heartfelt sigh as they heard the front door of Longbourn close behind them.

"Oh my," Jane said finally.

"We can never breathe a word of this," Richard said, and then his humour came to the fore. "Of course, it is one of those opportunities one dreams of with a boyhood friend, the chance to embarrass him utterly. But we must refrain from the impulse."

"Certainly," agreed Jane, then she giggled. "After all, you must leave early so you can get all the rest possible before tomorrow."

"Wait until then, my darling," Richard growled, "because I suspect that *you* will be the one begging for mercy rather than myself..."

"Is that a solemn promise, sir?" Jane said with a giggle that was almost girlish, and Richard laughed as he gave her his arm to return to the house.

CHAPTER 30

Marriage is an Athenic weaving together of families, of two souls with their individual fates and destinies, of time and eternity--everyday life married to the timeless mysteries of the soul.

— Sir Thomas More

Wednesday, May 20, 1812
Hertfordshire

Wednesday morning dawned, and a cock crowed behind Netherfield Hall as the first glimmers of sunlight peeked over the horizon. Richard was already awake, lying back in the barbering chair while Sergeant Bascomb shaved him. Behind them, servants filled the metal bathtub with hot water.

Richard knew his ritual of daily bathing was looked at somewhat askance by Bascomb, who held to the general view that a bath once a week on Friday night was more than sufficient. But his disapproval left Richard unmoved. He had gone unwashed for a great many days—even weeks—when campaigning, and he much preferred being freshly bathed.

When his orderly finished, Richard lost no time in immersing himself in the hot water and working up a fine lather of soap on his arms, chest, and legs while Bascomb did the same for his short hair. When he was through, he stood up while clean water was poured over him to wash away the soap before he stepped out into the welcome embrace of a thick, warm robe.

Then came the details of dressing, and he was pleased to be donning his uniform after Jane had opined that no attire could be more appropriate for him. This particular uniform had only been delivered the day before, a gift from his mother, sewn from the finest fabric available and carefully tailored to his personal dimensions.

Though Bascomb was rather ambivalent about his marriage, he was completely pleased with this new uniform, which he thought only right and fitting for his colonel. He had polished Richard's boots to a glistening shine, and the dragoon helmet gleamed brightly. And, while Richard had flatly refused to exchange his heavy cavalry sabre for a more ornate dress sword, he had allowed Bascomb to wind decorative leather around the starkly functional wire-wound grip and to replace the usual boiled-leather scabbard with a version painted a glossy black and decorated with sufficient gold leaf to satisfy a general.

Richard examined his appearance from all angles in a mirror and nodded his satisfaction, though he again made a mental note to have Bascomb receive instruction in tying a cravat. From this point on, he would be wearing gentleman's attire more often than he was used to, and he did not wish to break in a new orderly.

"Mr. Darcy sent word he is waitin' in his coach to take ye to the church, sir," Bascomb said as Richard finished his inspection in the mirror. "Most everythin's packed, sir, and I'll be gettin' what's left into yer trunk so it'll be waitin' at yer house."

"Very good. Now, are you certain you would not like a furlough for the next week? I am certain you will not be needed until then."

"There's nuttin' fer me to go see, sir, but thank'ee anyway. I'll be happy to jest sit around with Sar'nt Jones and the boys and yarn about the ole days."

"Very well, then. I shall see you in about a week."

"Good luck, sir," Bascomb said, and the expression on his face was so doleful that Richard had to laugh.

"Good Heavens, man. I am getting married, not getting hanged. It is a happy occasion."

"If you say so, sir," Bascomb said doubtfully. "But good luck anyway."

Shaking his head in amusement, Richard went downstairs to meet Darcy for the short ride to the Longbourn chapel and a new life.

"MY STOMACH FEELS VERY UNSETTLED," JANE SAID AS SHE SAT IN front of her mirror watching Elizabeth put the finishing touches on her hair. Sarah had begun to skilfully comb and pin her hair into an elaborate and fashionable style, but she had not been finished when Mrs. Bennet called her away to attend to Lydia's hair. Elizabeth muttered imprecations under her breath as she worked, irritated at another demonstration of her mother's preference for her spoiled youngest sister. Mrs. Gardiner sat with the two girls and kept Jane's hand firmly clasped in her own to comfort her.

"Of course your stomach feels somewhat queasy, my dear. Today is the demarcation of your life. Before today, you were a maiden, unmarried, and innocent. Tomorrow, you will be a married woman, defined by your husband and yet assumed to somehow possess wisdom, judgement, and all manner of mysterious knowledge because of that marriage and the intimacies shared with your husband."

Jane believed she kept her expression unchanged at the thought of those intimacies, but she saw the merest hint of a satiric arc of Elizabeth's eyebrow in the mirror.

"It is all nonsense, of course," Mrs. Gardiner said cheerfully, "but such is the way of the world, even with those who have already experienced these events and should know better. And thus, we are unable to completely keep some part of this myth from infecting our own thinking, with the result that you have the sensation of butterflies in the stomach. I assume it is not misgivings because of your choice?"

"No," Jane said instantly. "Never that. I cannot conceive of marrying any other man."

"Then the audacity and determination of a single man has certainly wrought one momentous event in our family. And perhaps there may soon be news that he has accomplished his original errand, as well as his unexpected one?"

Mrs. Gardiner looked significantly over at Elizabeth as she said it, and Elizabeth coloured as she continued her task.

"There has been no announcement, Aunt," she said quietly.

"There does not have to be, my dear. The last your uncle and I knew, you were adamantly decided against Mr. Darcy, to the point that the mere mention of his name brought forth some rather uncharacteristic behaviour on your part. Then we received your startling letter announcing that you had decided to receive him at Longbourn, and now we see that he has been your constant companion since we arrived. And, I must say, I have never seen you in finer beauty than when the two of you are together."

"I regret my actions in town, Aunt, and I can only say I was very confused. But I am confused no more, and yes, you are right: William and I do have an understanding. But Father will not make a general announcement until the wedding breakfast. Not even my mother knows of it."

"Your uncle thought as much from speaking with Mr. Darcy. He likes him very much, and you know we both approve highly of Jane's Colonel Fitzwilliam. One can only approve of such a determined young man."

Elizabeth stepped away to give her efforts a considering look from all angles before she turned to seek Jane's opinion.

"It looks wonderful, Lizzy. Thank you."

"I agree," Mrs. Gardiner said. "You look like a veritable angel this morning, and I hope your colonel knows what a lucky man he is."

"From the way he speaks of her, you could believe nothing else, Aunt," Elizabeth said lightly. "I am convinced he thinks the sun would not rise in the morning if Jane desired to sleep late."

"Good," Mrs. Gardiner said, ignoring the sudden flush of Jane's cheeks at such fulsome praise. As Sarah came bustling back into the room, she asked, "Now, is everything packed?"

"Yes, ma'am," replied Sarah. "I saw to everything earlier, even the nightgowns you gave me last night as well as the evening gowns Mr. Darcy and his sister brought this morning." She gave a quick curtsey, gathered her combs and brushes, and left quickly since Mrs. Bennet had given her a long list of tasks to be completed during the morning.

Jane knew about the four elegant and enticing nightgowns her aunt had brought. Despite the simplicity of the gowns' designs, she had never seen such fine material and workmanship, and their exotic cut made them unique in her experience. She had modelled one for Elizabeth the night before, and her sister had commented on the way the diaphanous muslin clung to her body and made her look more than a little unclothed. And the cut of all of them was not English at all. A narrow slit was cut into the several layers of the sheerest silk of one gown, from the hem all the way to her waist, and the cuts were offset in different layers, so her bare legs and hip were intermittently revealed as she moved about the room.

But Jane had known nothing about any gowns from Mr. Darcy, and her eyebrow rose as she looked at her sister.

"William asked me not to say anything, for he was not sure they would be ready. When he first came to call on me and saw you and Richard together, he immediately sent an express to his sister to have a selection of fashionable gowns prepared. He knows our father has not had a chance to provide for wedding clothes, and he wanted to make amends for the sadness he has caused you."

"I do not blame him for that. I do not even blame Mr. Bingley any longer."

"But William believes he acted improperly, and it troubles him. When he first told me of his plan, I said what you just said, and he replied, 'I should at least have made certain that your sister's heart was not engaged by my friend rather than depending solely on my vaunted powers of observation.' So, at his request, I provided your general measurements, and Miss Darcy oversaw the sewing of the gowns. They can be tailored more exactly later after the wedding is complete."

Jane was still not satisfied, and Mrs. Gardiner laid a hand on her arm. "It is a generous gift, Jane, and it is given with a good heart by a man who will soon be your brother."

Jane considered what she said for a moment before somewhat reluctantly nodding her acceptance.

"Good. Then let us be about it since your father's carriage is at the door waiting to take you to the chapel. Your mother has had rugs laid from the door to the carriage so no dirt will attach itself to your dress, and she has already walked ahead with your other sisters."

Now that the moment was here, Jane grimaced as she stood up, for her butterflies had returned with a vengeance.

Wednesday, May 20, 1812
Longbourn Chapel, Hertfordshire

THE SUNBEAMS OF A GLORIOUS SPRING MORNING LANCED THROUGH the high windows in Longbourn chapel as the curate ignored Mrs. Bennet's sobs and turned to Colonel Fitzwilliam to continue the ceremony he knew by heart.

"Wilt thou have this woman to thy wedded wife, to live together after God's ordinance in the holy estate of matrimony? Wilt thou love her, comfort her, honour, and keep her in sickness and in health; and, forsaking all others, keep thee only unto her, so long as ye both shall live?"

Richard's voice was firm as he replied in a clear, carrying voice, "I will."

The Reverend Palmer remembered christening the lovely young woman before him when she was a mere infant more than twenty years earlier, and he could not help wondering where all those years had gone. But he resolutely forced his thoughts to stop wandering and turned to Jane for her part in the ceremony.

About them were gathered the small group of friends and family. Jane's sisters and mother stood behind her while her father stood by her side. Darcy stood close by Elizabeth, and Richard's parents stood in a loose group by the reverend along with his sister.

Bingley stood in the group in a bemused state. He had not really planned to attend the wedding, but somehow, when conversing with Elaine the previous night, she simply took it for granted that he would attend.

So here he stood in an assemblage where, only days earlier, he had believed he could never be more than an outsider. But today he did not feel like an outsider at all. He could not determine quite how it had happened, but it seemed to have something to do with Colonel Fitzwilliam's intriguing and rather perplexing sister.

"Who giveth this woman to be married to this man?" said Reverend Palmer, turning to Mr. Bennet, who held Jane's right hand in his. He passed her hand to the reverend who in turn placed it in Richard's larger one.

"Please repeat after me," Reverend Palmer said. "I, Richard…"

With the mutual affirmation of troths complete, Richard held out a folded paper with a gold ring on it and placed it on the Bible the curate held. Reverend Palmer took the ring and bowed his head over it for a few moments before handing it back, while the folded paper, which included the accustomed duty payment for both him and his clerk, disappeared into his pocket with the skill of long practice.

Lady Matlock felt a deep sense of fulfilment as she looked on Richard and Jane. She had been happy enough in her own marriage, but she had hardly known the earl before they were married. Afterwards, they had lived much of their lives in separate spheres. Her inability to influence him to change his adamant orders concerning Richard all those years ago was an example of the limits of her influence with her husband. But obviously Jane and her son would have a much more interwoven and, she hoped, much happier life together.

For his part, her husband was feeling the pangs of guilt that his wife had never been able to inspire. He had known for some years that he had been wrong when Richard refused a church education. In fact, he now believed a part of him had even known it then. But, in his pride, he had simply refused to admit it, and there was no one who could force him to change his mind. Now, as he saw the gaze his son bestowed on his chosen wife, he realized what he had missed. He had chosen to exercise his prerogatives as a father, husband, and peer of the realm…and he had sacrificed all feelings of tenderness and humanity to do so. No one in his life—not his wife, not his sons, and not even his daughter—would ever look at him the way this country lass looked at his long-estranged son.

The sense of desolation he felt was one that had never afflicted him before, and suddenly his whole life seemed useless and empty. If he had had the capability, he would have shed a tear, but it would have been a tear of remorse and despair, not a tear of happiness for the joy of a loved one. And such was his blindness that the Earl of Matlock had not a single inkling of the difference.

Meanwhile, Richard took Jane's left hand and paused, suddenly and unexpectedly transfixed by the laughter lurking in her sparkling violet eyes. The pause continued for some seconds before Jane gave a soft laugh and whispered softly, "Pray continue, dearest, or we shall never be married."

Richard shook himself and smiled ruefully before sliding the ring onto her fourth finger.

"With this ring, I thee wed," he said intently, his eyes locked with hers, which had now gone serious. "With my body, I thee worship, and with all my worldly goods, I thee endow. In the Name of the Father, and of the Son, and of the Holy Ghost. Amen."

He felt he could melt into the smile that suddenly blossomed on her face, and he forced himself to turn back to the Reverend and kneel beside Jane.

"Let us pray," the reverend said. "Oh eternal God, Creator and Preserver of all mankind…"

Richard felt the accustomed words wash through him, and a deep sense of peace and thankfulness swept over him. He added his own heartfelt prayer to the words of Reverend Palmer, conscious of the blessings with which he had been gifted.

When the curate was finished, he joined Richard and Jane's hands together, saying, "Those whom God hath joined together let no man put asunder. For as much as Jane and Richard have consented together in holy Wedlock, and have witnessed the same before God and this company, and thereto have given and pledged their troth either to the other, and have declared the same by giving and receiving of a ring, and by joining of hands; I pronounce that they be Man and Wife together, in the Name of the Father, and of the Son, and of the Holy Ghost. Amen."

It is done, thought Richard thankfully. *All I have to do is kneel here holding this precious hand while the pastor says all the usual things, and the first and most barren part of my life will be over. I shall put all bitterness and sadness behind me, for nothing can ever be hopeless with this woman by my side.*

Darcy looked on Richard and Jane as they knelt, not five paces away, while Reverend Palmer continued with the blessing, and he felt the most intense longing he had ever felt in his life sweep through him. Sudden doubt gripped him that he could ever be as transcendently happy as his cousin appeared to be, and he must have flinched or otherwise given sign of the emotions that afflicted him, for he suddenly felt Elizabeth's eyes on him. Looking her way, he saw her eyebrow arched in question while a smile of what seemed infinite tenderness graced her lips.

As quickly as his doubts and apprehension had come, they left him, and he was again confident that he would kneel on the same cushion in not too many days.

I can last, he thought as Elizabeth turned back to her sister while the pastor continued. *It shall come to pass in the fullness of time just as God promised. She has given me her promise, and I shall not let doubts assail me.*

The remainder of the ceremony quickly concluded, and at last Richard rose and put out his hand to his wife, who accepted it and rose gracefully.

Everyone was about them in an instant. Mrs. Bennet clasped Jane to her as tears ran down her face while Darcy shook Richard's hand firmly. Mr. Bennet caught his eye and nodded gravely, and Richard responded in kind. He knew his new father-in-law was not a demonstrative man, but he was certain of the older man's approval of this match.

Behind them were his parents and his sister, and he noticed that Bingley was now at Elaine's side. He wondered whether his father was still unaware of a possible attraction between them but firmly put the thought aside. Elaine was her own person, much as he had been but without his aggressive nature. He knew she would do as she willed, and if events turned out as they might, he hoped his father would not react as he had done in his own case.

Mrs. Gardiner pressed up behind them and embraced him warmly, kissing him on both cheeks.

"Congratulations, Richard. I simply cannot express how happy Mr. Gardiner and I are for both you and Jane."

"Thank you…Aunt," Richard said, his mind fumbling to adjust to the reality of his new family members. "There will be many new names and relations for me to learn."

"You shall not have much difficulty," Mr. Gardiner said with a happy smile, putting out a hand and gripping Richard's firmly. "Just call all the men 'sir' and all the women 'ma'am' until you get it sorted out. That was the advice my father gave me, and it served me well."

"I shall remember that, Uncle. Now, I shall expect you next Saturday for dinner as we agreed last night. My cook has been lamenting the fact that the family to whom I rented my house did not entertain, so she is expecting me to give her a chance to demonstrate her capabilities."

"We shall be there, Richard—"

"Son! Oh, Richard, let me give you a kiss!" Mrs. Bennet interrupted as she thrust herself between the Gardiners to embrace Richard and plant a sloppy kiss on his cheek. Mr. Gardiner rolled his eyes in mortification at the behaviour of his sister, but Richard simply smiled.

You cannot expect a leopard to change his spots, and you cannot expect Mrs. Bennet to act properly, he thought phlegmatically, turning his head to allow her to kiss his other cheek. *Besides, I owe her a debt for being the mother of my wife. I shall just have to think of her as similar to the wife of the major general, a woman who has to be endured as part of my duty.*

Gradually, everyone left the church to walk back to Longbourn, leaving Richard and Jane, with Darcy and Elizabeth in attendance, to sign the parish record. Afterwards, Reverend Palmer congratulated the newlyweds again and then turned to Elizabeth and Darcy.

"And is there a chance I may be able to perform a similar service for you at some time in the not-too-distant future, Miss Bennet?"

Elizabeth smiled gaily, looking up at Darcy. "I suppose I really am 'Miss Bennet' now, sir. But, to answer the question, I believe my father will be making an announcement during the breakfast."

"That is excellent news," Reverend Palmer said, beaming broadly. "Simply excellent. After all, I have known you all your life, and I am no longer a young man. I was hoping you would make up your mind soon since, otherwise, I might not be able to preside over the service."

"I believe you are directing your words at the wrong person, Reverend," Richard said sardonically, "since I believe my cousin was prepared for a much longer courtship than Miss Bennet came to believe was warranted. I *was* becoming a bit impatient, Darce. I detected Miss Elizabeth's change in attitude long before you did, and I believe I even informed you of it."

"You did, but I was too blind to see." Darcy nodded. "It seems I am an incomplete person, but I have hopes my deficiency shall soon be rectified."

"Due to the most resolute cousin a man could have," Elizabeth said seriously. "It was very courageous of you to take the steps you did to correct my own failings, Richard. You have my thanks for all your efforts, as well as those of Mr. Darcy. And that is even before I attempt to extend my gratitude at having made my sister so deliriously happy."

Richard turned red with embarrassment, and he could not seem to find words to answer such lavish praise.

"I believe Richard would not call it courage, Elizabeth," Jane said. "Perhaps we might more aptly describe it as boldness."

Richard looked over at the man who had just married them; he looked on with a bemused smile.

"Perhaps you could help me out of this, sir?"

"Oh, I think not, young man. I think you have been described with admirable accuracy."

"Having grown up with Richard, I have known few occasions when he was at a loss for words," Darcy said. "I never imagined I might shut him up by praising him."

"Perhaps this would be a good time to refrain from taking unfair advantage of your cousin, William," Elizabeth said. "Soon, you shall be in the same situation, and he will have had time to think up something suitable to say."

"Hmm. I believe you are right, my dear. Discretion may be called for in this case."

"Always your strongest suit, Darce," Richard said with an amused snort, and then he cocked an eyebrow at Reverend Palmer. "Perhaps you see now why I believe they will be such a fine, boisterous couple—once they are safely married, of course."

"Of course, young man. I completely agree. Now, we had best be on our way. There is still the wedding breakfast Mrs. Bennet has planned. She must be wondering what is keeping us."

"Certainly, sir. We should be on our way."

As Jane and Richard followed Darcy and her sister from the church, Jane held Richard's arm quite tightly. She also took the opportunity to make her eagerness to get the morning behind her known to him by the possessive way she pulled his arm firmly against her breast, smiling warmly as he glanced at her with eyes that had widened slightly. It was only for a moment, and then they were out in the sunlight with none of those they followed being aware of this interplay.

As for Reverend Palmer, who followed somewhat behind them, whether he had seen or interpreted anything would never be known. In any case, he would have considered it to be none of his concern since the intimacies between newly married couples were part of their Lord's plan.

Wednesday, May 20, 1812
Longbourn, Hertfordshire

As Darcy saw Bingley leave Elaine's side in the front room at Longbourn, he quickly excused himself from Elizabeth and made his way across the room. Elaine saw him coming, and she also observed the grim look on his face.

"I would ask whether you are enjoying yourself, Cousin," she said as Darcy joined her, "except that, judging from the expression on your face, you have not come to exchange pleasantries."

"I have not," agreed Darcy, rather more harshly than he had intended, and Elaine raised an eyebrow in query at his breach of decorum.

"Then perhaps you should say what you have to say," Elaine said calmly, though it was clear she was not pleased with Darcy's manner.

"It is just this, Elaine. Bingley is my friend—my best friend, in fact. And I do not wish to see him hurt."

"Hurt? What would make you believe I would hurt him?"

"I know your playful and teasing manner. I have seen how you handle those young men whose attention you do not desire, and though you do not act cruelly or maliciously, I still would not have Charles treated in a similar fashion."

"I see," Elaine said, but her voice was now cold, and two spots of colour high on her cheeks showed her anger. "First of all, I might enquire what gives you the arrogance to simply assume that I would treat your friend as I might some foolish and conceited young man whose only interest in me is the size of my fortune? And second, just what tragedy in your friend's life would inspire you to defend his welfare in such an insulting manner to your own cousin?"

"It is not arrogance that drives me—it is guilt. Do you see Richard's new bride and your new sister over there? Well, at one time Charles was very interested in her, and she felt similarly. But I made a grievous mistake. I thought she was indifferent to his attentions, and I thought it best to so inform him. Since his sisters did not want their brother to marry a young lady without fortune, family, or connexions, they aided me in convincing him to stay in town and not return to Netherfield.

"But," he said, drawing a ragged breath, "I was wrong on both sides. Miss Jane Bennet was as attracted to him as he was to her. She simply did not show it as other young ladies might. That was last November, six months ago, and her heart—both their hearts—still ached when Richard chanced to be introduced to her. He cured the wound in *her* heart, but not that in Charles's. Now my friend realises what he allowed to escape him, and his pain is my fault. Accordingly, he is still vulnerable, and I feel the necessity of intruding even though my actions might seem overly protective to some."

Elaine's resentment had dissipated as Darcy told his story, and she laid her hand on his arm. "I am sorry for my anger. I did not know any of this. But you should understand that I am not playing with your friend. In fact, I like him very much, not least for the fact that he does not need my fortune yet still gives every indication of enjoying my company."

Darcy looked at her closely and saw the sincerity in her face, and he nodded slightly.

Elaine looked away to where Richard and Jane were laughing amiably with Jane's aunt and uncle from town. "Richard's new wife has no fortune, as you say, but she is beautiful. I do have a fortune, but I am not close to being beautiful, even if I am not as plain as my brother. Yet I am plagued with an unending stream of suitors who act as if I am Helen of Troy reborn. Do you realize how greed such as that revolts me?"

Her voice grew softer as she continued. "But your Mr. Bingley enjoys being with me, and I see admiration in his eyes when he looks at me. And, I repeat, he does *not* need my money. So I can come to no other conclusion than that he truly enjoys his time with me, the person, rather than Lady Elaine Fitzwilliam with a fortune of forty-five thousand pounds."

She looked back at Darcy and smiled brightly before continuing. "So you may rest easy, Cousin. I think Mr. Bingley might do very nicely, and if he shows any interest, I plan to encourage his attentions. And if he ever feels inclined to make me an offer, I assure you I shall give it the most careful attention."

"Do you love him?" Darcy asked quietly.

"How should I know? If I had not seen the besotted evidence of both you and Richard, I would previously have denied the possibility that such an emotion even exists. But I do like your friend, and he is so amiable and possesses such an easy disposition that it is impossible to believe any woman would not be happy and satisfied as his wife. I also believe I could make him happy should such an event ever occur. You know I do not have an unhappy character. I would much rather laugh than anything else."

She looked back at Darcy with a twinkle in her eye. "Now that I know you have been watching over him, I can only applaud your good intentions, even if you did make a mistake with Jane. He desperately needs a gentle hand to assist him in making decisions. He is as amiable and civil a man as I have ever met, but it is clear that he needs a guide through this life."

"I see Lady Catherine's heritage is still alive in the Fitzwilliam family," Darcy said satirically.

"And why should it not be? Our aunt has done quite well in managing Rosings since she lost her husband. But do not worry. If such an eventuality arises, I shall make sure your friend is guided but not ruled. But you know yourself that such a man as your friend needs a strong, decisive woman at his side. You and Richard do not, and Richard is probably the more fortunate because Jane appears perfectly happy to leave most decisions to him. You, however, if you ever marry Miss Elizabeth…"

"*When*, Elaine—*when* I marry her," Darcy said complacently. "As I told your mother, we have an understanding."

"An understanding, is it? Well, that seems believable given the way she looks at you. In any case, your Miss Elizabeth does not appear to be a young lady who can be ruled."

"Of that you can be completely certain," Darcy said emphatically. "But I would not have it any other way. She is exactly what I want and need, and we are going to reach decisions in our family in an altogether unprecedented way." He smiled beatifically at his cousin as he concluded this statement, but he appeared to be waiting for something.

"Unprecedented, you say," Elaine said suspiciously, eyeing him carefully. "And what might this unprecedented approach be, if I might be so bold as to ask?"

"We are going to talk about important matters—the two of us," Darcy said smugly.

"Oh, dear Lord!" cried Elaine in mock horror. "The two of you will '*talk* about important matters.' We have a radical in the family! A revolutionary! One who would bring the walls of our civilization tumbling about our ears. What will Father say when he finds out?"

Darcy only smiled wider at her comments.

"Never mind," Elaine said, making pushing motions. "Go do something rash and unreasonable such as plotting against the Kingdom with your Miss Elizabeth. Here comes Mr. Bingley, and I have no need of you to watch over him. Now, shoo, shoo. It appears Mr. Bennet is trying to get everyone's attention. In the meantime, rest comfortably—your friend will be in good hands."

MR. BENNET WAS INDEED TRYING TO GET EVERYONE'S ATTENTION by striking one of the glasses with a fork, but it was several moments before he achieved a modicum of quiet. He glanced over at his wife, who was seated beside him, for he wanted to ensure she was not standing when he made his announcement.

"Thank you, thank you," he said finally. "I can see from the volume of the conversation that everyone must be enjoying themselves, and I can also see from the fidgeting of my eldest daughter and my new son that at least one couple is very eager to be gone."

He beamed at the gust of laughter that washed through the room. Jesting about the intimacies of marriage was normally a subject that had to be approached with due discretion in polite conversation, but an exception was made in commenting on the eagerness of newly married couples to finally achieve some privacy. In fact, it was rather an obligatory jest, and it never failed to receive the same enthusiastic response.

"But in addition to losing my eldest daughter, it seems I have been approached by another young man, who appears to have developed an attachment to another daughter."

Mrs. Bennet sat up straighter, her eyes flashing over to Elizabeth and Darcy.

Can it be? she thought in exultation. *I thought the day would never come! Why, oh why, did Lizzy wait so long to accept him? I simply do NOT understand that girl.*

"So, in addition to giving our good wishes to Colonel and Mrs. Fitzwilliam, I would also like to announce the engagement of the new Miss Bennet to Mr. Fitzwilliam Darcy of Derbyshire."

Mingled applause and good-natured laughter and shouts rang through the room, and Darcy rose to his feet and bowed to the assemblage. His face was flushed bright red, but the smile on his lips was one of good cheer and acceptance of their attention. He held his hand out to Elizabeth, who took it and rose to his side. To the cheers of all in the room, he bowed deeply and kissed her gloved fingers.

When the noise subsided somewhat, Mr. Bennet continued. He wanted to state the next announcement in front of the many witnesses since he knew it would not please his wife.

"Mr. Darcy and I discussed setting a date for the wedding, and we have decided on two weeks from today." Mrs. Bennet's gasp of dismay was clearly audible, and Mr. Bennet hurried on.

"In fact, Mr. Darcy would have been happier with an earlier date, but since Lizzy wants her sister Jane to stand up with her, it would have been impossible to schedule it sooner. Colonel Fitzwilliam has informed me he will not be receiving visitors until Friday week."

Cheerful and earthy laughter swept the room, and Jane flushed bright red this time. But she still smiled as she looked up at her husband, holding his arm tightly.

Mrs. Bennet was displeased at again having a wedding date set without her advice, but she could not blame Mr. Darcy, not when he would be the salvation of her other daughters. If he wanted to take Lizzy back to his estate so soon, then that was an end to it, and she would just have to make the best of it. Besides, she would soon be able to talk about her two married daughters, Mrs. Darcy and Mrs. Colonel Fitzwilliam, to all her friends. Her prestige would be without bounds!

Perhaps Lord and Lady Matlock might come to this wedding also? she thought as sudden and unexpected hope blossomed in her bosom.

"AT LAST, MY ORIGINAL TASK IS ACCOMPLISHED," RICHARD SAID with a sigh of relief. "I hope you are not surprised to know I had my doubts about the success of that particular endeavour."

"Lizzy does have firm opinions whether they are right or wrong," agreed Jane with a smile. "It will feel most peculiar to no longer share a room with her. Perhaps she can visit us in town before the wedding."

"She may visit, dearest, but not for at least a week. My butler has already taken down the knocker from the front door, and it shall not go back up for at least that long."

Richard's expression was bland, but there was laughter in his eyes at seeing the pretty blush on the cheeks of his new bride. However, even if she had blushed at the roguish teasing of her husband, Jane was not afflicted with false modesty.

"Then how much longer shall we stay, Husband?" she asked quietly.

"Ah, then you are anxious to go, are you?" Richard asked playfully.

Jane's answer was to stand up and take his arm, and given such a clear statement of his wife's desire, he lost no time in escorting her from the room and outside to Darcy's coach.

CHAPTER 31

Marriage has many pains, but celibacy has no pleasures

— Samuel Johnson

Wednesday, May 20, 1812
London

Jane came awake as she felt the coach come to a jerky halt. Richard's arm around her kept her from flying forward, and at first she did not recognise the interior of the coach. But sudden realisation returned as she saw a tender smile on her husband's dark-eyed face.

"Welcome back to the world of the living, my sweet," he said, and she could hear the good humour in his deep voice.

"I cannot believe I fell asleep so quickly. I do not even remember getting beyond the drive."

"I believe you were still awake past the drive, but your head was already nodding. You were well asleep before we got to the main roadway, and you did not stir until now."

The driver opened the door and put down the step. "Sorry about the sudden stop, sir. A boy and his dog took off across the street just as we were coming up to the door."

"No harm done, Johnson," Richard said as he stepped down and extended his hand for Jane.

Obviously, someone had been watching for their arrival since the front door was already open, and Richard's small retinue of staff was already outside, accepting the trunks and other luggage from the top of the coach.

Jane inspected the house with interest as Richard helped her down from the coach and they climbed the steps. As Richard had said, it was a brick-and-mortar town house of four stories, similar in fashion to her uncle's house though it was narrower across the front. A spare, grey-haired man and a plump woman of similar age waited for them to the side of the front door while the stream of servants carried the luggage into the house.

"Good morning, Sergeant," Richard said to the man.

"Sir!" the old man barked, his voice still loud and firm despite his age. His eyes twinkled with excitement as he braced to attention with a click of his well-shined cavalry boots.

"My dear, this is Sergeant Jones, formerly of the Sixth Dragoons and now the head of my household. And this is his wife, Mrs. Jones, our housekeeper and the person who really makes sure everything runs smoothly.

"Very pleased to meet you, Mrs. Fitzwilliam," Sergeant Jones said, giving her a deep bow. "Welcome to the colonel's—and now your—home."

"Honoured, ma'am," his wife said, giving a curtsey.

Jane responded with a nod and a warm smile. "Thank you, Sergeant, Mrs. Jones. I am glad to be here."

"Would you like to meet the rest of the staff now, ma'am, or would you rather wait until later?" asked Jones. "I have had hot water prepared for a bath, and the kitchen stands ready to prepare whatever you might like."

"Thank you very much, Sergeant, but I would prefer to meet everyone at a later time. I am rather fatigued from the journey."

Not to speak, she thought archly, *of how anxious I am to get to my bedroom and remove Richard's uniform pants...among other items...*

"Certainly, ma'am. My daughter, Betsy, is waiting upstairs to attend to your needs for the nonce. You can make a decision about a permanent maid once you have settled in."

"Thank you, Sergeant. I am sure I could not find a more fitting maid than the daughter of the man who first taught my husband how to be a soldier when he was a young lieutenant."

Richard noted the way Jones stood up straighter at the compliment, his eyes bright in remembrance, and he knew that his new wife had just won a lifelong defender. It was obvious that the rest of the staff were similarly affected, and they bowed and curtseyed as he escorted Jane through the front door.

"That was well done, my love," Richard said softly as the staff filed in behind them. "All the men are former enlisted men who served with me, and several suffered crippling wounds and could no longer serve. I cannot employ them all, but I do what I can. Now, are you sure you would not like to have something light to eat?"

"I need only to get to my bedroom and into more comfortable attire, darling. I have already bathed this morning, so I should need no more than ten minutes."

"I am at your disposal, my dear," Richard said with a grin.

"That is good," Jane said, with a saucy lift of one eyebrow. "That is very, very good."

Richard smiled again, remembering how they had both heard Elizabeth make the same comment to Darcy just the previous night.

He had trouble restraining himself to a dignified tread as he mounted the stairs beside his wife. What he really wanted to do was to throw her over his shoulder and bound up the stairs to his room, but he knew he could not do that. The staff would be embarrassed. Jane would be embarrassed.

As for himself, he was not altogether sure…

Sometimes I think our Norse ancestors may have had some good ideas that should not have been discarded in the rush to be 'civilised,' he thought with contained amusement as he sedately escorted his new wife to her rooms.

"That is good enough, Betsy. You may leave those in place," Jane said, stopping the anxious young girl from removing the pins from her hair. It was still curled around her head in the elaborate style Sarah and Elizabeth had arranged just that morning.

"Yes, ma'am," the girl said obediently though she did feel certain doubts about leaving Mrs. Fitzwilliam's hair as it was. But she controlled her doubts and held up the outer robe for the nightgown her mistress was wearing.

As Mrs. Fitzwilliam slid her arms into the long-sleeved garment, Betsy smiled inwardly at the thought of such a garment being called a 'robe.' It was so inappropriate since its material was a fine muslin similar to that of Mrs. Fitzwilliam's nightgown in softness and especially translucence. She had already noted that the nightgown was so sheer that every curve of her body could easily be discerned through the translucent fabric. And the slits in the various layers were so daring!

It must have been copied from a French design, she thought. *The Frogs are called depraved, but they are far more passionate than we English.*

"That will be all for tonight," Jane said. "I shall ring if I need anything."

"Yes, ma'am," Betsy said, thinking how strange it was to hear the early afternoon hours referred to as 'night.'

After giving Mrs. Fitzwilliam a curtsey and turning to depart, she caught a last glimpse of her mistress in the mirror, leaning forward to inspect her face before jumping to her feet and striding swiftly out of sight. From the direction her mistress had taken, Betsy knew she was going to the door that led to the master's bedchamber. Suddenly,

Mrs. Fitzwilliam's reference to 'night' did not seem nearly as strange.

Obviously, the master's new bride is not at all unwilling. And, judging from her bewitching nightgown, he will likely greet her with equal eagerness.

It was an intriguing insight into the character of the master of the house and his new wife, but it was an insight Betsy never even considered sharing with anyone else. Her father had been adamant when he told her that whatever passed in her mistress's chambers was her mistress's business only and was never to be shared—not with him, not with her future husband, and especially not with the staff.

She had a last wistful thought as she descended the servants' stairs to the lower floor. *Shall I even meet a young man who will make me feel like Mrs. Fitzwilliam?*

RICHARD WAS PACING THE FLOOR OF HIS ROOM, CASTIGATING himself for his discomfiture, when the door to his chamber opened. It was much the same feeling as when he called on Jane the first time at Gracechurch Street, and he was deep in memory as the door opened and Jane walked into his room.

"Welcome, my love," he exclaimed, whirling to meet her. "I have been—"

Whatever else Richard had meant to say caught in his throat as Jane walked across the floor towards him, her hips swaying gracefully and her unrestrained breasts bobbing under the most unbelievably enticing nightwear he had ever seen. The outer garment was open, revealing the gown beneath as she walked. Her long legs were easily visible through the sheer fabric as well as the slits in the separate layers that allowed him to catch flashes of pale skin as she moved. He could see the outline of her nipples through the sheer material, and he tried to swallow through a throat that was suddenly as dry as the desert sands.

"Hello, my husband," Jane said, smiling in delight at the effect she was having on her new husband, and she walked into his embrace, throwing her arms about him and holding him tightly. She looked up at him with her lovely violet eyes wide in the cool semi-darkness of his bedroom. She was already excited, with various warm and tingling feelings washing through her, and her blood was singing in her ears as Richard slowly smiled down at her.

"Hello, my wife," he said, his normally deep voice made raspy by the obvious emotion in his face. "You are simply too beautiful for words, you know. That was a most dramatic entrance."

Jane smiled happily and nodded in acknowledgement of the clear emotion of the compliment. She had grown accustomed to such praise since accepting his proposal, but this was special. Now they were truly husband and wife, and seeing the obvious love and desire in Richard's eyes made her heart throb in her chest.

"I left my hair pinned up for you."

"So I see. It was very thoughtful of you," he said, and his hands were already busy, carefully feeling through her dark tresses to discover the sharp implements holding it in place.

"There, I believe that is the last one, my dear," he said, brandishing a handful of gleaming steel.

"It would be best if you put those somewhere safe. I have reason to know what it feels like to step on one in bare feet."

"A wise suggestion. Here, I shall put them in this drawer in my desk. That should be safe enough."

"Excellent," she said, returning to his embrace. "Now, sir, I am wondering what happens next. Ah, I have an idea!"

She stepped back and slid her sheer robe off her shoulders, allowing it to fall to the floor. She reached down to gather her nightgown, and in a single smooth move, she gracefully raised her garment over her head and tossed it on a nearby chair.

Richard's breath froze in his throat at this unexpected action on Jane's part, and she smiled sweetly as she put her hands above her head and slowly twirled about, trying to imitate her own internal image of a Persian dancing girl showing herself off to her sultan.

"So, may I assume that your present stricken condition is an example of how one of His Majesty's finest reacts to an unexpected situation?" She undulated and twirled again, a sly smile on her lips.

"Minx," Richard said with a huge laugh. She was still moving seductively as he reached out for her, and she laughed delightedly as he bent and swung her nude body into the air. "Where did this unforeseen and sportive playfulness come from? I thought your sister Elizabeth was supposed to be the one with the assertive and mischievous sense of humour."

"Well, I have never been married before, so I suppose you may have awakened unexpected urges in me. If it is not to your liking, I suppose you have no one to blame but yourself."

Richard laughed delightedly. "Such impishness in addition to such beauty is more than I deserve. Though I had anticipated a certain amount of blushing when I peeled your nightgown from you myself."

"I thought as much, but I had an impulse to surprise you—"

"—which you did!" Richard exclaimed delightedly. He ran his eyes over her displayed charms as he walked to the bed, attempting a leer of lust.

Jane laughed in delight at this. "You should not attempt a career in the theatre, Husband," she said as he laid her carefully onto the bed, which already had the blankets peeled back. "You do not do justice to your attempt to look lascivious. Honest soldiering is much more suited to you."

"Likely so. But I was trying to do justice to your enticing attire—or lack of it. I have never seen its like before."

"That was the safest answer you could have given," Jane said as he discarded his dressing gown and got in bed beside her. "I know you have more experience than I, but I would not desire *too much* experience."

Without conscious thought or hesitation, their lips met in a kiss of passionate fulfilment, the first of many, as they embraced tightly, hardly daring to believe that this moment had finally come. Richard was careful to remember Jane's innocence as he began to guide her in the manner of a man with a maiden, and the almost unbearable sweetness of their lovemaking that night was a memory that neither forgot in the years that followed.

CHAPTER 32

Didst thou but know the only touch of love, Thou wouldst as soon go kindle fire with snow, as seek to quench the fire of love with words.

— William Shakespeare,
The Two Gentlemen of Verona

Friday, May 29, 1812
London

The rays of the rising sun slanted through the windows, illuminating Richard's bedroom with the first light of dawn. Jane stretched and yawned, inching herself upward as the quilt slid down from her chest. She looked over at her sleeping husband and smiled fondly as she thought back on the days and nights of the past week.

Despite her declaration on their wedding night that she would not allow Richard to leave the bedroom, she had been forced to relent and allow a few excursions since it proved somewhat impractical to spend the entire first week of their marriage in bed. He had given her a tour of the house and introduced all of the staff, and they had twice dressed formally for dinner, just the two of them, though afterwards they had skipped gaily up the stairs to his bedroom. Twice he had taken her for a drive about town in the new carriage Sergeant Jones had bought for them, and they had even considered attending the theatre. Still, they had spent the overwhelming majority of the week in his bedroom, often reading or talking for long hours until the attraction of marital intimacies drew them back to his bed.

It had been a wonderful week, but now it was over. The knocker would be replaced on the front door after breakfast, and undoubtedly, visitors would soon come to call. In addition, she had to begin learning what was needed to keep the household functioning. But there was no urgency about that task; Richard's staff had kept affairs in order quite competently before she arrived and could continue to do so without any fumbling attempts to help on her part. However, despite her inexperience, she had no doubt that all of them, starting with Sergeant Jones and his wife, would hew strictly to the precepts of their society.

She was now Mrs. Colonel Fitzwilliam, mistress of this house, and questions and requests for decisions would be brought to her from now on. The sooner she mastered what needed to be done and formed a working relationship with the staff, the better for the health and harmony of all who lived there. She had nothing from her own experience to guide her since her mother had been completely inept in managing the Longbourn household, but she could not let that daunt her. She would not be satisfied until she had learned what was necessary.

But at just this moment, as she looked at the sleeping face of her husband, it came to her that she did not have to embark on her education immediately. It would be some time before breakfast, and on their first night together, she had vowed to drive Richard to exhaustion despite his robust physique and reserves of energy. She had tried her best, but she was not entirely sure of her success though he did seem to be sleeping very deeply...

She leaned over and uncovered a small bowl of water on the bedside table. Several lemon slices floated in the water, and she put one of them into her mouth, sucking on it to freshen her breath.

She turned back to her sleeping husband and pressed her bare body against him, sliding her thigh over his legs.

"Richard, my darling," she said softly into his ear while she let her hand roam over his broad chest and down over his stomach. "Are you still asleep, my love? Please wake up. Our first week of marriage is not quite ended."

Richard opened one bleary eye, which did seem to be somewhat more bloodshot than usual, she thought. Her fingertips moved lower, and she felt his involuntary arousal.

She laughed deep in her throat as her mouth descended on his, and he could not help reacting to her eager advances, despite his foggy state of mind. In fact, the feel of her velvety soft skin as she moved atop him was enough to clear away the shards of sleep. Jane's soft laugh of triumph showed her delight as he began to respond as she had hoped.

WELL AFTER BREAKFAST, COLONEL RICHARD FITZWILLIAM SAT in his study, a steaming cup of coffee in his hands as he took a grateful sip. He was sitting slouched far down in his chair, and the door to his study was open, allowing him to listen to the pleasant sounds of his household bustling about.

The sound of the knocker at the front door did little to jar his reverie. He scarcely moved as he heard Sergeant Jones answer and greet a visitor, and it was not long before his cousin Darcy entered his study.

"Good morning, Richard," he said cheerfully. "And how does married life suit you so far?"

When Richard did not respond immediately and merely sat unmoving, Darcy looked closer. He took in his cousin's stance, sitting slouched in his chair, as well as the dark circles under his eyes and the way he took another long sip of his coffee. His eyebrows rose and one corner of his mouth quirked up in amusement. He closed the door quietly behind him before taking one of the comfortable chairs on the other side of Richard's desk.

"You appear to be somewhat the worse for wear, Cousin," he said in amusement. He poured himself a cup of coffee from the decanter on the desk and helped himself to one of the appetizing little cakes that were still warm from the kitchen.

His last comment was enough to make Richard open one eye and gaze at him before closing it again. Darcy chuckled softly as he added cream and sugar to his coffee.

"Trying week, was it?" he asked cheerfully.

Richard never opened an eye as he responded. "Darce, if I were you, I would make a point of getting as much sleep as I could before your wedding. Please remember that your intended and my wife are sisters, and everyone would likely agree that my Jane has a much quieter and milder disposition than your Elizabeth."

Darcy only laughed lightly and took an appreciative bite of his cake.

"Excellent cake, by the way. I can see that your cook has lost none of her skill. Come, have one with me. You need energy, man! You cannot let the staff see that your new wife has reduced you to a shell of the man you once were."

Richard was quiet for a moment, and then he put his hands on the arms of the chair and heaved himself fully upright in his chair. He was dressed in a comfortable, well-worn duty uniform with trousers rather than breeches, and he was clean-shaven and groomed. Even so, Darcy thought there was a general air of untidiness about him that was not his cousin's usual wont. His hair appeared to be trimmed in the short style he preferred, yet it still looked to be a bit in disarray. His uniform was perfectly clean and serviceable, but it just seemed to be the slightest bit crumpled. His cheeks had hollows to match the darkness under his eyes, and he seemed to be having difficulty opening his eyes all the way.

"It appears that your wedding week was quite satisfactory, I would say." Darcy's face was composed, but he was unable to completely contain the mirth that bubbled in his voice.

"Just remember my warning," Richard said, taking a bite out of one of the cakes. "*Satisfactory* is a completely insufficient word to describe the past week."

"And my cousin Jane? I hope she was equally pleased at being a married woman?"

Richard finally opened his eyes to look upon the amused countenance of his cousin. "I believe I may safely say that she is as pleased as I to be married," he said carefully, taking another sip of his coffee. "So, has anything happened while I was out of touch?"

"The plans for my wedding proceed apace, and Mrs. Bennet appears to be having a delightful time in all the bustle and disorder," Darcy said with a shrug. "However, I have grown quite fond of Mr. Bennet, who has been most hospitable about inviting me into his library when his wife has need of her daughter. We are both content to sit quietly and read in the midst of all the turmoil until such time as Elizabeth is able to regain her freedom."

He was not altogether pleased by this last part since he and Elizabeth had not been able to manage a single afternoon picnic during the entire week, despite their earlier plans. But he was most anxious to get the next week behind him though he was conscious of a little inner voice warning that he ought to give more attention to his cousin's admonition. But he was not inclined to pay it heed, remembering only the feel of Elizabeth's smooth skin against his and her fevered kisses on the day of their betrothal.

He shook his head inwardly to clear his mind of these memories, pleasant and engaging though they were, and tried to concentrate on his cousin.

"There is, however, one point that may interest you. Georgiana and I dwell by ourselves at Netherfield while Mrs. Bennet luxuriates in her position as the most fortunate mother in the entire county. But my friend Bingley has abandoned Netherfield and is residing again at the Hurst town house along with his two sisters, who have somehow managed a return from Scarborough."

Richard nodded absently, wondering idly why such a model of civility would have left his closest friend alone at his estate. However, Darcy's next words sharpened his attention.

"In fact, it seems Bingley has visited Matlock Hall to call upon Elaine. And the word I hear from my aunt is that he was received most cordially, both by my aunt and uncle as well as by my cousin."

"Really? I know we discussed the possibility of an attraction the day before my wedding, but later I wondered whether we were not deceiving ourselves. All I really observed was that they spent a good deal of time talking."

"Which was perfectly understandable because their pairing was so predictable. You had Jane, I had Elizabeth, and my aunt and uncle had each other. What could be more natural than that the two unattached persons would be thrown into each other's company?"

"In any case, it was none of my business. Elaine is quite capable of looking after herself."

"True, but I discussed the matter with her at your wedding breakfast. I wanted to make sure she did not toy with Bingley's affections. He had already been hurt enough."

"Elaine would never do such a thing. You know that."

"Not intentionally, no, but I had to make sure." Darcy looked distinctly uncomfortable. "But Elaine told me she was well aware of Bingley's interest and found his attention pleasing. She considers him much more intelligent and well mannered than the herd of useless young men who have been chasing her from breakfast to dinner to ball during the entire Season. And the fact that he has no need of her fortune makes him even more appealing."

"This is very interesting, Darce. I am not as familiar with Bingley as I am with you, but I would not have expected anything this precipitous."

"Well, he has always been quick to fall in and out of love, but this is quite unusual. I have to wonder whether he has been affected by your example and is taking steps he never took with Jane."

Richard had to smile at this though Darcy thought the smile was rather strained. Then his expression grew serious, and he leaned forward.

"What you say is interesting, but I feel compelled to mention that Elaine shares a common heritage with Lady Catherine. As much as I love my sister, if Bingley ever does decide to make an offer of marriage, I predict it will be the last decision he will be burdened with for the rest of his days. Elaine is a young lady of decisive temperament. She will care for him properly, but she will also rule her family."

"Such is my belief also, but discussing it with her, I have concluded it might not be the worst decision for Bingley. I cannot look out for him forever, and I am not sure that my care has been everything it ought to have been. So having someone to plan his life for him might be the best means of ensuring his future happiness."

"Well, you know him better than I do. Lady Catherine did the same for her husband, and he appeared to be rather satisfied with their arrangement. But it would not do for me or for you."

"Of course. Now, where is your new wife? I should at least pay my respects before riding back to Netherfield."

"She is upstairs with Mrs. Jones," Richard said. "Let me send for her, and you can inform us of all the plans for your wedding so you do not have to repeat yourself."

Friday, June 12, 1812
London

TWO WEEKS LATER, AS FITZWILLIAM DARCY OPENED BLEARY EYES to regard the cheerful countenance of his cousin in the doorway to his office, he did indeed have cause to remember his warning that his Jane had a "much quieter and milder disposition than your Elizabeth."

"Do not say a word," he said wearily. "The coffee is on the sideboard next to the brandy. I am having brandy with a dash of coffee in it, but you may do as you please."

Richard's booming laugh rang through the room as he leaned over Darcy's desk to cuff his cousin (and now his brother) affectionately on the shoulder.

"You *were* warned, you know," he remarked cheerfully as he added cream and sugar—but no brandy—to his coffee before sitting down across from Darcy.

"Too true," said Darcy through closed eyelids though his lips quirked in a slight—a very slight—smile.

"In any case," Richard said briskly, "Mother will be returning Georgiana before noon. I would imagine she plans to stay to dine, and I think it is likely Elaine and Bingley will accompany her. So be warned: there will be a party at your table this evening."

Darcy nodded mutely then opened one eye. "And what about you and your lady fair?"

"Mrs. Fitzwilliam will be stopping by later to see her sister, but I have to leave from here directly. Duty calls, and I have to be on my way back to the regiment. I have to arrange quarters so Jane can join me soon."

At that moment, a discreet knock sounded on the door, and one of the maids entered carrying a small tray with a folded piece of paper.

"A note from Mrs. Darcy," the maid said with a curtsey.

Darcy took the note and read it in one quick glance. As soon as the door closed behind the maid, he rose to his feet, crumpling the note and dropping it in the container by the desk.

"Ah, a matter of some importance, Richard," he said, his eyes bright. "You...umm...will have to excuse me. You can see your way out, of course."

Without waiting for a response, he walked quickly out the door, and Richard heard his pace quicken as he reached the hallway. Bemused, Richard walked to the door of the office in time to see Darcy mount the stairs to the next floor two and three at a time.

Shaking his head in resignation, he walked to Darcy's desk and retrieved the note. Without even the slightest hesitation, he opened it to read:

Dearest heart,

It has only been an hour and already I miss you terribly. Please come to me as soon as may be.

There was no actual signature at the bottom of the note, only a small picture of a heart with an arrow through it.

Dropping the note back in the container, Richard left the room with a broad but understanding smile on his rugged features. After all, it was not as if he had needed the note to ascertain the cause of Darcy's precipitous departure.

EPILOGUE

Married love between man and woman is bigger than oaths guarded by right of nature.

— Aeschylus

Friday, December 29, 1865
Rosings, Kent

"Unto Almighty God we commend the soul of our brother, Sir Richard Spencer Fitzwilliam, and we commit his body to the ground, ashes to ashes, dust to dust, in sure and certain hope of resurrection into eternal life through our Lord Jesus Christ."

Jane Fitzwilliam stood silent and without a tear as the parson delivered the familiar words from her prayer book. Her six sons stood to her left, all of them a full head taller than her, and even her daughter topped her by two inches. Two of her sons wept openly for their departed father, and one stood silent while tears coursed down his deeply tanned cheeks.

However, her eldest son, William, godson of Darcy and Elizabeth, stood as dry-eyed as his mother did, for he was of the same mind: that tears were not needed in remembrance of a life lived to the fullest. He

412

would mourn his father and would certainly miss him dreadfully, but his father had been his closest friend as well as his sire, and he would not weep for him.

William's sister, Elizabeth, the only living daughter of his parents' eight children born and his father's greatest joy, did weep openly, and neither he nor his mother begrudged her that. She had loved her father dearly, and her husband, Richard Fitzwilliam Darcy, second son of his aunt and uncle Darcy, held her close and comforted her. He attempted to emulate his aunt, though with mixed success since the glitter of unshed tears marked the corners of his eyes.

At last, the service was over, the grave was filled, and the headstone placed. "General Sir Richard Fitzwilliam, KB," it read at the top, and below, in smaller letters, it said, "Beloved husband of Jane, father of William, Arthur, Steven, Charles, Nelson, Richard, Elizabeth, and Mary."

Jane did feel the temptation to shed a tear at that, for Mary had been her last child and had lived only a few weeks after birth. Her small grave lay to the left of Richard's, next to that of his cousin Anne and his aunt Lady Catherine de Bourgh.

Richard had been astonished when Lady Catherine had written after Anne's death and informed him of her intention to bequeath Rosings to him. Even so, he had not anticipated that her bequest would become reality since Lady Catherine had never "owned" Rosings. She merely had the use of it after the death of her husband, Sir Lewis de Bourgh. It had not been entailed away to a male relative, but Fitzwilliam anticipated that it would be inherited by one of those male relatives after his aunt died. However, legal proceeding had determined that, since Sir Lewis had no immediate male relations, the bequest by his aunt provided the clearest possible path for the court, and ownership had eventually been invested in him.

Jane had not been sure she wanted to live there since the town house had been her first home with Richard and had also been the birthplace of three of her sons. She was not sure at first whether Rosings could ever feel like home to her, considering the ornate style of decoration that was so at variance with her own desire for simplicity. But, since the ownership of Rosings had brought with it a considerable increase in income, they had been able to make alterations that eventually made it more closely resemble the elegant style of Pemberley. And now, after almost fifty years in residence, it had truly become her home.

As she finally started back to the house on the arm of her eldest son, Jane was surrounded by scarlet coats. It was still hard to believe that every one of her sons had been determined to follow in their father's footsteps, and they ranged in rank from lieutenant colonel to brigadier general. All had seen action in the Crimean War, and the youngest, Lieutenant Col. Richard Avery Fitzwilliam, wore the Cross of Victoria on his chest, awarded by the Queen herself.

"You are now the owner of Rosings, William," she said after they had returned to the house and found comfort in front of a warm fire. "Have you given thought to when you will take up residence?"

"I had not even thought of it, Mother. I had not intended to retire so soon, but I am well aware that I cannot manage the estate if I do not live here."

"Your godfather managed Pemberley from Cambridge all by himself for several years, you know."

"I seem to have a vague memory of having heard the story once or twice before, Mother," William said with a grin. "Father absolutely loved to tell the story of his courtship of you, but I know that I am not nearly as smart as Uncle Darcy—none of your sons are. Elizabeth is the only one of us with any real pretensions to intelligence."

Elizabeth gave a snort of amusement at the comment. Growing up with six older brothers—all vying to outdo the others in the protection of their sister—had led to a certain immunity to their attempts to exaggerate her accomplishments.

"Nevertheless, you must make plans to take over management no later than the spring," his mother continued. "As soon as it becomes warm enough, I am going to travel to Pemberley to see Lizzy. You know your uncle is unable to travel, and she will never leave his side, so I must travel there if I am to see her. In fact, it is likely that I shall reside there since all of you are much more able to travel there than I would be to visit you."

"Father hardly showed his age until this last month," Arthur said. He was their second son and the godson of the Duke of Wellington, with whom Fitzwilliam had served on the continent as the tyrant Bonaparte was finally and completely brought down. "Until then, he never missed his daily ride or his walk with you through the gardens."

"And Nelson and I can remember listening to him chasing you around the bedroom any number of times," Richard said with a grin. "His room was right above ours, and we did not even realize what we were hearing at first."

"Richard!" his mother said sharply, but she had to repress a smile when she said it. She could not be truly angry, for she also remembered.

"Tell us truly, Mother," Nelson said, with a sly grin. "Did you have to slow down to allow him to catch you? Father was always a big man and rather slow."

"Now you two boys just be quiet," Jane said. "Neither of you has any idea what was going on. Why, the idea of your father chasing me is ludicrous."

The brothers simply looked at each other and smiled. They would never contradict their mother, but their memories of their father's love for her were one of the cornerstones of their lives.

"Mother is right, you know," Elizabeth said, as she sat holding her husband's arm. "You were completely wrong all those years, despite all the amusement you gained from it." She put down her cup of tea carefully. "You see, it was really Mother chasing Father—and I daresay she always caught him too."

Charles was drinking tea at that same moment, and while his

brothers gaped at their sister in silent astonishment, he instantly choked on it. Richard pounded on his back to help him clear his throat, then all six brothers looked at Elizabeth and their mother in open-mouthed shock. They saw their sister and mother share a slight, secretive smile, and they all wondered in that way that children have of imagining a physical intimacy between their parents: *Could it really be?*

They looked closely at their mother, who only smiled and rang the pull for a servant.

"More tea, anyone?" Jane Fitzwilliam asked sweetly, a smile of fond remembrance on her face.

Finis

ABOUT THE AUTHOR

By training, C. P. (Colin) Odom is a retired engineer, born in Texas, raised in Oklahoma, and graduated from the University of Oklahoma. Sandwiched in there was a stint in the Marines, and he has lived in Arizona since 1977, working first for Motorola and then General Dynamics. Colin raised two sons with his first wife, Margaret, before her untimely death from cancer, and he and his second wife, Jeanine, adopted two girls from China. The older of their daughters recently graduated with an engineering degree and is working in Phoenix, and the younger girl is heading toward a nursing degree.

Colin has always been a voracious reader and collector of books, and his favorite genres are science fiction, historical fiction, histories, and in recent years, reading (and later writing) Jane Austen romantic fiction. This late-developing interest was indirectly stimulated when he

417

read his first wife's beloved Jane Austen books after her passing. One thing led to another, and he now has five novels published: *A Most Civil Proposal* (2013), *Consequences* (2014), *Pride, Prejudice, and Secrets* (2015), *Perilous Siege* (2019), and *A Covenant of Marriage* (2019).

Colin retired from engineering in 2011, but he still lives in Arizona with his family, a pair of dogs (one of which is stubbornly untrainable), and a pair of rather strange cats. His hobbies are reading, woodworking, and watching college football and LPGA golf. (The ladies are much nicer than the guys as well as being fiendishly good putters.) Lately, Colin has reverted to his younger years and taken up building plastic model aircraft and ships—when he can find the time!

Facebook: https://www.facebook.com/colin.odom

Amazon author page: http://www.amazon.com/C.-P.-Odom/e/B00BPT2BQQ/ref=sr_tc_2_0?qid=1393834353&sr=1-2-ent

Goodreads: https://www.goodreads.com/author/show/7073904.C_P_Odom?from_search=true

Meryton Press author page: http://colinodom.merytonpress.com/